When No One Else Will

Books by Amanda Skenandore

BETWEEN EARTH AND SKY

THE UNDERTAKER'S ASSISTANT

THE SECOND LIFE OF MIRIELLE WEST

THE NURSE'S SECRET

THE MEDICINE WOMAN OF GALVESTON

WHEN NO ONE ELSE WILL

Published by Kensington Publishing Corp.

Praise for the novels of Amanda Skenandore

The Medicine Woman of Galveston

"A wonderful story about seizing second chances—and who doesn't love those? Amanda Skenandore has a keen eye for developing characters who transform while keeping the endearing, relatable qualities that made us root for them in the first place. A charming cast of misfits and a devastating hurricane were just the ingredients I needed to completely lose myself in this book."

—Elise Cooper, author of *Angels of the Pacific*

The Undertaker's Assistant

"Effie's community of freedmen and Creoles in Reconstruction New Orleans is unforgettable. Skenandore's second novel is recommended for readers who enjoy medical historical fiction reminiscent of Diane McKinney-Whetstone's *Lazaretto*, and historical fiction with interpersonal drama."

—*Library Journal*

"Readers who like complex characters amid a roiling historical setting will be fascinated by Effie's quest. . . . Teen readers will empathize with a young woman's search for identity and love."

—*Booklist*

"Our immersion in that world—from the particulars of baking marble cake to the grisly minutiae of embalming corpses to the messy and violent politics of the Reconstruction South—is so complete that the reader never doubts it once existed. That said, one of this novel's many virtues is how it subtly conveys how many black citizens in the post-Civil War era took it upon themselves to improve their own lives."

—*Historical Novels Review*

Turn the page for more praise.

Between Earth and Sky

"Intensely emotional. . . . Skenandore's deeply introspective and moving novel will appeal to readers of American history, particularly those interested in the dynamics behind the misguided efforts of white people to better the lives of Native Americans by forcing them to adopt white cultural mores."
—*Publishers Weekly*

"A masterfully written novel about the heart-wrenching clash of two American cultures . . . a fresh and astonishing debut."
—V. S. Alexander, author of *The Magdalen Girls*

"By describing its costs in human terms, the author shapes tension between whites and Native Americans into a touching story. The title of Skenandore's debut could refer to reality and dreams, or to love and betrayal; all are present in this highly original novel."
—*Booklist*

"A heartbreaking story about the destructive legacy of the forced assimilation of Native American children. Historical fiction readers and book discussion groups will find much to ponder here."
—*Library Journal*

WHEN NO ONE ELSE WILL

AMANDA SKENANDORE

kensingtonbooks.com

KENSINGTON BOOKS are published by

Kensington Publishing Corp.
900 Third Avenue
New York, NY 10022

ISBN: 978-1-4967-4170-7
ISBN: 978-1-4967-4171-4 (ebook)

First Kensington Trade Paperback Printing: June 2026

10 9 8 7 6 5 4 3 2 1

Printed in the United States of America

The authorized representative in the EU for product safety and compliance
is eucomply OU, Parnu mnt 139b-14, Apt 123
Tallinn, Berlin 11317, hello@eucompliancepartner.com

For Jenny, Angelina, and Wendy.

I'm a better writer, thanks to you.
And a better person.

CHAPTER 1

Chicago, 1939

"You're sure your husband approves of this?"

Mimi shifts atop the thinly padded examination table. "Mm-hmm."

She's relieved he can't see her face. Her too-wide eyes and taut smile. The look of someone unaccustomed to lying.

"Perhaps we ought to wait until he can join us."

"No." Her voice echoes through the small room, high-pitched and piercing. Mimi takes a calming breath. "His leg. You remember. He still can't fully walk on it."

"Well, if you're sure."

"I'm sure." Now her voice sounds like her own. Soft, friendly, harmless.

The doctor wheels his stool closer and lifts the sheet covering her legs. "A little wider, dear."

Mimi spreads her knees, wincing at the cold pinch that follows.

"He'll be healed up in time for spring training, won't he? A strong fellow like him."

His words come muffled through the sheet, and his breath prickles her thighs. Must they talk while he does this? She'd just as soon close her eyes and imagine herself far away, the heroine of some daytime radio serial, until it's over. She can almost hear the radio announcer's smooth voice in her head:

Welcome to The Mimi Lukas Show! Today's episode is brought to you by Holland-Rantos. Women have more to worry about than bright complexions and soft hands. For those intimate concerns, there's Holland-Rantos, maker of hygienic preparations and appliances for all your feminine needs. Ladies, ask your doctor about Holland-Rantos products today!

Mimi would laugh but for the uncomfortable pressure between her legs. The scale in the corner, the glass-fronted supply cabinet, the jars of gauze and bottles of iodine, the vision chart tacked to the exam room wall—it all comes back into unwelcome focus.

What had the doctor asked? Oh yes, about her husband.

"Fully recovered come spring," she says. "That's the hope, anyway."

A fool's hope. Stan will be lucky if he's able to run the bases again by midsummer.

"Good. They'll need him if they want to beat those Yankees."

Mimi doesn't have the heart to tell him that the Sox cut Stan from the team. He'll read it in the papers soon enough.

She endures another few minutes of baseball talk before the doctor wheels his stool back and sits up straight, his bespectacled eyes meeting hers. His hairpiece has slipped back a few inches, revealing sparse patches of gray hair. Sweat dapples his brow, even though the room is decidedly cool. Surely, he's finished his exam, but the metal speculum he inserted remains uncomfortably in place.

"You know, in my day, we let God decide these things."

God? What does he have to do with baseball?

The doctor continues, lecturing her about motherhood being a woman's natural role and the joy children bring to the home, and Mimi realizes they're no longer talking about baseball. She's tempted to interrupt him and ask what God thinks about medical advancements like sulfa drugs, tank respirators, and infant incubators. Or perhaps she ought to remind him that she *is* a mother. He delivered both her children, for heaven's sake!

Surely, she needn't mention last year's miscarriage. God had decided that one, hadn't he? Another girl, Mimi was certain. She'd already picked out a name.

Mimi never told her husband. Not before. Not after. Stan hadn't broken his leg yet, but things were already getting hard. Best not to bother him with it. That was the advice of Bonnie Knows Best at *Ladies' Home Journal*, anyway. She'd wept at that first spot of blood, overcome with both loss and relief.

"It's only for right now," Mimi tells the doctor once he's finished his lecture. "While things are a bit—er—unsettled."

She's not sure if it's pride or shame that keeps her from saying more. That she hasn't been able to treat the kids to an ice cream soda in months. Or that their new school clothes came from the second-hand stalls on Maxwell Street. Or that she plundered the last few dollars from the old coffee tin in the back of her closet to pay for today's appointment.

The doctor sighs and removes the speculum. Mimi's relieved not to have the cold metal inside her anymore. She's further relieved when he pulls over a creaky side table. A small paperboard box, three tin canisters, and something that looks like a short, steel crochet hook sit atop the table. He opens the canisters. Each contains a different-sized rubber ring. Mimi grits her teeth as he descends beneath the sheet and begins probing again, this time with his fingers.

"How many grand slams had your husband hit before his injury? Four, was it?"

Again with the chitchat.

"Something like that," Mimi says, wishing he'd just get the darn thing fitted.

In truth, Stan hasn't hit like that in years. But if nursing school taught her anything, it's that you never contradict a doctor, even if you're talking about something as silly as sports.

He pops his head up, grabs one of the rubber rings, measures it against his index finger, then grabs another. She feels his fingers inside her again, clumsy and dry.

"Bear down," he tells her when he finally gets the ring inserted. She does. The ring slides out and hits the linoleum floor with a wet *smack*. From the corner of her eye, she watches it wobble on its edge to a stop halfway across the room, leaving a faint slick behind it.

"Damn it," he mutters, not bothering to pick it up before trying another size.

Mimi's cheeks burn. A root canal would be better than this.

At his command, she bears down again. Thankfully, the new ring remains snugly in place.

"Good," he says. "A seventy millimeter should do the trick."

Mimi starts to sit up, but he flaps a liver-spotted hand and bids her stay put while he putters around the office, rifling through desk drawers and peeking beneath stacks of paper. At last, he finds what he's looking for: a foldout chart of the female anatomy.

She remembers such charts from her nursing school days, recalls looking at them with wonder, trying to envision those strange passages, folds, and recesses inside her own body.

Mimi looks away, her gaze settling on the far wall, where his yellowed credentials hang. The rumble of automobiles and the crossing cop's shrill whistle sound from outside.

How young and silly she'd been back then. She'd never so much as kissed a man, let alone made love to one. The idea of growing and birthing a child was as bleary and mysterious as that of God.

Never you mind, had been Ma's reply when Mimi asked where babies came from. *Don't let a man touch you, and you won't have to find out, you hear*?

So Mimi thought babies were spread the same way as chickenpox or ringworm until her older sister set her straight. You could hold a fellow's hand, Ginny told her, and still be safe. Wear his jacket. Let him kiss you. (Watch out for fellows with bad breath, though!) Making a baby required a special kind of touching. But in the end, even Ginny hadn't known the full truth of it. The full cost.

Now, Mimi turns her attention back to the old doctor as he fumbles with the chart. His brow is sweating again, and his eyes are skittish. Mimi chokes back a bitter laugh. Why should he be uncomfortable? She's the one with her legs splayed.

Still, she waits for a break in his stammering description of the fallopian tubes and uterus before reminding him of her training.

"Nursing school?" The relief is plain on his face as he folds the chart. "I plum forgot. And afterward?"

"A private duty assignment on Lake Shore."

He nods approvingly. Mimi doesn't tell him her assignment lasted all of three months. Stan wasn't keen on career girls, and the old man who employed her wasn't keen on married nurses. So that was that. Love had seemed an acceptable trade-off at the time.

"Don't suppose they taught you about these?" He holds up the rubber diaphragm.

She shakes her head. They had hours of lecture about obstetrics in school, but not one mention of birth control.

With the same bumbling discomfort as before, he explains how to use the steel inserter to introduce the diaphragm into the birth canal and fit it snugly in place *over the . . . um . . . er . . . cervix.* Mimi lays back, grimacing at his cold touch as he demonstrates. Then he hands the instruments to her.

"Your turn."

Now Mimi is the one blushing and bumbling. Sure, this man delivered her children, but this is an entirely new level of intimacy. Her mother would balk at the idea, but it's Ginny she's thinking of as she fits the lip of the diaphragm into the notches of the inserter and guides it into her vagina under the doctor's watchful gaze.

Unless you were one of Mrs. Sanger's renegades, no one used diaphragms back when she and Ginny were girls. Heck, no one even knew about them, let alone how to get one. But it might have saved Ginny's life. And somehow, Mimi has the feeling it just might save hers.

CHAPTER 2

Mimi hurries from the pharmacy, making it to Halsted Street just in time to catch the L. There were two signature lines on the prescription—one where the doctor scribbled his name and one left blank for her husband. After fifteen minutes of hand-wringing, she'd surreptitiously signed Stan's name, then presented it to the druggist with a tight smile. He didn't even glance at the signatures.

Now, the Holland-Rantos diaphragm, in its paperboard box, sits snugly in her purse. She tries to look unbothered as she settles into her seat, ankles crossed and head high. The L lurches into motion. Next to her, a businessman reads the paper. Across the aisle, a colored woman bounces a toddler on her lap. Mimi smiles at the boy, but he turns away and buries his face in his mother's shoulder. The woman's eyes cut to her, and Mimi can't help feeling like the woman knows her secret. *I wouldn't lie to my doctor*, those brown eyes seem to say. *I wouldn't forge my husband's signature.* Mimi's hands tighten around the straps of her purse. She turns her head and looks past the man and his newspaper out the window. The slanting afternoon sunlight reflects off the passing buildings—a dense cluster of stone, brick, and steel stretching skyward.

She hadn't arrived at the doctor's office knowing she would have to lie. It was all far more complicated than she'd expected. The exam. The fitting. There's still a slight ache between her legs. Besides, it's not as if Stan's opposed to birth control. At least not that he's said. He's not half as religious as his mother. In fact, if it hadn't been for her and her constant eavesdropping, Mimi might have broached the idea with Stan before she made the doctor's appointment.

The man flips the page of his paper. Has he reached the sports section yet? Has news of Stan's release made it to print? Maybe it's not news at all—an injured player already well past his prime. Still, she fights the urge to look over the man's shoulder and see. He glances at her with disapproval. *Don't come any closer*, his gaze seems to say. *And for heaven's sake, be frank with your husband.*

Bonnie Knows Best would say the same thing.

Fine. Tonight. She'll tell Stan about the diaphragm tonight. Along with the other decision she's made. Her finger traces the outline of the box through the fabric of her purse. Perhaps Stan's just as worried as she is about their dwindling bank account. Perhaps he'll see the box and share her relief. Perhaps they'll even laugh about the shaky signature she passed off as his.

Mimi looks back at the woman and her child. He's ruddy-faced and chubby—a rare sight these past years, but just as a boy his age should be. This time, when she catches his eye, he gives her a shy smile. The woman, however, is still flat-lipped and staring. Mimi feels seven again, chalk in hand, standing before the blackboard. *Good girls do not tell lies. Good girls do not tell lies.*

Finally, just before Mimi's stop, the woman leans across the aisle. "I hope you don't mind me saying," she whispers, "but your dress. You've forgotten to fasten a few of the buttons."

Mimi glances down. Her dress gapes open above her navel, exposing her cheap rayon slip beneath. She gasps and crosses her arms over her waist. Has she really been walking around half-dressed since she left the doctor's office? She ought not to have left in such a rush.

"Thank you," she whispers back.

The woman nods. "We ladies got to look out for one another."

Mimi's cheeks still burn with embarrassment when she arrives home. No wonder the druggist didn't pay the signatures on her prescription any notice. No wonder the man beside her on the L eyed her askance.

Junior's bicycle lays on its side in the front yard, its back tire perilously close to her flower bed. The pansies have wilted with fall's arrival, but the asters and black-eyed Susans still stand tall. A sprinkling of leaves crunches beneath her feet as she mounts the porch steps. Hadn't she been out here just this morning with the broom? Paint curls away from the iron handrail, leaving flecks of black on her glove. There's no money for a fresh coat, though. At least you can't see the rust from the street.

Static greets Mimi when she opens the door. From the entryway, she can see Penny and Junior in the living room crouched beside the radio, fighting over the dial.

"Junior, your bicycle," Mimi calls.

He sticks his tongue out at his older sister as he stands and heads for the door. Mimi catches him on his way past, pulling him close for a quick kiss on the forehead before he squirms away.

"How was school?"

"Okay," he says, and is out the door before she can inquire further.

Mimi tucks her gloves into her pockets and hangs her coat on the stand. The catchy jingle of a soda commercial plays over the radio, followed by a man's smooth baritone announcing the next show. Penny wears a triumphant smile as she settles closer to listen.

"Is your schoolwork done?" Mimi asks.

Penny nods without looking away from the radio.

"And the table set?"

"You haven't even started cooking."

"You know the rules. Chores first, radio second."

Now Penny turns to her. "Pleeeease. *Little Orphan Annie* is about to come on." A new tooth is already filling in the gap in the right side of her smile. Mimi's gaze flashes to the armchair by the window, where her mother-in-law, Halina, sits. Her deep-set eyes—the same striking blue as Stan's—are fixed on the Polish daily, *Dziennik Chicagoski*, in her lap. No doubt it's filled with news of Poland's recent invasion. First the Nazis, now the Soviets. But whatever story's caught Halina's eye, Mimi knows her ears are still listening in.

"Five minutes, that's all," Mimi says to Penny.

Her mother-in-law shakes her head and flips the page of her paper. Mimi ignores her. She's always chiding Mimi for being too lenient with the kids. Never mind that it's her, their *babcia*, who slips them candy before dinner and lets them stay up late when Mimi and Stan are out.

Usually Stan's dragged himself from bed by this hour and is seated by the window, too, crutches leaned precariously against the floor lamp, his bum leg propped up on the fraying ottoman. But today's *Chicago Tribune* sits untouched on the coffee table beside the latest *Ladies' Home Journal.* A bad day, then.

"Five minutes," she reminds Penny before steeling herself and heading down the hall toward the bedroom.

Immediately after the accident—a spectacular collision between Stan and Detroit's second baseman after a line drive into right field—he'd been his usual jovial self, even telling the reporter who followed beside his gurney to the ambulance that he'd be back in time to finish the series. He stayed optimistic through the first weeks of recovery. Flowers and fan mail filled his hospital room. Boys from the pediatric ward snuck down to get his autograph. But the flowers soon wilted, and with them, his spirits. The season was shot, and though none of the doctors were brave enough to say it, likely his career.

He remained at the hospital with his leg in traction for six weeks. By the time he arrived home, the happy-go-lucky man she knew had become a bitter, morose stranger. Sure, some days were better than others. Days when he might ask after the kids' time at school or thank her for a rib roast cooked just to his liking. But there were other days when he didn't get out of bed at all. When he snapped at her for reminding him to do his calisthenics and grumbled that the supper she prepared was too salty or too dry.

Mimi fears today is one of those days.

Before she can turn the bedroom knob, there's a knock at the front door. She glances over her shoulder, waiting to see if Penny or Halina will get up to answer it. Another knock comes, a louder, double rap. Mimi sighs and goes to answer it.

Betsy from two houses down must be short a cup of sugar. That, or Mrs. Davenport from across the street wants to complain about Junior cutting across her lawn again. But when Mimi opens the door, two men in navy blue coveralls greet her instead. One carries a clipboard. The other rests an elbow on the top rail of an upright dolly.

"Is this the Stanislaw Lukasewicz residence?" the man with the clipboard asks.

Mimi hesitates. Stan hardly ever uses his given name. "Yes."

The other man straightens and wheels the dolly through the door, leaving Mimi no choice but to shuffle aside to avoid being run over.

"Kitchen in the back?" he asks her.

"What?" She looks to the man with the clipboard. "What's going on?"

"We're from General Electric, ma'am. I'm afraid you've fallen behind on your payments. We've come to take back your refrigerator." He holds the clipboard out to her. "Sign here, please."

"There must be some mistake." They'd missed a payment or two, it was true, but surely this could all be sorted out. She hears the thrum of rubber atop her newly polished parquet floors and turns to see the other man wheeling the dolly down the hallway toward the kitchen. "Wait!"

"No mistake," the man with the clipboard says. "A notice was mailed out last month."

Mimi thinks back. An official-looking letter from General Electric had arrived some weeks back. She'd set it aside for Stan like she did with all important mail.

The man thrusts the clipboard into her hands and fishes a pen from his breast pocket.

"Surely we can come to some sort of arrangement. I've got . . ." How much money does she have on hand? Ten . . . twenty dollars? She looks down at the paper on the clipboard, skimming the legal mumbo jumbo until she sees a number. A hundred and five dollars—that's how much they're behind. Mimi's stomach sinks. Even if she turned out every purse and pocket in the house, there's no way she could come up with that much money on the spot. She could run to the bank. If she withdrew their entire savings, it just might be enough. But then, how will they eat?

"Please. I've got some . . . some jewelry. Pearls and such. They're real. None of that cheap mail-order stuff." She glances down at her wedding ring, then hastily covers it with her other hand. Her necklaces and earrings she can do without. She's already pawned a few of them. But not her ring.

"You have to take that up with the office, ma'am. We're not permitted to take payments of any kind. Just the appliance. Sign here." With a grease-stained finger, he points to a line at the bottom of the page.

A clang sounds from the kitchen. Mimi scribbles her name on the line, hands back the clipboard, and hurries to the kitchen. She arrives just in time to see the other man yank the refrigerator's plug from the wall. The soft hum that's filled her kitchen for months dies. He moves toward her beautiful machine—top-of-the-line, with stainless steel sliding shelves and a super freezer compartment at the bottom—with his rusty dolly.

"Wait!" she cries again. He stops and looks at her with tired indifference. "At least . . ." She wants to tell him to use a drop cloth so he doesn't scratch the surface, but that's foolish. It's not her refrigerator anymore. "At least let me get the food out."

He opens the refrigerator door wide for her. "Be quick about it, will ya? We've got three more stops to make."

A rush of cold hits her. Mimi winces, even though it doesn't matter if they let all the cold air out now. She looks at the tidy shelves. Just that morning, she'd taken everything out and wiped down the interior, taking stock of what they had. Not as much as they used to, but enough to get by. Now, she grabs the jug of milk from the middle shelf, hesitating before twisting around and setting it on the kitchen table.

The man clears his throat, and she moves more quickly. Cream, eggs, yesterday's Jell-O salad. She sets them haphazardly on the table, then fills her arms anew.

The commotion draws her mother-in-law to the kitchen. Mimi hears the warning thud of her stiff gait and smells the wintergreen oil prescribed for her achy joints before she sees her.

"What's this?" Halina says from the doorway.

Mimi drops a bundle of carrots and half a head of lettuce onto the table. "They've come for our refrigerator."

"And you're giving it to them?" Halina's accent is even heavier than usual. She turns to the man and scowls. "Thieves!"

"No, Mamo. We fell behind on our payments."

Halina redirects her sour expression at Mimi. She leans against the doorjamb, a badger roused from its winter torpor, watching as Mimi clears out the last of the food without offering to help.

Then, unceremoniously, the man wedges the dolly beneath the refrigerator and wheels it out of the kitchen and down the hallway toward the front door. Mimi follows at his heels. The children glance at her with confused expressions as she passes the living room, then turn back to the radio.

It takes both men to navigate the dolly down the front porch steps. Her beautiful refrigerator clinks and rattles as they descend. Across the street, she sees Mrs. Davenport pressing her sharply pointed nose against the glass of her living room window.

As the men wheel the machine to the curb and load it into their truck, Mimi sinks down onto the top step. The concrete is hard and cold beneath her. She hadn't minded Mrs. Davenport's nosy stare eight months ago when the gleaming new refrigerator had been carted inside. They'd been the first family on the block to replace their icebox with an electric model. Now, shame burns beneath Mimi's skin. She'll be back to hanging a sign for ice in her front window, and everyone, not just Mrs. Davenport, will know it's gone.

The truck drives away, but Mimi can't bring herself to go back inside. The sky is starting to darken when the front door opens behind her.

"Mama," Penny says, "there's someone out back."

"One of them hobos," Junior adds.

Mimi grabs the iron railing and hauls herself up. "That's not what we call them, Junior—they're just like you and me, remember? But for the—"

"Grace of God go I," he finishes for her. "Yeah, I remember."

Today the well-worn words seem almost prophetic. The children trail her through the house to the back door off the kitchen. A man in ragged clothes stands on the stoop. It's been several months since anyone like him has come knocking. Long enough she'd almost begun to think the Depression might really be over. Today's a bitter reminder it's not.

"Good evening, ma'am," the man says to her, touching the brim of his worn hat. "Pardon for troubling you, but might you have a little supper to spare?"

She glances over her shoulder at the food on the table. Even if she and Halina can manage to haul the icebox up from the basement tonight, the iceman won't be by for another two days. By then, nearly everything will have spoiled. She might as well cook up what she can.

"Come back in half an hour, and I'll have a good meal ready."

A gap-toothed smile stretches across his face. It's almost enough to beat back her melancholy. Almost.

"Thank you kindly, ma'am." He touches his hat again. "I will."

"If you're traveling with others, bring them along, too. We've got plenty to go around."

Tonight they did, anyway. Tomorrow was another story.

CHAPTER 3

Three days later, Mimi hurries home after a busy day of marketing. Their old icebox is decidedly smaller than the electric refrigerator, and the freezer box doesn't stay nearly as cold. But they don't have money for frosted foods like Creamsicles, anyway.

After unloading the groceries, Mimi goes to check on Stan. When she left late this morning, he'd made it out of bed and into his well-loved armchair in the living room. Now that chair is empty, and she fears his bum leg has driven him back to bed.

She reaches for the bedroom doorknob like it's a hot coal and turns it gingerly. She blinks. It's not particularly bright inside, but she'd expected total darkness. The unmade bed is empty. Mimi opens the door fully to find Stan tottering before her vanity mirror, tying his tie. He's dressed nicer than she's seen him in weeks—navy blue slacks and a collared shirt. His jacket is draped over the vanity chair, and silver baseball cufflinks—the ones she bought him on their first anniversary—wink at her in the lamplight.

She starts to ask if he needs help but stops herself. The last time she asked, he hollered at her for treating him like a cripple. Instead, she settles for an even-toned, "You look nice." Still risky, but better than standing there gawking.

Stan turns and flashes her that megawatt smile of his. Here's the man she married.

"Be sure to put a little extra on for supper," he says. "Gibbins is coming."

Mimi feels herself deflate like an overmixed soufflé. *Extra.* What extra? They'd been getting by on less and less for weeks now. Never mind she hasn't had time to tidy the house.

Tell Gibbins to come another day, she wants to say. Instead, she straightens and dons her best happy-housewife expression. "Do you think he has news?"

"Sure does." Stan turns back to the vanity mirror and finishes with his tie. "Said he wanted to talk it over in person."

And squeeze a free meal out of them to boot.

Mimi hurries off to the kitchen to warm the oven, trying not to worry. Only two types of news need to be delivered in person: very good news and very bad.

"Thank you, Mrs. Lukas. That sure was delicious pie. Even my own mother's can't compare." Gibbins tosses the checkered napkin onto his empty plate and pushes back from the table. Mimi smiles. He said the same thing last time he ate over. And the time before.

"You sure you wouldn't like another slice?" Mimi asks. She hasn't taken one herself to be sure there's plenty to go around.

"No, no. Two's my limit."

She rises from the table and takes his plate to the sink. Gibbins isn't a bad fellow, just a bit too slick for Mimi's liking. The sort who's quick with a joke or wild story—like the time DiMaggio mistook Gibbins's topcoat for his own and wore it on his first date with Dorothy Arnold. *When he returned it, I could still smell her perfume!* Sure, you laugh. You might even believe him. But later on, you wonder what sort of stories he's telling about you.

Not that anything in Mimi's life is worth broadcasting. In her husband's life, perhaps. But not hers.

Still, she's glad he's here. Gibbins knows everyone in baseball. In his long career, he's been a manager, league organizer, promoter, and scout. If anyone can help Stan get a new contract, it's him.

"Want me to clear the kids out of the living room?" she asks Stan as she tops off their coffee.

"Nah, we'll talk here."

He's still smiling. Has been all supper long. And as much as she doesn't trust Gibbins's stories, it sure has been nice hearing Stan laugh again.

Mimi fills the sink with soap and water but leaves the dishes to soak so the two men can have privacy. Stan pats her on the rear as she leaves. He's sitting easier than he has since coming home from the hospital: shoulders relaxed, bum leg stretched out under the table, crutches leaning forgotten against the wall. Her hope swells.

She makes it four steps down the hall before temptation gets the better of her, and she flattens herself against the wall to listen.

"The missus won't mind if I smoke, will she?" Gibbins asks.

Mimi does mind. She's never liked the smell. But Stan must have assured him otherwise, because a matchbox rattles and a flame rasps to life. A few moments later, cigarette smoke drifts from the kitchen.

"Want one?" Gibbins says. "I hear they're good for your health. Gets the blood flowing."

She hopes Stan will say no and is grateful when she hears Gibbins stuff the matchbox and cigarettes back in his pocket.

"How goes it, anyway, the healing?"

"The docs are still saying I'll make a full recovery. Did you tell the folks in Washington that? Christmas if not sooner."

Christmas? Not a chance.

"I told them." Gibbins's cigarette crackles. Fresh curls of smoke float into the hallway. "I'm afraid they're not interested, Stan."

"Not interested? But I was having a damned good season before the accident. I was hitting—"

"It's not your stats. They're, well, not bad. But Stan, you're thirty-six."

"Earle Brucker is thirty-eight. Hell, Jo Heving's almost forty!"

"They're not coming off an injury and three months of bed rest."

"They never beat out Gehrig for the most grand slams in a single season, either."

"Sorry, pal, but that's old news. Fans want to see Foxx or DiMaggio smash one out of the park, not some old title holder hit a grounder and hobble to first."

A fist slams the kitchen table, causing the hallway pictures to rattle against the walls.

"I can still hit with the best of them. And I don't hobble, damn it!" Then, more calmly, Stan says, "At least I won't come spring."

"I know, I know. But they don't want to risk it. Philly, either, I'm afraid."

Mimi covers her mouth with a hand, stifling a gasp. The air around her grows thin. Stan must be feeling it, too, this sudden tightness in the lungs, the rev of panic in the veins.

She hadn't wanted to move to D.C. Or Philadelphia, for that matter. Aside from a two-year stint in Cincinnati when Stan was traded to the Reds, Chicago has always been their home. But for the promise of a paycheck, she'd pack up and move to Timbuktu.

Stan clears his throat. "What about St. Louis?"

"I rang Haney, too. No luck."

Mimi's hand presses harder against her lips. Even the Browns—the worst team in baseball—don't want him. She thought at least one of the teams would offer some sort of conditional contract. Invite Stan to spring training to see how he played. It wouldn't help much now, not money-wise, but the prospect of it would get him out of bed. And come spring, who knew? Stan could charm the socks off anyone when he wasn't in a sour mood. If his playing didn't razzle-dazzle them, his smile and wit would. Now, he won't even get the chance.

"What are you saying, Gibbins? Is this the end?"

"No, no. I put out feelers with a couple National League teams, and you can always . . ."

Mimi shuffles to the living room, not wanting to hear more. It *is* the end. Why can't Gibbins just come out and say it? Coward. Her eyes flash to her purse, hanging on a peg by the door. The paperboard box inside seems all the more critical now, and she doesn't regret lying and forging Stan's signature to get it.

In the living room, she sinks into one of the armchairs. The radio cabinet—a waist-high, lacquered affair—is playing *Captain Midnight*. Peggy and Junior are sprawled in front of it, listening.

"Something wrong?" her mother-in-law says, her voice just audible above the show.

Mimi shakes her head, though she wouldn't be surprised if Halina had been eavesdropping, too. She's been living with them ever since Mimi and Stan were newlyweds—after Stan's father died suddenly of a heart attack—and though she seldom lifts a hand to help with the housework, her ears are always open.

"Good," Halina says, and juts her chin toward the children.

The children. Mimi dredges up that happy-housewife expression.

She grabs *Ladies' Home Journal* and pretends to read until Gibbins is finally at the door, ready to leave.

Mimi gets up and hands him his coat.

"Always a pleasure to see you, Mrs. Lukas."

She meets his gray-blue eyes. Nothing about tonight has been pleasurable. Not for her, and she suspects not for him. They hold each other's gaze for several seconds, longer, perhaps than they ever have before. Surely, he can see her desperation. Hear her silent plea. *Do something!*

"Thanks for coming tonight," she finally says, though *thanks for nothing* is more like it. She closes the front door behind him and watches through the glass as he strolls to his Lincoln coupe. Its headlights flash on, the engine rumbles to life, and he's gone.

Mimi stares out at the quiet street a moment longer, girding her courage. The houses around them sit like the backdrop of a play, their curtains drawn and porch lights glowing. That snooty Mrs. Davenport notwithstanding, Mimi's friendly with all their neighbors. She knows the wives by name, the ages of their children, the occupations of their husbands. They've lent one another cake plates, complimented one another's flower gardens, passed around the clothes and toys their kids have outgrown. But how well does she actually know them? What's happening behind their shrouded windows and shut doors? Do they look at her house and wonder the same thing?

Mimi shakes her head. Wondering won't get the dishes clean or kids to bed. It won't fill their pantry or fatten their bank account.

Stan's still in the kitchen twenty minutes later when she returns to finish the dishes. The water in the sink is cold and the suds gone. Cigarette smoke lingers in the air. She reaches beneath the stack of plates and pulls the plug. Once the water fully drains, she turns on the sink and starts again.

"What did Gibbins have to say?" she asks over the running water.

"Nothing good."

"So . . . what's next?"

Stan shrugs, and Mimi turns back to the sink. She's halfway through the dishes before she works up the courage to say over her shoulder, "I was thinking, what if I went back to work as a nurse? Just until . . . until you land with a new team."

She's hoping he'll come clean about the news Gibbins delivered. That there won't be a new team. Instead, he says, "What?"

Mimi turns around, dripping dish in hand.

"A new team. Is Gibbins still making calls or—"

"No, before that."

"Oh, I thought I'd look for a nursing job."

His brow furrows, and she rushes to add, "Not a live-in position like before. Something . . . less demanding."

It's suddenly so quiet in the kitchen, Mimi can hear the soap bubbles popping in the sink behind her.

"So you're giving up on me, too."

"That's not it at all," Mimi says, even as a knot of guilt twists in her abdomen at the small paperboard box secreted in her purse.

"You think I can't provide for this family?" Stan's voice fills the kitchen. Mimi winces and glances through the narrow doorway down the hall. She put the kids to bed, but Halina is still up. And undoubtedly listening.

Mimi drops the dish back into the sudsy water. She crosses the kitchen and crouches in front of him, placing a wet hand on his knee. Not the knee of his bum leg. He still flinches when anyone touches it. Even her.

"Of course I don't think that. But Stan, we're running out of options."

"We've got plenty of options. Gibbins is just getting started."

"Washington's out. Philadelphia's out. St. Louis is out. Who else is there?"

Stan frowns down at her. "Listening, were you? You're as bad as my mother."

"Don't change the subject. Who?"

"Boston, Pittsburgh, New York."

Mimi laughs. "The Yankees?"

"The Giants," Stan says sourly. He tugs at the knot of his tie, fighting with it until it finally whips free of his collar. He balls it up and tosses it onto the table amid the dinner crumbs and stray flecks of cigarette ash. "And why not the Yankees? You think I ain't got it anymore?"

She bites her lip and wills herself not to glance at his crutches.

"If you think that, you might as well take the kids and leave right now."

Mimi flinches. He's never suggested such a thing before. Her eyes prickle, and a tear escapes before she can blink it away. "I see."

She rises on unsteady legs and returns to the dishes. The water's gone cold again, but she doesn't care.

"Aw, hell, Mimi. You know I didn't mean that."

She picks up a plate and drags her dishcloth in slow circles across its surface. She hadn't expected the conversation to go so poorly. Maybe she should have waited a few days for the sting of Gibbins's words to wear off before bringing up the idea of her going back to work.

She rinses the plate, sets it in the drying rack, and grabs another. They don't have a few days, though. The pantry shelves are already thinning out. She's been buying cheaper cuts of meat and day-old bread for weeks now.

Her dishcloth moves more frantically over the plate. Scrub, rinse, repeat. Did they really outrun the last nine years of the Depression, only to fall victim to it now?

Behind her, Stan's chair creaks, and his crutches knock together. Mimi doesn't look back. A few noisy steps, and he's close enough his breath warms the nape of her neck.

"I'm sorry, peach. You know I don't mean what I say when I'm mad. I'd be lost without you." He nuzzles below her ear. Mimi sighs and leans back against his chest.

"I don't care if Jimmy and the rest of the team think I'm washed up," he says, and snakes an arm around her waist. "I don't care if Washington and Philly agree. But I gotta know that *you* still believe in me."

Mimi turns to face him. "I do."

He leans down to kiss her, but she holds up a hand. "This isn't about belief, Stan. We're in trouble." After losing the refrigerator, she took it upon herself to open all those important-looking letters she'd been putting aside for him. They only confirmed what she already knew. "The bills from the hospital all but wiped out our savings, and more are coming due. We'll be out of money by Thanksgiving."

His hand drops from her waist, and he takes a hobbling step backward. "It's not as bad as all that. I can always ask Gibbins for a loan."

"A loan? How would we pay that back?"

"Not a loan. An advance."

"An advance against what?"

"My next contract. Worst comes to worst, I can hit the tryout field come spring. Show them just how much Slammin' Stach still has in him."

Mimi shakes her head. They're going in circles again. "You'd rather borrow money from Gibbins than have me work as a nurse again?"

"Who's gonna take care of the kids? The house?"

"Your mother can help out while I'm away. Penny, too."

Stan scrubs a hand over his face. "I'm going to bed. We'll talk about this later."

But Mimi knows they won't. Just like they don't talk about his baseball career being over. Or their refrigerator being repossessed. She watches him totter away on his crutches, then turns back to the sink full of dishes. The face reflected in the cloudy water is wan and tired. No more happy-housewife smile. Instead, grim, purse-lipped determination.

At least if they don't talk about it, he can't tell her no.

CHAPTER 4

Superintendent Hale stands at a file cabinet and pulls out a drawer. "Class of twenty-eight, you say?"

"Yes." Mimi smooths her skirt, nervous as a schoolgirl again. "Gunther was my maiden name."

Nerves aren't the only thing rattling around inside her. Being back at the nurse training school attached to Cook County Hospital has stirred up excitement, too. The days were long and the work difficult, but she loved being a student.

"Ah, here you are." Superintendent Hale pulls out a manila folder and seats herself at the desk. After a moment of leafing through its contents, she looks up. "Miriam, yes. I remember you. That was only my second year as superintendent, and you were one of the best students. You graduated, what, third in your class?"

"Second."

She'd studied hard for the honor. Unlike most of the other nursing students, Mimi didn't come from the city. Science and Latin weren't part of the curriculum at the one-room schoolhouse she'd attended as a girl. The only thing she knew of medicine came from the mouths of the traveling pitchmen who stopped by their farm every summer with their cure-all elixirs.

That is, until a Red Cross nurse visited their church when Mimi was seventeen. After the benediction and closing hymn, the nurse was ushered forward to speak about her time in France during the war. Later that afternoon, she gave a lecture for the womenfolk about hygiene and nutrition. Mimi had never met anyone as bright and worldly. The nurse reminded her of Ginny—or at least of the woman her sister might have become. Afterward, when she gave Mimi a Red Cross pamphlet and told her about the Illinois Training School for Nurses, Mimi saw a chance for a life beyond the farm. Saw a chance and seized it.

Things hadn't worked out quite the way she expected, though.

"I must say," Superintendent Hale says, closing Mimi's folder. "I was disappointed to hear of you leaving the profession so soon. A smart, eager woman like you could have made a real difference."

Mimi shifts in her seat, crossing and uncrossing her ankles. "I've made a difference in my own way." Her gaze drops to her hands. "In the home."

"I'm sure you have." Superintendent Hale's voice is sincere.

"I've two children—seven and ten. They're darling little things but certainly a handful. Always up to some antics. Not that I'm complaining. I always wanted to be a mother. Long before nursing school." Mimi forces a smile. She's rambling. Why does she feel like a lowly student again?

Superintendent Hale folds her hands atop her desk and returns Mimi's smile. "Why are you here, Mrs. Lukas?"

Kind but direct, just like Mimi remembers her. Now, as then, her manner has a strange way of putting Mimi at ease. Ginny was the same way. The one person Mimi always knew she could trust.

She stanches the thought and straightens. "I'm thinking about rejoining the profession. But honestly, I don't know where to begin. I've been scouring the help wanted pages but haven't found a thing."

"There are not many private duty assignments anymore," Superintendent Hale says. "Those that do come up are quickly filled by referral."

"Oh . . . I suppose that's to be expected in hard times."

"That's part of it, yes. But even the dwindling moneyed class prefers a private hospital room to home care these days. Though they often hire a special to assist."

Mimi leans forward in her chair. She hadn't considered a special duty position, but that type of assignment might be just the ticket. Short-term and not too grueling. Usually, a special was only needed for those critical first few days of a patient's admission. But those who could afford it often retained her service for their entire hospital stay, enjoying the luxury of a nurse at their bedside all hours of the day. "And those positions?"

"Largely by referral, too, I'm afraid."

Mimi sighs. She unpins her hat and places it in her lap, worrying the brim. The felt has begun to wear, and her fingers trip over the uneven fabric.

"You worked a private duty assignment after graduation. Have you contacted the client?" Superintendent Hale asks. "Let them know you've a mind to start working again? Perhaps they could refer you to someone. Or at least provide a reference."

"He's since passed, I'm afraid. His wife, too."

Superintendent Hale purses her lips, deepening the lines that bracket her mouth. Her hair—once a warm brown—is now heavily threaded with silver, and bags hang beneath her eyes. But it's her hands that most betray her age. Blue veins bulge beneath chapped and liver-spotted skin. Mimi's hands are chapped, too. But not from years of scrubbing with antiseptic. For her, the culprit is more mundane: dish suds and laundry soap. A good smear of lotion usually does the trick to hide it. But today she was in such a state of nerves, she forgot.

Mimi's face must look older, too, despite the powder and rouge. She has yet to find a gray hair, but Mimi knows it's coming soon enough. Her mother was entirely gray by forty. Ma blamed Ginny's death for that—all the heartache and trouble it caused. But by that account, Mimi should have gone gray, too, for she felt the loss far more deeply.

Perhaps she isn't being fair. A mother now herself, she can't imagine losing a child, what that would do to her soul. Losing a sister was bad enough.

Mimi rattles her head. She thinks of Ginny every day, but not her death. That she keeps tucked deep away. Damn her visit to the doctor for jostling it free.

"Could you provide a referral?"

"No," Superintendent Hale says. "You're not the only one out there looking for work, Mrs. Lukas. Other former students, some with years more experience than you, have requested the same thing. I've told them no, as well. The school cannot involve itself in such things. Not once a nurse is no longer under our supervision. We cannot afford the risk to our reputation should that nurse prove . . . unsuitable."

"But I—"

She holds her hand up. "While I like to think all our graduates are women of impeccable character, times are still hard. And hard times make for hard choices."

"Are you saying you think I'd steal from patients or take advantage of them in some other way?"

"No, Mrs. Lukas. I do not think you would. You always had a strong moral compass. That is something I remember of you. But I cannot do for one what I am unwilling to do for another. I hope you understand."

Mimi nods, even as her shoulders fall. "I suppose I must look for a job at a hospital, then. Do you know any that are hiring?"

Superintendent Hale pulls out a sheet of paper and writes down two names. She pauses, then writes down another.

"That's all?" Mimi asks when she hands her the paper.

"Presbyterian had an opening or two, but I think they've been filled. You can check, though. Nurse Reinhart handles hiring there."

Mimi glances down at the paper. To get to any of these hospitals from her home, she'll have to sit through dozens of stops on the L and transfer lines at least once. That means more time away from home, from her family, from all the housework she'll still have to do.

"I'm hoping to work only two or three days a week. Do you suppose any of those hospitals will agree to such an arrangement?"

Superintendent Hale leans back in her chair and gives Mimi a pitying smile. "Not when other nurses are willing to work six. If you can find such a situation, it will likely be a night duty position, I'm afraid, with little advance notice of your schedule."

"Night duty?"

"What did you expect?"

Mimi looks down, not trusting herself to hide her disappointment. She'd forgotten many hospitals had schools attached to them. Why pay a nurse to staff the ward when a student would do? She folds the paper slowly and tucks it into her purse. Her excitement has bled away. Her nerves, too. But not her resolve. "Thank you, Superintendent. This is most helpful."

They both stand.

"Good luck, Mrs. Lukas."

With no reference or referral, Mimi has a feeling she's going to need all the luck she can get.

CHAPTER 5

After more than a dozen inquiries and two not-so-successful interviews, Mimi finally lands a position at Chicago Memorial. Night duty, as Superintendent Hale predicted, with a schedule so erratic, Mimi often doesn't know more than a few hours in advance whether or not she's working the upcoming shift.

She's promised Stan it's only temporary. As soon as he signs with a new team, she'll quit. Neither admits—at least not to the other—how unlikely it is he'll sign with a new team at all. But as long as three meals a day appear on the table, Stan doesn't grumble. Not much, anyway.

Halina grumbles enough for the both of them, since she's the one making breakfast when Mimi's late getting home from the hospital. (If putting a box of cereal and jug of milk on the table can be called "making" anything.) But Mimi suspects her grousing is just for show. If there's one thing she admires about Halina, it's her tenderness and devotion to the children.

Besides, her mother-in-law's a shrewd woman. She's seen their cupboards emptying. Watched the electric refrigerator being wheeled away. She may not like the extra work, but it beats the alternative. If she weren't so stubborn, she might actually thank Mimi.

But *dziękuję* isn't in her vocabulary. Not as far as Mimi's concerned.

Thanks or not, someone in the Lukas household must make

money. Mimi's proud that someone is her. But that pride, along with her excitement at being back in the hospital, fades as quickly as her once bright uniform.

There are parts of the job she loves—talking with patients and rubbing their backs before bed, taking their temperature and blood pressure, readying the doctor's tray and assisting with an emergency procedure, checking the medication list and passing out the various pills and solutions. But much of her time is spent on other tasks—making out the diet sheet and census report for the next day, cutting paper for the night and day reports, scrubbing bedpans and urinals, dusting the ward, filling inkwells, stacking linen, straightening the medicine cabinet. It's her job to ensure the ward is in tiptop shape and ready for the day nurses and doctors when they arrive in the morning. This *and* care for patients who wake during the night needing a warm compress, a dose of pain medicine, or an emesis basin. When the night supervisor, Nurse Thumble, rounds at five A.M., Mimi's always behind. Never mind she's only been working at Chicago Memorial for a few weeks, and her skills are still a bit rusty.

Well, maybe that's an understatement. *Very* rusty.

This shift was particularly bad. Her uniform is stained with vomit, and her feet ache from hurrying back and forth to the washroom all night long. The day nurse gave her an earful for not refilling the patients' water pitchers or restocking the treatment room with fresh dressings. Nurse Thumble threatened to speak to the head nurse if Mimi's performance doesn't improve.

It's nearly eight-thirty A.M. before she leaves the hospital. It's been twenty-four hours since Mimi last slept—or maybe twenty-six. Her brain's so addled, it's hard to keep track. She'd meant to nap yesterday afternoon, but the laundry took longer than expected, and Penny needed help with her schoolwork.

Now, all she's thinking about is getting home and slipping into bed. Hopefully she can get a full three hours' rest before needing to get up to make lunch. She unpins her nurse's cap as she nears the back door and tugs on her coat. Her hand is on the knob when she hears someone call out behind her.

"Mimi? Mimi Gunther?"

She turns. A well-dressed woman hurries toward her, her patent leather shoes *click-clack*ing on the linoleum floor. Soft dark curls frame her face, and bright red lipstick paints her lips. Mimi doesn't recognize her, even as the woman pulls her close for a hug.

"Mimi! I knew it was you."

They pull apart, and then it dawns on her. "Emily!"

"Yeah, silly, didn't you recognize me?"

Mimi smooths down her frazzled hair, wishing she'd powdered her face or at least splashed some water on her cheeks before leaving the ward. "I—it's been a long night, and I didn't—I haven't seen you since . . ."

"Your wedding. You said we'd get together for a drink after you got back from your honeymoon, and you'd find me a handsome ballplayer, too, remember?"

Mimi doesn't remember. It still feels as if her thoughts are stuck together with chewing gum. These mornings, it's hard enough to remember where the L station is, let alone who said what over a decade ago.

"Sorry, I was . . ."

"Don't worry about it. That's love for you." She gives Mimi a wink. "You two were so smitten with each other, I doubt you made it much beyond the bedroom most days."

Heat blooms in Mimi's cheeks. Emily always did have the mouth of a flapper; *that* she remembers. "Do you work here?"

"Goodness, no. I'm just here dropping off some paperwork for a patient. I have an office job." Her words have a slight whiff of superiority. "With Dr. Millstone—you remember him, don't you?"

More of their nursing school days together are breaking through the cloud of Mimi's fatigue. Cheeky, yes, and sometimes prideful, but Emily could make even a skeleton laugh. She was kind. And a loyal friend. Mimi wishes now they'd gotten that drink after all and not lost touch.

"He was the doctor who lectured in a few of our classes, wasn't he? The one with those bright blue eyes?"

Now it's Emily's cheeks that redden, and her smile widens. No wonder she was so quick to bring up love. There isn't a wedding ring on her finger, but Mimi seems to remember one on Dr. Millstone's finger back when he'd lectured at the nursing school. That was a long time ago, though.

"Yep, that's the one. He's such a good physician. And swell guy to work for. He gives me a bonus at Christmastime and buys me flowers on my birthday. He even gave me two weeks off last year to care for my mom when she caught the flu. Two weeks! And he paid me same as if I'd been there."

Somehow, Mimi's pretty sure she made it up to him. "I don't suppose he's looking to hire a second nurse."

"Nope, sorry." She glances down at the cap in Mimi's hand, and her brow furrows as if she's only just noticed it. Good old Emily. Kind, yes. Observant, no. They used to joke in school that she would miss a patient's heartbeat and send him off to the morgue someday.

"Are you working again as a nurse? Here?"

Mimi glances over her shoulder at the door. Nice as it is to see Emily, every minute they stand here chatting is a minute she could be sleeping. And it's not as if there's anything glamorous about her new position. "Just a few days—er—nights a week. My children are both in school, so I thought it'd be nice to get back into the profession."

"What about your ballplayer?"

"Stan? Oh, he doesn't mind. Not really. He's . . . in between contracts right now, and it never hurts to have a little extra money coming in." She's coated the words in too much cheeriness—like a sundae drenched in strawberry sauce—but again, Emily doesn't seem to notice.

"I hear you there. Must be awful working nights, though. I can't imagine how my complexion would hold up with so little sleep."

"There are worse things than a dull complexion."

"Are there?" Emily laughs. It has that same infectious quality Mimi remembers—songlike and airy—but this morning, Mimi is immune. Watching the food in your cupboard dwindle—that's worse. Asking your children to stuff their feet into too-small shoes—just until you can save enough money to get new pairs secondhand—that's worse. Worrying you'll lose your home or have to sell your car to make ends meet. Mimi could go on and on. But this morning, she's too tired to lecture anyone. She knows Emily doesn't mean to give offense. Mimi was that blithe, too, before Stan's accident.

"I really should be going. I've got loads to do at home, and I'm back tonight for another shift." She reaches out and gives Emily's hand a squeeze. "It's truly great to see you. I'm so glad you're doing well."

"You, too."

Mimi turns from the pitying look in her eyes and hurries out the door. The day's sunlight blinds her, and she stumbles before finding her stride. The city is wide awake—bicycle bells ringing, automobile engines humming, train tracks rattling. People hurry to and fro around her. Mimi's aching feet can't match their pace. She's halfway down the block when she hears Emily's voice behind her again. Mimi turns around, holding her folded nurse's cap like a visor to block the sun from her eyes.

"Say, what about that drink?"

Mimi draws her bottom lip between her teeth. She doesn't have the time or money for a drink. But Emily's eager smile is just as irresistible as it was in nursing school. "Now?"

"No, silly. The evening sometime."

"Sure," Mimi says, exhaustion bleeding into her voice. "I'll ring you." She turns to go, but Emily stops her.

"You don't have my number."

"Oh, right."

Emily wags her head, then pulls a pencil and small pad from her purse. She writes down her phone number but doesn't hand the paper over to Mimi. Instead, she puts the pencil in her mouth, chewing on the end. Her kohl-rimmed eyes dart furtively about.

Mimi glances about, as well, but nothing about the bustling city is amiss. It's several seconds before Emily stops gnawing on the pencil and removes it from her lips.

"I might know of a clinic looking for a nurse."

"Really?"

Emily nods. "Dr. Millstone helps out there sometimes." Her once lusty voice is now barely audible above the morning din. She scratches something else onto the paper but pauses again before finally handing it over. Written beneath her telephone number is a physician's name and an address in the Loop.

"Don't give that out to anyone else, you hear?"

"Sure, of course." Though Mimi can't think why it would matter. Unless the doctor's one of those uppity types who can barely stand anyone's presence but his own. Even if he is, it would be better than

Memorial. Or maybe it's one of those specialty practices that cater to film stars and business moguls. Imagine that! "What kind of office is it?"

Emily looks around again. "You'll see when you get there. Tell them I sent you."

A prickle dances down the back of Mimi's neck. Something about this isn't right. Maybe it's not a specialty practice at all, but a shade more sinister. This is Chicago, after all. What is it Pa always said? *If somethin' seems too good to be true, you best believe it is.*

"Thank you," Mimi manages, her excitement draining away.

Emily pulls her into another hug. "That's what friends are for, right?" The wariness is gone from her eyes, and a smile brightens her face. "Remember what I said. And don't forget to call for drinks."

Emily turns and struts back toward the hospital, heels clicking and hips swaying. More than one passerby swivels his head to watch her go.

A chuckle builds in Mimi's chest. Same old Emily.

Her eyes fall to the slip of paper in her hand, and another shiver passes over her. This office—whatever type of work they do—isn't for her. And though it'd be nice to see Emily again, between nights at the hospital and busy days at home, when will Mimi have the time? Besides, what do they have in common anymore? It's plain Emily's done well for herself. And Mimi, well, her life's about as glamorous as a worn-out shoe. She crumples the paper into a ball and tosses it into a nearby trash can as she trudges toward the L.

CHAPTER 6

The sound of clanking metal startles Mimi awake. The instruments and supplies she set aside while she was cleaning the dressing cart lay scattered at her feet. She doesn't remember nodding off, but she must have, accidentally knocking everything off the table when she did. Her eyes dart around the ward. A few of the patients stir, but none awaken. And no Nurse Thumble. Thank goodness for that. If she caught Mimi with her eyes closed—even for a moment—it'd be another visit to the head nurse's office. Mimi already made one visit this week and endured a lengthy reprimand. On her way out of the office, she overheard the head nurse sigh and say to Nurse Thumble, "I should have known better. Mothers seldom make good nurses."

Now, Mimi rises from her chair and gathers up the supplies—scissors, forceps, tweezers, a scalpel, unraveled rolls of gauze. She'll have to clean and reorganize everything. At least she's not behind on her tasks—most of which are pure drudgery. All the excitement happens during the earlier shifts. Half the patients are already asleep when she arrives. Those who aren't are often querulous and hard to please. By the time she gets them settled with extra pillows, hot-water bottles, cups of warm milk, a few aspirin, or a sleeping draught, the light sleepers are waking with their own demands. It's usually past midnight before everyone's finally asleep, though she can expect a few to wake again, usually when her arms are full of linen, or she's down on her hands and knees scrubbing the floor.

Perhaps Mimi wouldn't mind if it weren't so like the work she did at home, only instead of taking care of four people, she's looking after twenty. She went to nursing school to do more than clean and help people to the toilet.

She finishes with the dressing cart and takes it to the storage room. Next, she'll start on the medication log. Each patient's medicines must be copied onto a new page for the coming week. She prefers to use the large table in the center of the ward rather than the cramped desk in the medication closet. The lighting is poor, but she can keep a better eye on the patients.

She tucks the heavy log under her arm and grabs a pen, her mind drifting to tomorrow. Can she stretch the chicken in the icebox into two meals instead of one? Can that tear in Junior's trousers be mended, or will he need a new pair? Halfway to the table, she trips over the mop bucket she'd left out after a patient spilled his milk on the floor. The bucket topples. The pen and logbook go flying. Mimi falls, landing hard on her hands and knees in a growing puddle of dirty water.

A few of the patients startle awake. One of them cries out, "Enemy fire! Take cover!" It's Mr. Burroughs. He's here for a flare-up of gout, but the day nurse mentioned to be careful of loud noises around him, too. Shell shock from the war.

Mimi clambers to her feet and rushes to his side. "It's all right, Mr. Burroughs. You're here at Chicago Memorial Hospital. You're safe." He thrashes within the cage of her arms and continues to yell. His elbow collides with her face. Not until she manages to turn on the bedside lamp does he still.

Her nose is bleeding. She stanches the flow with one hand while wiping the sweat from Mr. Burroughs's brow with the other. Once he's calm and his tangled blankets righted, she glances around the ward. Nearly every other patient is sitting up awake.

Nurse Thumble arrives a moment later, her face pinched with displeasure. "What is going on, Nurse—" She stops, her eyes widening.

"The blood's mine," Mimi reassures her.

But Nurse Thumble isn't looking at her blood-stained uniform.

Mimi follows her gaze past the overturned mop bucket to the medication log. It's lying open, face down in the pool of dirty water. They both rush toward it. Mimi reaches it first. Its water-logged pages drip as she picks it up. Ignoring the trickle of blood from her nose, she dabs at the book's edges with her apron to sop up the water. But before Mimi can fully survey the damage, Nurse Thumble grabs it.

She flips it open to a random page, and Mimi's stomach drops.

"Nurse Lukas, what have you done?"

It isn't really a question—it's plain what Mimi has done. The logbook is ruined. The entries are nothing more than messy blots of ink. "It was entirely an accident. I tripped on my way to the table and—"

"And who left the mop bucket in the middle of the ward?"

"Well . . . I did, but—"

"How are we to administer patients' morning medicine without a legible record?"

"I'll use the patients' charts and make a new log." Never mind the hours it will take. No hope of getting out on time today.

"Indeed you will. But what if a doctor wishes to know whether a patient received their full regimen of medication yesterday or the day before? What are we to tell him?"

Mimi blots at the ink-smeared page with her apron and points at one of the rows. "Some of the entries are still legible. Once it dries, I can copy those, too."

Nurse Thumble slams the book shut, nearly catching Mimi's fingers. Her eyes rake over Mimi's uniform, and her expression puckers, as if she's just noticing the blood. "Clean yourself up and see to your patients. You've woken the entire ward with your foolery." She holds up the medication log, still dripping ink-stained water. "As for this, we'll see what the head nurse has to say in the morning."

Mimi swallows. Whatever the head nurse says, it won't be good.

CHAPTER 7

Mimi arrives home just as the mailman is leaving, bright-eyed and whistling. He waves to her, and it's all she can do to return the gesture, never mind his smile. Her nose is sore, and her uniform ruined—but that hardly matters now. Waiting in the mailbox is another one of those important-looking letters, the kind she used to set aside for Stan.

She puts off opening it until that evening, after the dinner dishes are washed and the children asleep. Stan and Halina relax in the living room, listening to Glenn Miller and His Orchestra play over the radio. From where she sits at the kitchen table, Mimi can just make out the swinging rhythm. It's the sort of music that makes her feet itch to dance. But tonight, Mimi is immune.

Before her is splayed a mess of papers and receipts. Her budget book lays open to one side next to the long, slender Addometer. Bite marks pock the end of her pencil.

This newest letter is from the Cook County Treasurer's Office. The second installment of their property taxes was due last month. Now, in addition to the 105 dollars they owe in taxes, they must pay a delinquency fee of two dollars and seventy-five cents. If they don't, that fee will keep rising, and eventually they'll lose the house.

Her stomach clenches at the thought. She remembers the Sullivans from down the street who lost their home in '34. And the Clarkes, two blocks up, whose house was sold out from under them in '37. She can still picture the bewildered look on their faces as they stood amid a sea of furniture on the curb. It's hard to imagine it happening to you. Until it does.

Mimi shudders and turns her attention to the other bills. They're still paying down Stan's hospital bill, with another fifteen dollars due at the end of the month. They owe five for the stove. Four for the telephone, and ten seventy-five to the utility. Even without the refrigerator, their electric bill remains high. Perhaps she needs to switch their light bulbs to a lower wattage. Run the vacuum less. Limit how often they use the toaster.

She tallies each expense in her notebook. There's still enough for the marketing if she shops the weekend sales and switches to brown eggs. Enough for this week, anyway. Next week, too, if they keep the oil burner in the basement on low. But what then? They won't just come for her electric stove, but their home, too, if they can't scrape together the money to pay the taxes.

Mimi gnaws on the end of the pencil, then sets it down and rubs her temples. Perhaps she could ask her parents for a loan. Mimi frowns at the thought. They never approved of her "big city lifestyle." Fingernail polish, knee-length skirts, the occasional evening of dancing or bridge—it was all sinful. And they'd draw a straight line from that to her current situation. *For he that soweth to his flesh, shall of the flesh reap corruption*, and so on. But she'd stomach the browbeating, stomach the memories a visit home is sure to stir up, if it means a new coat for Junior and warmer stockings for Penny. If it means saving their home. But asking them is no use. Even if they did care to help, all their money is tied up in the farm.

She tucks the bills and receipts into her notebook and closes it. She's getting better with all this figuring—what bill is due when, how much to budget for gasoline and laundry soap. Those ten-cent fares on the L and monthly newspaper subscriptions add up. It's depressing how quickly the money she made at Memorial is vanishing. A few weeks, and it will be gone.

In the bathroom, she washes her face with icy water—hot water will raise the electric bill—and ties up her hair. Her nose is still slightly swollen, though no one in the house gave it a lick of notice. Nothing sounds better than curling up in bed, but she and Stan can't put off talking about their troubles forever.

The radio continues to hum. Smoke drifts from the living room into the hallway, thanks to the new habit Stan picked up after Gibbins's last visit. Mimi coughs and waves it away. She stops in the doorway, glancing at Stan and his mother. Were it not for the flutter of Halina's crochet hook and the smoldering tip of his cigarette, they could be statues.

"Mamo, can I talk to Stan a moment?" Mimi says. Stan insists she calls her that, *Mamo.* Mother. Neither of the women like it.

Halina doesn't move. "Go on."

Mimi sighs. In her mother-in-law's mind, there are public matters—things anyone may hear—and there are family matters—things only the adults of the house should be privy to. There are no husband-and-wife matters.

"In private."

"I'm listening to the music."

Mimi holds back another sigh. Halina couldn't tell Glenn Miller from Bob Wills and the Texas Playboys. She doesn't care about the music, only about making Mimi miserable.

Mimi had once hoped they might be close. That Halina might fill the gulf that grew between Mimi and her own mother after Ginny's death. The night Stan first took her home to meet his parents, Mimi splurged on an expensive bouquet of lilies and roses, presenting them to Halina along with her best smile. Halina took the flowers without thanks, frowning down at them as if they were weeds. Later that night, while Mimi helped bring the dirty dinner dishes into the kitchen, she noticed the beautiful bouquet crammed into the trash bin.

She'll warm to you, Stan promised. But she never did. No one was good enough for her *aniołek*, her little angel, certainly not Mimi, who didn't have a drop of Polish blood in her body. And Mimi's long since given up trying to win her affection.

"Fine." Mimi looks at Stan. "In the bedroom, then."

Stan flicks his cigarette over the ashtray and takes another drag.

"Please," she must say before he stubs out the cigarette and reaches for his cane.

As she watches him rise, Mimi can't help but recall an earlier time when the mere mention of the bedroom would have drawn a smile from Stan's lips. When he would have leaped from the sofa and followed close at her heels.

Her thoughts drift back further still. Him, a young man in a hospital bed. Her, a nursing student one month shy of graduation. She studies his chart as she enters his room, then looks up to find him grinning at her.

"Good morning, Mr. . . . Mr. . . ." She glances back down at his chart. "Luka . . . Lukasewicz."

"I go by Lukas. Stan Lukas. Ever heard of me?"

"It says here, Stanislaw Lukasewicz. Unless it's incorrect, that's what I shall call you."

"Please don't. Only my mother calls me that."

The head nurse is a stickler for formal address. She'd read Mimi the riot act if she overheard her use anything but the man's proper name. But his doggone smile wins her over. "All right, Mr. Lukas. How are you feeling this morning?"

"Stan. Call me Stan."

Mimi glances over her shoulder. "I can't."

"Fine. What can I call you?"

"Me?"

His smile widens, and she decides she doesn't like it after all—those full lips and straight teeth. The dimple in his left cheek. Too cocky and decidedly distracting.

"You may call me *nurse*."

"Nurse what?"

"Just nurse. Now lay back so I can examine your incision and change the dressing."

Stan does as she asks. "You really ain't heard of me?"

"No."

She's careful to draw the blankets over his hips before raising his gown. His stomach is smooth and well-muscled, with a line of soft hair only a shade darker than the sandy blond of his head. It's not the first man's stomach she's seen. With nearly three years of schooling behind her, she's seen hundreds. Plenty of them smooth and muscled. It's only that gosh-darn grin of his that has her cheeks still burning. At least, that's what she tells herself.

She removes the dressing from the right side of his abdomen and studies the three-inch incision beneath. The skin is drawn together with a careful row of stitches. Pink and a little puffy, with flecks of dried blood at the edges. No pus. No odor. No separation. Warm, but not hot to the touch.

"You're lucky," she says.

"I am? How?"

"Appendicitis. It can be deadly at any age, but it's rare in adults, so it's often overlooked."

"Guess I am lucky, then. Any chance of getting more lucky and learning your name?"

She makes a quick note in his chart, ignoring his question. Fraternizing with patients is strictly forbidden, and she's not about to be expelled because of him.

He fights back a wince as she cleans the incision, and again when she pats it dry. "It doesn't disgust you?"

"What?"

He waves vaguely around the room. A callused ridge marches along his palm just below his fingers. "All of this. The blood. The guts. The gore."

"I was raised on a farm, so, no."

"A farm?"

Another thing she shouldn't have said. He'll think her a bumpkin for sure.

"You don't sound like you're from a farm."

"And just how do farmers sound?"

No more smile. Good.

"Listen, I didn't mean—"

She slaps a clean dressing over his incision. This time, he can't keep his face from scrunching in pain. She's more careful applying the tape.

"I just meant to say, well, you sound real smart. Not that farmers ain't smart. Heck, they gotta be to know how many seeds to put in the ground and when and how long before it's time to . . . to . . ."

"To harvest?"

"Exactly!"

Now she's the one smiling.

"I was just trying to pay you a compliment, is all. But I ain't smart like you, so I guess I bungled it."

She pulls down his hospital gown.

"How about this one," he says. "You sure got lovely eyes. The color of a well-done steak."

"A well-done steak?"

For a moment, that easy confidence in his own eyes—cornflower blue—seems to falter.

"Sure. Just the way I like it."

She chokes down a laugh. "Save your strength, Mr. Lukas. The night nurse has lovelier eyes than I do."

"I doubt that. But if you don't like steak, how about this one? You're as pretty as peach pie."

Before she can ask him what's so pretty about peach pie, one of her classmates pokes her head into the doorway. "Mimi, can you help . . ." Her gaze locks on Stan as her voice trails off. "Say, don't I know you from somewhere?"

"Well, I don't know. Do you watch—"

"My help with what?" Mimi interrupts, looking between the two of them. Her classmate's eyes have gone wide, and Stan—Mr. Lukas—is positively preening.

"Umm . . . just a sponge bath. My patient in bed ten is due for surgery and—"

"I'll be there to help as soon as I'm through here."

"Thanks," her classmate says, without bothering to peel her stare away from Mr. Lukas.

Mimi clears her throat.

Her classmate startles and rattles her head. "Nice to meet you, Mr. . . ."

"Lukasewicz," Mimi says before he can speak. She waits for her classmate to drift away before turning back to him. She's curious what he was about to say after *do you watch*, but doesn't ask. He's handsome enough to be a film star, but even though Mimi hasn't seen many movies, she's certainly read enough *Picture Play* magazines to recognize him if he were. Maybe a stage actor, then, or—

"So that's your name. *Mimi*. What's it short for?"

"It's short for none of your beeswax."

He chuckles, and it's a surprisingly rich sound, one that skitters pleasantly over her skin.

"All right, Mimi."

"Nurse."

"Nurse Mimi."

"Just nurse."

"All right, just nurse. Can I take you dancing when I get out of here?"

Her gaze shoots up from the metal tray table where she's gathered up the leftover dressing supplies.

"No."

"Why not?"

"I don't know how to dance."

It's true. Ma and Pa forbade such things. But Mimi regrets saying so. If he didn't think her a country bumpkin before, now he surely does. And then, of course, there's the correct answer, the one she's managed to give before when other male patients got fresh—namely, that it's against school policy.

"I'll teach you," he says, his voice almost a purr. Mimi's sturdy legs go momentarily weak. He's cocky as all get out, but there's a kindness to him, too. A gentleness his wide shoulders and stocky thighs belie. Not that she noticed in any way beyond her nursely duty. The thought of fox-trotting with him, of feeling his hand on her back and breath on her cheek, isn't helping her legs any.

She grabs the last of her supplies along with his chart. "No."

"Please."

"Mr. Lukas—"

"Stan."

"Mr. Lukas, it's not uncommon for a patient to develop misplaced feelings for his nurse. Why, you only came out of surgery yesterday. Likely as not, your words are the aftereffect of ether. I've no doubt you'll say the same thing to the night nurse and to tomorrow's nurse, should it not be me. By the time you leave, you'll have made so many offers, your social calendar will be filled for weeks. So let me save you a day and spare us both the embarrassment when you can't remember my name the next time you see me."

Mimi turns to leave, but the waggish note in his voice stops her.

"That sounds like a challenge."

She doesn't look back, but she has to bite her lip to keep from grinning. It wouldn't do for the head nurse to see her mooning over a patient.

Of course, Stan won that particular challenge. Two weeks later, when he was discharged from the hospital, he took Mimi to the Sunset Café and taught her the Charleston and the Lindy Hop and the Texas Tommy and, yes, that foxtrot she'd been imagining.

Now, as Stan limps from the living room to the bedroom and Mimi follows behind, a foxtrot plays over the radio. But dancing is far from her mind. After setting his cane down by the bed, Stan pulls out his cigarettes and lights one.

"I wish you wouldn't, Stan. Not here in the bedroom. You know how the smoke bothers me."

He tosses his pack of Camels onto the bedside table and takes a long drag before snuffing out the end with a pinch. Ash rains down onto their quilt. Mimi hurries over to his side of the bed and brushes it away before it can singe the fabric.

"Please be careful." She makes another pass with her hand, feeling the charred edges of a small hole. Mimi has never been overly fond of the quilt's colors—mustard yellow and brick red—but it was a wedding present from her grandmother.

Stan drops the cigarette onto the table, heedless of the smudge of ash it leaves on the lacquered surface.

"Really, Stan, why can't you just—"

"Is there no place in this goddamn house where I can be free from your nagging?"

His loud voice echoes off the walls.

Mimi winces. He's never called her a nag before, and she finds her eyes smarting with tears. Not only from his words, but from everything this awful day has heaped on her. He reaches for her. A slow, half-hearted gesture, as if raising his arm is a Herculean effort. Mimi steps away, and he lets his arm fall.

"What did you want to talk about?"

She hesitates, wrapping her arms around herself. "I was . . . I was fired today, Stan."

"Oh," is all he says. He looks away from her and begins unbuttoning his shirt.

Mimi waits for him to say more. Prays for more.

His fingers work slowly, maneuvering each button through its hole. One, then the next, and the next, and the next, until he's shrugging out of his shirt and peeling off his undershirt. His stomach isn't as firm as it used to be. His once trim waist has expanded a little over the years. Mimi doesn't mind. She likes the soft parts of him as well as the hard. But there's a new bulge to his belly. Slight, it's true. Mimi wouldn't mind this either if it didn't mirror their current situation. The creeping bulk of their problems. Not just money problems, but this souring between them.

He hobbles toward the hamper and tosses his clothes inside. His pants and belt, he hangs over the back of the nearby armchair to wear again tomorrow. It's better than heaping it on the floor, as she often finds his clothes these days. Then again, he's probably just trying to save himself from her nagging.

"What about our bills, Stan? We're late paying taxes on the house, and we've got over thirty dollars coming due at the end of the month."

There's no change in his expression as he limps back to the bed. Sure, at one time, thirty dollars was nothing to bat an eye over. Back in the early days of their marriage, when he was the hottest player on the team and the effects of the Depression were still far off, they sometimes spent more in a single night. But that isn't the case anymore. Why can't he see that?

"There's the telephone bill and electricity bill and two different hospital bills and—" She stops when he closes his eyes and breathes out slowly.

"I'll figure it out."

"How?"

He pulls down the covers and sits on the edge of the bed. He moves like a man of sixty, not thirty-six. "I'll call Gibbins in the morning."

The same answer he always gives. But tonight, it isn't enough. Mimi cannot bear all this on her own. "What's he going to tell you that will make a goddamn difference now, *this* month, with *these* bills? We could lose the house, Stan."

Even cussing at him—something she never does—doesn't get a rise. Instead, he just shakes his head. It's as if he used up all his stuffing with that first cutting remark. She'd rather him call her a nag again than this . . . this apathy.

It's something Mimi has never had to navigate before. Not with him. Since their first meeting in his hospital room all those years ago, he's been dogged and assured, rising to every challenge. This man seated before her now is a stranger.

But stranger or not, he's still her husband. Still the head of their household. Still a man with responsibilities he ought to uphold. And, somewhere in there, still the man she loves.

"What about selling the Packard? You're not back to driving yet, and I can manage the marketing without it. I bet it would fetch—"

"We're not selling the car." His voice is tired. "I'll need it when I'm playing again. I can't take the L to Armour Square on a game day."

"But—"

"We're not selling the car, Mimi."

"Then what about going to the public assistance office? There's a new program where families on relief can exchange special stamps for surplus farm products. Rice, beans, butter. I read about it in *Ladies*—"

"The Lukasewiczes don't take handouts," he says, his eyes narrowing with anger again.

So much for that idea. Mimi would apply herself if she could. But it would take more than a forged signature to convince the relief agency that *she* was head of the household and not just some housewife looking for a little extra pin money.

She approaches Stan like she would a skittish pup, sitting gingerly on the bed beside him, close enough to take his hand in hers, but not so close their legs are touching. He offers no resistance when she turns his hand face up in hers and traces the callused ridge at the top of his palm. "I know these last few months haven't been easy for you, darling. The season ending so abruptly, your leg not healing as it should. But maybe it's a sign." She swallows. "A sign that you should give up baseball and find something else you'd like to do."

Stan rips his hand away from her. "Baseball is my life. There's nothing else I want to do."

"Baseball isn't your life. *We're* your life." She shifts her position, turning and drawing a knee up onto the bed so she can face him head-on. "Me. The kids. Your mother. We're your life, and we need you. You did offseason work before. How is this any different?"

"You think I can dig postholes for the telephone company or run around a service station pumping gas with that damn thing?" He nods toward his cane. "It would only make my leg worse."

There are other jobs he could take that wouldn't require him to be on his feet all day, but Mimi doesn't say so. "I'll look for another nursing position, but I can't do this all on my own."

Stan doesn't look at her. "I didn't ask you to get a job."

"One of us needs to. We can't—"

"I said I'll call Gibbins in the morning, and that's what I'll do." He lies down, swinging his legs up and onto the bed so quickly, Mimi has to scramble to keep from being kicked in the gut. He reaches for his matches and the loose cigarette. "Turn off the damned light, will you?"

Mimi swats at the light switch as she storms from the room, slamming the door behind her. Tears regroup at the corners of her eyes, and her lungs frantically suck in air. What are they going to do?

No, there's no *they* anymore. Until Stan comes back to his senses, it's up to her.

She leans against the wall and tries to steady her breathing. Music continues to play on the radio in the living room—a slow, sweeping tune that ought to calm her. It doesn't.

Then she remembers the scrap of paper Emily gave her. Mimi hurries to the entryway and snatches her purse off the peg on the wall, upending its contents onto the floor. A few loose pennies tumble out, alongside her handkerchief and a tube of lipstick. Another shake, and a handful of receipts flutter out, followed by one of Junior's baseball cards.

Mimi kneels and begins to rummage through the mess before remembering she threw the address Emily had given her in the trash.

How had she been so stupid?

She doesn't care if the Chicago Outfit runs the clinic and she becomes the private nurse of Frank "The Enforcer" Nitti himself—Mimi has got to find another job.

Closing her eyes, she tries to picture the address Emily scratched down. The office was in the Loop; she remembers that much. On State Street. The doctor's name began with a G . . . Greene? Gale? Gerber?

She leaves the spilled contents of her purse on the floor and hurries to the kitchen, where they keep the telephone directory. Over a hundred doctors are listed whose last names begin with G. But only four have an office on State Street in the Loop. She writes down their addresses, praying that one of them is the mysterious doctor Emily told her about and that he's still in need of a nurse.

CHAPTER 8

The next day, Mimi takes the L to the south end of the Loop, alighting at a station on the corner of State and Van Buren. She makes her way down the stairs to street level and glances around to get her bearings. Buildings stretch toward the sky all around her. Automobiles swerve around the streetcar as it rattles past.

The first address on her list is only a block up State Street in the Lytton Building. She keeps her eyes ahead as she passes Goldblatt's Department Store. No point in admiring the fancy shoes and stylish dresses in the storefront windows when she can no longer afford them.

Arriving at the address, she realizes the telephone directory hadn't provided an office number. Mimi cranes her neck to take in the building's full height—all eighteen stories of it. There must be hundreds of offices inside.

"Two hundred and fourteen offices, to be exact," the elevator attendant tells her when she enters. He's a friendly man with a well-lined face and strands of silver in his coily black hair. But he's new—only two weeks on the job—and can't tell her which floor, let alone which office number she's looking for.

So Mimi rides to the very top and wanders the halls, one floor at a time. She passes beauty parlors, barbershops, real estate offices, a detective agency, a carpet wholesaler, a tailor shop, a photograph studio, a bank, a millinery school, and four dentist offices. Some businesses have plaques beside their doors with the proprietor's name and trade. Some have just a name. Others—like Mr. Hotchkiss, the fireworks manufacturer, and Mr. Owens, the cigar dealer—operate out of unmarked offices. Most are kind enough to open the door when she knocks. But it makes for slow going, and her feet begin to ache.

One hour and ten floors later, Mimi finds the office she's looking for: S. J. Greenblatt, M.D. She smooths her skirt and straightens her hat before entering, determined to make a good impression.

Whatever Mimi was expecting—a luxe office for the rich and famous, or a gangster hideout—this isn't it. The waiting room is spartanly adorned with blank walls and worn wooden chairs. A middle-aged woman sits beside a feverish-looking boy with snot dripping from his nose. Across the room, an old man with a bandaged eye has fallen asleep in his seat.

Mimi makes her way to the reception desk, where a rosy-cheeked woman who can't be a day over twenty is seated. She smacks her gum and flips through the pages of a magazine, not looking up until Mimi clears her throat.

"I'm here to see Dr."—Mimi fishes the paper from her pocket—"Dr. Greenblatt about a nursing position. Miss Ranus sent me."

"Who?"

"Miss Emily Ranus. She's a nurse. She said Dr. Greenblatt might be—"

"Never heard of her." The woman drops her gaze back to the glossy pages of the magazine.

"Are you sure? Perhaps Dr.—"

"I'm sure."

The wad of gum in her mouth pops loudly, and Mimi fights back a huff of frustration.

"Might I see him anyway? I'm a nurse myself and—"

"He ain't lookin' for any help."

Mimi stands there a moment, hoping someone else might magically appear with whom she could talk. But the door to the back office remains firmly shut. Behind her, the sleeping man begins to snore. The boy gives a wet sniffle.

"You're quite sure the doctor isn't looking for another nurse? I'm willing to work evenings, Sundays, even nights if need be."

The woman flips the page of her magazine without answering. Mimi sighs and leaves.

She fares no better at the next two offices on her list. Neither is easy to find, and blank stares greet her when she mentions Emily's name. The receptionists eye her like she's a panhandler at the mention of work and are quick to tell her no, the doctor isn't hiring.

By the time she makes it to the final address on her list—190 North State Street—her feet are throbbing, and the wind has whipped her carefully styled hair into a rat's nest. Somewhere between here and her last stop, her stockings snagged on something sharp, and a run streaks up her calf.

The afternoon sun has already slipped behind the hulking State Lake Building that occupies much of the block. Twelve floors' worth of windows gape down at her. Behind one of them is the office she's looking for, or so Mimi hopes. She's started to doubt her memory of that morning with Emily. Maybe the office hadn't been in the Loop. Maybe the doctor's name started with a *C*, not a *G*. Maybe her sleep-deprived mind made the whole thing up, and she hadn't run into Emily at all.

She has no choice, though, but to keep looking.

The State-Lake Theatre occupies much of the building's ground level. HENRY FONDA AND CLAUDETTE COLBERT IN DRUMS ALONG THE MOHAWK is scrawled across the marquee.

Stan used to love the pictures, and they came here often in the early days of their marriage. They'd sit toward the back and snuggle, Stan's arm draped around her shoulders or resting on her knee, sometimes inching higher when the lights went down. The thought makes her chest ache, but she pushes the feeling aside.

She passes the theater and finds a secondary entrance to the floors above. The double-wide glass doors open into a brightly lit lobby with polished stone floors. Stairs curve upward to her left, but Mimi opts for the elevator to spare her feet.

"Where to, ma'am?" the elevator attendant asks, opening the bronze gate and ushering her inside.

Mimi has little hope he'll be able to direct her to Dr. . . . Dr.—she glances down at her list—Dr. Gabler's office. She'll likely end up wandering the halls for an hour, like she has at the other buildings. But when she gives the attendant the doctor's name, he recognizes it immediately and ferries her to the sixth floor. "Office six-oh-four," he tells her when they arrive, pointing left down the hallway.

Mimi thanks him and trudges off in that direction. Halfway down the hall, she comes to a door marked 604. Beside it hangs a brass nameplate: J. GABLER, M.D. The name doesn't look any more familiar than the others, and she doesn't bother smoothing her skirt or trying to untangle her hair. What's the point, when some cheeky young receptionist is just going to turn her away again?

She twists the knob, wishing for the umpteenth time she hadn't thrown away the paper Emily gave her. Beyond the door is a small waiting room. It's warmly decorated with peach-colored walls and watercolor seascapes in lacquered frames. A cherrywood coatrack stands in one corner, and a Khalabar rug covers the floor. Of all the offices Mimi's visited, this one is decidedly the most . . . homey. It doesn't look like the kind of place run by gangsters—though Mimi's experience with the mob is nil.

Whatever the doctor's disposition, he's taken pains to make the room comfortable. Yet the three women who sit waiting seem anything but. Two have their arms tightly crossed, and none of them meet her gaze.

There's another door across the room, presumably leading to the exam room and the doctor's private office. Beside the door, a woman about Mimi's age sits at a sturdy cherrywood desk, the same shade as the coatrack and polished to the same high sheen.

No, this office bears no resemblance to a gangster's den. It's not quite posh enough to be the type of clinic that caters to the rich and famous, either. The women waiting here aren't film stars or society-page socialites. Nothing about them or the office would make someone look over her shoulder before writing down the address. Slim chance, then, that this is the place Emily told her about.

Mimi's heart falls, but she plods over to the receptionist nonetheless. The woman greets her with a smile, her hands folded atop a closed ledger. With her sweeping shoulder-length blond hair, she resembles Marlene Dietrich. She's got the starlet's bedroom eyes, too, but they're framed by a stylish pair of silver-rimmed eyeglasses.

"Can I help you?" the Dietrich lookalike asks.

"I'm here to see Dr. Gabler."

"Do you have an appointment?"

"No. A friend, Miss Ranus, sent me."

"And you're . . ." the woman says, with the inflection of a question.

Maybe it's her aching feet or the prospect of an entire day wasted (not to mention the cost of the L), but words spill from Mimi's mouth, unchecked by decorum. "Please, I'm desperate. I've got no place left to go. If I could just speak with Dr. Gabler, I'm sure—"

"I understand." The woman retrieves an index card from the desk drawer. "I'll just need to get a few details from you. Name?"

"Miriam Lukas."

"Address?"

Mimi tells her where she lives, along with her telephone number and age, when asked. She expects the next questions to be about her schooling and experience, but instead the woman says, "Date of your last menstrual period?"

"What?"

"How far along are you?"

Mimi stands there for a moment, dumbfounded, before making sense of the confusion. "Oh, no, I'm not a patient." She gives an uneasy laugh. "I'm here to see about a job. My friend—Nurse Ranus, that is, from Dr. Millstone's office—she said Dr. Gabler had a nursing position he's looking to fill."

There's a soft *ahem* to Mimi's right, and she turns. The door to the back rooms has opened, and a stout, grave-faced woman stands there.

"She," the woman says.

"Excuse me?"

"Dr. Gabler is a woman."

"Oh! I'm so sorry. Nurse Ranus didn't say, and I just assumed . . ." Mimi flashes the woman an apologetic look, hoping she hasn't dashed her chances right out of the gate.

The woman's gaze slides from Mimi to the receptionist, and her lips flatten. It's the same look Halina gives Mimi any time the soufflé falls or the roast turns out dry. "Really, Miss Kuder, you must be more careful."

The receptionist wilts.

"You're a nurse, then?" the woman says, returning her attention to Mimi. There's a slight lilt to her voice. Scottish, perhaps? Irish?

"Yes," Mimi answers.

"Do you have any surgical experience?"

She hesitates. Surgical experience? What need would there be for that in an office? "Some, but it was—er—quite a while ago."

The woman studies her, eyes traveling from head to toe and back, no doubt noticing the run in Mimi's stockings and the frazzled hair sticking out beneath her hat. "Well," she says after a moment. "Some experience is better than none." She turns on her heels and starts through the open doorway, saying over her shoulder, "Come on, then. I'll introduce you to Dr. Gabler, and we'll see what she thinks of you."

Mimi hurries after her. The doorway leads to a narrow hallway off which sit several other rooms. The woman pauses long enough to introduce herself—Ada Martin, office manager—before marching onward.

First they pass what looks to be a utility room with a deep sink and long metal counter. Atop the counter sits a stainless-steel container about the size of a bread box. An electrical cord snakes away from it to an outlet on the wall. It's an instrument sterilizer—if Mimi's memories from nursing school serve her.

The next door they pass is closed.

"This is the anteroom," Mrs. Martin whispers. "Patients rest here before and after their procedure."

They must perform some sort of minor treatments here, then. Before Mimi can ask about it, they pass another room, much larger than the first. An exam table sits at the center, draped in a crisp white sheet. Metal stirrups protrude from the end, reminding Mimi of her recent doctor's visit. Do they fit diaphragms here, too?

Her eyes drift to a pair of tall gooseneck exam lights standing on either side of the table. A basin of water rests on a nearby supply table beside a small tray of surgical tools.

No, the doctor hadn't needed more than a speculum for her fitting. Whatever happens here is more involved.

The sound of running water draws Mimi's attention to the far side of the room, where a nurse stands scrubbing her hands over a porcelain sink. She wears an ankle-length smock over her white uniform and a cloth cap over her hair. Clearly, cleanliness and asepsis are a priority here.

Another *ahem* pulls Mimi's attention from the room, and she hurries along behind Mrs. Martin. They pass two more closed doors—a coat closet and bathroom, Mrs. Martin tells her—then arrive at the end of the hall, where yet another door awaits them.

Mrs. Martin raps twice before turning the knob. The room they enter is tiny, made even more so by everything crowded inside—a desk, a bookshelf, a lamp, a filing cabinet, a pair of chairs, and now Mimi and Mrs. Martin. The only thing keeping Mimi from feeling claustrophobic is the impressive tidiness of it all. Not so much as a pencil seems out of place.

A woman is seated at the desk. She looks to be in her late fifties, with pale, lined skin and thin, unpainted lips. Strands of white hair spill out of her surgical cap. Her hazel eyes flit from Mrs. Martin to Mimi and back with mild impatience.

"This is Mrs. Lukas," Mrs. Martin says to the woman. "She's a nurse. Dr. Millstone sent her."

"Ah!" The woman stands, her face brightening. "You're here about the nursing position?"

"Yes," Mimi eagerly replies.

"And you have experience?"

"Private duty and hospital experience, yes."

"Any time in the operating theater?"

"Yes." She glances sidelong at Mrs. Martin. "Well, that is, some."

"Where did you do your schooling?"

"Illinois Training School for Nurses."

The woman nods appreciatively and extends a hand. "I'm Dr. Gabler. When can you start?"

Mimi stands there, mouth agape, before remembering herself and shaking the woman's hand. She'd expected a lengthier interview. "Well . . . I . . ."

"We're in a bit of a lurch since one of our nurses left last month. The pay is forty-five dollars a week. With a five-dollar bonus every other Sunday, when you'll have to be available to field patient phone calls. Mrs. Martin can fill you in on all the details."

Dr. Gabler returns to her desk, as if it's all settled.

Forty-five dollars! Mimi was making half that at Chicago Memorial. Mrs. Martin takes her by the arm and steers her toward the door. *Forty-five dollars.* And no more night duty to boot!

"Nurse Lukas," Dr. Gabler says, and they stop in the doorway. "I trust it goes without saying that discretion is of the utmost importance for us here. The fewer people you tell about the nature of our work, the better."

Mimi's palms are suddenly clammy. "What—er—is it exactly that you do here?"

Dr. Gabler's lips draw together and she looks pointedly at Mrs. Martin.

"Nurse Ranus didn't tell you?" Mrs. Martin says.

"No."

The women exchange another weighty look. After a moment, Dr. Gabler says, "We provide abortions, Mrs. Lukas."

"Therapeutic abortions? Like for women with tuberculosis and heart conditions and—"

"For any woman," Dr. Gabler says.

Mimi's lips part, and she breathes a soft, *oh.*

"Is that something you can assist with, or are you no longer interested in the position?"

"But that's . . . illegal," Mimi says, thinking aloud, still trying to wrap her head around the news.

"Yes," Dr. Gabler says, her voice firm and unapologetic.

Mimi recalls the rooms they passed. It all makes sense now—the table of instruments, the examination lights, the anteroom, the edge of reserve in the waiting room. A weight forms in the pit of her stomach. She knew places like this existed, but had never imagined they would look like any other doctor's office. In her mind, nontherapeutic abortions were performed in dark alleyways or the back seat of an automobile or the basement of some dilapidated house on the edge of town. This was a bona fide medical office. In the middle of the Loop, no less.

Both Dr. Gabler and Mrs. Martin's eyes are on her. She opens her mouth but doesn't know what to say.

"Perhaps you ought to take more time to think about it," Dr. Gabler says. "In the meantime, you'd do well to keep your mouth shut. None of us, including you, Nurse Lukas, want the police to come calling."

Mimi nods, and Mrs. Martin steers her out of the room. She makes a *tsk-tsk* sound as they walk toward the exit. "I'll have to talk with Dr. Millstone," she says, seemingly to herself. "He can't be sending us girls who don't have the backbone for it."

"It's not Miss Ranus's fault," Mimi says, though Emily ought to have at least hinted she was sending Mimi to the office of an abortionist. An angel maker. A criminal. "I . . ." She's still too shocked to make heads or tails of her thoughts. They've reached the door to the waiting room, but Mimi's hand hesitates above the knob. "I . . . I'm sorry for wasting your time."

Another *tsk*; then Mrs. Martin opens the door for her and shoos her out.

Mimi's pace quickens as she makes her way to the elevator. She presses the button but soon abandons the wait, taking the stairs instead. Flight after flight, she descends, the rapid patter of her feet echoing off the walls, until a rush of dizziness forces her to slow.

She'd been a fool to think a nurse out of work for ten years could find work at a *real* office. Hopefully Emily won't get in trouble for sending her there. Why did she think Mimi would take such a position? It's illegal, for heaven's sake!

Outside, the sun has disappeared behind the towering buildings, and the temperature has plummeted. The air cuts through Mimi's stockings and nips at her exposed neck. Of course, she forgot to bring a scarf.

There's an L station only a few hundred feet away, at the corner of State and Lake Streets. After a glance around the busy street and sidewalk, Mimi hurries in that direction.

An abortion clinic here, just a few floors above a movie theater—she can still hardly believe it. Not only is it illegal, but wrong. An abomination. First, last, always.

Isn't it?

She thinks back to her girlhood in Iowa. No skyscrapers or movie theaters there. Certainly no abortion clinics. The tallest things around were grain silos and the weather vane–topped steeple of the German Lutheran Church they attended every Sunday.

Most of what the pastor said during his sermons, she's forgotten. But whenever he preached about sin, Mimi remembers hiding her eyes in her Service Book and sinking low in the pew, fearful his fiery gaze would find her and penetrate her secrets. They were Ginny's secrets, really. But she carried them, too. That's what sisters did.

Often as not, his ranting would wend its way from sins like dancing, drinking, and card playing to more heinous offenses. By this point in the service, most in the chapel had grown bored. They fanned themselves with their hymnals and stared out the window, or picked at the dirt beneath their fingernails. There were fields to tend at home. Chickens to truss and get into the oven for supper. But one Sunday—just as the pastor said, *and those who delight in wicked pleasures then destroy the fruits of their lust before the innocent babes even draw breath*—a baby one row in front of Mimi, hitherto sleeping in her mother's arms, began to wail. The entire congregation straightened and turned their heads toward the noise. *A sign,* the pastor exclaimed, *a lament for her brothers and sisters murdered in their mothers' wombs!*

Even now, Mimi remembers the sound of that baby's cry, though she knows the line between good and evil isn't quite as stark as the pastor said. But abortion?

Her feet slow as she nears the metal steps leading up to the L platform, and a man in patched trousers and a threadbare jacket catches her eye. He stands beside the stairs, holding out his cap to passersby. The tips of his ears are red with cold.

Mimi knows his story well enough. She's heard it dozens of times from the men she's fed at her back door. They had jobs once. Homes. A dollar or two tucked under the mattress. Until they didn't. Until life's hard knocks landed them on the street.

How long before the same thing happens to her family? Before this man's story becomes hers? Only she had the chance at work and didn't take it.

She fishes inside her purse for a few spare coins. All she has are the ten pennies she needs for the L. She stares down at the money in her palm as people brush past, hurrying to catch the train rattling toward them on the tracks above.

No, she and her family will not end up like that. Not while Mimi can help it.

She tosses three pennies into the man's hat, then turns around. Riding the streetcar home will take twice as long, but it only costs seven cents. And first, Mimi has a job to accept.

CHAPTER 9

The next day finds Mimi back at the office on North State Street, dressed in her starched white uniform. A woman who introduces herself as Roberta greets Mimi when she arrives. She, too, wears a nurse's uniform, but it looks better against her rich, dark skin than it does on Mimi. Or maybe it's Roberta's easy confidence that makes it a better fit. Either way, Mimi can't help but tug on her collar and fidget with her cuffs as Roberta leads her to the back suite of rooms.

"Here's where you can hang your coat and store your bag," Roberta says when they reach a small closet at the far end of the hall.

Mimi glances back toward the door that leads to the reception room. A few hundred steps and six flights of stairs, and she can be gone. Yesterday she was so certain of her decision. Today that certainty has fled. She pictures herself standing downstairs outside the lobby's glass doors, automobiles racing by, busy pedestrians pushing past her, the nearby L tracks rumbling with an approaching train. But where does she go? Home empty-handed?

Roberta rests a hand on her arm and squeezes. "You're gonna do just fine here."

She's a few years younger than Mimi—mid to late twenties, maybe—with kind, deep-set eyes. Her neatly trimmed nails are painted a vibrant red. It's the only flashy thing in her otherwise unassuming demeanor.

Mimi manages a thin smile. It's not the work that worries her. Sure, her skills are no longer up to snuff, as her last position made painfully clear, but she's always been a quick study. It's the nature of the work. The sin she'll be complicit in. Most worrisome of all, though, is that by walking into this office, by hanging up her coat and pinning on her nurse's cap, by joining this staff in their morally dubious work, she's becoming a criminal.

Her hands tremble as she unfastens the first button of her coat. By the last button, they are steady. She can do this. She *must* do this. It's only temporary, after all. She'll keep looking for other positions. Keep nudging Stan to find work, too.

Roberta begins Mimi's training at the reception desk. It's only a few minutes past eight, and the reception area is still empty.

"Josephine ought to be here soon," Roberta tells her. "Usually, it's her or Ada who sees to the patients when they first arrive. But in a pinch, we fill in, too."

She shows Mimi the scheduling book and the intake cards that are filled out for each patient. There's a locked cashbox in the bottom drawer and a stash of pens and pencils in the drawer above. Behind the desk is a lacquered wooden chair on wheels with a brocade seat cushion. Roberta pulls it out and gestures for Mimi to sit. "Pretend I'm a newly arrived patient. What would you say to me?"

Mimi hesitates. It seems a silly request. Like being asked to sit down for a make-believe tea party. The kind Penny has with her dolls. Surely, a medical clinic is no place for such games.

When at last she sits, Roberta moves in front of the desk and nods at her expectantly. Mimi sighs, glancing about the empty room, before saying, "Um . . . good morning. . . ? Do you have an appointment?"

"No, ma'am. It's my first time here."

"All right. You're here to have . . . er . . . an abortion, is that right?"

Roberta frowns. "Don't say it like that. Don't mention the procedure outright."

"Why not?"

"Someone could have arrived here by accident. Gotten the office numbers mixed up or something. She could even be an undercover cop. We don't want to telegraph to the whole wide world what goes on here. Understand?"

Mimi swallows and nods. "What do I say?"

"Ask them why they're here."

"Okay . . . um . . . good morning, ma'am. How can I help you today?"

"I'm here for the procedure."

"A dilation and curettage?"

"A what and what?"

Now it's Mimi who's frowning. Of course Roberta knows what a dilation and curettage is. Any nurse would know. Certainly one working in a—*ah*, the game, and Mimi's failed again. She's got to get better at thinking like a criminal. "I mean, what sort of procedure?"

"Well, I'm pregnant, see, and hoping you could help me."

"Help you how?"

"You know." Roberta lowers her voice. "Make away with it."

"Yes, we can help you with that. Let me get an intake card and—"

"Don't promise we can help until you're sure. If the gal's too far along, the procedure can't be done."

Of course. Mimi should have known that. Why is she so bad at this?

"Don't worry, you'll get it," Roberta says.

"Is my face that easy to read?"

"We see a lot of women at this clinic. Women from every walk of life you can imagine. You'll get to be good at reading faces, too."

Mimi won't be here long enough for that. But she doesn't say so.

Roberta grabs one of the waiting room chairs and sits beside her. "Now, one of the first things you need to know is how far along a woman is. Ask her how many months it's been since her last period. More than two, or, if the woman doesn't know, the doctor will want to examine her first."

They go through the other details on the intake card—name, address, telephone number, age, marital status, number of children, past procedures—nothing out of the ordinary, until they get to the line for reference.

"This is important," Roberta tells her. "Make sure you ask who told them about the clinic."

"Why?"

"Dr. Gabler likes to reward those who pass along business to her."

"You mean they get a cut of what the women pay?"

"A small cut, yes. We can't advertise our services in the paper like we're selling soap or something. So we've got to do it this way. Simple as that."

Mimi's heard of commission payments among other professions. Even among other doctors. But somehow, it adds to her unease about the illicitness of what they're doing. Her eyes slide to the door, and she thinks again how easy it would be to grab her coat and leave. Mimi's not cut out for this kind of subterfuge. She's never broken the law. Not once! Well, maybe forging Stan's signature on her diaphragm prescription was illegal, but that was diddly-squat compared to this.

Roberta grabs the arms of Mimi's chair, pulling her from her thoughts. She swivels the chair so they're face-to-face, knees nearly touching. "Look, I didn't feel good about it either when I started here. But you and I didn't make the rules. Not the rules that govern this city, and not the rules about how this business operates. And it *is* a business. Everyone's got bills to pay. You, me, Dr. Gabler, the doctors and druggists and beauty shop owners who send us patients. But it's not about the money. It's about these women needing our help."

Mimi nods, but a knot tightens in her stomach. For her, it *is* about the money. About putting food in her cupboards and keeping the heat on this winter. Does that make her a bad nurse?

She swivels back to face the desk and looks down at the intake card. "How much do we charge?"

"That depends. Fifty if the woman isn't too far along and otherwise in good health. After three months, the procedure's riskier, and they need more aftercare, so we charge more. A hundred. A hundred and fifty."

A hundred and fifty dollars? Mimi would have to sell everything left in her jewelry box to scrape together that amount of money. Even then, she'd probably come up short. The women who come here must be desperate. Even fifty dollars is no trifle. "What if they can't pay?"

"We can go as low as thirty-five for those women really hard up. And for those who aren't, a gold watch or pearl necklace works as collateral if they can't get the money together all at once."

"How can I tell? Those who are hard up, I mean."

"You'll know, trust me. And if you're ever unsure, just ask Ada."

The door opens then, and the receptionist Mimi remembers from yesterday, the Marlene Dietrich lookalike, hurries in. "Ada's not here yet, is she?" she asks, breathless.

Roberta shakes her head. "You beat her in."

"Phew! It wasn't my fault this morning, I swear. The L skipped my spot. Didn't slow down one bit. I had to wait twenty minutes for the next one." She unpins her hat and turns to Mimi. "You're the same gal who came by twice yesterday, aren't you?"

A flush creeps into Mimi's cheeks. "That's me."

"Mrs. Lukas is our new nurse," Roberta says.

The woman smiles at Mimi and holds out her hand. "I'm Josephine Kuder, but call me Jo."

"Mimi."

"Sure will be swell not being the newest one around here anymore," Jo says after they shake hands. She throws a glance over her shoulder and whispers. "Ada's nice enough, but she sure does hover."

Before she can say more, the morning's first patient arrives, and Roberta steers Mimi into the back to prepare the operating room. Mimi tries to remember everything she's told—where the sterile instruments are stored, how Dr. Gabler likes them arranged for the procedure, how to check the amount of nitrous oxide left in the gas tanks—but her nerves are getting the better of her brain. Thankfully, all she has to do today is watch.

When everything is ready in the operating room, Roberta escorts the woman from the waiting area to the small anteroom in the back. Mimi trails behind. The room is empty save for a cot covered with a crisp sheet and wool blanket. A shaded window stands alone on the far wall, letting in only a halo of pale light and a few muffled sounds from the busy street below.

Roberta hands the woman a white hospital gown. "Undress completely, then put this on. You can rest on the cot until the doctor is ready." Her words are matter-of-fact, but her voice is warm, and Mimi can see the woman's tight body relax in response. "It will be just a few minutes."

They close the door and return to the operating room. Another nurse has arrived and already donned a floor-length smock over her uniform. Her hair is hidden beneath a cap, and a cloth mask dangles from her neck. Roberta introduces her, though Mimi quickly forgets her name as she tries to keep up with everything.

Roberta readies the tanks of oxygen and nitrous oxide. Meanwhile, the other nurse wheels two steel basins seated in metal stands to the center of the room, arranging them alongside the instrument table. One sloshes with water; the other is empty.

Mimi thinks back to her nursing school days, trying to remember what she learned about operating room procedures. Though much of the supplies and equipment around them are familiar, a lot's changed in the intervening years. Thank goodness it's only a simple D&C and not heart surgery.

"Do you always work in pairs?" Mimi asks, marveling at how quickly they finish readying the room.

"Usually," Roberta says. "One of us takes charge of the patient and the gas. The other, the instruments. Ada helps out when there's only one of us. She can't assist with the instruments but knows enough to manage the gas."

"Glad you're here," the other nurse says.

That makes one of them.

"We've been running short for weeks," she continues. "Ain't easy to find nurses for this line of work, ya know?"

Mimi manages something between a smile and a grimace. Luckily the woman has turned her attention to the instrument table.

After donning cotton smocks and caps like the other nurse wears, Mimi and Roberta return to the anteroom to fetch the patient. She's an ordinary-looking woman—dull brown hair, close-set eyes, chapped lips. She wears a thin gold wedding band and dime-store perfume. As they lead her back to the operating room, the woman begins shaking slightly.

"You nervous, honey?" Roberta asks, taking her arm.

"Will it hurt?"

"You might be a little sore for a few days afterward, but you won't feel a thing during the procedure." They reach the operating table in the center of the room, and Roberta gives the woman's arm a squeeze before letting go. "You ready?"

The woman nods. There's still a hint of fear in her eyes, but no hesitation.

She's not what Mimi expected. Not some careless career girl or red-light district floozy. Still, Mimi feels the stirring of her strict upbringing, contempt rising unbidden like bile in her throat. She swallows it down, but the burning remains. This is not the sort of thing good women do.

What does that say about Mimi? Isn't she an accomplice in all this now?

She watches Roberta help the woman onto the operating table. The other nurse puts her legs in stirrups, knees bent and wide apart, while Roberta straps down the woman's hands.

"It's just so you don't move during the procedure," Roberta reassures her. If she feels any contempt for this woman, it doesn't show.

Nor in the other nurse, as she grabs a razor and carefully shaves the hair from the woman's mons pubis and labia. Roberta folds a towel over the woman's eyes. Mimi wonders what the towel is for but doesn't want to ask in front of the patient. A minute later, Dr. Gabler enters the room and begins scrubbing her hands at the sink against the far wall. The woman turns her head toward the noise but cannot see who's entered on account of the towel.

The knot in Mimi's stomach twists tighter still. She'd momentarily forgotten what they're doing is illegal. The towel prevents the woman from being able to identify the doctor. Mimi and the rest of them have been afforded no such protections. Sure, they're not the ones doing the actual procedure, but isn't aiding and abetting a criminal offense, too?

Dr. Gabler nods at Roberta, who places the rubber mask attached to the anesthetizer over the woman's nose and mouth. In less than five minutes, the woman is relaxed, nearly asleep. The others don their masks, and Mimi does the same. Dr. Gabler is quiet, steady, and efficient. Barely twenty minutes go by before it's over.

The woman awakens a few minutes later. Roberta and Mimi unstrap her and help her back to the small room with the cot.

"Everything went just fine," Roberta tells the woman, her voice gentle. "Lie down, and we'll be back to check on you in a few minutes."

When they return to the operating room, the other nurse is gone, along with the dirty instruments.

"That metal box in the supply room—it's a sterilizer, right?" Mimi asks.

"Yep."

"And we run it after every case?"

"Of course."

Mimi's relieved they don't just wipe down the instruments and pass them off as clean. "I . . . er . . . I remember using one in nursing school, but it's . . . it's been a while."

"Don't worry, it's easy. I'll show you this afternoon. But it's pretty tight back there, so be careful not to burn yourself."

In less than half an hour, the dirty linens have been thrown in the hamper, the tables and basins wiped clean with Lysol, and the floor mopped. It's not unlike Mimi's routine at home, and she's happy to be able to help without having to be told what to do.

They return to the anteroom, taking the woman's vital signs and peeking beneath the sheets and blankets to check the sanitary belt and napkin they fitted her with in the procedure room. There's a little blood, but not much. When asked if she's in any pain, the woman shakes her head. "A little cramping's all."

They bring her a hot-water bottle, then let the woman rest for another half hour. When they return, Roberta takes a quick set of vitals, then deems the woman ready to go home.

"Who's picking you up, honey?"

"My husband. He said he'd be back in two hours. Has it been that long?"

"Just about." Roberta gives the woman a card with instructions about how to care for herself in the coming days. Eat and drink as normal. No intercourse or hot baths. "Call or come by in three days so we can check on you. Can you do that?"

The woman nods.

"We've got a twenty-four-hour telephone service, so if you start feeling unwell or bleed more than you would during a heavy period, telephone immediately. Do not call your doctor or go to the hospital, you understand?"

She waits for the woman to nod again.

"That's very important. If something's wrong, we'll send someone to you right away."

Roberta gives her a packet of douching pills, then tells her to dress.

"That's it," she says to Mimi once the woman has left with her husband. "Not too hard, right?"

Mimi's at a loss for what to say. During her schooling, she spent a few weeks on the septic ward of the hospital. Several of the patients were there because of abortions. One woman's uterus had been perforated and her bowels accidentally drawn through. She died shortly after arriving. Another had so serious an infection, the doctors were forced to do a hysterectomy. Another still had the knitting needle she used on herself lodged in her vagina.

Of course, Mimi hadn't expected Dr. Gabler to use a knitting needle, but she hadn't expected it to be so . . . so ordinary, either. It was like any other operating room procedure. Clean linen, scrubbed hands, sterile instruments. No furtive glances over the shoulder. No rushing or cutting corners. No sneaking out the back door under the cover of night.

But there's no time to dwell on the strange normalcy of it all. Another woman's waiting in the reception area. They strip down the cot and redress it with clean linen. Then the whole process begins again. And again. And again.

By the end of the day, they've seen eight women. Mimi's feet are tired, but she doesn't feel nearly as rundown as she did all those mornings leaving the hospital.

Ada catches her as Mimi's shrugging on her coat. "See you tomorrow."

It's a statement, not a question, but her shrewd gray eyes are searching Mimi's face.

"Yes, see you tomorrow." It's the truth. Mimi has no intention of quitting now. Not until she has somewhere else to go. But the lightness with which she speaks belies the heaviness she feels, the weight of so many conflicting thoughts and emotions. Is this how all criminals feel? It's like she's stepped through a one-way door. No matter how short her sojourn, she'll never be the same person who crossed the threshold.

CHAPTER 10

Mimi trains alongside Roberta one more day, then is scheduled on her own. She's slower than the other nurses but doesn't make any mistakes worthy of being dragged before the head nurse, or in this case, Ada. Nevertheless, she often feels Ada watching her. *Hovering*, as Jo put it. But though Ada is direct and likes everything just so, she's never unkind.

Mimi's still getting to know the other nurses. In addition to Roberta, there's Edna, who stands a full head taller than the rest of them and styles her graying hair in a short bob like it's still 1925, and Annie, who's dainty as a china teacup. Annie's chatty, while Edna's all business, but both women are quick to help Mimi when she gets the tubing for the gas tangled or forgets how to operate the sterilizer.

Even Dr. Gabler is patient, calmly correcting Mimi when she hands her the wrong instrument—dressing forceps instead of the uterine dilator the doctor asked for. Mimi gets it right the next time and is rewarded with what she suspects is a smile beneath Dr. Gabler's mask.

If any of them harbor reservations about the work like Mimi, they don't show it.

After three straight days working at the clinic, Mimi knows her household chores have piled up. (Literally, in the case of the laundry.) But she isn't as tired as she was those weeks on night duty at the hospital, and by Sunday morning, thc house is in order again. Just in time to get breakfast on the table and hurry off to church.

Stan, however, hasn't bothered to get out of bed to eat, even though Mimi forwent buying a new tube of hand cream—she can squeeze the dregs out of the tube she has—and bought a thin slice of ham steak—his favorite—instead.

Things have remained tense between them since their argument. No, not tense. Cold. The diaphragm she went to such trouble to get five weeks ago sits hidden in the far corner of her dresser drawer, but she's used it only twice. (There was a third time, when he didn't want to wait for her to "freshen up first" in the bathroom. Afterward, she fretted for a week straight until her period came.) Most days now, she feels like they're not living together, but around each other. She catches herself moving past him, as if he's an inanimate part of the house, no different than the sofa or icebox or hat rack.

If he ever made that call to Gibbins, he didn't say. Nor did he ask how she found another nursing position so quickly. When she returned home from her first days at the office, he didn't inquire how they'd gone. Mimi tells herself that if he *had* asked, she would have told him the truth about what she was doing instead of letting him believe she found work at another hospital. Honestly, silence is easier. But it can't go on forever.

The ham steak is an olive branch. She knows he can hear it sizzling on the stove. Smell the aroma even from the bedroom. It's hard to tell the children, "This is a special treat only for your father," when he doesn't come to the table. So she cuts a small piece for both of them and leaves the rest to grow cold alongside Stan's bowl of creamed wheat and glass of orange juice.

On the way out to the car, she knocks on the bedroom door. "Are you coming to Mass?"

When he doesn't answer, she opens the door a crack and peers in. He's lying on his side in bed, facing away from her. She might think him asleep, except for the stench of a newly smoked cigarette. It's the third week in a row he'll miss church.

The others are waiting for her in the Packard, bundled up against the late November cold. Halina is sandwiched between the children in the back seat, as if she'd fully expected Stan to come along, despite not showing for breakfast and the vacant, I-don't-give-a-darn look he's worn all week long. She glowers when Mimi slides into the front seat alone.

Mimi's mother-in-law hates her driving—a fact she's made no secret of over the years. Stan stops and goes much more smoothly, according to Halina. He never gets stuck behind a lousy driver and always finds the best parking spot. Never mind that Mimi was driving her pa's tractor when Stan was still riding a bicycle. She suspects Halina would prefer Junior to drive rather than Mimi, even though his feet can't even reach the pedals.

But the venom behind Halina's eyes can't all be chalked up to her driving. She blames Mimi for Stan's absence, too. Were Mimi a better wife, he'd be here with them. But what does Halina expect her to do? Drag him from bed?

Years ago, when Mimi and Stan broke the news of their engagement, his father congratulated them, shaking Stan's hand and wrapping Mimi in a one-armed hug. He wasn't much of a talker, Stan's father, or much for shows of affection, so these gestures meant a lot. Halina, however, stood and stalked to the kitchen, saying nothing. Stan followed. For the next twenty minutes, Mimi listened from the living room as they argued. It wasn't just that Mimi wasn't Polish, Halina said, loudly enough even neighbors must have heard. Not just that she wasn't Catholic. She was *tchórzliwa*, Halina said. Then she repeated herself in English, undoubtedly for Mimi's benefit: *without backbone.*

Seated beside her in the living room, Stan's father shifted uncomfortably and made some comment about the unseasonable cold they were having. Mimi nodded, willing herself not to cry.

Now, Halina glares at her in the rearview mirror a moment longer, then turns her gaze pointedly to the window. Mimi's hands tighten around the steering wheel. Twice she catches herself speeding on the short drive to Holy Trinity. She's not spineless. It's not her fault Stan won't get out of bed.

Is it?

In truth, Mimi isn't sure, but by the time they arrive at church, she's pinned a Sunday smile to her face.

She parks the car, and they join the thick of people streaming toward the cathedral. Halina takes both children's hands, leaving Mimi to walk alone behind them as they mount the stone steps. Even without Stan here, she feels like little more than his shadow. She's always felt that way inside this hulking church.

The first time she'd attended Mass here with him, Mimi found all the columns and arches impressive. The painted ceiling and gilded altar beautiful. But her feelings of awe were soon dwarfed by the sidelong stares, the whispers in a language she didn't understand, the awkwardness of not knowing when to stand, sit, and kneel.

At home in Iowa, the chapel was small and the services simple. She knew every person seated in the pews. Not only their names, but what kind of crops they grew. Who made the best strawberry pie and who brewed illegal beer in his barn. They knew as much about her. It was smothering sometimes, especially after Ginny's death, but comforting, too.

Of course, there were Lutheran churches in Chicago. But Mimi never went. Not once during her three years of nursing school. Nor after. She'd gone to Christmas service at a Methodist church with Emily one year. That was it. She hadn't forgiven God for what he'd done to Ginny, and she suspected he hadn't forgiven her.

Back then, Stan never skipped Sunday service. When the Sox were on the road, he and a teammate named McIntyre would find a Catholic church near the ballpark and squeeze in Mass before their game.

Despite her impasse with God, Mimi admired Stan's devotion and had been more than willing to tag along. If it were important to him, it was important to her, too. Wasn't that how love was supposed to work? So, despite her unease that first Sunday and every Sunday after, they got a dispensation from the bishop and married at Holy Trinity. They baptized their children here. But much to Father Kowalski's chagrin, Mimi hasn't yet converted.

Now, she knows by rote when to sit, stand, and kneel. Speaks enough Latin to piece together what Father Kowalski is saying from the chancel and enough Polish to recognize the insults her mother-in-law's friends still occasionally fling her way. But she still feels like an outsider, all the more so today. Not only because of Stan's absence. In the seven days since last she was here, she's become a criminal. A new type of sinner: murderess of the innocent.

At least according to His Holiness in Rome. Even in cases where the mother will surely die, abortion is forbidden.

But what would God himself say? She stares at the painting of the

Holy Trinity above the altar as those around her shuffle off to receive Communion. Only Junior remains at her side. He'll receive his first Communion this spring, and then she'll be all alone.

When God doesn't answer her, she turns away from the painting and looks down at her son. He's got her brown hair but Stan's blue eyes. His legs swing back and forth beneath the pew, the tips of his shoes tapping against the folded-up kneeler. The chords of the pipe organ drown out the sound, but he's still getting disapproving looks from the older parishioners as they pass their aisle. No, not him. Her. Normally, Mimi would scold him to sit still. Instead, she puts an arm around his shoulders and pulls him close. He's not yet old enough to want to squirm away like Penny has begun to do. He smells of soap and, ever so faintly, of ham steak. She says nothing to him about swinging his legs.

After the service, Father Kowalski greets them on the top step as they exit the church, kissing Halina's cheek and shaking Mimi's hand. When she first met him, she'd been surprised by how young he was. How warm and energetic. Nothing like the white-haired, pinched-faced priests of her imagining. He even joked about how hot and heavy his vestments were and how, without his collar, he was sometimes mistaken for an altar boy.

She doubts anyone would make that mistake now, a decade on, but his warmth and vigor are bright as always.

"Where's Stanislaw today?" he asks.

"Bad cold, I'm afraid," she answers quickly. Last week, it was a headache. Before that, an early case of the flu.

"I could come by and bring him Communion this evening."

"Oh, no, I'd—er—hate for you to get sick, too." Mimi glances at Halina, hoping to find her nodding in agreement. Instead, her mother-in-law has conveniently turned away to fuss with Junior's tie, leaving Mimi to make up excuses on her own. "I'm sure he'll be right as rain by next Sunday."

She can tell Father Kowalski hasn't bought her lie, but the kindness in his eyes doesn't falter. "Well, you can always call me if he'd like some company. You know I'm as good at talking baseball as I am God's word."

Mimi nods. The line behind them has swelled, and she puts a hand on the children's backs to usher them onward, but Father Kowalski continues, "I'm here for you, too, Mrs. Lukas. My Father's house has many rooms, and anytime you're ready, I'm happy to delve into our Catholic teachings with you so that you can fully join our fold."

"Thank you," Mimi says. "I'll—er—keep that in mind."

They move on down the steps, making way for other parishioners to greet Father Kowalski. Mimi waits at the bottom, while the kids dash off to say hello to their school friends and Halina makes her rounds among the dowdy parish matrons. Every Thursday afternoon, one of these graying women takes her turn hosting the others for tea and *drożdżówka*, a coffee cake Mimi finds much too sweet. She can't imagine what's happened in the intervening days that requires so much yapping, but she waits as patiently as she can, fighting the urge to check her watch or tap her foot. The smile she pinned into place when they arrived grows heavy.

It's not just annoyance she feels. Something else twists inside her. Halina is in her element here. Smiling, laughing, trading bits of gossip. Even during Mass, Halina sits serene, bathing in Father Kowalski's words. If she's a briar at home, here, she's a rose. And that feeling twisting inside Mimi—if she's honest with herself—is envy.

Would she feel less lonely here if she gave in to Father Kowalski and converted? At first, she hadn't been ready to renounce her Lutheran upbringing. Now, it's stubbornness. A way to show Halina she can be just as contrary as her. Besides, she'd still stand out. Stand alone. And while God certainly speaks to Halina here, Mimi has yet to hear him. Never mind that if Father Kowalski knew what Mimi was doing at the clinic on State Street, he'd skip over baptism right to excommunication.

Mimi's eyes drift to the top of the steps. Next in line to greet Father Kowalski are Zofina Dabrowski and her husband. In addition to a set of twins born last year, Zofina has two children the same age as Mimi's, so they're constantly running into each other—here, at school, at the playground or Humboldt Park. But they hardly ever speak beyond the obligatory hello. Years ago, Mimi had hoped they might be friends and tried to join the Catholic Daughters charity group Zofina ran. They were both pregnant for the first time, and Mimi thought they might be able to commiserate over swollen feet and the unending need to pee. But Zofina turned her away, saying only true congregants were allowed to join. Since Mimi wasn't Catholic, she didn't fit that bill, never mind that she attended Mass every Sunday same as the rest of them.

Mr. Dabrowski works at a bank, but if the rumors Mimi overheard the last time Halina hosted teatime are true, he's recently been let go. Unemployed husbands—something else she and Zofina have in common. But Mimi doesn't even bother to freshen her smile when the other woman looks her way. Zofina doesn't smile at all. Her narrowed eyes seem to say, *at least my husband is here.*

CHAPTER 11

On her fifth day at the clinic, Mimi finds herself alone at the reception desk for the first time. Edna is readying the operating room for their next case, and Jo is on her lunch break down the block at Pixley and Ehlers with a new beau. Mimi knows enough already not to expect Jo back until five or ten minutes after the hour, when she'll hurry in, cheeks flushed and hat askew, blaming the slow elevators or lazy traffic cops. Mimi doesn't mind her lateness—it's never more than a few minutes—or her excuses, but she's still nervous about keeping an eye on the reception desk while Jo's away.

Luckily, the lunch hour's nearly passed, and no unexpected visitors have arrived. She's spent the time memorizing the code they use in the schedule book—a series of letters, numbers, and symbols that stand in for the woman's name and telephone number.

Mimi glances at the small clock on the corner of the desk. Five past one. Jo should be back any minute. And sure enough, footsteps sound in the hallway beyond the office. But they're not the *rap-tappity-tap* of someone in a rush. No, these are steady and smooth. They stop just before the clinic's door. Half a minute passes, as if whoever's standing outside is having second thoughts. That, or she's paused to powder her nose. Then the doorknob turns.

The woman who enters looks as if she just stepped out of the pages of *Vogue*. She has dark, glossy hair and coal-black eyes to match. Full lips painted a deep shade of red Mimi's never been bold enough to wear. A stylish velvet hat. A fur coat is slung over her arm.

Her navy blue dress fits her nipped waist and slim hips perfectly. It's the sort of dress you'd see on a mannequin in the storefront window of Marshall Field's or Mandel Brothers. The sort of dress Mimi splurged on once or twice when Stan's career had been red hot, and neither one of them gave a fiddle about money.

Now, most of her clothes come from the secondhand stalls on Maxwell Street. Mimi's handy with a needle and thread and can let out a seam or freshen up a tired style, but nothing in her closet would hold up next to this woman's attire.

"Good afternoon," Mimi remembers to say after several seconds of staring. She's grateful to be wearing her nursing uniform. At least, that's supposed to be plain. Still, her hands are suddenly restless, smoothing the starched cotton and tugging on her cuffs. "How can I help you?"

The woman saunters over to the desk. "I didn't know there was more than one thing you could do for me."

Mimi shifts, the chair creaking beneath her. What does she say to that? Before she can think of a reply, the woman laughs.

"Oh, don't get your stockings in a bunch. I'm here for an abortion." She says it loud enough that the other woman in the waiting room—their next appointment—looks up from the magazine she's nervously been flipping through.

A frown lands on Mimi's face before she can help it. She pulls out an intake card from the top drawer. "What's your name?"

"Rosaline Simms." She peels off her gloves and tucks them in her black satin purse, answering Mimi's next questions about her address and telephone number with bored indifference.

"Are you married?"

"Does that matter?"

Mimi grits her teeth to keep from frowning again.

"I need to know to complete your intake form."

"Fine. No."

She tells Mimi her age: twenty-four. Her occupation: typist. And the date of her last menstrual cycle: oh, back in September sometime. Mimi's eyes travel from her chic hat to her pearl necklace to her polished leather shoes. Such finery can't be bought on a typist's salary, but Mimi doesn't say so.

"Do you have children?"

Another laugh. "Good heavens, no."

Mimi bristles. Just the type of woman she expected to encounter here.

"Have you had—er—a procedure like this before?"

"An abortion? Yes. Two years ago."

Mimi makes a note on the intake card, then opens the scheduling book. "The cost will be—"

"A hundred dollars," a voice says from behind her. She turns to see Ada softly closing the door to the back.

Ada crosses the short distance to the desk and stands behind her. "A hundred dollars," she repeats. Double what Mimi was going to say.

The woman's red lips flatten. "Sixty."

"Eighty."

"Fine, but I want it done today."

Ada leans over Mimi's shoulder and glances down at the scheduling book. "We can squeeze you in at four."

"Four?"

"That's the earliest we can manage."

The woman huffs but opens her purse. She hands Ada the money, then takes a seat in the far corner and pulls a silver cigarette case from the pocket of her fur coat.

"I'll handle things out here until Miss Kuder returns," Ada says to Mimi. "Go make sure Edna's got everything ready in the procedure room. We can't afford to fall behind today. Not with this extra case."

Mimi nods. She can't help feeling like she's being shooed to the back so she doesn't make any more mistakes at the reception desk. But how was she to know to ask for such a steep fee? The woman couldn't be more than two months along.

Now isn't the time or place to ask about it, though. Ada's right. With another procedure added, they'll barely have time to sterilize the instruments between cases, and Mimi best not dally.

"It's four ten," Miss Simms says as Mimi leads her to the anteroom. "My appointment was supposed to be at four."

Mimi takes a moment to school her temper before responding. She's unsure what it is about this woman that's so grating, but the afternoon's punishing hustle hasn't helped. "I'm sorry. We got you back as quickly as we could."

Miss Simms goes directly to the window and lifts the shade. "You're not sorry."

It's something a child would say. Something her children *have* said. Penny, most recently, when Mimi told her she couldn't have a piece of pineapple upside-down cake before dinner. "You'll need to undress, so the shade must stay down."

"You'd have to be quite the Peeping Tom to see up here." She lowers the shade just as Mimi is about to ask again, then plops down on the cot and takes out her cigarettes.

"You can't smoke in here. The reception area only."

Miss Simms closes her cigarette case with a loud snap. "Sheesh, I can't do anything back here, can I?"

What is it with this woman? Most of the women Mimi has brought back to this room hardly say a peep. She hands her a folded white hospital gown. "Put this on and rest a few minutes until we're ready for you."

Miss Simms holds the corners of the gown, letting it unfurl before her, and frowns. "How chic."

Mimi ignores her sarcasm. "I'll be back for you soon."

When Mimi returns, Miss Simms is sitting on the cot, powdering her nose. She hasn't changed, and the window shade sits askew. The room reeks of smoke. Mimi flaps her hand to wave it away, her pulse thrumming against her temples.

"I tried to open the window, but it wouldn't budge," Miss Simms offers with a shrug.

"What if the next patient is an asthmatic? Do women like you ever think about the consequences of their actions? About the people who suffer on your account?"

The words fly from Mimi's mouth before she can stop herself.

Miss Simms flinches, and her cheeks bloom with color. For once, she is silent.

Mimi covers her mouth with her hand. Nurses are never supposed to criticize their patients. She ought to apologize. Instead, she points to the heap of white fabric at the corner of the cot. "Is there something wrong with the gown?"

"The fabric is itchy. I didn't want to wear it any longer than I possibly had to."

Mimi waits while Miss Simms changes into the gown, then leads her back to the procedure room, where Edna's waiting. She still feels a throb of irritation and leaves Miss Simms to clamber onto the operating table herself. As soon as she's lying down, Mimi fastens the straps around her waist and wrists, while Edna guides her legs into the stirrups.

As Mimi buckles the last strap in place, Miss Simms screws up her face and lets out a soft cry. Mimi hasn't cinched it overly tight, but she sees now that Miss Simms's left wrist is red and swollen.

"A bicycle accident," she says, before Mimi can ask about it. "It's . . . er . . . still a little sore."

"Do you need me to loosen the strap?"

Miss Simms shakes her head. For the first time, Mimi can see a hint of fear in her dark eyes. She lays a hand on Miss Simms's shoulder. "It won't take more than twenty minutes, and you won't feel or remember a thing."

"I know," Miss Simms says coolly. But the look is still there when Mimi covers her eyes with the towel.

Dr. Gabler enters the room and readies for the procedure, while Mimi administers the gas.

"Tell me about this one," the doctor says, pulling on her elbow-length rubber gloves.

"Twenty-four, unmarried, no children, good general health, one previous abortion two years ago," Mimi tells her. "Last menstruated in September."

Dr. Gabler nods and begins the procedure. Everything Mimi told her is relevant to the case, except that Miss Simms is unmarried. It's nothing Dr. Gabler wouldn't have seen if she'd had the time to look over the intake card, but still, Mimi isn't sure why she said it. Why it matters to her. This isn't the first unmarried woman Mimi has seen in her short time here. And she knows better than most the shaming such women face. But must this woman be so flippant about it all?

Mimi pushes the thought away and focuses on her job, on Miss Simms's slow breathing, her strong and steady pulse. The procedure ends quickly and without incident. Once the gas has worn off enough for Miss Simms to walk, Mimi loops an arm around her waist and helps her back to the anteroom. She has the sloppy, stumbling gait of a drunkard, but that's to be expected. When they arrive, Miss Simms lies down on the cot, curling into a ball beneath the blanket. The gas will be fully cleared from her system by the time she leaves, though sometimes a headache or nausea remains.

After cleaning the procedure room, Mimi returns, knocking softly before she enters. Miss Simms is already dressed, and a fresh coat of lipstick brightens her otherwise pale face.

"Can I go?"

"Not yet. How are you feeling?"

"Fine."

"Any cramping?"

"Nothing I can't handle."

Mimi checks her pulse and makes her lie down again so she can see how much blood is on her pad. "All right, you can go as soon as we review the home care instructions."

She pulls the instruction card from the pocket of her uniform. Miss Simms plucks it from her hand and tosses it in her purse without reading a word. "I've done this before, remember?"

Mimi sighs. "Be sure to call if you start to feel ill. And you'll need to return after three days for a quick checkup." When Miss Simms frowns, Mimi adds, "If you don't come in, a nurse will telephone your home or come by to check on—"

"No," she says, in a voice too loud for the small room. "No. I'll return after three days, as you say."

Mimi fishes in her pocket again for the packet of douching pills. "Dissolve these in warm water and—"

"I know, I know." Miss Simms reaches for the packet, but Mimi closes her hand.

"Why are you in such a rush?"

"Sheesh. I gotta get home, is all."

"Your fellow doesn't know about this, does he?"

Miss Simms glares at her and holds out her palm for the packet of pills. Mimi hands them over, then steps aside so she can leave. On the way out, Miss Simms snickers. "Only a fool tells her lover everything."

That evening, Mimi and Edna stand by the main door to the office, waiting for Jo. At the hospital, she'd rarely left in time to walk out with the other night staff. Those rare days she did, they'd all been too tired to chitchat. She can't even remember a single nurse's name, besides the dour Miss Thumble.

Here, the nurses and Jo always walk out together. They part on the corner of State and Lake Streets, each toward her respective home—Jo taking the bus uptown; Mimi, Edna, and Annie all heading for different L stations; Roberta catching the streetcar to the South Side. But those few minutes making their way to the elevator and out through the lobby are always filled with easy conversation.

"Sorry," Jo says, hurrying from the back. "I almost forgot my hat."

Edna smiles and shakes her head. She's older than Mimi and Jo, but only by a handful of years, the puffy, drooping skin beneath her eyes and gray hair being the only clues.

The three of them are almost out the door when an *ahem* sounds behind them. "Mrs. Lukas," Ada says from the far end of the room. "Might I have a quick word before you go?"

The other women flash Mimi apprehensive looks and slip past her out the door. Ada motions for her to take a seat in one of the waiting room chairs and comes to sit beside her. Mimi's insides squeeze. This must be about Miss Simms's intake interview. It hadn't exactly gone smoothly. And she'd almost asked for half what Ada demanded in payment.

Ada reminds Mimi of her grandmother. Not her father's mother, who'd been frail and doting, but her maternal grandmother, a hefty woman with hands strong enough to wring the head off a chicken and eyes that missed nothing. She could guess the price a bushel of corn would sell for the following year within five cents and add and subtract numbers in her head faster than Grandpa could on the abacus. Mimi feared her, yet never felt as cared for and protected as when Grandma was around.

Ada isn't quite so old—late forties, Mimi guesses—but seems just as indomitable, and it's all Mimi can do not to squirm.

"I overheard you today."

"My interview with Miss Simms. I know it wasn't very good. I should have gotten her to speak more quietly and—"

"In the anteroom. When you berated her for not thinking about the consequences of her actions."

The warmth bleeds from Mimi's face. "I didn't mean—it wasn't in regard to her . . . er . . . condition. She smoked a cigarette after I explicitly told her not to."

"Be that as it may, you cannot speak to clients that way."

Mimi's stomach squeezes again. "Am I . . . are you letting me go?"

"Firing you?" The hearty laugh that follows startles Mimi. "Good heavens, no. I don't exactly have nurses beating down my door to work here. It'd be months before we could find a replacement for you. Besides, I like you, Mrs. Lukas."

"Mimi, please."

"Mimi. You're smart and a hard worker. And, despite what you said to Miss Simms, I know you care about the women who come here."

Mimi looks away, glancing at the wall clock behind the receptionist's desk. She doesn't really care what time it is. Halina will have seen that the kids are asleep by the time Mimi gets home. They know better than to give Babcia grief about bedtime. But Mimi doesn't want Ada to see the doubt in her face. She doesn't care about these women. Not like Roberta or Edna seem to do. It's a job. A paycheck. A temporary solution.

It has been nice these past few days to escape the house, though. Stan's blue moods are suffocating. But he'll pull out of it soon enough and realize he's got to move on from his accident. From his spiraling self-pity. From baseball. As soon as he's gainfully employed again, she'll be gone.

"I won't keep you from your family," Ada says, patting her hand. "But when Miss Simms returns for her checkup, I want you to apologize."

Mimi nods, though she doesn't relish the idea. Her words might have been sharp and easy to misconstrue, but women like Miss Simms never change unless their selfish ways are pointed out to them.

Mimi stands, and Ada rises, too. "And perhaps you might consider what it is about Miss Simms that vexes you so."

"What? Like I told you, it was only the smoking. I was clear it was forbidden in that room."

Ada smiles—a smile Mimi knows well from childhood visits to

Grandma's house. A smile that says, *you can lie to yourself, but you can't lie to me.* "I've often found that when we criticize someone, the words are usually not meant for them, but for someone else."

She pats Mimi's arm again and heads toward the back of the office. Mimi watches her go, trying to shrug off the weight of her words. At least she still has her job.

"Mrs. Martin."

Ada turns.

"Why did you charge Miss Simms so much money? She wasn't but two months along."

"She could afford it," Ada says simply.

When Mimi leaves the State Lake Building, a gust of cold air greets her. It's not as sharp and biting as it's bound to become in the months ahead, but Mimi's glad she remembered her wool scarf today. She thinks of Miss Simms with her fine fur coat and frowns, shoving her hands into her pockets as another gust pulls at the hem of her skirt. Miss Simms doesn't deserve an apology, but Ada is right. A nurse should never criticize her patient. How had Mimi let her temper get the better of her like that?

It must be nearly eight-thirty at night, but the city is awash in light. Streetlamps cast pools of soft yellow on the sidewalk while overhead, the marquee glows a brilliant white around the tall black letters proclaiming the title of tonight's picture. Across the street, the Chicago Theater boasts the name of a rival film, its façade twinkling in an array of red and yellow lights. A line of people has gathered outside the box office just in time for the late show.

A similar crowd waits here at the State-Lake Theatre, couples arm-in-arm, friends huddled close, chatting. Mimi threads her way through them on her way to the L. Her thoughts suddenly turn to Ginny, though she can't say why. Maybe it's the teenage girl with auburn hair. She stands a few feet apart from the crowd. Waiting, Mimi thinks. For a beau? For a girlfriend? For a sister who promised to meet her here after evening typing classes?

Maybe it's not the girl. She isn't that similar to Ginny. Only when the light strikes her hair just so. Maybe it's the light itself. Mimi hadn't minded the darkness of the country. She sometimes misses how clear and bright the stars shone. How easy it was to slip into slumber beneath their watchful gaze. But Ginny longed for something far brighter than the stars or the moon. Brighter than the occasional lakeside bonfire or moth-swarmed porch lamp.

Chicago was her dream, not Mimi's. And despite all the people here—over four million, if the radio newsman is correct—it's never felt full enough without Ginny.

The train arrives just as Mimi makes it up to the platform. A lucky break. The long day has caught up with her, and all she wants now is a cheese sandwich and a hot bath. Halina will be up when she gets home. Hard to say about Stan. His sleep is erratic these days. Sometimes he's up until four and sleeps past noon. Sometimes he goes to bed before the children.

He needs something from her, but Mimi isn't sure what. A better wife would know. A better wife wouldn't secretly hope she'd arrive home and find him already asleep. Mimi sighs and rests her head against the cool glass window. The glittering city is a blur outside.

She still hasn't told Stan what sort of work she's doing. He's got enough on his mind right now. He doesn't need to worry about her and the risk she's taking to keep them afloat. At least, that's what Mimi tells herself. Deep down, she suspects he wouldn't understand.

The train slows, its wheels screeching atop the rails, as it approaches her stop. As she peels her cold cheek from the window, Miss Simms's words come back to her. *Only a fool tells her lover everything.* Perhaps they're more alike than Mimi realized.

CHAPTER 12

Maybe it's the auburn-haired girl she saw last night or the newspaper headlines about the growing war in Europe, but as Mimi rides the L to work the next day, her thoughts tumble back in time, leaping over one decade, then another. She stares out the train car window, but even the dawn-lit skyscrapers aren't enough to anchor her in the present.

It's no longer fall, but summertime. The day is warm, and crops grow tall in the field. Another war, not unlike today's, rages in Europe. Even in faraway Worth County, Iowa, they feel its effects. From "Meatless Mondays" to "Wheatless Wednesdays," Mimi's family does its part to conserve food for the young men like her oldest brother, fighting on the front line. Today, she's in the kitchen helping Ma make blackberry jam.

"Hand me that can of corn syrup," Ma says.

Mimi wrinkles her nose but does as she's told. She liked it better when Ma used sugar. After they finished cooking, Mimi could lick her finger and swipe it across the counter, capturing any stray specks of sweetness. Corn syrup is goopy and sticky and doesn't taste as good on Mimi's tongue. But she hasn't seen a sack of sugar on the shelves of Bauer's General Store in town all summer. Mimi knows she can't complain—not when it's all going to the soldiers—but how much sugar do those boys need? She pictures her brother in a mess tent somewhere in France eating spoonful after spoonful of the stuff, the lucky duck.

She sneaks a slick of corn syrup from the rim of the can after Ma opens it—not as tasty as sugar, but it's better than nothing—then returns to the bowl of berries she's been crushing with a fork. Maybe she'll get lucky, too, and when they're done, Ma will give her one of the Hershey's Kisses she keeps hidden in her closet.

Kisses have also been missing from the store shelves this summer, but Ma's got to have at least one or two left in her secret stash. The hope is enough to keep Mimi working long past when her arm begins to ache. The blue sky winks at her through the kitchen window, and she longs to be outside.

"After lunch, can I go to the lake with Ruthie?" she asks.

Ma's lips flatten. She grabs the bowl of berries and tosses the mash in the huge pot on the stove. It's so hot in the kitchen that Mimi's underclothes cling to her sweaty skin.

"Who else is going?"

"I reckon just us."

Ma stirs the pot with one hand and uses the other to fan herself with a dishtowel. "Did you get the chicken coop cleaned out?"

Mimi nods.

"What about the weeds in the vegetable garden?"

"Yes, ma'am."

"All right. But don't get in above your ankles. I don't need you holding up your skirts and showing off your legs to any ol' Joe passing by."

Mimi frowns but says, "Yes, ma'am."

As they continue their work, Ma hums "A Mighty Fortress Is Our God," but Mimi's in no mood to join in. Last summer, she swam in the lake up to her neck in nothing but her chemise. This summer, she's hardly been allowed out to the lake at all. Ginny's to blame for that. To blame for all the extra chores. To blame for all these boring nights Mimi spends alone. No stories. No staying up late brushing each other's hair. No flipping through pages of forbidden magazines, reading about the lives of adventurers and film stars by candlelight.

Her brothers—the two still at home—think Ginny's visiting one of Ma's cousins in Mason City. Seems like every day, one or the other of them is complaining how it ain't no fair Ginny's off in the city having fun while they're stuck here on the farm. Not when she got to leave school a month early, to boot.

Mimi knows the truth. Knows that wherever Ginny is, she's not having fun. Mimi knows because she's the one who tattled to Ma and Pa about Ginny in the first place.

But that was almost four months ago. Before she realized Ginny had a baby growing inside her. If Mimi's done her figuring right, Ginny should return in a few weeks, just in time for school. Then things will go back to normal.

Except for the baby, that is.

Ma motions for her to take over stirring the pot while she adds the corn syrup. Last summer, Mimi would have had to stand on her tiptoes to do it. Now she's almost as tall as Ma. If she keeps growing, she might even beat out Ginny.

"Who's gonna look after the baby when Ginny's at school?" Mimi asks as she stirs.

Ma's humming stops. She slams the can of corn syrup down on the counter and grabs Mimi's arm so tight it hurts.

"Hush now, you hear?"

"Yes, ma'am," Mimi says, hoping Ma will release her arm.

She doesn't.

"I told you not one peep about that."

"Yes, ma'am."

"We don't need the whole county knowin'. A shameful thing like that ain't something people forget." Her grip loosens. "I don't want to hear one more word about it. Not now. Not ever." She gives Mimi's arm another tight squeeze, then lets go. Her face is as red as an apple, and Mimi knows it ain't just on account of the hot stove. "When Virginia gets back, we're all gonna go on like it never happened. Understand?"

"Yes, ma'am," Mimi mutters, rubbing her arm.

Ma begins to hum again, but the sound is forced and reedy. No hope of getting a Hershey's Kiss now.

And that still doesn't solve the problem of the baby.

Mimi hadn't known that's what was wrong with Ginny. Not at first. Last October, when all anyone could talk about was the upcoming Reformation celebration, Mimi caught Ginny sneaking out their bedroom window one night.

"I'm going to Bible study," her sister said.

A very important man and his family had come to town from some college in Minnesota to deliver the evening address on Reformation Sunday. *Doctor*, everyone called him, even though he didn't have nothin' to do with sick people. He had a stout, mousy wife, a pimple-faced son, and twin girls Mimi's age. Mimi reckoned these newcomers would be at the Bible study, too, and wanted to tag along, but Ginny said she couldn't. Grown-ups only. But Ginny wasn't a grown-up. She'd only just turned fifteen. And how come she needed lipstick to study the Lord's word?

Mimi didn't tell on her then. That came later. Almost six months later, when Ginny wouldn't let her borrow her favorite pink ribbon for Easter service.

Ginny had been acting strange for weeks, all moody and mopey. At night, she went straight to bed, no brushing Mimi's hair or reading a magazine together from their secret stash. She hogged all the warm bathwater, too, insisting they get it so hot the water was near boiling when Ginny stepped in. Then she'd linger in the tub until the water was so cold, Mimi's teeth chattered when she climbed in herself. Twice, Mimi overheard Ginny throwing up in the outhouse. Once, she caught her jumping up and down in the barn like one of those crazy Shakers Mimi read about in school. When she tried to join in, Ginny yelled at her and stormed out.

The pink ribbon was the last straw.

Mimi stewed about it all day, barely enjoying the Easter cake Ma made special for after supper. When Ginny reached across the table for more, Mimi said, "Another piece? That's why you're getting so fat."

Ginny's face went white as the frosting. "I a-a-a-m not."

"Are so. You can barely lace your corset."

Ma's eyes turned to Ginny and darkened in a way Mimi'd never seen before.

She sent the boys outside to do their evening chores, even though it was an hour yet till sunset. As soon as they were out the door, she grabbed Ginny's arm and hauled her upstairs to the bedroom Mimi and Ginny shared. Mimi snuck up behind them, peeking through the gap between the door and the jamb as Ma made Ginny undress.

Ginny's hands shook while unbuttoning her dress and unhooking her corset. The laces were let out as far as possible. Tears leaked from her eyes. Before she could remove her chemise, Ma grabbed the hem and wrenched it up over her round stomach. She gasped.

Ginny was fully sobbing now. "It's not . . . I didn't mean to—"

Before her sister could finish, Ma slapped Ginny hard across the face.

Mimi sucked in her breath, feeling the sharp sting of it, too, deep in her chest.

"You wicked girl!" Ma spat.

"I'm sorry," Ginny said, cradling her face.

"It's too late for sorry. You should have thought of the consequences of your actions before you lay down in sin."

That's when Mimi understood Ginny wasn't getting fat. Someone had put a baby inside her.

Now, as Mimi stirs the bubbling jam, she tries to shake off the awful memory. It doesn't work. It sticks to Mimi like corn syrup, leaving a far worse taste on her tongue.

Ma takes the spoon from her. "Ginny ain't keepin' the baby. So don't go asking about it again."

The sudden lurch of the train car jolts Mimi back to the present. She looks up through watery eyes and sees she's missed her stop.

CHAPTER 13

Mimi closes the front door quietly behind her and hurries to the L. In her two days off from the clinic, she's managed to squeeze in four days' worth of housework, help Penny with her English homework, and finish Junior's costume for the school's Thanksgiving pageant. He wanted the part of the Indian but is stuck playing the turkey. A small but important role, Mimi assured him. Penny is Pilgrim #3. She'll wear Mimi's nursing cap, and helped stitch her own apron. The rest of her costume was cut from a black dress Mimi pulled from the back of her closet. The fabric had long ago lost its luster, and the waist was a few inches too small, but that first *snip* of the scissors still pained her.

How many gay evenings had she passed in that old rag? Too many to count, though one in particular came to mind: meeting Stan at the train station after an away series in Detroit. They were so happy to see each other, they made love in the back seat of the car before joining a few of the other players and their best gals for a late-night dinner in the Loop.

Now, what scraps of the dress remain are tucked away in Mimi's sewing basket. The floors are washed and waxed. The curtains vacuumed. The kitchen table is set with bowls for breakfast cereal. Lunch—a stack of four sandwiches covered by a cloth—sits in the icebox beside a casserole of canned greens and leftover chicken that Halina can warm in the oven for dinner.

She arrives at the State Lake Building right on time. The theater box office sits empty. Last night's ticket stubs and popcorn bags litter the ground. The usually bustling street is quiet, taking its time to awaken like the rest of the city. She enters the lobby and walks to the bronze-caged elevator without a backward glance. Instead of hiding her face, she offers the attendant a distracted smile as they whir upward to the sixth floor. She doesn't look over her shoulder before opening the office door. Has this new life of crime become normal so soon? Or is it merely that it's Saturday, and the building, like the street outside, still seems to be shaking off its slumber?

Mimi can't say. Her mind is already on her work. On the conversation she had three nights ago with Ada. On the impending visit of Miss Simms. On the apology Mimi must begrudgingly deliver.

But morning passes into afternoon, and Miss Simms doesn't arrive. Mimi forgets her worry and focuses on the new cases—a rosy-cheeked twenty-one-year-old who arrives with her fiancé, a thirty-six-year-old mother of two who spends her nights packing sausages at the meat plant, a frazzled twenty-five-year-old with a four-month-old baby at home.

It's nearly four o'clock when Ada raps on the doorjamb of the sterilizing room where Mimi's readying the instruments for the next case. "Miss Simms is waiting in the anteroom for her checkup."

Mimi checks the time on the sterilizer, swallowing a groan. When they're busy, Ada often does the checkups, and could easily have seen to Miss Simms herself. Mimi needs no reminder why she hasn't.

"I'll be right there."

Mimi waits two minutes for the machine to finish, then removes the instruments and dries them with a sterile towel. Outside the room, she unties her smock and plucks the cap from her head. No one is around, so she allows herself a heavy sigh, then heads to the anteroom.

Miss Simms stands waiting for her at the foot of the cot. She wears a different coat than last time—navy blue wool with a plush velvet collar and cuffs. Her hat, a wide-brimmed affair with matching velvet band, sits low and angled over her face.

"About time," she says in greeting.

Mimi bristles at the curt greeting but does her best not to show it. "I apologize for the wait and my . . . er . . . terse words when last you were here."

Miss Simms waves a gloved hand as if she can't be bothered with niceties, even as the corners of her lips tug upward in a soft smile.

"How have you been feeling?"

"Finc."

"No fever or chills?"

"No."

"No unbearable cramping or heavy bleeding?"

"No."

"Nothing else out of the ordinary."

"No," Miss Simms says, her voice clipped and smile gone. "Can I go now?"

She tips her chin upward and brushes a strand of hair from her temple. That's when Mimi sees it. The dark bruise around her eye.

"What happened to your face?"

Miss Simms meets her stare but says nothing.

Mimi's stomach tightens as she remembers the red, swollen wrist Miss Simms had at her last visit. The coffee she drank at lunch inches up her throat. "Another bicycling accident?"

"Something like that."

"Do accidents like that happen often?"

She doesn't reply.

"Miss Simms, if you need—"

"I don't." She grabs her purse from the cot. "May I go?"

Mimi nods, and Miss Simms shoulders past her toward the door.

"I'm sorry," Mimi says softly. This time, her words are sincere.

Miss Simms stops, her hand slipping from the doorknob and coming to rest atop her womb. "I . . . I don't regret my decision. But I regret everything else about this damn situation." She reaches for the door again but hesitates before turning the knob. "Do you think it ever goes away? That feeling? That weight?"

There are several things in Mimi's life she regrets, but none more than what happened with Ginny. "No. Not completely."

Miss Simms nods slowly. Then, her shoulders square. She adjusts her hat downward and strides out of the room.

Mimi watches her go, a mix of bile and coffee burning her throat while that old, familiar pain stirs in her chest.

CHAPTER 14

Two weeks later, Ada calls to her from the office at the far end of the back hall. Mimi dumps the dirty sheets she's carrying into the laundry bin and shuffles down the hall to the office. In the late afternoon bustle, an unruly strand of hair has sprung free again from her pinned-back curls. She hooks it behind her ear, not bothering with the bobby pin that should be holding it in place. In the four weeks she's been working for Dr. Gabler, Mimi's learned there's no use fussing over her hair. Donning and doffing a surgical headcap six or eight times a day invariably leaves her curls flattened and disheveled.

But she doesn't want to look unkempt, either. Not in front of Ada. That woman misses nothing. So Mimi stops just before the doorway, smoothing her skirt and dragging a thumb beneath her eyes to catch any flecks of mascara. Hopefully she hasn't done anything to catch Ada's shrewd eye again. Mimi's still getting a feel for assisting with the procedure—when to give a patient a little more gas, which instruments the doctor needs and when, how to angle the overhead lamp to afford them the best light. And she's made a few small mistakes at the reception desk. But nothing Ada has seen fit to comment on since their conversation about Miss Simms.

"Yes, Mrs. Martin?" she says, entering the office.

"Can you drive?"

It's an odd question, but Mimi nods.

"Good. I need you to take the motor car and go check on one of our patients."

"The car?"

"The office keeps a motor car in case we need to transport a client somewhere or run a quick errand."

"Which patient?"

Ada hands her an intake card filled out in Mimi's handwriting. Name: *Dorothy Bates*. Age: *41*. Married: *Yes*. Employed: *Yes*. Children: *7*.

She remembers the woman from last week, her plain, thin face and graying hair. Her dress, impeccably clean but so faded the tiny pink and blue flowers that dotted the fabric were barely visible. When she told Mimi how far along she was—three and a half months—Mimi told her it would cost sixty-five dollars. Less than she should have charged. More than she suspected the woman could pay.

They set a date for the next day, and when Mrs. Bates returned, she handed over forty dollars and a tarnished brass pocket watch. Mimi doubted the watch was worth the remaining twenty-five dollars, but to her surprise, Ada took it without consternation.

"Has something happened to her?" Mimi asks now.

"I don't know. She didn't show up earlier this week for her checkup. Miss Kuder's tried to telephone her, but it appears the number's no longer in service." Ada fishes through the desk drawer and pulls out a set of keys. She hands them to Mimi. "Had she not been so far along, I might let it pass. But we can't have her falling ill and landing in the hospital." She shakes her head. "I should never have let her go home directly after."

Mimi remembers their argument. Ada told Mrs. Bates she'd need to stay with Nurse Edna for at least two days after the procedure so Edna could look after her and ensure there were no complications. The woman refused. Insisted she must go home. Ada consulted with Dr. Gabler and finally relented on the condition that Mrs. Bates lay in bed and not return to work for three days.

Mimi's heart quickens. If Mrs. Bates fell ill and went to the hospital, the police would soon be at her bedside, pressing her for the name of her abortionist. During those weeks in nursing school Mimi spent on the septic ward, she saw it happen. Officers stomping in without any regard for the cleanliness and quiet of the ward. Standing over the women's bedsides, demanding names and details. Telling the women they were going to die and might as well fess up. Ignoring their pain and fear.

Even so, most women held on to their secret. Most, but not all.

"What do I do if—"

"If anything is amiss, find a pay telephone and call right away."

"What about the rest of today's cases?"

"Annie can handle the instruments. I'll step in for everything else."

Ada describes the car and where it's parked. Mimi grabs her coat. As she's heading out the door, Ada gives her the brass pocket watch. "If you get there and everything's fine, try to get that twenty-five dollars she still owes us."

Mimi nods and pockets the watch, though there's hardly any room amid her racing thoughts for such trivial concerns. She finds the black DeSoto sedan just where Ada said it was parked. Mimi's never driven this model before, and it takes her a moment to find the shifting lever mounted on the steering post instead of the floor. She starts the car before realizing she doesn't know where she's going. The address on Mrs. Bates's intake card is unfamiliar. Thankfully, Mimi finds a folded-up map in the glove compartment and charts her course as the engine idles.

Once on her way, she forces herself not to speed. She liked Mrs. Bates when she met her. The woman had been polite and done everything Mimi asked of her. No complaining about the wait or smoking in the anteroom. Even afterward, when she'd argued with Ada, she'd kept her voice low and words respectful. But now, Mimi finds herself silently cursing her. Cursing the worry and trouble she's caused.

Their last case today at the office is scheduled for five o'clock, and Mimi hoped she might leave early after the woman departed. Thanksgiving's only two days away, and she still has a few things to buy. But any chance of making it to the grocer tonight before they close is gone. She'll have to squeeze in a trip tomorrow between baking pies and readying the children for the evening's school pageant. The store will be a nightmare of crowds and picked-over shelves, but there's no helping that now.

Mimi sighs and whispers *dagnammit.*

Her route takes her out of the Loop and deep into the Near West Side. The farther she drives, the more rundown the houses and apartment buildings become. Shanties and tents crowd open lots. Stray dogs dart from one shadowy alley to the next.

She finds the house she's looking for—one among a long stand of crumbling row houses. Mimi parks the car but hesitates before getting out. Her skin suddenly feels too tight around her bones. She can tell the home was once white, but little paint remains. The front steps have been patched with bits of scrap wood, and rust weeps down the iron railing.

Mimi hesitates again before knocking on the door. Takes a steadying breath. What if Mrs. Bates is terribly sick? What if Mimi's too late to do any good? What if the police have already been summoned and await her inside? Finally, her knuckles find the weathered wood. A young boy about Junior's age answers. Freckles trail across his nose and dot his cheeks. The overalls he wears are two inches too short, and his feet are bare. He looks up at her with wide blue eyes.

Mimi meets his stare with a smile. "I'm looking for Mrs. Bates. Is that your mother?"

He nods.

"Is she home?"

He shakes his head, and Mimi's stomach sinks.

Just then, a young woman appears in the doorway beside the boy. A baby rests on her hip.

"I'm looking for Mrs. Bates," Mimi says again.

"Ma's not here," the woman says, her voice tired. "Who are you?"

"I . . . er . . . I'm a friend of hers." It's a clumsy lie. The young woman gives her a dubious look, but Mimi continues. "It's very important that I see her today. Is there someplace I can go to find her?"

"You're a friend of hers, you say?"

Mimi nods and continues to smile.

"You sure you're not one of those women from the collection agency?"

"No, I promise."

A cold wind stirs the air. The skin on Mimi's legs turns to gooseflesh beneath her stockings. The baby begins to fuss. He's wearing an oversized cotton jumper with the sleeves and pant legs rolled up to keep from swallowing his feet and hands. The woman sighs and bounces him on her hip. Another lick of wind steals past them. She looks past Mimi down the street. "Ma ought to be getting home soon. You can come in and wait."

"Thank you," Mimi says.

It's nearly as cold inside the house as outside. To the left sits a parlor, dimly lit and sparsely furnished. Two more children play jacks by an empty fireplace. The boy who answered the door runs off to join them while the young woman with the baby leads her back to the kitchen.

Another two children—a boy and a girl in their early teens—sit at the kitchen table. He's reading a battered Superman comic, and she's doing math homework with a nub of a pencil. A single dim bulb glows in the overhead fixture, offering them scant light. They look up as Mimi enters. Their eyes travel from her head to her shoes, then drift back to their work and reading. The young woman takes the last chair at the table, bouncing the fussing baby on her knee.

Between an unvarnished cupboard, a chipped enamel sink, a soot-blackened stove, and the table, there's no place to stand but in the center. Mimi clasps her hands to keep them still. She wants to ask about Mrs. Bates. Where she is and if she's well. But to ask might reveal too much. She doubts even the young woman knows about her mother's visit to Dr. Gabler.

Mimi's eyes slide to the cupboard. There's a stack of plates, a few mixing bowls, a sack of oats, and a few cans of food. Otherwise, the shelves are bare. The sight is almost painful, and Mimi drops her gaze. The floor is a patchwork of scuffed linoleum and bare wood. How do so many people get by on so little?

Heat pricks Mimi's cheeks even as gooseflesh remains on her legs. She knows the Bateses are not the only family in the city who live like this. There must be thousands. Those who make do in shanties and tents and rusted-out automobiles are worse off still. But this is the first time Mimi has stood so close to such poverty. Her worries these past months since Stan's accident shrivel beside it.

What is the shame of putting the card for ice back in your window compared to having no icebox at all? What is the discomfort of too-small shoes compared to going barefoot?

Mimi hears the front door open and all but sighs in relief. A moment later, Mrs. Bates shuffles in. Her shoulders slump with exhaustion. Her cheeks and nose are wind-chapped and red. Otherwise, she seems in as good health as last week.

Her eyes widen at the sight of Mimi, and she shoos the others out of the room, telling them to go wash up while she gets dinner on.

When they're gone, she turns to Mimi. "How long have you been waiting here?"

"Only a few minutes," she says, though it felt much longer.

"What do you want? I don't have the rest of the money, if that's what you're after."

Mimi slips a hand in her pocket, her gloved finger grazing the watch. "I'm here to make sure you're all right. You didn't return to the office."

The woman shrugs. "I had to work." She gestures for Mimi to sit in one of the now-vacant chairs and looks around the kitchen. "I'd offer you tea, but I don't have any."

Mimi sits, even though she doesn't mean to stay long. One chair leg is shorter than the rest, and she has to lean to one side to keep from rocking. "What do you do?"

"I work for a woman a few blocks up. Cooking, cleaning, minding her children."

"I hope it's not too strenuous. You really should take it easy after . . ."

"I'm fine. And, as I'm sure you can see, we need the money."

"Does your husband work?"

Mrs. Bates opens the stove door and uses an iron poker to shift around pieces of half-burnt wood. "He's got a WPA job painting houses," she says over her shoulder. "We'll see how long that holds up. He was out of work most of last year and the year before."

"My husband's been out of work, too. Not so long as that. Just since the summer." Mimi rubs her arms, though the cold no longer bothers her. She doesn't know why she brought up Stan. There's little similarity in their situations. But when Mrs. Bates turns to look at her again, her eyes are less guarded.

"And what about your job with Dr. Gabler? Is it enough to get by on?"

"It is."

"You're lucky."

Mimi hasn't thought about it that way. Not in those terms. But one look around this barren kitchen, and Mimi knows how very lucky she is indeed.

Using a page of old newsprint as kindling, Mrs. Bates lights the stove. The flame gutters before finally taking hold. She pours two cans of beans into a pot atop the stove, followed by four cans of water, before coming to sit beside Mimi at the table. She kicks her feet out in front of her and lets out a heavy breath. Mimi realizes it's likely her first chance to sit all day.

"If you must work, try to take it easy when you can. At least until your body's had a chance to recover."

Mrs. Bates nods.

"And if you do have trouble—bleeding or fever or chills—you must telephone right away."

"Ain't got no phone. Not one that works, anyway. We can't afford it."

"Oh . . ." No wonder Jo couldn't get hold of her. "Well, if you can't call, come in."

Mrs. Bates closes her eyes and releases another long breath. When she opens her eyes again, she doesn't look at Mimi but stares down at her dry, cracked hands. "I suppose you think the easiest way would be just not to do it. But it ain't. You know what it's like when your husband's out of work. He's gloomy and unhappy all the time. Life is terrible. And somehow it's your job to keep him from going crazy. Many times—that's the only way. I thought I was old enough not to have to worry anymore."

Mimi's throat grows tight. She places a hand over Mrs. Bates's. Nothing about her situation is easy. And she doesn't owe anyone—certainly not Mimi—an explanation. "I'm not here to judge. I just stopped by to make sure you're okay."

"Well, I ain't dead, and I ain't . . . in trouble that way no more. So I reckon that means I'm okay. As okay as I'm gonna get, anyway."

CHAPTER 15

The next day, Mimi does her marketing early. On the way home, she drives back to the Near West Side and leaves a basket of food at the Bateses' door. It's not much. Some sausages and cheese. Rolls and butter. A few cans of vegetables. Nothing resembling a true Thanksgiving dinner. But at least they'll have something. She slips the pocket watch inside the basket, too, knocks on the door, then hurries away.

Mrs. Bates remains on her mind all day, even as she sits in the school's darkened auditorium, waiting for the children to appear on stage in their costumes. How bleak the Bateses' home had been—cold, dingy, stripped of anything but the bare necessities. And yet, there are still plenty of families in Chicago who'd look upon their situation with envy. Who'll pass Thanksgiving with no meal at all. Had Mimi not found the clinic on State Street, would hers be among them?

The curtain rises, and she does her best to shake off such thoughts. A jumble of children dressed in pilgrim black appears, squinting and smiling in the bright stage lights. Penny and two other girls step forward and begin reciting a Keats poem. "Season of mists and mellow fruitfulness . . ." Mimi's heart swells. She reaches for Stan's hand, only to remember it's Halina sitting beside her. Stan begged off last minute, saying he still wasn't steady enough with his cane. Mimi knows it's pride more than balance holding him back, but didn't say so. Now, as Junior waddles on stage in his overstuffed turkey costume, she wishes she'd pressed Stan to come.

The pageant is a great success, though Junior forgets his one line—*Gobble, gobble!*—until June, who's playing a stalk of corn, elbows him and whispers, "It's your turn." At the end, all the children crowd onto the stage and sing "Over the River and Through the Wood" before the curtain falls and the auditorium's harsh overhead lights come on.

Among the crowd of parents and grandparents now standing and shrugging on their coats, Mimi spies Zofina Dabrowski and a few of the other members of the Catholic Daughters. They wave and smile and trade compliments about their children. None of them glance her way or mention how beautiful Penny's recitation was or how adorable Junior looked dressed as a turkey. Mimi reminds herself she doesn't care. It was plain to anyone watching that Penny and Junior stole the show. She knots her scarf, tugging sharply on the ends, then buttons her coat. It's hard to breathe, but she doesn't loosen the knot until everyone's loaded into the Packard and they're on their way home.

The next morning, Mimi's up early to get a jump on supper. By noon, the rich smells of roasting turkey and freshly baked rolls fill the kitchen. Mimi's too busy mashing potatoes and sieving gravy to think about Mrs. Bates or Zofina Dabrowski. When supper's nearly ready, she wrangles Penny into filling the water glasses and asks Halina to keep an eye on the oven so she can slip away to change her dress and freshen her lipstick. Then she calls everyone to the table, resisting the urge to spread her arms wide and say, *ta-da*!

Curls of fragrant steam waft from the gravy boat. The brussels sprouts glisten with melted butter. Their good dishes were one of the first things to go when Stan's medical bills began piling up, but she's still managed a smart spread. Polished candlesticks, neatly folded napkins, and her grandmother's lace runner work wonders to camouflage the cracks and chips in their everyday plates.

Junior and Penny each light one of the candles, then turn to their father. In years past, Stan's always led Thanksgiving prayer. But today, he reaches for the turkey without saying a word. Mimi hastily fills in with a Lutheran prayer she remembers from her girlhood, earning a scowl from her mother-in-law.

"Where's the cranberry relish?" Penny asks, after all the serving dishes have gone around.

"And the yams with marshmallows," Junior says. "I want yams!"

Mimi glances at Stan, but he's busy salting his meat, seemingly oblivious to the children's complaints. She holds back a sigh and straightens. "Thanksgiving's a time to be grateful for what we have, not to whine about what we don't have." The Bateses' dilapidated house flashes in her mind. "Some children have next to nothing to eat. Do you suppose they're complaining about cranberries and yams?"

The children look chastened, their eyes falling to their plates, and Mimi regrets the sharpness of her words. For the next several minutes, the room is silent save for the clinking of forks and occasional crackling of the candle flames. No one mentions how beautiful the table looks or how juicy the turkey is, though Mimi does overhear Halina mutter that the mashed potatoes are gluey and the gravy lumpy.

"Tell your father about the pageant last night," Mimi says when the quiet becomes unbearable. Penny and Junior talk over each other, eager to recount their part in the play. The only thing Stan says in reply is, "Pass the stuffing."

He leaves the table before dessert in favor of a cigarette in the living room. Mimi watches him go, torn between begging him to stay and throwing a spoonful of *gluey* potatoes at his back. All supper long, she'd waited for a smile, a nod, some acknowledgment of the work that went into the meal. For making it come together on such a modest budget. For being the breadwinner and homemaker all in one. But he doesn't spare her so much as a glance over the shoulder.

Mimi's hand tightens around her spoon, knuckles blanching, then slowly releases. Hurling mashed potatoes at him wouldn't be worth the mess.

The Monday after Thanksgiving, Mimi returns to the clinic. Ada calls her into the back office to ask about her visit with Mrs. Bates. She also asks about the watch.

"I . . . er . . . I gave it back to her."

Ada purses her lips. "This is a business, Mrs. Lukas, not a charity. If word got around that we don't hold firm to our debts, every woman who comes in would expect a free procedure. How would we pay our rent? The office telephone bill. The salaries."

She looks pointedly at Mimi with those last words, as if she can tell how much Mimi relies on each week's pay. Mimi shifts in her chair. She wants to tell Ada how wretched the Bateses' house was. How thin and poorly clothed her children appeared. How little they had in the cupboard. Mimi still feels that skin-tightening discomfort when she thinks of them. But instead, she says to Ada, "I'm sorry. It won't happen again."

"Good."

"I understand if you want to subtract the value of the watch from my pay." Mimi knots her hands together and swallows. "Twenty-five dollars, I believe it was."

Ada leans back in her chair, studying Mimi for a moment. It's all Mimi can do not to squirm. "That watch wasn't worth twenty-five dollars," Ada says at last. "At best, I could have gotten ten. I'll tell my bookkeeper, Frank, to subtract two dollars from your pay for five weeks starting in January."

Mimi holds in a sigh of relief. If Ada wanted the full twenty-five dollars and demanded it be paid back immediately, Mimi isn't sure how she'd manage Christmas presents for the children. "Thank you, Mrs. Martin."

Ada's expression softens. "I admire your generous spirit, Mrs. Lukas. But don't forget, every woman who comes here has a story. A past. A burden she's carrying. You cannot take those burdens upon yourself. We help them in this one way. That is all. That is enough."

Mimi nods. It doesn't feel like enough. But it *is* something.

There's a lightness to her step as she leaves Ada's office. A purpose. The next case is waiting, and Mimi scrubs her hands and forearms at the operating room sink with care. Maybe this is more than a job. A paycheck. Maybe they are helping.

CHAPTER 16

A few weeks later, Mimi and Roberta are cleaning the operating room after a case. With the patient resting in the anteroom, they talk softly of the coming Christmas holiday. Of the garlands and baubles that trim the storefront windows and bright red bows decorating the streetlamps.

Roberta's also a mother—two small boys younger than Junior. Her husband works nights at the steel plant. So Mimi knows she's got her hands full managing things at home. As lovely as the decorations are, the holidays mean juggling more trips to the store and stretching the budget as far as it will go.

All the more reason Mimi shouldn't go out tonight. After the lonely ordeal of Thanksgiving, she'd gotten Emily's telephone number from Dr. Millstone, who helped at the clinic sometimes when Dr. Gabler was out, and finally called her.

"Took you long enough, you goose," Emily had chided her, then laughed in that infectious way of hers, and they set a date to meet for drinks in Greater Grand Crossing. The restaurant was close to Emily's work and cheaper, Mimi hoped, than the swanky places here in the Loop.

Now, imagining the trek halfway across the city, she's regretting her decision.

She places the speculum, traction forceps, curette, and other instruments Dr. Gabler used in the last case into a steel water basin to soak, then turns to Roberta. "How long do you suppose it takes to get to Seventy-fifth Street from here?"

"What's all the way down there?"

"I'm meeting a friend at a restaurant there tonight." Roberta raises an eyebrow, and Mimi quickly adds, "A girlfriend, that is."

"Forty-five minutes or so."

Mimi bites her lip. Maybe she ought to beg off.

"You can ride the streetcar with me," Roberta says. "It'd be nice to have some company for a change. That is, if you don't mind going through Bronzeville."

"No, that'd be swell. I haven't been to the South Side since . . . well, since Stan's accident."

"I get off in Washington Park, but you shouldn't have more than a dozen stops after mine." Roberta wheels the canisters of gas to the corner of the room. "How is he, your husband?"

Mimi forces a smile, one so thin she knows Roberta can see right through it. "He's walking with a cane now instead of crutches. It's progress, I guess."

Roberta nods and graciously steers the conversation back to holly berries and evergreen boughs.

As soon as the office closes for the night, Mimi follows Roberta to the streetcar. It's been ages since she's had a night on the town. Stan's accident put a stop to their moviegoing and dancing. Back when they *had* gone out, Stan's teammates and their wives sometimes joined them. Mimi got on fine with these women. A few of them she even liked. But they weren't friends. She learned that quickly after the accident, when not one of them came around. Mimi didn't blame them. In their shoes, she probably would have done the same. But it did leave her feeling . . . lonely.

Roberta's company is a welcome balm for that. Emily's will be, too, even if she has to cross the city to see her.

As the streetcar rattles along, she and Roberta chat about their children. Roberta's youngest recently brought a tadpole home.

"Lord knows where he found it this time of year," she's saying, then stops abruptly.

Mimi follows her gaze to a white woman standing at the front of the car. The woman eyes Roberta with a prune-faced scowl.

"What's wrong?" Mimi asks. "Do you know her?"

Roberta's jaw tenses as she holds the woman's gaze. "No, but she thinks I ought to get up and move along to the back."

"Oh." Mimi doesn't know what else to say. She's never thought about what it must be like for Roberta and the other Negroes in the city, just going about their daily lives. "Would you like me to—"

"No. Best just ignore her."

"Does this . . . happen often?"

"Too often to count."

A knot twists in her gut. Too often to count, and Mimi'd never noticed. She reaches out and takes Roberta's hand, giving it a squeeze.

Roberta remains stock-still for a moment, then squeezes back. She straightens in her seat and turns to Mimi. "Where was I?"

She finishes the story about the tadpole, which ended up in a mason jar on her son's bedside table, but the levity is gone from her voice. The prune-faced woman gets off after only a few stops, and Mimi's glad to see her go. The farther south they travel, the more Negroes fill the streetcar. Many smile and greet Roberta warmly. Mimi feels a conspicuousness not unlike what she feels at Holy Trinity. Not unlike what Roberta must have felt only a few blocks before. Except no one's scowling at Mimi with the unspoken expectation she give up her seat.

After a stretch of silence, Mimi asks, "Why did you come to work for Dr. Gabler?"

Roberta pulls at a loose thread on her handbag, then turns and looks out the window. Mimi can see her solemn face reflected in the glass and worries she shouldn't have asked.

"There was a girl I knew growing up," Roberta says, her voice quiet but steady. "She found herself in trouble and couldn't see no way out. So she jumped off a bridge." She turns back to Mimi. "It didn't seem right to me that she should have to do that. After I got my schooling, I heard about Dr. Gabler and asked her for a job."

Mimi nods slowly, then finds her own gaze pulled to the night-shadowed city beyond the window. She ought to tell Roberta about Ginny. Feels the words unspooling on her tongue. Feels that familiar ache in her chest, dying to be let free.

But she doesn't.

And then Roberta's stop is upon them, and the moment to pull Ginny's name from the darkness is gone.

* * *

Mimi spends the next twenty minutes glancing at her watch. It's nearly nine o'clock when her stop at last arrives. One drink. She'll have one drink; then she simply must be getting home. She kicks at the crust of gray-tinged snow edging the sidewalk where the streetcar deposited her as she gets her bearings. The December wind lashes her cheeks. Thankfully she spies the warm glow of the restaurant's windows only a block away.

"Mimi!" Emily squeals as soon as Mimi enters. Before she can shrug out of her coat and hand it to the attendant, Emily wraps her in a hug. "You came."

"Of course I came." Never mind that she'd been about to cancel only a few hours before and intends to hightail home as soon as she can.

When Emily tells the host they'd like seats at the bar, his lips compress into a frown. "We don't serve unescorted ladies at the bar, I'm afraid. You can try the beer hall down the block, or perhaps you'd like a table in our dining room?"

A flush creeps up Mimi's neck, but Emily appears unbothered. "And here I thought prohibition had lifted for gents and gals alike."

The host's frown deepens.

"Oh, don't work yourself into a dither. We'll take a table in the dining room."

He shows them to a small table at the back of the room. Lamps with cut-glass shades dangle from the ceiling, but little of their light reaches them. The clank of pots and pans carries from the nearby kitchen. Mimi feels like a dunce banished to the corner of the classroom. Still, it beats trudging another block to the beer hall.

When the waiter arrives, Emily orders a Manhattan.

"And to eat?" he asks.

"I never eat this late," she says, flashing him a dazzling, red-lipped smile. "Gotta look out for my figure, ya know."

The waiter throws a glance over his shoulder, blushing. "I'm afraid I really must insist."

"Fine." Emily glances down at the menu. "I'll take a plate of sardines."

Mimi orders a rum and eggnog and the cheapest food on the menu: stuffed celery.

"Sorry about all the fuss," Emily says after the waiter leaves. "Henry and I come here all the time and never have a problem."

"Henry?"

"Dr. Millstone, I mean."

"For drinks?"

Emily's gaze flickers away, and she pulls at the collar of her blouse. "Oh, you know, every now and then, after a long day at the office."

Her nails are painted a deep burgundy color in the half-moon style, with the base of the nail bare. It's been months since Mimi's had the time—or money—for a manicure. Emily looks back and catches her staring. "Remember that fusty old Head Nurse Wilkerson who thought painted nails were the mark of the devil?" Emily sits up straight and blinks rapidly, the way Nurse Wilkerson always did behind her thick spectacles. "A nurse never draws attention to herself."

Mimi can't help but laugh. "Remember when she thought Louisa had rouged her cheeks and made her go wash her face?"

"Boy, do I! All that scrubbing only made poor Louisa's rosacea worse."

"Or when she told you to stop flouncing about the ward like a flapper?"

"That old bag had never even seen a flapper."

"You don't know that. Maybe she wore polka-dotted stockings under that starched skirt of hers."

They're both laughing when their drinks arrive. Mimi catches her breath and takes a sip. There's only a hint of rum, but it tastes good nonetheless. "And you were, by the way."

"Were what?"

"Flouncing."

"A girl's gotta make an impression somehow."

Mimi manages another sip despite her chuckling. "Do you think she's still there, tormenting students?"

Emily shakes her head. "I heard they let her go when the university took over, and she died the following spring."

"Oh," Mimi says, the laughter drying up inside her.

"She'd been a nurse for doggone near fifty years. I don't think she knew how to be anything else."

Thoughts of Stan invade Mimi's mind, but she pushes them away.

Nurse Wilkerson might have had nothing else to live for, but Stan certainly does. She raises her glass. "To Nurse Wilkerson."

Emily clanks her glass with Mimi's. "To Nurse Wilkerson. May her ghost continue to haunt the wards."

They drink, and silence falls between them. Mimi glances at her watch. She's not all that hungry but wishes their food would hurry up and arrive. How long does it take to upend a can of sardines and smear cheese on a celery stick?

"And what about you?" Emily says, after draining most of her drink. "Bet you're glad I sent you to Dr. Gabler."

Mimi hesitates. *Glad* isn't the right word. Grateful, yes. Resigned. Perhaps even resolute. But not glad. "I certainly never would have found her on my own."

"Too bad she's leaving."

"You know about that?"

After Thanksgiving, Dr. Gabler had announced to everyone at the clinic she was leaving at the end of the year. Little else was said. Things would operate as they always had, she told them, except with new doctors. It was all Mimi and the other nurses had whispered about since, but she's surprised word has gotten around to Emily. Then it hits her.

"Dr. Millstone. Is he going to take over the clinic?"

Emily shakes her head. "He'll be working there more, sure, but what I heard is—" She stops as the waiter arrives with their food. Emily thanks him and orders another round of drinks before Mimi can stop her. So much for pinching pennies and getting home at a reasonable hour.

Emily forks a sardine onto a cracker and eats it before leaning in and continuing. "I heard Mrs. Martin is buying the clinic from Dr. Gabler. The deal's all but done and signed."

"Ada? But she's not even a nurse, let alone a doctor."

"She's not the one who's going to do the procedures, you goose. Henry will. And other doctors. But she'll run the place."

Mimi leans back and takes a bite of one of her celery stalks. The filling is a blend of cream cheese and chopped olives. There's a hint of cayenne, too. Not the best pairing with eggnog, but Mimi absent-mindedly takes another bite.

Ada buying the clinic. The more Mimi thinks about it, the more sense it makes. Ada already runs the day-to-day operations. She's smart, efficient, and seems to have a head for business. And Emily's right; so long as Ada can get a few doctors to sign on, she doesn't need a medical degree to manage the place. Mimi finishes her celery stalk and grabs another. Roberta and the others will sure be surprised tomorrow when she tells them.

As Mimi chews, something else Emily said catches in her mind. "You called him Henry again."

"Did I?" Emily polishes off her Manhattan and looks around for the waiter, no doubt hoping he's on his way over with their fresh drinks. "Just a slip of the tongue."

"Was it?"

"Oh, all right. We're sort of . . . on friendly terms."

"How friendly?"

Emily shrugs as if it's nothing, but a smile pulls at her lips. Mimi can't help but smile, too. Then she remembers the wedding ring he'd worn when he lectured for their class. She leans in. There's really no need to whisper—only a few patrons remain in the dining hall, and the businessmen seated at the bar are too far away to hear—but Mimi lowers her voice anyway. "Isn't he married?"

Emily waves a hand dismissively. "Divorced. Years ago."

A dozen more questions spring to Mimi's mind. How long have they been working together? How long have they been "friendly," and what exactly does that mean? But before she can ask, Emily says, "Anyway, now that Dr. Gabler's leaving, Henry will be taking more cases at the clinic. You and I will get to see each other all the time."

"You'll be coming along, too?"

"That's the plan."

"And you don't mind?" She leans in again. "Doing that kind of work?"

"Someone's got to do it. That's how I see it. Better us than any old Tom, Dick, and Harry. Don't you agree?"

Mimi certainly agrees with the latter. Only last week, she read in the paper about a woman in Peoria—the mother of five small children—who died after getting an abortion from an electrician. An *electrician*! But the first part of what Emily said, that someone must do it, sits less easily with Mimi. "Wouldn't it be better if no one did it? I mean, if there wasn't a need."

"Wasn't a need? Maybe on the moon!"

Mimi thinks back to what Roberta said on the streetcar. Some women's situations were so desperate, death was the only way out—theirs or the unformed protoplasm inside them. That was the world they lived in. Still, Mimi asks, "You don't think it weighs on Dr. Gabler's conscience?"

"Does it weigh on yours?"

"I . . ." It had in the beginning. Or, she thought it would. Now, she isn't sure.

"Look, Dr. Gabler's moving to Florida. That's what Henry told me. If she's running away from anything, it's this god-awful weather." She nods toward the windows lining the far wall of the dining room. Outside, the wind hurls flurries of dead leaves and stale snow at the frost-skirted glass. Mimi shivers even as she laughs.

"Enough work talk," Emily says, after the waiter brings them new drinks. "What about you? How's that ballplayer of yours?"

Now Mimi's the one shrugging and hiding her eyes in her glass.

"I forget—what position does he play? And is he with the Cubs or the Sox?"

He doesn't play anything anymore but the damned radio, Mimi wants to say, but she drowns the words in a gulp of eggnog. This drink has more rum than the first, and it hits the back of her mouth like a punch. Luckily, Emily doesn't wait for her to respond.

"Henry's a total baseball nut. Talks my ear off about the sport, so I know everything about the game. What's your fella's . . . um . . ." She flaps her hand. "You know, that number everyone's always spouting."

"His batting average?"

"Yeah, that's what it's called."

"Stan played for the White Sox. First base. In his best year, he averaged three-sixty-two." Mimi's surprised at how readily the number comes to mind. "But he hit above three-fifty another two years besides that. There, did I answer all your questions?"

"Hardly!" Emily rests her elbows on the table and leans close, like they're schoolgirls again, whispering about boys when they should be studying. "What's it like? Are the two of you treated like royalty wherever you go?"

Mimi laughs. "Sure, I just forgot my crown at home today."

"I'm serious."

She thinks for a moment. There certainly were times when Stan's bat was on fire and the manager of a restaurant would cover their dinner or bring them a free round of champagne. When young boys would ambush Stan on the street, clamoring for his autograph. One Sunday before a pennant game, Father Kowalski singled out Stan in his closing prayer. The prayer had been in Polish, so Mimi didn't know what he said until after. But she caught the other parishioners' murmurs of agreement and the shy smile on Stan's bowed face.

Mimi would give anything to see that smile again.

"It was fun," she says at last. "But also . . . hard."

Emily raises a thin, darkly penciled brow. "Hard?"

"Sure." Mimi takes another sip of her drink, letting the rum warm her throat before speaking. "He was gone a lot, for starters. On the road for games. Spring training. There's always the possibility of a trade, too. You never know when you might have to uproot the family and move."

"How come you're talking like it's over?"

"He broke his leg this summer and was cut from the team."

"Golly, that's awful."

"Baseball's all he's ever known. Ever done." The words, *ever loved*, come to mind, too, but Mimi doesn't say them aloud. "The adjustment to normal life has been . . . challenging."

"But he'll play again, right?" Emily asks.

Maybe it's the alcohol, but the truth spills out before her standard lie. "No. He never will."

Saying it aloud is like coughing up a fish bone, painful as it comes up but a momentous relief once it's expelled.

"That's why you became a nurse again."

Mimi nods.

"Well, there's your silver lining."

"Silver lining?"

"Sure. Isn't it nice to make your own money? To have that small bit of freedom. To know that if you had to do it on your own, you could?"

Mimi doesn't think of the checks she receives as *her* money. It's the family's money. And whether he acts like it or not, Stan is still the head of that family. But it has been nice to fill her days with more than housework. To put her nursing skills to use again. To make new friendships and rekindle old ones. Most of all, it's nice not to have the threat of poverty stalking her like a shadow anymore.

"You're right." Mimi raises her glass. "To silver linings."

To her surprise, there's still a light on in the living room when Mimi arrives home. She tosses her coat on the rack and fumbles with her hat, making a mess of her hair as she clumsily removes the pins. Maybe a third drink wasn't such a good idea. But golly, it felt good to laugh with Emily tonight.

She tiptoes to the living room doorway and finds Halina seated in her favorite chair by the window. Otherwise, the room is empty. Stan hasn't waited up. Mimi didn't expect him to but feels a prick inside her chest just the same.

A book rests in Halina's lap, but she isn't reading. Instead, her frosty blue eyes cut to the wall clock, and her lips twist into a scowl. "Where have you been?" Her voice is not only sharp, but drowning in that Polish accent of hers, the way it sounds whenever she's angry.

"Shh. Keep your voice down."

"It's almost midnight o'clock."

In the hopes of getting her mother-in-law to stop shouting, Mimi crosses the room and sinks into the chair beside her. Stan's chair. It used to smell pleasantly of his cedarwood and vanilla cologne. Now it reeks of smoke.

"No note. No telephone call. No nothing."

"I'm sorry," Mimi says. "Next time, I'll ring."

"Next time?"

If anything, the level of her voice has risen. Mimi flaps a hand and shushes her again.

"Next time? Were you out with a man?"

"What?"

Halina leans closer and sniffs—actually *sniffs*!—as if Mimi might smell of sex or another man's cologne.

"I wasn't with a man."

"Ah, but you were drinking."

Mimi recoils. There's no way Halina can smell the rum and eggnog she drank. Is there? "Not that it's any of your business, but I met a friend, a *gal* friend, after work for a drink."

Halina wags her head, eyeing Mimi as if she were a rotten fish pulled from the back of the icebox. "What kind of a mother are you?"

The words hit Mimi like a blow. Any other night, Mimi might hang her head and wait for the next blow to land, telling herself there's no point in arguing. Telling herself she's the better woman for not fighting back. Telling herself the dark looks and snide comments don't hurt. All the while conceding that Halina is a teensy bit right.

But they do hurt. And tonight, Halina is wrong.

Mimi stands. Her hands are tingling, so she balls them into fists at her side. "I am not a bad mother. Every day that I'm not here cooking and cleaning, I'm at work, earning money so there's food on the table. You like eating, don't you? And having gasoline in the car? And oil in the heater? And it's not just for you. I'm earning money so Penny and Junior can have new winter coats and presents under the tree come Christmas." Mimi realizes she, too, is shouting, but doesn't lower her voice. "This is *my* house. I can come and go as I please. If I want to go out after work and have a drink with a friend, I will."

Halina looks up at her slack-jawed.

"And one more thing," Mimi says. "If you think the gravy is lumpy, next Thanksgiving, sieve it your damn self!"

Her mother-in-law sits momentarily stupefied; then she hisses something in Polish and crosses herself.

Whatever it is she said, Mimi doesn't care. "Goodnight, Mamo. I'm going to bed."

She holds her head high and strides from the room. Her hands still tingle, but her body feels lighter than it has in days. Weeks, even.

Triumphant, she slips into her bedroom and closes the door. There's a louder-than-usual click as it latches, but Mimi doesn't care about the noise. She almost hopes to find Stan awake. Hopes he's been listening.

Her eyes adjust to the darkness, and his body takes shape on the bed. His broad chest rises and falls in a low, steady rhythm. His breath whistles in and out of his nose in soft snores.

Disappointment rolls in like a storm cloud, the air around her heavy and charged. She *could* have been out with another man. Stan doesn't know she wasn't. Is her meddling mother-in-law the only one who cares when she comes and goes?

Mimi leans against the door and sinks down until her bottom hits the floor, swiping tears from her eyes.

So much for silver linings.

CHAPTER 17

On Christmas Eve, the children eagerly await the appearance of the first star in the sky, then scurry to the dining room table, where all the *Wigilia* favorites are laid out—carp and cabbage rolls, pierogi and poppyseed cake. After supper, the family attends midnight Mass at Holy Trinity. Not even Stan can get out of going on this special night. The next morning, Penny and Junior awaken to a special present from Santa Claus under the tree. For Penny, it's a Shirley Temple doll. For Junior, a windup train. Mimi beams at the delight on their faces.

There are more presents under the tree, too. A bowl of oranges. Another brimming with ribbon candy and nuts. Halina crocheted a new set of mittens for both children and a winter cap for Stan. There's a new skein of yarn for Babcia and a new shaving set for Father that Mimi helped the children pick out from the Sears and Roebuck catalog. When Junior asks Mimi, "How come Santa didn't bring a gift for you?" she swallows the lump in her throat and pulls him close, kissing the top of his head. "You're my present, darling."

A week later, Chicago welcomes the new year with a blanket of white. Mimi's glad to be leaving the dreary 1930s behind. Hopefully the Depression is at last behind them too.

These days, Mimi is especially busy. The children are soon back in school, so in addition to the cleaning and cooking and marketing—

not to mention her work at the clinic—there are uniforms to mend and homework to check.

Mimi doesn't mind the busyness. Some days—many days—she's glad to be going to the clinic. Glad to be getting away from Stan's constant moping. Glad to be spending the day among colleagues who've quickly become friends. Glad to bring a check home each week and no longer open her budget book with dread. She still sets aside the help wanted page to peruse for other nursing positions, but spares it little more than a glance.

At the end of January, Stan gets a telephone call from Gibbins, who invites himself over for dinner the next evening. Mimi will be at the clinic but readies the roast she'd been saving for Sunday. Halina can put it in the oven that afternoon. Stan's clearly annoyed she won't be there to do it herself, and she promises to come home early if she can. She stays up late making a pie with the last of their cherry preserves.

The next day's a hectic one at the clinic. The staff is still getting their feet under them after Dr. Gabler's departure. By one o'clock, four women are waiting in the reception area. Jo is late coming back from lunch—again. Annie left early with the stomach flu. Ada is at the administrative office she keeps on Dearborn Street, filing away their latest records. Dr. Brodie—one of a few doctors who now rotate through the office—is impatient to get the next case started, and Mimi is scrambling to get the procedure room ready on her own.

She's just gotten a clean tray of instruments from the sterilizing room when she hears the main office door open. Thank God. It's about time Jo returned. She sets the tray on the instrument table. She'll wait to unpack it until she fetches the next patient and gets her ready in the anteroom. Jo will have to help with the gas. She's done it a time or two before, but Mimi will have to watch her closely to ensure she gives the right amount.

When Mimi opens the door to the reception area, it's not Jo she sees, but three policemen. One stands by the door, blocking anyone from leaving. The other two are prowling around Jo's desk. The four women waiting for their procedures all wear looks of white-faced dread.

Mimi feels the blood draining from her face as well, but manages to say, "Can I help you officers?"

The men at the desk turn to her. One must be six feet tall, while the other has barely an inch on Mimi, but by the smug-faced look on him, he's the one in charge.

"Ah," he says, his pale eyes traveling up and down her white uniform. "I was just about to ring for you." He gives the silver bell on the desk a jab anyway. A high-pitched clang echoes through the reception room. Mimi jolts at the sound. The officer laughs.

She sucks in a shaky breath, willing her nerves to calm. But they don't. It's as if every cell in her body is ping-ponging against the underside of her skin. It's only the women—the fear in their eyes—that gives her courage to speak. "I'm here. What do you want?"

Another chuckle. "We got a telephone call today from a doctor at St. Mary's Hospital. There's a woman in his care who had an abortion at this very office. You wouldn't happen to know anything about that, would you?"

A woman sick at the hospital? How sick? Mimi's thoughts fly through the patients she's seen over the last few weeks. Dozens come to mind. And those are just the ones she assisted with. She can't remember anyone having a difficult procedure or not keeping their follow-up appointment. A delayed hemorrhage was unlikely, but one of them could have since developed an infection.

The officer sounds the bell again, startling Mimi from her thoughts. "I asked you a question."

"No, I don't know anything about that," she manages to say.

"This isn't an office where a gal can come to get a criminal abortion?"

"No, sir." The lie rolls off her tongue with surprising ease.

He gestures to the women. "So they're just here for . . . a regular checkup."

Mimi's mouth has gone too dry to say anything more, so she nods.

The smile he gives in return makes her limbs go cold. He saunters toward her. "So if I went in the back, I'd find just a regular old exam room."

He's so close now, Mimi can smell pastrami and sauerkraut on his breath. See the dribble of mustard on his collar. His wife will have a terrible time lifting the stain.

He slips a hand around her and cups her rear. "What if you take me back there and show me?"

"Vinegar!" she blurts.

He steps back. "What?"

"Vinegar," she says again. Her pulse is thudding so loudly in her ear, she can hardly think. "The stain. On your collar. Vinegar will help."

He looks down at his shirt and frowns. His fat thumb swipes at the mustard, succeeding only in smearing it further. He huffs, and his smug expression darkens.

Mimi backs away, running into Dr. Brodie just as he enters from the back suite of rooms.

"What's all the commotion—" His voice dries up as he looks from Mimi to the police.

The short officer's frown deepens, but Mimi can't help but feel a whoosh of relief.

"You a doctor?" he says.

"I am."

"You work here?"

"I . . ." Dr. Brodie looks from one officer to another. "I . . ."

"That's enough of an admission for me." The short cop pulls a set of handcuffs from his belt. "All right, boys, round 'em up."

The officers throw Mimi, Dr. Brodie, and the four women into the back of their police wagon. They sit in slack-jawed silence until the engine rumbles to life.

"Are they taking us to jail?" one of the women asks, her voice edged with hysteria. "I haven't done anything wrong."

"My husband," another says. "He can't find out."

Mimi looks to Dr. Brodie. He sits with his head down and shoulders shaking. A hitching sob is the only reply he makes to the women.

Panic stirs inside her at the sight of him, but Mimi pushes it down. They can't all lose their heads. She knows that well enough from being a mother. Nothing frightens a child more than seeing their fear reflected back in the eyes of an adult. If Dr. Brodie won't be the adult here, Mimi will.

She turns to the women, fighting back a shiver as the wagon lurches into motion. "Don't worry. It will all be okay."

"How can you say that? We've been arrested."

Mimi nods at the first woman who spoke. "She's right. You've done nothing wrong. Even if they brought in another doctor to examine you, they'd find nothing has happened."

"They'd do that? Force us to submit to an examination?" one of them says, her voice high pitched with alarm.

"I don't know," Mimi says. "I don't think so." She's heard of such things happening, read about it years ago in the paper when another clinic was raided, but saying so would only frighten the women further. "The point is, you have nothing to confess. You've committed no crime. They have no grounds to hold you."

She doesn't know if that's true, either. Abortion is a crime, but is the intent to have an abortion? She's never read of *that* in the papers. But who knows what sort of thing the stodgy old men who wrote the laws might have come up with.

She meets each woman's stare, nodding reassuringly. The fear doesn't disappear from their eyes, but it lessens. If only Dr. Brodie would quit his crying. Mimi pats his knee, the same soft touch she's used with Penny and Junior a hundred times. He doesn't look up, but eventually quiets.

The drive takes considerably longer than Mimi expects. The Central District jail isn't but a few blocks away. Three small windows line either side of the wagon, but Mimi can't make out much through the bars. With each passing minute, it becomes harder to tamp down her dread. Where are they taking them?

Mimi has her answer when they stop at last in front of a wide, towering building of gray stone. Columns line the front façade like teeth in a gaping mouth. COOK COUNTY CRIMINAL COURT HOUSE is etched above.

The officers make no attempt to be gentle as they haul Mimi and the others from the back of the wagon. The short one's fingers squeeze so tightly around her arm, she can feel a bruise blooming.

Aside from what she's read in the papers and heard on the radio—sensationalized stories about gangsters and bank robbers—Mimi knows nothing about how an arrest works. But the photographs in the *Tribune* or *Chicago Daily News* usually show the police dragging criminals to the jailhouse, not the courthouse. Is she to be arrested, tried, and sentenced in one great swoop? Will she ever see her children or Stan again?

A sob claws up her throat, but she clamps her lips shut. The other women must be thinking the same thing. They may not be at the clinic, but they're still her patients, and she must hold herself together for them.

When she's calm enough to speak, she asks, "Why are we here?"

"We're just the clean-up crew," the cop says, his smug smile returning. "The state's attorney will decide how he wants to charge you." His meaty hands had loosened but now tighten again. "Don't worry, you'll see the inside of a jail cell soon enough."

Mimi wants to spit in his face. She's never done a thing like that, but the urge is so strong, she drops her head and focuses on the concrete steps leading up to the massive building. Better this way, too, so the others can't see the panic warring with her anger.

The marble-tiled lobby is crowded with every sort of person—rich, poor, Black, white. Voices echo off the travertine walls, drifting up to the coffered ceiling. No one seems to pay Mimi and the others much mind. The officers take them up a back staircase to the second floor.

It's quieter here, but that only increases Mimi's worry. They're led past several doors before finally entering into what appears to be a waiting room. Tall windows look out upon a band of train tracks and the sprawling city beyond. A vacant desk with a typewriter and three-tiered file tray sits beside a set of closed double doors. She suspects those doors lead to the state's attorney's inner office. Before Mimi can ask, the officer shoves her into a hard wooden chair against the far wall. The others are made to sit, as well.

Her handcuffs remain tightly in place as the shorter officer saunters away, not toward the double-wide doors but out of the room and down the hall. The other two coppers remain, stationed like sentinels on either side of their chairs.

How long will they be made to wait here? The roast should be going in soon. Hopefully, Halina hasn't forgotten. Gibbins will be arriving for dinner at seven, and he's never late. Not when a home-cooked meal is involved. Why he never married remains a mystery to Mimi. If anyone could do with a woman's touch, it's him. And Stan, he all but insisted she make it home in time to see to dinner's finishing touches.

A laugh builds in her throat. There's no hope of that now. No hope of even making it home before they cut the pie. By the time the laugh reaches her lips, it's more a strangled cry, and the others—including the coppers—look her way. She tries to cover the sound with a cough, but they must see how her shackled hands tremble as they cover her mouth.

A moment later, two men in suits enter the room. Police badges hang around their necks. The shorter cop follows them into the room, looking a bit chastened.

"You can remove their handcuffs," one of the men says. His crooked nose looks as if it's been broken more than once, and his eyebrows need a good trimming. But, like the other man who entered with him, his eyes are kind.

When none of the officers move to retrieve their keys, the other man says with more force, "They're not bandits, for criminy sakes. Remove their cuffs."

Begrudgingly, the men comply. Mimi breathes in deeply and rubs her wrists. It feels like the first full breath she's taken since the cops appeared at the clinic.

"Water?" the second of the two suit-wearing officers asks them. He's a slender man with dark brown hair slicked back from his tall forehead. Mimi and two of the other women nod. He returns a moment later and hands them each a paper cup. The water is lukewarm and tastes slightly of rust, but Mimi drinks it greedily. It sits uneasily in her empty stomach.

The two officers in suits stand apart from the others, speaking in hushed voices. The dark-haired one leaves, and the other knocks on the double-wide doors. He disappears into the room beyond for several minutes, then returns.

"It'll be a minute," he says. Mimi isn't sure to whom he's speaking until he adds, "Why don't you fellows go get some grub."

The short cop frowns, but the other two look relieved.

"No funny business," he says to Mimi and the others as he leaves.

A minute turns into thirty. Then an hour. A clock hangs on the far wall above the desk, and Mimi watches the hands tick away.

The double doors open, revealing a sliver of the room beyond. A woman slips out, her arms weighted down by a stack of files two feet tall. She's dressed as if she just stepped from a storefront window display—a smart blue jacket and matching wool skirt, fine leather shoes, a dainty silver wristwatch.

She unloads the files onto the desk and flashes the crooked-nosed officer a weary smile. His return grin reaches all the way to his ears. The woman's expression turns cold and businesslike when she regards Mimi and the others. A practiced look, Mimi can tell, and she can't blame the woman. She must see all manner of criminals in this line of work.

Criminals. The word rattles inside Mimi's mind, threatening to shatter her calm façade. She knew what she was getting herself into. Knew this could happen. But she hadn't truly expected it ever would.

It's almost five o'clock before the double doors open again. A man in a tailor-made suit steps out, leaving the doors open behind him. He crosses the room and stands before them, his narrowed eyes moving down the line of chairs, starting with the four women seated to Mimi's left. He takes his time assessing each of them, his face revealing nothing. One of the women begins to cry. None of them meet his stare. Their downturned faces hold a mix of fear and shame.

When his gaze reaches Mimi, her lungs freeze mid-inhale. He takes in her white uniform before his eyes travel to her face. It's all she can do not to look away. He holds her there, frozen, for a long, uncomfortable moment before shifting his gaze to Dr. Brodie.

He gives the doctor only a cursory glance, then turns to the crooked-nosed officer. "These four can go." He waves a hand at the women, then retreats to his office.

The women look from one another to the officer, who nods to the door.

"You heard the man."

They're up from their seats and out the door as fast as children at the sound of the recess bell. Not one of them spares a look back at Mimi or Dr. Brodie.

A gaping quiet descends on the room again, punctuated only by the tick of the clock and tap, tap, tap of the woman's typewriter. A renewed panic creeps over Mimi, turning her skin to gooseflesh. The women, her patients, gave her reason to be strong. Or at least to appear so. In their absence, that strength erodes. It doesn't help when Dr. Brodie falls into a fit of crying again.

The clock nears six, and the woman at the desk tidies her files. She pulls a stylish purse from her bottom drawer and grabs her coat from the rack in the corner. The thought of her, too, leaving fills Mimi with a rush of dread. The woman hasn't glanced Mimi's way once since sitting at her desk, but her presence was nevertheless a comfort.

"Wait!" Mimi blurts out. "Can I use the telephone?"

The woman stops buttoning her coat and glances at the officer. He shrugs. She turns to Mimi, that cold, practiced look back in place.

"Please," Mimi says. "I just want to call my family. To tell them"—her voice breaks—"tell them I'm all right."

The woman flattens her lips and looks over her shoulder at the double doors.

"I have a daughter. She's ten. And my son, he just turned eight. They were expecting me home tonight in time to tuck them into bed."

The woman sighs and waves Mimi over. "Keep your voice down and make it quick."

"Thank you." Mimi picks up the telephone and dials before the woman changes her mind. It rings several times before anyone answers—Mimi hopes it will be Stan, but instead, Penny's voice sounds on the line.

"Good evening. Lukas residence." She speaks in the polite, clear way Mimi taught her to use when answering. Hearing it is like a nail driven straight into Mimi's chest.

She takes a deep breath to steady herself.

"Hello?" Penny says, politeness veering into impatience.

"It's Mother, darling."

"Mama!"

"Can you put your father on, please?"

"He's in the shower."

Mimi shakes her head. Of course he'd wait until the last minute to get ready for his dinner with Gibbins.

"Babcia, then."

No reply.

"Penny?"

"You didn't say *please*. I *always* have to say please. Last time when I didn't you—"

"Please, Penny. Please, get Babcia."

"All right."

The line is silent for a moment. The woman is watching her, furrows deepening across her brow. Mimi gives her a grateful smile and nods in understanding of her unspoken command: *hurry up*.

Mimi hears the thud of footfalls over the line, then Penny's voice again.

"Babcia says she's too busy with the roast."

Too busy with the roast! All she has to do is put it in the oven. Mimi saw to everything else. She takes another steadying breath. "Tell her it's important."

Another stretch of silence.

"She said, *Daj mi spokój*."

"What does that mean?"

"Um . . . she wants you to leave her alone."

Mimi sighs and glances again at the woman. She's tapping her foot and eyeing her watch.

"Fine. I need you to write down a message for me. Go get a pen and paper. Hurry now."

As the line goes quiet, Mimi tries to think of what to say. Certainly not the truth. That would frighten Penny. Frighten all of them. Stan would cancel his dinner. Halina would never let her hear the end of it about the perfectly good roast Mimi ruined. But what if she isn't as lucky as the other women? Surely if the state's attorney wanted to let her go, he would have done so already.

"I'm ready, Mama."

"Okay, write down . . . write that there was an emergency at the hospital and . . . they need me to stay and work night duty, too. I likely won't be back before morning." Who knows when she'll be let go. How she'll make bail. If the judge will even grant bail. If she'll see a judge at all. But this, at least, buys her a little more time. "Did you get all that?"

"Yes."

"Be sure to give that note to your father as soon as he's out of the shower."

"I will."

"And one more thing. I—"

"I have to go. Babcia's yelling for me to set the dinner table."

"Penny, I love you. You hear me? Tell your brother I love him, too."

"Bye, Mama."

Mimi hears a click, before she can say *bye* in return. She places the handset back on the base. Tears leak from her eyes. "Thank you."

The woman's cool, practiced expression falters, and she nods.

Mimi returns to the hard wooden chair beside Dr. Brodie. It's another twenty minutes before the double doors open, and the man waves them into his office. The crooked-nosed officer follows them inside, closing them in.

The room is richly furnished with a large, polished oak desk and a high-backed leather chair. Watercolor paintings of the lakeshore adorn the walls. There's one for every season, but Mimi's eyes are drawn to summer and the red-and-white umbrellas dotting the beach. Penny and Junior love the shore in the summertime. Before Stan's injury, they went at least once a week. Mimi had been looking forward to going again. Come summer, she'd have money enough to take the car and buy them each an ice cream cone from one of the beachside vendors. Now she wonders if she'll ever see the shore again.

"Have a seat," the man says to them, gesturing to the two chairs in front of his desk. They're not nearly as nice as his chair, but at least there's a seat cushion.

"I'm Assistant State's Attorney Moynihan. The Central Police claim to have been tipped off about—"

"They've got it all wrong," Dr. Brodie interrupts. "You've got to believe me. I don't know who told them what, but I've only just started working at the clinic, and I—"

Mr. Moynihan holds up his hand. "Let me finish, sir."

"But I can't possibly be—"

"Doctor," he says, with the kind of force you'd expect from a man used to dealing with criminals worse than them.

Dr. Brodie goes quiet, slumping in his chair and hanging his head. Mimi leans away from him. Any minute now, he's bound to start bawling again.

"Now, where was I?"

"The Central Police," she reminds him, her voice flat. They might as well get on with the interrogation.

Mr. Moynihan looks at her, the corner of his mouth twitching upward. "Ah, yes. The Central Police. They were tipped off about a doctor's office on North State Street performing abortions without medical justification. I trust you know that such an act is illegal." He pauses, and Mimi nods. Dr. Brodie only grunts. "Now, if such a racket were occurring in said office, it'd be my sworn duty to prosecute all those involved."

He leans back in his chair and looks directly at Mimi again. "You wouldn't know anything about such a racket, would you?"

Mimi skirts his gaze. She'd kill for another cup of water. "No, sir."

"I didn't think so." He turns his heavy stare on Dr. Brodie. "And you?"

"It's like I said, sir. I—"

"I think you should take a cue from your nurse here. A simple 'no, sir' will suffice."

"No, sir."

"Very well. Let's see what the morning holds. One of my officers is doing a bit of investigating on his own." He stands.

Mimi is too stunned at first to move. Is that all? And what did he mean by *let's see what the morning holds*? Mimi gets half an answer when Mr. Moynihan turns to the crooked-nosed officer and says, "Take them to jail for the night."

CHAPTER 18

At the Central Station jail, Mimi shares a drafty cell with a bedraggled woman picked up on Clark Street for prostitution. There are no beds in the cell, only two long wooden benches. A small barred window sits high up in the back wall. The dank air smells faintly of urine.

The woman introduces herself as Bea, and as the night wears on, Mimi learns her story.

Her full name is Beatrice Rose Delany. She grew up in Appleton, Wisconsin. A farm girl, like Mimi. She came to the city with a man who heard her sing in church and promised he could make her a radio star. Her voice *is* really something, and she might have had a shot if the man actually knew the bigwigs at WMAQ and WGN, like he said. When she sings for Mimi, the cold jail cell with its rock-hard benches and musty urine smell falls away. So does Mimi's fear, her panic, her thirst and hunger. But the night guard, whose job it must be to ensure that no comforts—not even a simple song—are enjoyed here, bangs his billy club on the cell's bars and hollers for her to stop.

She's been working the streets for three years now, ever since the man ran out on her. There's no way she can return to Appleton, she tells Mimi. They'd chase her out of town like Cain from Eden, her father and brothers leading the charge.

Mimi learns from Bea that they're both casualties of the morals squad, a specialty unit set up by the mayor to police crimes of vice, to seek out delinquents and deviants and harass them into submission. "But a gal's gotta eat, don't she?" Bea says.

She guesses from Mimi's uniform the sort of moral offense Mimi's been picked up for. Bea's availed herself of such services a time or two, she tells her.

"Done it once myself, too," she says flatly. "With the rib of an umbrella. That same trick landed a friend in the morgue, though. So I ain't keen to try that way again. Plus, it hurt like the very devil."

"I'm sorry." Mimi doesn't know what else to say.

Bea shrugs. "Desperate times and all that."

The two women talk half the night away, Bea doing the lion's share of the chattering. Then Bea curls up on the bench and falls asleep as soundly as if it were a feather bed. Mimi doesn't even try to sleep. Her thoughts are a cacophony of worry. Her empty stomach a tangle of knots. What did the assistant state's attorney mean by *let's see what the morning holds*? What did his officer's "investigation" yield? Bea's soft snoring is her only comfort as night's wee hours march slowly to dawn.

Mimi's back is stiff and her rear sore by the time morning sunlight finds its way into the cell. Bea still snores, curled up on the bench opposite her. Mimi watches her, marveling at her ability to sleep here. It's not just the cold and the smell and the hardness of the bench. It's the threat of what's to come. Mimi isn't sure how these things work, but she recalls from listening to shows like *Gang Busters* that some official business is supposed to occur. Fingerprinting, picture taking, the recording of her name and details. Odd that they didn't do it last night. But maybe the clerk, or whoever gathers and records such things, had already logged off for the day. Or maybe the police want it that way. No official trace, so they can cart her off to prison, lock her up, and toss away the key without having to bother with a trial. Those kinds of things also happen in radio dramas. But in real life, there'd be no hero to save her. Even if Stan were up to the task, he'd never find her. That was the point.

Thinking about Stan and the children brings fresh tears to her eyes. She wipes them quickly away when she hears footsteps coming down the hall. It's the crooked-nosed cop and his dark-haired partner from the state's attorney's office. Better them than those brutes from the morals squad. But her heart inches up her throat nonetheless. The guard who'd banged on the cell bars last night when Bea was singing is with them. He opens the door and points at her. "This one?"

The cops nod.

"You," the guard says to her, "let's go."

Mimi glances at Bea, who's still sleeping soundly. Her story is not unlike Ginny's. Both begin with a man and his hollow promises. Only the ending is different.

She'd like to say goodbye to Bea. Wish her good luck. Tell her to never stop singing. But it seems wrong to wake her from so peaceful a sleep. Reality will come back to her soon enough.

Mimi expects to be handcuffed the moment she leaves the cell. Instead, the dark-haired cop takes her upper arm and leads her down the hall. Compared to the bruising she received yesterday, this man's grip is a whisper. But then, there's little worry of her getting away in a place like this.

They stop at another holding cell at the far end of the hall. Over half a dozen men are crowded inside. Dr. Brodie squats in the corner. His lip is bloodied and swollen—an injury he didn't have last night when they parted. Did these officers take him to a little room somewhere and interrogate him? (A tactic the investigators in *Gang Busters* often employ.) Is this what the assistant state's attorney had meant when he said his officer—the officer whose hold she now finds herself in—was doing some investigating of his own? Is she the next part of that investigation?

Her breath starts to come in shallow, ragged pulls. She knows hyperventilating will only make things worse, but that tiny rational voice is no match for her fear.

The officer squeezes her arm gently. A threat? A promise of what's to come? Or was it meant as a reassurance? Mimi isn't sure.

The doctor is called from the cell. He gives the other men inside a wide berth as he exits, flinching when one of them makes as if to rush him. Perhaps that was who gave him the bloody lip. Indeed, he seems relieved when the cell door closes behind him, and the crooked-nosed cop takes his arm.

Mimi's breathing slows—not to a normal rhythm, but steady

enough that she's no longer in danger of passing out. The cops lead them from the holding area, up a flight of stairs, and out through the lobby.

No fingerprints or pictures, then. It's either off to Oakdale or back to the county courthouse. Despite her stomach being empty, Mimi thinks she might be sick.

The morning light stings her eyes. The cold bites through her stockings and the thin cotton of her uniform. They reach the officers' car and stop. The dark-haired man releases her arm but makes no move to open the back door and force her inside. Instead, he dips a hand into his pocket, fishes out a dime, and presses it into her hand.

Mimi stares down at it, confused.

"For the L." He opens the front passenger door and gets inside. Mimi glances over her shoulder at the station house half a block away, then back at him. Is this some sort of trick?

The other officer lets go of Dr. Brodie and makes his way toward the driver's side, leaving them alone on the sidewalk. Dr. Brodie looks just as confused as she is but says to the officer, "Hey, don't I get a dime, too?"

"Find your own way home," the crooked-nosed officer says, before climbing into the car and starting the engine.

Home? Are they really letting her and Dr. Brodie go free? Mimi's feet remain rooted to the sidewalk as the car pulls away from the curb and drives off. One block. Two blocks. It stops at a traffic light before the third. Mimi holds her breath. The light changes, and the car continues on.

They're free.

Mimi turns to Dr. Brodie and finds him already gone.

She makes it home by midmorning, long after Penny and Junior have left for school. Before climbing the porch steps, Mimi glances over her shoulder, still half expecting to see a police car driving down the road. She's looked back every half block or so since leaving the L. She takes a deep breath and starts up the stairs. The police have no way to find her, she reminds herself. They don't even know her name.

The house is quiet when she enters, but she smells a freshly lit cigarette and sees a curl of smoke coming from the living room. Smoke or no, Mimi's so glad to be home, she almost squeals. She's hungry enough to eat a horse and tired enough to sleep straight through till tomorrow. But first, she wants to see her husband, to rush into his arms and bury herself in his embrace.

Three strides, and she's in the living room. Three more, and she'll be beside his chair. But her step falters at his sour expression as he turns his head from the window. She hoped to see worry in those blue eyes of his. Concern. Joy at her return. Not contempt.

"Are you abandoning your responsibilities to this home altogether now?" he says.

"What?"

"Mama's had to do everything around here these past few days—cook dinner, pack the kids' lunches, make breakfast. You know how bad her rheumatism is."

Mimi's mouth opens, but she can't untangle her thoughts enough to speak. Has she walked into the wrong house? At last, she says, "Didn't you get my telephone message?"

"You should have told them no."

The police? She almost laughs, thinking about saying no to that foul-breathed officer. "I'm sorry, you can't arrest me, sir. I have responsibilities I must attend to at home." But then she realizes by *them*, Stan means the hospital. That's where he thinks she works. That's where he thinks she's been. That's the lie she told him.

Here's her chance to come clean.

She searches his face again for some shred of the feelings she hoped to see there. Some indication he wants to understand. Nothing.

"It was an emergency. The night nurse didn't show and—"

"It was an emergency here."

She takes a step closer. "Did something happen with the children? Are they—"

"My meeting. With Gibbins. Does that ring a bell?"

Mimi can't help the laughter that rises inside her again. She pivots away from him and sinks onto the sofa across the room as the sound spills out of her. The sofa's cushions don't have the bounce they used to. The fabric has grown shabby at the corners. But right now, it's the softest, most comfortable sofa she's ever sat upon. This makes her laugh harder. There's a grape juice stain on the armrest she keeps covered with a doily. The wood feet are dented from one too many run-ins with Junior's toy fire engine. They'd planned to go shopping for a new sofa the very week Stan broke his leg.

She's laughing so hard she's crying now. The scowl on Stan's face deepens, but she doesn't care.

Funny how fate makes his entrance when your eyes are drawn to the opposite side of the stage. When you're thinking about what kind of sofa you want to buy. Or when your colleague will return from lunch. Or how come your sister won't let you borrow that pretty pink ribbon.

Her laughter begins to recede, but the tears continue.

"It's not funny, Mimi. This is my career we're talking about."

"I know. I'm sorry," she says, even though his nonexistent career is the last thing on her mind, and she isn't sorry. Not for that.

"You're my wife, and I needed you here last night. Gibbins never would have . . . never would have quit on me had you been here."

Mimi sits up and swipes the water from her eyes. "Quit on you? What do you mean?"

"He couldn't get me one tryout. Not one! And he's done asking. Says he's got his reputation to think about. The good-for-nothing bastard."

"Oh, Stan." She rises from the sofa and goes to him, reaching out her arms. He turns his head away and angles his body toward the window.

Mimi stops at the foot of his chair. He might as well have spit on her. She watches him take a long drag on his cigarette and blow out the smoke with a heavy exhale. "What are you going to do?"

"I don't know."

"Did Gibbins have any—"

"Fuck Gibbins!"

Mimi flinches.

He grinds the butt of his cigarette into the ashtray, then reaches for another.

"Spring training's out then?"

"I don't know."

"What about—"

"I said I don't know. I don't know! I don't know."

Mimi looks down at her hands. Her shoulders bow with the weight of her fatigue. What can she say to him to make this better?

The truth? At least then, he might feel sorry for someone other than himself. But Mimi doesn't want his pity any more than this anger. Telling him what happened last night would likely rouse both. Or maybe nothing at all. Perhaps that's what she fears the most. A callous shrug before turning his attention back to the window and his damned cigarettes.

How did they get here? This impasse. He's so close, she could reach out and stroke her hand along his stubbled jaw. But the tiny space between them seems impenetrable.

Mimi follows his gaze out the window. Last week's snow still covers the lawn—a hard crust of white, tinged gray in places by the fumes of passing automobiles.

What about her? What is *she* going to do? She'd hoped they'd figure it out together. No, that isn't true. She'd hoped he'd figure it out for them. *Father knows best* and all that silly advice they spew in the homemaking magazines she reads. Or used to read when she had a moment free to herself.

She turns and starts toward the bathroom. What she's going to do is shower. Then wash the dishes that are undoubtedly piled in the sink. Then sleep. She'll figure out the rest later. Alone.

CHAPTER 19

The next day, Mimi returns to the clinic on North State Street, her decision made. Two women wait in the reception area. Jo sits at the desk, looking over the day's schedule. It's strange to see everything operating as normal. As though police officers hadn't barged in two days ago and arrested everyone.

Jo looks up and greets Mimi with a relieved smile. Mimi doesn't smile back. She walks straight through the reception into the back hallway. Jo follows through the door a moment later and trails behind her.

"Are you okay? I called Ada the minute I got back and found the office empty. She told me to lock up and go home. I didn't learn until yesterday that"—her voice lowers to a whisper—"that coppers came by."

Mimi stops in front of the closet and grabs the coat and purse she had to leave behind when the cops dragged her out in handcuffs.

"Hey," Jo continues. "Why aren't you in your uniform? You're not quitting, are you?"

Mimi closes the closet door and turns to face her. The concern in Jo's eyes sends an ache through her chest. They've known each other for barely three months, but Mimi will miss her dearly. Miss everyone here.

"I just came to get my things and say my goodbyes."

"Was it that bad? Ada will be furious if they mistreated you."

"They didn't mistreat me. But it was still awful. I spent the entire night in jail."

Jo takes her hand. "You poor dear! Your family must have been beside themselves with worry."

Mimi doesn't correct her. After their argument, she and Stan didn't speak for the rest of the day. And Halina only eyed Mimi with her usual suspicion. For the children, what was for dinner and who got to pick the radio program was of greater importance than where Mimi had been the night before. Of course, she wouldn't have wanted them to worry. But she might have liked to be missed. "That's why I can't stay. What will happen to them if I wind up in prison?"

Jo looks down and sighs. "If only I hadn't been running late."

"They just would have arrested you, too."

"At least you wouldn't have been alone."

Mimi squeezes her hand before letting go. That Jo would brave arrest to stand beside her—that she would even contemplate it—makes the aching in her chest even worse. "Is Ada in her office?"

Jo nods. "I wish you'd reconsider, but I understand."

"Thanks for being such a great friend." She turns and heads to Ada's office before Jo's earnest expression erodes her resolve.

The office door is open, and Ada sits at the small desk within. When Mimi knocks on the jamb, Ada waves her in. "Close the door and sit down."

Once Mimi's seated, Ada leans forward and folds her hands atop the desk. "Tell me everything that happened."

Mimi recounts the raid, their time at the county courthouse, her night in jail, and the officers' strange behavior the next day. She leaves out Dr. Brodie's blubbering and her own paralyzing fear. Ada listens without interruption, and Mimi gets the sense she somehow already knows much of the story.

When Mimi finishes, Ada leans back and sighs. "I'm sorry you had to spend the night at Central Station. I got to work as soon as Miss Kuder telephoned and told me her suspicions, but I couldn't get things arranged until the next morning."

"Arranged?"

After a moment's hesitation, Ada says, "I have an understanding with a few of the men at the state's attorney's office."

"That's why they let us go?"

Ada nods. "It's as if the whole thing never happened. Legally speaking, of course. Two of the women have already returned and rescheduled their appointments." She glances at the coat balled in Mimi's lap alongside her purse. "I imagine for you, though, the ordeal is not so easily forgotten."

"No," Mimi says.

"And you've come back today to tender your resignation."

"I have to think about my family. I can't risk being arrested again."

"Technically, you weren't arrested. Only anonymously detained. But I understand family comes first. You won't be easy to replace, you know. Even if it were easy, I'd be sorry to lose you. You're a good nurse, Mrs. Lukas."

A warmth spreads through her at the sincerity of Ada's words. *A good nurse*. It's been ages since she's been told she's good at anything. "Thank you."

"Where will you go?"

"Back to hospital work."

Ada could point out how difficult that will be, but she doesn't, and Mimi's grateful.

"Can you stay and finish out the day? Annie's the only other nurse scheduled, and we have a particularly . . . delicate case this morning I was hoping you could attend to."

"Me?"

Ada slides an intake card across the desk. Mimi frowns but picks it up. The name *Annabelle Johnson* is printed at the top. She skips over her address and telephone number. Notes that she's not married and has never had an abortion or previous illness. It's been two months since her last period. The name of a local druggist is written in the referral line. Nothing out of the ordinary.

Mimi's about to hand back the card when her eyes snag on the woman's age: *12 years*. She's not a woman at all, but a child. Mimi glances back at Ada.

"It's not a mistake. And I suspect she's further along than two months, but Dr. Snyder agreed to do the procedure without a prior exam. No need to put her through more than she's already endured."

Mimi sets the card down on the table with an unsteady hand. Twelve. That's barely older than Penny. "I didn't wear my uniform."

"Edna keeps a spare in the closet. It won't be a perfect fit, but it will do."

Mimi looks down at the coat and purse bundled in her lap. She'd made up her mind to fetch her belongings and leave. But what if *she* were the one waiting in the reception room alongside her daughter? "All right. I'll stay. Just for the rest of the day."

At the end of the day, Mimi returns to Ada's office.

"Thank you," Ada says to her. "Had it been my daughter, I would have wanted a nurse like you."

Mimi's throat tightens. It might just be the greatest compliment she's ever received. One she wishes Ada didn't have cause to bestow.

"What happens to her now?"

"She goes back home."

"And the man?"

Ada shrugs. "I talked to the mother. Told her I knew people in the police department and elsewhere who could help her. Help them. She insists Annabelle's no longer in danger."

"But what if it's her father or—"

"We cannot be everything to everyone, Mrs. Lukas. This is how we help people, by what we do here in the clinic. The rest we must leave to someone else."

It's not an answer Mimi likes, but she hears the truth in it. And at least they could offer the girl something. A gentle touch. A reassuring smile. A way out of this one part of her troubles.

"Will you be back on Friday to pick up your final week's pay, or shall I mail it to you?"

"No," Mimi says. "I'll see you for work tomorrow."

CHAPTER 20

Has she made the right decision to stay at the clinic? Mimi isn't sure. It's past Valentine's Day before her heart stops jumping into her throat at the sound of the main office door opening. And she still glances over her shoulder now and then as she enters the State Street Building.

At home, things settle more quickly, though not for the better. As spring training approaches, Stan becomes quiet and surly. The children grow skittish of him. Mimi contrives all manner of activities to keep them out of the living room whenever he's there, which he often is. Art projects at the kitchen table, snowman-building contests in the yard. She even saves up and buys a second radio so they can listen in the cellar. The reception isn't as good, but they make do, sipping mugs of warm Ovaltine and wrapping themselves in blankets against the cold. It's their very own underground clubhouse, Mimi tells them. And though it's become hard to iron the laundry without stepping on a teddy bear or train engine, it keeps the peace.

She knows Stan would never hurt them. But she hates for them to witness his decline. Wants their memories of him to be of happier times. Playing catch in the yard. Riding the roller coaster at Riverview Park. Reading bedtime stories. As soon as he's his old self again, they'll move the clubhouse upstairs.

For now, they wait, tiptoeing past the living room whenever he's there, eating dinner in silence, holding their breath until he goes to bed. Only Halina's words, spat out in a fiery string of Polish, get him up and dressed for church or into the bathroom for a shower and shave after three days in the same wrinkled shirt and trousers.

Mimi hoped their mutual concern for Stan would draw her and Halina closer. Instead, it's only deepened the rift between them. It's easier to blame the other and her failings as a wife or mother than rotten luck or Stan himself.

The clinic is quiet as Mimi gives the procedure room a good scrubbing. Ada left early to see her son—newly enlisted in the Army—off to the train station. Edna's gone, too, having taken their last patient—a woman four months along—to her home to watch over for the next few days. So Mimi and Jo are left alone to close up for the day.

While Mimi finishes sterilizing the last tray of instruments, Jo copies tomorrow's schedule and organizes the day's records, leaving both on Ada's desk. The records, Mimi knows, will soon find their way to the Dearborn Street office, where all the records are stored. The schedule will be reviewed and posted in the back hall before the first case gets underway. But those are tomorrow's cares.

Once everything is clean, tidy, and smelling sharply of antiseptic, Mimi grabs her coat and waits for Jo in the empty reception room. She smiles as Jo glides in, having traded her working-gal's wool skirt and jacket for a starlet's A-line velvet dress with a sweetheart neckline. She wears a fresh coat of lipstick, a strand of pearls, and elbow-length satin gloves. Her hair hasn't suffered beneath a cotton cap all day as Mimi's has, and frames her face in smooth waves.

"Don't you look a picture," Mimi says.

Jo twirls once, her skirt flaring, and they both laugh.

"But really, you think it's all right?"

"For Chez Paree? It's perfect. You'll turn heads at every table."

"I only care about turning one head tonight." Jo opens her purse and fishes through its contents. "I know my key is in here somewhere."

"I'll get the lock," Mimi says, easily finding her key in the small zipped pocket inside her bag. She can't help but feel plain standing beside Jo. It's not just her cotton uniform, her workaday coat, or her simple handbag. Compared to dinner and dancing at Chez Paree, her entire life feels plain.

Jo switches off the reception room light and steps into the hall, Mimi locking the door behind them.

"You and Stan should join us some night," Jo says, as they make their way to the elevator. "Didn't you say you liked dancing?"

"I'm not sure Stan's leg is up to it."

"You could still come out. Stan could enjoy the music, and we could take turns dancing with Edgar. Stan isn't the jealous type, is he?"

"No," Mimi says. She always liked that about him. He never hassled her about past fellows she'd dated. Never minded if she took a turn on the dance floor with one of his teammates who'd joined them stag. Never asked where she'd been and made her produce the grocer's or butcher's receipt to prove it. But these days, she'd happily take a flash or two of jealousy over Stan's indifference.

They take the elevator down to the first floor and are halfway through the lobby when Jo stops.

"Oh, horse feathers!"

"What?"

Jo glances back at the large clock near the elevators and utters another, far less ladylike curse.

"What?" Mimi asks again.

"Before Ada left this afternoon, she asked me to run a quick errand tonight. I forgot all about it until now."

"Can't you do it tomorrow?"

"No." Jo's expression is pained as she looks between the clock and the lobby's glass doors. "Ada will kill me if I don't get it done, but Edgar will be here any minute."

"Why didn't you tell Ada about your date? I'm sure she would have understood."

"I forgot."

Mimi shakes her head and says with a teasing smile, "How does someone so forgetful get a job as a receptionist?"

"At least I remembered before Ada has my head for it tomorrow." She sighs and starts back toward the elevators.

Mimi follows her. "I'll do it."

"Really?"

"Sure. The kids are already in bed, and Stan . . . well, Stan won't mind. You said it's just a quick errand, right?"

Jo hurriedly tells Mimi about an envelope in the top center drawer of her desk. After retrieving the envelope, Mimi must take it to the LaSalle Street Tavern across from City Hall and deliver it to a man named Mr. Moriarity.

"That's it," Jo says when she's finished.

Before Mimi can ask any questions—like what the envelope contains, or how on earth she's supposed to recognize this Mr. Moriarity—Jo gives her a quick hug and rushes out the lobby to where Edgar's car is waiting at the curb.

Mimi takes the elevator back up to the office and retrieves the envelope. Had she known the errand involved going alone to a tavern this late at night, she'd have been less eager to volunteer. But Jo seemed to think it terribly important, and if Mimi doesn't go through with it now, Ada will have both their heads tomorrow. Besides, she's glad to let Jo go off and have her fun. It's not like Mimi has anything to look forward to at home except a sink full of dinner dishes.

On the elevator ride down, she studies the envelope. It's a standard white envelope the size of her hand, with no markings or stamps. The flap is only partially sealed. It's none of Mimi's business what's inside, but curiosity gets the better of her. She carefully wedges her nail beneath the flap and works it free. Inside is a hundred-dollar bill.

The elevator chimes as it reaches the first floor. Mimi startles, nearly dropping the letter. Who is this Mr. Moriarity, and why is Ada giving him a hundred dollars? That's more than twice what Mimi spends on groceries each month. She hastily licks the flap and reseals it before tucking the envelope into her purse.

Outside, the winter wind picks up swirls of newly fallen snow and flings it into the night. The city's bright lights reflect off the gray-black clouds above, casting everything in a strange faint glow.

Unnatural, her Pa would say about the overabundant light. As if the city had no shame. Now that she's an adult, Mimi might counter: a sin's a sin, whether it happens in the dark or the light. And perhaps all those shameful things he imagines happen in the city aren't so sinful after all.

Or maybe Mimi's grown blind to the difference.

She pulls her scarf higher up her neck and starts toward the tavern, grateful when the city's din drowns out Pa's voice in her head.

Mimi's never been to the LaSalle Street Tavern, but it isn't difficult to find. A rush of air pushes past her as she opens the door. It smells of smoke and beer and dust, but she ignores the stench in favor of the warmth and hurries inside. A long bar runs the length of one wall. Against the opposite wall, a line of beer barrels squat beneath a bank of fogged windows. Tables and chairs—nearly all of them occupied—fill in the center.

Mimi removes her gloves and unwinds her scarf but leaves her coat on. She already feels out of place, being one of only a handful of women in the room. Baring her white nursing uniform would make her stand out all the more.

After a glance around, she heads toward the bar, hoping the bartender can point Mr. Moriarity out to her. If not, she'll have to go table to table, never mind the eyebrows it will raise. Next time, Ada will just have to run her own errands. That, or Jo and Edgar will have to change their dinner plans. Trade champagne and caviar for beer and peanuts.

There's no music but a steady stream of chatter and the occasional peal of raucous laughter. Tin lamps hang from the low ceiling amid a cloud of cigar and cigarette smoke. Mimi's halfway to the bar when her eyes snag on a familiar face. Her feet stop of their own accord, and the tavern's warmth vanishes. She averts her gaze, then slides it quickly back to be sure. The dark-haired man sitting at the corner table—he's one of the coppers from the state's attorney's office.

A city of millions, and she walks into the same tavern as him. What if he's changed his mind about letting her go free?

Her first thought is to run, to turn around and hightail it from the bar before he recognizes her. But that would only draw more attention to herself. And with these shoes and snow-slickened sidewalks, she could never outrun him, even with a head start. Still, it's all she can do to uproot her feet and keep moving toward the bar.

She trains her gaze on the wall behind the bar. A picture of President Roosevelt hangs above the cash register. Beside it is a sign advertising ten-cent Budweiser and a bawdy calendar depicting a half-dressed woman riding on the back of a nymph. From the corner of her eye, she sees the copper stand up. Her gut squeezes, but she keeps walking.

He could be getting up to leave. Or standing to greet an old friend. She doesn't dare look.

Mimi makes it to the bar, grabbing the lip to still her shaking hands. Now what? She can't go forward with her plan and risk the copper's attention. Whoever this Mr. Moriarity is, he'll have to get his hundred dollars another day. But she can't just turn around and leave. Maybe there's a side exit she can slip out of. Or—

The bartender strides over before Mimi can make up her mind. "What can I get you, doll?"

"I . . . um . . ." She glances behind him at the beer advertisement, then to the liquor bottles cluttering the back counter. Should she order something? A woman sipping a drink at a bar is far less likely to draw attention than one beelining it for the door. But the longer she's here, the greater chance the copper will see her. If he hasn't already. "Actually, I—"

"She'll have a gin rickey, and I'll take another beer," a voice says beside her.

Mimi turns and sees the copper. Her fingers tighten around the lip of the bar. He's going to arrest her again. Mimi knows it. She should have run when she had the chance.

As the bartender scuttles away to get their drinks, the copper leans down and whispers in her ear, "You got something for me?"

Mimi blinks. Has she heard him right? "Are you . . ."

"Daniel Moriarity. Go sit down at the table in the corner."

Her thoughts are ascramble. It doesn't help that her pulse is racing, and her stomach is somewhere down by her knees. "But I—"

"I'll be right behind you with our drinks." He gives her a pointed look, then nods toward the table.

Mimi's fingers slowly uncurl from the lip of the bar. The table in the corner couldn't be farther from the door, the exit, home, but she does as he's directed her. What other choice does she have? At least she's fairly certain he's not going to arrest her.

Half a beer remains on the table alongside a folded section of the *Chicago Tribune*. She sits in the chair opposite the beer. The seat is well-worn and surprisingly comfortable, despite its lack of cushioning. It's less smoky in the corner of the tavern, too, thanks to the vent she spies high up on the nearby wall.

Her heart starts to slow, and her thoughts untangle. This—the money in the envelope—it's a bribe. This is the reason no charges were filed after the morals squad raided the clinic last month. Mimi unshoulders her handbag and flings it onto the table, not wanting the envelope inside anywhere near her. The work she does at the clinic is one thing, but this is the sort of thing gangsters do. Immoral, illegal, not to mention dangerous.

The minute Officer Moriarity arrives at the table with the drinks and sits down, Mimi opens her bag. She reaches inside like she's sinking her hand into a slimy, stopped-up drain. The sooner she's done with this awful "errand," the better. But before she can grasp the envelope, Officer Moriarity leans across the table and takes hold of her wrist. His grip is firm, but not to the point of pain. His gray eyes meet hers, and he shakes his head.

"Relax. We'll get to that later."

"Later?"

He lets go of her wrist and pushes the gin rickey toward her.

"I agreed to deliver an envelope, not to sit here and have a drink with you."

"More than a dozen people are watching you right now. Do you really want to hand me that envelope right out in the open?"

A chill skitters down Mimi's neck, as if she can suddenly feel those eyes upon her. She withdraws her hand and sets the bag in her lap. "Why are they watching?"

Officer Moriarity leans back and takes a sip of his half-drunk beer. "You're a new face around here. And a pretty one to boot."

Mimi scowls at him, frustration getting the better of her fear. Racketeer was not a role she signed up to play.

"It's just an observation. You stand out like a sore thumb, and not just 'cause of that face."

"Stand out how?" she snaps.

He shrugs. "Like it's your first time stepping into a tavern. You know prohibition ended half a dozen years ago, right?"

"I've been in plenty of taverns, thank you very much." It's not exactly true, but she's not some country bumpkin, either. Not anymore. She's been in plenty of dance halls and drunk her share of cocktails—even back when it was illegal. To prove it, Mimi picks up her gin rickey and takes a deep drink.

It's a bad idea. Her face puckers and eyes water. The soda is nearly flat, and the gin tastes like rubbing alcohol. Swallowing is worse. Half goes down her windpipe, sending her into a fit of coughing. The rest slides down her throat, burning as it goes.

Officer Moriarity chuckles.

Mimi's face burns, and not just from the alcohol. If people weren't watching her before, now they certainly are. She straightens and forces down another sip.

"Don't worry," Officer Moriarity says. "In a few minutes, everyone will be paying more attention to themselves and their drinks again than you and me."

Mimi hopes he's right.

"Where's Ada tonight?"

"Her son is off to Camp Forrest. She asked me—well, actually, not me but my colleague—to come in her stead."

"And where's this colleague?"

"She had dinner plans with her beau."

"Not you?"

Mimi shakes her head. He offers her a consoling smile, then glances down to where her hands rest atop the table. She follows his gaze and realizes she's fidgeting with her wedding ring. She pulls her hands apart and thrusts them into her lap.

Silence falls between them. He finishes the first beer and pushes the empty glass aside but doesn't start on the other. Mimi wishes he and Ada could have at least picked somewhere with music for their dealing. At least then, the quiet between them wouldn't feel so empty. She uncrosses her ankles, then crosses them again. If the silence bothers him, he makes no show of it but seems content to stare at her with those unnerving gray eyes.

He doesn't look like a cop. Not really. Not like those men from the morals squad, anyway. If she didn't know he was a cop and could arrest her here on the spot, she wouldn't be the slightest bit intimidated by him. He's not small or weak-looking, but he lacks that tough-guy swagger. Had they met under different circumstances, Mimi would have thought him a tailor or author or architect.

She remembers the glass of water he'd brought her at the courthouse. How he'd insisted their handcuffs be removed. Those were the actions of a kind man, a self-assured man. Not someone who needs to prove his strength or superiority with violence.

But those eyes. They've got a cop's sharp alertness, even if there's a gentleness to them, too.

Mimi takes another sip of her drink, remembering how awful it tastes after the liquid hits her tongue.

"Scoot closer to me," he says, at last breaking the silence.

"Why?"

"So that in a few minutes, when we get up and leave together, people won't think I've got you at gunpoint."

"Do you?"

Another chuckle. "No."

"I'm not leaving with you." Then she remembers the envelope tucked inside her handbag. Remembers that she's soon to add bribing a police officer to her list of capital offenses. Better that they seem on friendly terms than, well, what they actually are: strangers. She scoots her chair a tiny bit closer.

Officer Moriarity shakes his head and moves his own chair, shrinking the distance between them to mere inches. "Try to act naturally."

"Is this how you and Ada do it?"

"No. But she's . . . better at blending in."

"Well, I'm sorry I'm not more of a natural criminal."

He raises an eyebrow.

"That's different. We're helping those women when no one else will." She's parroting what Ada and the others have said, but it feels . . . true. She can't read in Officer Moriarity's face whether he agrees. "I'm doing it for my family, too."

"Most criminals will tell you that," he says. "Me included."

"You?"

"What, you don't imagine someone like me could have a family?"

Mimi opens her mouth, then closes it again. She hadn't imagined him with a family. A glance down, though, reveals he, too, is wearing a wedding ring.

"You have children?"

"Daughters. Four of them."

"Four!" Mimi can't help but smile. No wonder he's got such a gentle demeanor. "And no sons?"

He shakes his head.

"How old are they?"

"Let's see." He rubs a hand over his chin, his fingers rasping over a day's worth of dark stubble. "The oldest, Joan, she's twenty-one. My wife had her before we married, but I adopted her. Marie is fifteen; Margaret's thirteen; and the littlest, Carole, she just turned six."

There's a warmth in his voice as he speaks of them, and Mimi feels more at ease than she has all night.

"I have a daughter, too. She's ten. My boy's almost eight. They're great, but a handful. I don't know how your wife manages with four."

His expression tightens. "My wife . . . she's not well. Nerves, lumbago, melancholy."

"I'm sorry."

He shrugs. "I do what I can. The girls are a big help, too. Even little Carole does her share of chores."

"Still, that can't be easy. Holding everything together yourself. Last summer my husband broke his leg and . . ." Mimi looks away, her gaze settling on the frosted windows across the room. She shouldn't be telling a stranger about her family. About Stan.

"And you've had to hold everything together, too?"

Mimi nods.

Officer Moriarity sighs. "Well, here's to health and better days." He picks up his beer, and Mimi, her gin rickey. They clink their glasses together and drink. She's ready for the burn but can't help but wince as it goes down.

"Next time, I'll get you a beer."

There won't be a next time, Mimi ought to say. Instead, she just smiles.

They sit in silence again, but this time it doesn't feel so strained. After a minute or two, Officer Moriarity scans the room. "You can hand me that envelope now. Under the table."

Mimi fishes around her bag until she feels the envelope.

"This is what it costs to keep the state's attorney from bringing charges against the clinic?"

"No. It costs a lot more than that."

"Then what is this for?"

"Think of it like a retainer. A monthly payment, so when Ada calls and needs something, I answer."

"So you're a . . ." What was the word they used in *Gang Busters*? "Fixer."

He doesn't reply, but the fact he isn't denying it tells her it's true. That feeling from earlier—revulsion at this whole business—stirs again. But it doesn't sour her stomach like before. She knows this is wrong. But also that it's not that simple. And Officer Moriarity is not the man she assumed him to be.

His hand brushes against her leg beneath the table, but she knows he's not getting fresh, just waiting. Mimi withdraws the envelope and passes it to him. He leans back as if stretching and slyly slips the envelope into his back pocket.

"Shall we?" he says, jutting his chin toward the door.

Mimi nods, glancing at the clock on the far wall as she stands. It's nearly ten o'clock. A flash of panic jolts through her. What will Stan think at her returning home so late? The ensuing disappointment is worse than that jolt of panic. Stan isn't worried. He's probably already asleep. Even if he isn't, she doubts he's paid her a passing thought.

Outside looks colder and darker than before. The clouds must have cleared, and with them, any trace of the day's warmth. She wraps her scarf snugly around her neck and follows Officer Moriarity out of the tavern. They're headed in opposite directions, but he insists on walking her to her L stop.

As they wait for her train, he turns to her. "I never asked you your name."

Mimi hesitates, but only a moment. For better or worse, they're confederates now. "Mimi Lukas."

CHAPTER 21

With spring approaching, Mimi gets a telephone call from one of her brothers in Iowa. They don't talk outside of their once-a-year Christmas Eve call, so Mimi knows before he says it that something is wrong. That something is their mother. Emphysema, an ailment she's had for years but of late has worsened. Worsened how, he can't say. He's a farmer, not a doctor. But he's never been one for exaggeration, and even if he can't describe her symptoms, the concern underpinning his voice is enough. She promises to bring the children and come home for Easter.

How long has it been since she's visited the farm, she wonders as she packs their bags. Halina has taken Penny and Junior to Good Friday service. She's horrified they'll be celebrating Easter in a Lutheran church instead of Holy Trinity, but Mimi brooked no argument. Stan is napping in his armchair in the living room, so the house is quiet, a welcome receptacle for Mimi's unspooling thoughts.

Four years since her last visit? Five? Mimi feels a prick of shame when she realizes it's been six years since she's been back to the farm. Junior was barely walking. Penny, going through a shy phase, clung to Mimi's leg the entire three days they were there. The only time she ventured away—to press a few keys on the out-of-tune piano—Ma had scolded her, then scoffed at her tears. But later, Ma made it up to her with a piece of chocolate from her secret stash.

Stan had gotten along swimmingly with her brothers. They talked baseball from sunup until sundown. And even though he didn't know a rake from a thresher, Stan was eager to help with whatever tasks were at hand. Even Pa softened toward him, saying to Mimi their last night there, "He ain't so bad for a city slicker."

The topic of religion came up only once—a muttered comment by her mother about vile pope worshipers—which Stan sportingly ignored. Considering Mimi's parents had refused to attend their wedding and the children's baptisms out of scorn for the Catholic Church, Mimi half expected the visit to end in fisticuffs. So three days and only one slur was a victory on par with the Battle of Amiens.

But for Mimi, those three days had been torture. Her mother's critical eye missed nothing. Not Junior's thumb-sucking or Penny's picky eating. Not the hole in Stan's sock that Mimi forgot to darn. Not the girdle Mimi now wore instead of a corset.

And Ginny. She was everywhere in the house. The family picture above the fireplace—the one they took just before her brother left for the war. The paperboard jewelry box gathering dust atop the dresser in their old room. The old sycamore tree beside the barn where Ginny carved her initials. Yet no one spoke of her.

This time will be different, Mimi tells herself now as she packs. Still, she inspects each piece of clothing before folding it and placing it in the luggage. Is that a stain on Penny's skirt? A balding patch on the knee of Junior's trousers? The beginning of a run in Mimi's stockings? Those articles she sets aside. Only their best will do. Thank goodness she saved enough this month to buy the children new outfits for Easter.

When their clothes are neatly packed and shoes impeccably shined, Mimi loads their luggage into the back of the Packard. She makes sandwiches for the road while she waits for Halina and the children to return from church. Stan awakens, and she fixes him a sandwich, too. She doesn't ask again if he wants to go with them. He won't change his mind. Besides, even though Mimi dreads explaining his absence to her family, seeing him now, slumped in his chair by the window, hair disheveled and day-old clothes smelling of smoke, she can't help feeling a tinge of relief.

"What happened to Ginny's jewelry box?" Mimi asks the day after their arrival at the farm.

"What jewelry box?" Ma's voice is raspy, and there's a high-pitched wheezing sound when she breathes. She sits at the kitchen table, opening the package of Hershey's Kisses Mimi brought her, while Mimi stands at the counter, mixing the ingredients for a pie crust.

"The one Aunt Shelley gave her for Christmas. She kept it atop the dresser."

"I have no idea." Ma pauses to breathe, then says, "Don't overwork it. The crust will come out tough."

I know, Mimi wants to say. She hears the crinkle of foil, followed by a contented sigh. Kisses always were Ma's favorite.

"There was a necklace inside," Mimi prods. "The silver one with the pearl."

"It wasn't a real pearl."

"Just the same, I thought Penny might like it."

"That's enough water."

Mimi's hand clenches around the spoon. This isn't her first pie crust. She's tempted to add more water just to spite the woman. "Would Pa know what happened to the necklace?"

Ma snorts. Or maybe she's just clearing the mucus from her throat. Her brother was right to be worried. Mimi remembers cases like this from nursing school. Ma could live for years like this—each breath an effort—or be gone before the fall harvest. Mimi should be grateful for this time.

"Your Pa wants nothing to do with any of that. There's a box—" Her words are cut short by a fit of coughing. Mimi wipes her hands on her apron and brings Ma a glass of water from the sink. She waits at her side until the fit is over.

"Sit forward. It will help you breathe better."

"I know what helps." Ma flaps a hand—all bones and skin—toward the counter. "That pie isn't going to make itself." She unwraps another of the Hershey's Kisses and plops it in her mouth like it's a menthol cough drop.

Mimi shakes her head and returns to the dough, rolling it thin, then flipping it over into the pie pan. "You were saying something about a box."

"Upstairs closet. Top shelf. You're welcome to whatever's in it."

Mimi works in silence for a few minutes, trimming the excess crust and fluting the edges. Through the window above the sink, she can see Penny playing fetch with Pa's old mutt, Bluey, while Junior and two of his cousins squat around a bald patch of the yard, shooting marbles. In total, her three brothers have twelve children. The youngest is only three months old. Mimi's sister-in-law brought the baby around last night, and Penny squealed at the chance to hold her. Mimi happily took her turn, too. The baby had her brother's warm brown eyes and her sister-in-law's button nose. Her hair, wisps of reddish-brown, favors neither of them. Of all the Gunther line, only Ginny had hair that color.

When the crust is ready, she opens the cupboard and scans the jars of preserves. "Cherry?"

"No, blueberry."

The lid of the first unscrews easily. The second, she wrestles with for a minute, then gives up and runs it under water until, at last, it loosens. "Ma, how come Ginny didn't marry that boy?"

Mimi doesn't need to say which one. Ginny was popular with all the boys, but somehow it was the pimple-faced son of that visiting "doctor" who stole her heart.

"What's with all this talk about your sister?" She takes a wheezing inhale. "Don't think it will keep me from noticing what's going on with you."

"Me?" A stab of panic shoots through her. Does Ma know about her arrest? Mimi loosens her grip on the jar of preserves. Of course not. No one knows. "Nothing's going on with me."

"Then why isn't your husband here?"

"I told you, his leg is still healing, and he didn't want to leave his mother alone on Easter."

Ma makes another sound—this one definitely a snort. "If his leg hasn't healed by now, it's never going to heal."

Mimi scoops the preserves into a bowl, willing herself to stay calm. Somehow, this will work its way to her. How she's a bad wife.

"You remember that Jersey cow we had who broke her leg."

Mimi whirls around. "Are you suggesting I shoot my husband?"

"Of course not. But what good is a baseball player who can't play baseball?"

"He's not *just* a baseball player. He's a father. A husband. A good and decent man." If only Stan would see things that way.

"Those things don't pay the bills. You need to help him find something new to be."

"I'm trying!" she shouts, then winces as her voice echoes through the house. Thank goodness it's only her and Ma inside. Something cool dribbles onto her hand. Preserves from the spoon she hadn't realized she was still holding. She sighs and turns back to the counter, wiping her hand on her apron. "He won't . . . he doesn't seem to hear me anymore."

"Then you need to make him hear you."

If only it were that easy. "I have a job now." Ma makes no reply, so she continues. "I'm working as a nurse again. The money's more than enough to keep us going until Stan . . . decides what he wants to do next."

Mimi adds a little sugar and cornstarch to the preserves and stirs. She doesn't have to look behind her to know Ma is shaking her head.

"Your job is in the home."

"I can do both."

At this, Ma laughs. It quickly leads to more coughing. Mimi closes her eyes, strangling the spoon handle. "I like my job. I like the other women I work with. I like having time away where I can think about things beyond what to cook for dinner and whether the drapes need vacuuming."

Ma's still coughing. Did she even hear what Mimi said? A lightness blooms in her chest as she realizes it doesn't matter. The words weren't just for her mother. They're for her, too. She *does* enjoy working at the clinic. And without this job, she couldn't have afforded new Easter clothes for the children or even the gasoline it took to bring them here.

She lets the spoon fall against the side of the bowl and brings her mother more water.

"I never understood why you went away to that school anyway," Ma says once she's caught her breath. "The city was Virginia's dream. Not yours."

Mimi opens her mouth, then lets it close. It's true. The city had been her sister's dream. But nursing had been Mimi's. And they'd both wanted to get away. Needed to get away. It wasn't until she got to the city and felt her lungs fully expand for the first time in years that Mimi realized how suffocating life at home had become.

Mimi returns to the mixing bowl, not bothering to check if the preserves need more sugar before dumping them in the empty pie shell. "I don't regret my decision."

"Your sister said the same thing. Look where that got her."

Mimi flinches at her words. She grabs the rolling pin and sinks it into the remaining dough.

"You know why Pa didn't insist she marry that boy?" Ma sucks in a deep breath, and her voice grows louder. "Because it wasn't that boy she did the devil's deed with." Another rasping inhale. "It was his father."

Mimi stills. "The doctor?" Her vision goes in and out of focus. "But he was twice her age."

"He wasn't a *doctor* doctor. He was a professor. More to the point, he was already married."

Mimi thinks back to the week he and his family had been in town for the Reformation celebration. She can't quite picture him—the doctor, professor, whatever he was—though she remembers the slick timbre of his voice. The way his words filled the church with an almost quaking intensity. Her stomach turns at the thought of him using that charm on Ginny. The flattery and false promises he must have whispered in her ears.

To Mimi, Ginny always seemed so wise and mature. But she'd only just turned fifteen. Hardly more than a child.

"Why didn't Pa go after him?"

"And alert the entire county of her shame? No. Besides, he was long gone by the time we knew. It's not like he forced himself on her."

Mimi spins around. "How do you know?"

"Because she was still mooning over him when we sent her away."

Mimi's hands are covered in flour, so she wipes her eyes on the shoulder of her dress. "There must have been another way. What about an—" She catches herself before saying, *abortion.* Only one physician lived within driving distance of the farm at the time. Mimi can still recall his wiry mustache and beady eyes. He refused to give women chloroform during their labor. The pain, he believed, was penance for Eve's curse. No, he certainly wouldn't have helped Ginny. And whom did that leave? The stodgy old veterinarian or the town druggist? Ginny herself?

Her eyes can't help but drift toward the front room, where Ma keeps her knitting basket. She shudders. When she looks back at Ma, she knows the woman has read her thoughts.

"There was no other way."

Mimi turns back to the pie. *No other way.* Maybe not, but there should have been.

After the pies are made, Mimi helps Ma to the front porch. They have to stop twice along the way for Ma to catch her breath. When she's seated in the wicker chair, a faded blue blanket draped over her lap, Mimi goes back inside and makes a pitcher of lemonade. She brings it outside with a tray of jam jars, and the children come scrambling from the yard. Penny shows her a blue jay's feather she found by the barn, and Junior holds out a shiny new marble he's won.

They gulp down their lemonade and return to their games. Ma's already dozed off in her chair. With Pa in the barn, repairing equipment for the coming spring planting, Mimi has the farmhouse to herself. She leaves the empty lemonade pitcher and jars in the kitchen and heads upstairs. The closet door's hinges are stiff and squeal as she opens the door. The smell of mothballs drifts out. She glances past the stacks of folded linen and a basket of sewing scraps to the top shelf, where a box sits. Mimi stands on her tiptoes and coaxes it out.

It weighs less than a twenty-pound sack of flour, and as Mimi carries it to her bedroom, she can't help but wonder how an entire life can be reduced to a single box. She sets it on the bed and sits beside it, working up the courage to open the lid. Inside is a jumble of odds and ends. Ginny's 4-H cap and pin. Her prayer book. The tablecloth and quilt she'd stitched for her hope chest.

Near the top is Ginny's high school report book. The pages have yellowed and begun to curl at the edges. Inside, the record shows high marks in English, music, and algebra. Middling grades in civics, history, and home economics. But her scores in deportment were excellent. There's not a single mark for tardiness, and she had perfect attendance every month but one.

Mimi leans back and closes her eyes, remembering how Ginny had loved school (anything to get off the farm) and prided herself on her exemplary attendance. They look at those things—attendance, deportment, industry—when you apply to secretary school, she told Mimi. It shows that you're dependable. Responsible. Agreeable. More than just a pretty face.

It was the start of Ginny's freshman year—her last year—and she already knew where she wanted life to take her. Mimi, in sixth grade, wasn't so sure. Or so pretty. Not with all her freckles and those ugly pimples that had just started to appear. Not like Ginny. But if Mimi wanted to join her in the city when they were grown-ups, to wear silk stockings and lipstick and go to secretary school and do all the things they read about in fashion magazines, she'd better have good attendance, too.

Mimi thinks forward several months to the summer Ginny was away. Pa said it was on account of that red lipstick he'd found at the bottom of Ginny's book bag that she'd gotten herself into such a mess. But Mimi knew that wasn't true. And for the life of her, she couldn't figure out how a man who'd spent his entire life on a farm could be confused about such things.

Still, Mimi was careful to hide the glossy magazine she'd bought in town with the two nickels old Mrs. Schmidt had given her for helping with her canning. She was tempted to buy an ice cream soda instead, but she wanted something to surprise Ginny with when she got home. Mimi didn't take so much as a peek at the inside pages before hiding it at the bottom of her dresser drawer, beneath her socks and spare nightdress.

As the new school year drew close, she squirreled away other things. A shiny rock she'd found down by the river. The third-place ribbon she won at the county fair. Half of the Hershey's bar Aunt Myrna had given her.

She'd peek at these treasures before bed and smile, imagining how it would be when Ginny got home. How proud she'd be that Mimi's canned asparagus had beaten out twelve others at the fair. How much she'd like the flecks of silver that shimmered in the rock's surface when you held it up to the light. How fun it would be to stay up late, eating chocolate and flipping through the magazine.

Just like old times.

And Ginny would forgive her.

Tears stream down Mimi's face when she opens her eyes. She sucks in a steadying breath and returns to the box, not bothering to wipe her cheeks. As she tucks Ginny's report book beneath her 4-H cap, she spies the paperboard jewelry box nestled in one corner. Mimi lifts it out and brushes the dust from the white and blue lid. Inside is a pair of silver barrettes, a few tarnished school pins, a tiny bouquet of dried cornflowers held together by string, and, at the bottom, the pearl pendant.

As Mimi reaches for the pendant, she notices something else in the jewelry box: a small red tin. DR. CHESTER'S PENNYROYAL PILLS is embossed on the lid. She picks it up and reads the black lettering beneath the name. *A never-failing remedy. The only reliable pill of its kind. For all female complaints.*

It's harder to get pills like these today, but Mimi knows they're still out there. The women they see at the clinic report trying all kinds of things before coming in—castor oil, quinine, ergot, snakeroot, foxglove, slippery elm; homemade douches with Lysol, turpentine, or Clorox.

A never-failing remedy, indeed. She drops the tin back into the box and grabs the pearl pendant. She hadn't known Ginny was taking these pills. Even if she had, Mimi wouldn't have guessed why. Just like she hadn't guessed why Ginny was jumping in the barn or taking scalding-hot baths.

She might not have known the reason for Ginny's strange behavior, but surely Mimi should have seen her desperation. Her fear. Had Ginny meant for her not to see, or had Mimi just been blind to it? It pains her to think that for all their closeness, there were still secrets between them. But then, Mimi's no stranger to secrets of her own. Not anymore.

She stands and walks to the window, holding up the necklace. The afternoon sunlight glints off the silver chain and solitary pearl. A little polish, and it will look good as new. She smiles, thinking of Penny wearing it, and knows Ginny would approve.

Out the window, farmland stretches clear to the horizon. The occasional grain silo and windmill juts above the unsown fields. She remembers finding this land beautiful once, even in these late winter months when it's little more than snow and dirt and naked trees.

Now, she misses the city. It may have been Ginny's dream, but it's become Mimi's home.

A glance toward the sun tells her there's time yet before she'll need to start on supper. She might as well go through the rest of the box while she's got the stomach for it. The next time she returns to the farm, it will likely be in funeral black.

They didn't have a funeral for Ginny. Her brothers believe she's buried in a family plot in Mason City, where she was staying when she caught influenza and died. Only Mimi and her parents know the truth: Ginny lies in a potter's field near the unwed mothers' home in Des Moines, along with her stillborn baby. Mimi's thought of visiting a hundred times, but never had the courage.

She pushes the thought aside and slips the pearl pendant into her apron pocket. Standing over the bed, she looks down at the jumble of Ginny's things and sees what the jewelry box previously concealed. Mimi's heart squeezes, and her hands turn cold. There in the corner, atop the embroidered tablecloth, is the pink ribbon. The ribbon Mimi wanted to wear that Easter. Time has dulled its luster, or maybe it was never as shiny and pretty as Mimi thought. Did Judas think the same of his silver?

Mimi steps away from the box as if the ribbon is a viper. She hasn't the fortitude after all. Tears well in her eyes again, and her legs lose their strength. Only the sound of the children barreling through the front door keeps her from falling.

"I'll be down in a minute," she manages when they call out, hungry for a snack. She tosses the jewelry box back inside and hurriedly replaces the lid.

If only it were that easy to box up her guilt.

CHAPTER 22

"I brought the next patient back to the anteroom," Jo says, placing an intake card atop the glass-fronted cabinet near the door.

Mimi thanks her, then returns her attention to the instrument table. Two days have passed since she returned from Iowa. After the trip and yesterday's frenzy of unpacking, washing, and grocery shopping, she's relieved to be back at the clinic. Here, she doesn't have to worry about being the perfect daughter, the perfect wife, the perfect mother. She need only be herself and do her job well.

Since Dr. Gabler's departure, half a dozen physicians have rotated through the clinic, and Mimi's had to learn the peculiarities and preferences of each. Dr. Snyder is left-handed and likes the instruments arranged by size. Dr. Wetherby prefers the instruments be grouped by type and is so tall, the exam bed must be cranked up to its full height.

Today, Dr. Millstone is in residence. He's the most frequent doctor scheduled and doesn't care how the instruments are arranged, so long as the overhead light is tilted just so. Mimi likes working with him best, because Emily frequently accompanies him. It lightens the load around the clinic and allows the other nurses more time off. But mostly, Mimi's happy to see her because it means a day of easy chatter and smiles.

Emily and Dr. Millstone stepped out for a quick lunch but should be back any minute. Mimi covers the instruments with a sterile sheet and double-checks the gas while she waits for them to return. When she hears Emily's singsong voice in the reception room, Mimi grabs the intake card Jo left and goes to get the patient.

After six months here, Mimi can glance at the card and glean all she needs to know: age (those in their early teens and forties have increased chance of complications), number of children (it's more difficult to dilate the cervix of a woman who's never given birth), date of last menstrual period (the further along the woman is, the greater the risk), and previous illnesses and abortions. The other details—address, telephone number, marital status, employment, referent—don't matter in the procedure room.

This case looks pretty standard: thirty-two years old; four children; last menstruated two months ago; no history of illness or prior abortions.

She passes Emily and Dr. Millstone in the hallway on her way to the anteroom. He's at least ten years older than she and Emily, with receding brown hair, big ears, and a large, squarish nose. When not in Emily's company, he's serious as the plague, his thin lips set in a flat, unmoving line. Mimi isn't surprised by the color Emily brings to his cheeks nor the twinkle she lights in his eyes. Emily's always affected men that way. What surprises Mimi is the comparable effect Dr. Millstone has on Emily.

Love is funny that way. No telling where it will lead you. Or to whom.

"I'll be right in with the patient," she tells them.

Dr. Millstone nods.

"I'll get my gown and mask on," Emily says over her shoulder.

Their fingertips brush—the doctor's and Emily's—as she turns into the procedure room and he continues down the hall toward Ada's office. It's so slight a touch, Mimi may well have imagined it. But there's no imagining the smile on her friend's face or the flush creeping up the nape of the doctor's neck.

Mimi smiles, too, even as she pushes down a pang of jealousy.

After a soft knock, Mimi opens the anteroom door and slips inside. The woman is seated on the cot, her back straight and hands folded in her lap. She looks up, and it's all Mimi can do not to gasp.

It's Zofina Dabrowski.

Mimi glances again at the intake card as if her eyes might be playing tricks on her. They're not. Has Zofina recognized her, too? Perhaps her cap and smock are sufficient disguise. But when Mimi looks up from the card, she sees her own shock mirrored in Zofina's slack-jawed expression.

"Mrs. Dabrowski, what are you—" Mimi stops and rattles her head. There's no point in finishing the sentence. There's only one reason women come to the clinic.

Panic stirs inside her. If the other women at Holy Trinity learn she works here, it will only be a matter of time before Halina knows, too.

Zofina seems to be having a similar thought. "I . . . I'm not . . . it's not what you . . ." Her eyes dart frantically around the room, finally settling on her purse and the neatly folded clothes beneath, as if she might grab them and flee.

Mimi's panic morphs into dark satisfaction. At church, Zofina is the picture of haughty poise. Now, she squirms and sputters like a child caught stealing. How many times has Mimi had to swallow her own discomfort on account of the woman? How many times has she been made to feel small and unworthy?

Zofina bites her bottom lip and reaches for her clothes. "This was a mistake." In her trembling haste, she knocks over her purse, spilling its contents onto the floor. Something between a gasp and a sob escapes her mouth as she crouches down, snatching at her things. Her hospital gown falls open at the back, bearing her naked rear to the room. She tries to close it with one hand while reaching for a tube of lipstick with the other. Her stretched fingers glance off the tube, sending it rolling. As she grabs for it, the hem of her gown catches on her knee, tugging the flap back open.

Another sob, and Mimi's satisfaction vanishes. She bends down. "Here, let me help you."

"I can do it myself," Zofina snaps, but Mimi's hand reaches the lipstick first. She holds it out, palm open, and Zofina seizes it in her fist. Their eyes meet—Zofina's wild and wet with tears. After a moment, her shaky breathing slows. "Thank you," she mutters.

They collect the rest of her scattered things in silence. Zofina sits on the cot again, returning the items to her purse one at a time. "You can go," she says. "I'll just get dressed and leave."

"You don't need to do that. I'll get another nurse to care for you." Mimi turns toward the door.

"It's just that . . . the twins are still so small, and Peter still hasn't found work. We're on relief, for heaven's sake. Relief!"

Mimi turns around. "You don't need to explain yourself to me. To anyone here."

"Peter—he doesn't know."

"Stan doesn't know I work here."

Zofina looks up at her.

"He thinks I work at a hospital." Mimi joins her on the cot. "He hasn't found work, either. He's not even looking."

They sit in silence for a moment.

"You won't tell anyone, will you?" Zofina asks.

"Not if you don't."

Zofina gives a soft chuckle. "Does it . . . does it hurt?"

Mimi takes her hand. "No."

CHAPTER 23

The last Saturday of April is unseasonably warm, and Mimi suggests a visit to the zoo. Penny and Junior cheer at the idea and rush to put on their shoes.

"Mamo?" Mimi asks, but Halina shakes her head. She's working on the children's costumes for the upcoming Polish Constitution Day Parade. All that embroidery and ribbons must surely make her stiff hands ache, but the children haven't missed a parade yet.

"Stan?"

He grunts.

"Is that a yes or a no?"

His face is to the window. He doesn't bother to look her way or even grunt again. A "no," then.

Perhaps Stan's thinking of the parade, too. It's the first year he won't ride front and center with his bat and glove. A new player with the Cubs has that honor, even though he's only a quarter Polish, and his batting average has yet to break .300.

Still, Stan could have at least answered her and wished them a good time. Sure, he's hurting, but can't he see that he's hurting her, too?

When they get to the zoo, Mimi does her best not to let Stan's absence sour the day. They've seen a dozen animals and are on their way to the primate cages when Mimi and the children pass by a cart selling ice cream. It's nearly noon, and ice cream will spoil the children's appetite for the sandwiches and apples Mimi packed, but she's no match for their cries of *pretty please*. So they line up behind the dozen others eager for a cold treat.

In front of them stands a man and his two daughters. When he turns around, Mimi's chest tightens, and a prickle of alarm skitters over her skin.

"Officer Moriarity," she manages to say, her voice a bit squeaky.

"Mrs. Lukas." The smile he flashes is wide and genuine.

She looks around, but for what? More policemen? They're at the zoo, for heaven's sake, not the clinic. And this man is on their side.

"Are these your children?" he asks.

"What? Oh, yes." She wraps an arm around their shoulders, pulling them in close. "This is Penny and Junior. Children, this is Officer Moriarity."

"A pleasure to meet you both," he says.

Before Mimi can think of some excuse for a hasty exit from the line, Junior asks, "Are you a policeman?"

"I am."

"Can I see your gun?"

"Junior," Mimi scolds, but Officer Moriarity laughs.

"I left it at home today, but I promise to show you another time." His gaze returns to Mimi, then to the two girls at his side. "These are my daughters. Two of them, anyway. Margaret, Carole, this is Mrs. Lukas and her children, Penny and Junior."

Registering the girls for the first time, Mimi feels the tightness in her chest ease. In her momentary panic, she'd forgotten he was a family man. She loosens her grip on Penny and Junior's shoulders and smiles at the Moriarity girls. They have their father's rich, dark-brown hair. The older girl, Margaret, shares his Roman nose, while Carole favors him around the eyes. They're both pretty girls, slight in stature, and Mimi finds herself wondering what their mother looks like.

As the children exchange shy hellos, Mimi glances at the people crowding the nearby cages and those seated on the benches lining the walkway. "Is the rest of your family here with you?"

"Not my wife, no." A look of pain flickers across his face, but just as quickly, it's gone. "Marie's here with a schoolmate."

"A boy," Margaret adds.

Mimi swallows down a laugh. "A boy?"

The sisters both wrinkle their noses and nod.

"We promised not to bother them so long as they stay in sight," he says, discreetly pointing to two teenagers at the front of the line. The boy looks back over his shoulder at them. Officer Moriarity's lips flatten and eyes narrow. It reminds her of the look he gave the officers in the morals squad when they hesitated to unfasten her handcuffs. The boy's cheeks drain of color. He quickly turns around and takes a half-step away from the girl.

This time, Mimi doesn't bother to hold back her laughter. "I'm sure glad my father wasn't a cop."

"It has its perks."

Mimi cocks her head, and he smiles, clearly aware of the double entendre in his words. She looks away, unsettled by the normalcy of it all. She's a criminal. He's a cop on the take. And yet here they are, standing in line for ice cream with their children. Maybe her recent trip home has her overly conscious of such things. She forgot how rigidly her parents view the world. Things are either black or white. Good or evil. Right or wrong. For them, there's no in-between.

But if not for the in-between, where is she standing now?

Officer Moriarity clears his throat, and she realizes she's gone silent.

"So, where are you off to next?" he asks, as they shuffle a few steps forward in line.

"We're going to see Bushman the Gorilla!" Junior replies for them.

"Oh? I hear he can be quite scary."

"I'm not afraid," Junior says. "I saw him last summer, and I was only seven then. Papa said so long as I don't put my hand through the bars, he can't hurt me."

"That's good advice." Officer Moriarity looks from Junior to Mimi. "Is he here today, your husband?"

She shakes her head. She ought to make up some excuse but finds she doesn't want to lie.

Officer Moriarity's gaze shifts back to Junior. "I'm sure he's looking forward to hearing all about Bushman when you get home."

"He is," Junior says. "I'm going to tell him about Bushman and the zebras and the elephants . . ."

Officer Moriarity listens with interest while Junior lists every animal they've seen so far. Penny chimes in when he forgets the bighorn sheep and the family of ducks they saw in the pond. By the time the children finish, it's the Moriaritys' turn to order ice cream.

After they order, Officer Moriarity turns and says, "What are you having?"

"Oh, no," Mimi says. "I couldn't."

"Are you sure? I'm happy to treat."

Mimi shakes her head, and he doesn't press her further. When it's her turn, at the stall, she orders a chocolate cone for Penny, vanilla for Junior, and strawberry for herself. Then they join the Moriaritys in the shade of a nearby elm tree.

"Thank you for the offer to buy our cones. I didn't mean to be rude in refusing, but I . . ." She glances toward her children, who stand a few feet off, talking with the Moriarity sisters. "It's just a silly ice cream cone, I know, but I . . . I work hard to be able to afford it, and I'm proud that I can."

"I understand," he says.

Silence falls between them again as they eat their ice cream. From the corner of her eye, she spies a glob of vanilla dribble onto Junior's shirt. He wipes it away, then licks his fingers. Mimi winces.

"No point letting it go to waste," Officer Moriarity says.

"I was hoping you didn't see that."

"I'm a cop, remember. I see everything."

"Right."

They return to their ice cream. Mimi takes her time, telling herself it's so she can enjoy the bright, creamy taste. But strangely, she's also enjoying the company. A glance at Officer Moriarity, and it seems he, too, is taking his time, his tongue lapping at his ice cream in slow, lazy strokes.

A flush warms Mimi's neck, and she looks away to see that the children are on the last bites of their cones. Junior's fingers are a sticky mess, and she welcomes the excuse to break away from Officer Moriarity's orbit to wipe them clean.

"I guess we better be off," she says when she's done wiping Junior's hands. "Say goodbye to Officer Moriarity and his daughters," she tells her children.

"Call me Daniel, please," he says to her, as the children exchange goodbyes.

"Daniel." The name rolls pleasantly off her tongue. "Where are you all headed next?"

"That depends on them." Daniel juts his thumb toward a nearby bench, where his teenage daughter and her schoolmate sit angled toward each other, heads bent and knees touching. Daniel gives a loud *ahem*, and they straighten and scoot apart.

"Good luck," Mimi tells him, a laugh in her voice.

"I think I'll need it."

Mimi, Junior, and Penny depart for the primate house, while the Moriaritys head toward the penguins. Their paths cross again at the giraffe cage. Mimi and Daniel fall into easy conversation, while the children watch the zookeeper feed the giraffes handfuls of hay. When the spectacle is over, they all follow the lovestruck teenagers to the black bears' enclosure and then on to the exotic bird house.

Mimi and Daniel talk first of simple things—the weather, the latest pictures playing at the theaters, the best place in town for a good milkshake. But as the afternoon stretches on, they share more about themselves. Daniel tells her about his upbringing in the city and his early days as a cop. He and his wife, Elizabeth, met through a friend and married six weeks later. Her daughter, Joan, was four years old at the time and served as the flower girl at the wedding. She'd always been prone to melancholy, his wife, but it wasn't until after Carole's birth that she began to suffer from nervous attacks and bouts of crippling pain. She goes weeks sometimes without rising from bed.

Mimi, in turn, tells him about growing up on the farm. About meeting Stan in nursing school and her family's objections to her marrying a Catholic. She talks about the high days of his baseball career and the low days since his accident.

The children are so absorbed in the animals, they don't pay them any mind. She and Daniel speak softly, nonetheless, careful of their words when anyone's within earshot. Twice, Mimi has to stop midsentence to remind Junior not to climb over the cage railings. More than once, Daniel has to clear his throat loudly when the teenagers get too close. There are also interruptions for bathroom breaks and questions from the younger girls about words like *pachyderm* and *omnivore* and *diurnal*, which Mimi or Daniel are happy to answer. Then their conversation resumes as if they were old friends, not near strangers.

Mimi knows she ought to feel guilty about sharing such private things. A wife should never complain about her husband. Certainly not to another man. But she isn't complaining. Daniel seems to understand her fears and frustrations without her even naming them. And he can relate in a way her friends at work can't.

At Junior's request, they visit Bushman a second time before the zoo closes. Earlier, the gorilla had put on a show, swinging from the barred roof of his cage to the thick chain of his tire swing and back. Now, he squats in the back corner on an iron stool, glowering at them through the bars.

Mimi goes silent, watching him. Even at rest, he's a magnificent creature, keen eyes and flaring nostrils, barreled chest and massive limbs, dark glossy fur that turns from black to silvery red atop his crown. How bleak to wake day after day in the confines of such a small, spare cage. She'd read in the paper that as a baby, Bushman was saved from hunters and raised by American missionaries in Africa. When he was three, he was sent to the zoo.

He likely has no memory of life before capture, if he has the capacity to remember anything at all. Mimi isn't sure whether that's a blessing or a curse.

Daniel moves closer and whispers into her ear. "I hope you're not thinking about that night at Central Station."

Mimi shakes her head. Perhaps this cage should have called to mind that awful night. About the terrible risk she takes each day she goes into the clinic. But sometimes, taking no risks has its own terrible consequences.

"I'm sorry you had to endure that," he says, his breath dancing along her neck.

"Iron bars aren't the only thing that can cage people," she says. Then, more lightly, "Just see that it doesn't happen again."

CHAPTER 24

May passes in a blur for Mimi. She's stopped reading the help wanted ads or wondering if Stan will find a new job. If she's careful with the marketing and sets aside a few dollars every month toward next year's property taxes, they can get by on what she makes. At least for now.

She hasn't bought a new hat or dress for herself in months, but finds she no longer cares if the people at church notice her cycling through the same four outfits week after week or if the color of her hat doesn't perfectly match her shoes or if the styles don't match those pinned to the mannequins in the storefront windows on State Street. She no longer cares if the neighbors see the sign for ice in their window or about having to take the streetcar or L instead of the Packard. The money saved on gasoline, electricity, and clothes—plus what she earns—allows them to keep the house and buy food. It even allows for the occasional cherry soda or ice cream. And the satisfaction Mimi feels in that is more than enough.

So, too, is her satisfaction when Zofina greets her at Mass with a smile. Mimi hasn't been welcomed into the Catholic Daughters or anything like that, but a simple smile suits her just fine. She has other friends now, anyway—Jo, Emily, and the other nurses. Even she and Ada are on friendly terms.

Mimi counts Daniel among her friends, too, though she's seen him only once since the zoo. This time, she entered the tavern and walked straight to his table. They talked over beers (no more gin rickeys, thank you very much) for hours before she surreptitiously slipped him the envelope. The others at the bar must have thought them lovers, but Mimi doesn't mind, if it keeps them from guessing their true purpose.

Halina thinks she's taken a lover, too. She eyes her like overboiled pierogi whenever Mimi's more than ten minutes late getting home. Halina can think what she wants, though. She hasn't raised her concerns with Stan. Or if she has, he doesn't care.

On the last Friday in June, Mimi is filling in at the reception desk when a man enters the office. Mimi recognizes his stocky build and snow-white hair. She's seen him in the office a time or two before with Ada but doesn't know his name. He swaggers to the desk with a wide grin.

"Afternoon, doll. Fetch Ada for me, will you?"

He smells strongly of cologne—expensive cologne—and his suit is of fine worsted wool. His surefire cockiness reminds her of Babe Ruth and Ty Cobb, neither of whom she particularly enjoyed meeting. But at least they were great sportsmen. What's this man's talent?

"Is she expecting you?"

His smile falters, but only for a moment. "She will be when she learns I'm here."

It takes conscious effort for Mimi not to roll her eyes. "Very well. What name can I give her?"

"Louis Piquett."

His name stirs something in the back of her mind. She's heard it before but can't remember where. Mimi takes her time putting away the schedule book and locking the desk drawers before heading to the back of the clinic. She hopes Ada will be too busy to see him or will at least make him wait a few minutes. But when Mimi gives her the name, she tells Mimi to send him in right away.

Back in the reception room, Mimi finds Jo, returned from lunch, chatting with Mr. Piquett. He steps closer and whispers in her ear. Jo laughs and bats his arm playfully.

He leans in as if to speak again, but Mimi interrupts him. "Ada will see you now, Mr. Piquett. Right this way."

He holds Jo's gaze a minute longer, his smile no longer just confident but positively rakish. Then he turns to Mimi and follows her back to Ada's office. Ada stands to greet him, and they hug like old friends.

"Close the door, please, Mrs. Lukas," she says as Mimi leaves.

Tempting as it is to linger and listen, Mimi seeks Jo out instead. Their next appointment isn't due to arrive for another fifteen minutes, so the reception room is empty save for them.

"Who is that man?" Mimi asks.

Jo pulls a compact from her purse and examines her reflection. "Why, that's Louis."

"I know his name, but what's his business here?"

Jo closes the compact and shrugs. "He's a friend of Ada's. Fetching, don't you think?"

"He's old enough to be your grandfather."

"Don't let that hair fool you. He isn't a day over fifty."

"Did he tell you that?"

"Come on, Mimi, there's no harm in a little innocent flirtation."

"He looked like he wanted to eat you."

Jo's smile widens. "Really? I might let him if I wasn't worried about Barney finding out."

"Barney? What happened to Edgar?"

"Edgar's old news."

Mimi shakes her head. "At least tell me Barney was born this century."

"Maybe."

They both laugh.

"I bet you wish Stan looked at you that way. Like he wants to eat you."

Mimi's gaze falls to the floor, the laughter dying in her throat.

"I'm sorry," Jo says quickly. "I didn't mean . . . I was only teasing."

"It's all right." Mimi sighs. "It's been so long, I don't think I'd know what I'd do if he looked at me that way."

"Well, I doubt he's looking at anyone else that way, either, so you can be glad for that."

"Yeah." She starts for the door.

"You're a real catch, Mimi Lukas. The bee's knees and all that."

Mimi can't help but smile. She hasn't heard that phrase in years. "Now you're making me feel old."

"I'm serious. Stan will remember soon enough."

Will he? Mimi isn't so sure. She gets to work readying the procedure room, but her thoughts are stuck on Jo's words. Maybe she's just not trying hard enough. She can't remember the last time she remade her hair or touched up her lipstick before leaving work at the end of the day. Jo always looks sharp before heading out to meet Edgar or Barney or whoever her beau of the month is. Maybe tonight she'll spend some time in front of the mirror before heading home.

A rap on the doorjamb startles her from her thoughts. Ada stands there with Mr. Piquett at her side.

"When's Edna due back from lunch?" Ada asks.

Mimi glances at the wall clock. "Half an hour."

"And how are things here?"

"Just about ready."

"Good. I want you to go with Mr. Piquett to County Hospital and check on a patient there."

"One of ours?"

Ada nods, her face grave.

"Is she . . ."

"Dying? I don't know. That's what I want you to find out. The police have been by to question her, too. We need to know if she talked."

Mimi looks from Ada to Mr. Piquett, still trying to process what she's heard.

"He'll be there to straighten things out with the husband," Ada says, plucking the question straight from Mimi's mind. "And to see that you get safely away if the police come sniffing around again."

Mimi's stomach knots at the mention of the police.

"Don't worry," Ada says. "I don't expect any trouble. I wouldn't send you if I did. Besides, you'll blend right in. If anyone asks, tell them you're from another ward in the hospital."

Mimi hates the idea of lying like that. But there's no escaping the urgency of the situation. She nods.

"Good," Mr. Piquett says. "It's all settled." He kisses Ada on the cheek, then turns to Mimi. "Grab your things, doll. I'll be waiting with the car out front."

"Nurse Lukas," Mimi says.

He raises an eyebrow.

"You may call me Nurse Lukas. Or, if you must, Mrs. Lukas."

"Sure thing, dol—er, nurse. Whatever makes you happy."

He flashes that wide smile again, but Mimi only purses her lips. "I like her," he says to Ada, then walks out.

Mimi removes her smock and cap, balling them up to toss in the laundry, even though she'd just put them on.

"Don't mind him," Ada says to her. "He plays the part of the rascal well, but he's harmless. And he's very good in situations like these."

"How often do situations like these arise?"

"Not very often, thank God. Our doctors are very good." She hands Mimi a slip of paper with a name scrawled on it: Mrs. Betty Rawlings.

Mimi doesn't recognize the name, but they see so many women, it's impossible to remember them all. Or the woman could have come in on one of Mimi's days off. Either way, Mimi hopes she's okay.

A shiny Pierce-Arrow coupe is pulled up to the curb when Mimi steps outside with her hat and purse. Mr. Piquett gets out of the driver's seat and comes around the car to open the door for her.

The inside smells of leather, cigar smoke, and Mr. Piquett's cologne. As they drive away, Mr. Piquett turns a small white dial, and a crackly voice fills the silence. She follows the sound to a wooden octagon-shaped radio speaker protruding from the dashboard.

"You don't mind, do you?" he asks. "I'm hoping to catch the score of the game."

Mimi shakes her head. "Are you a Sox fan or a Cubs fan?"

"White Sox, naturally." He turns down Harrison Street toward Cook County Hospital. "Didn't peg you for the kind of gal interested in baseball."

"I've watched my share of games."

"The Sox used to have a player by the name of Lukas, you know," he says, above an advertisement for Lucky Strike cigarettes. "Slammin' Stach, they called him. A great hitter in his day."

Mimi can't help but smile. "I think I may have heard of him."

Maybe Mr. Piquett isn't so bad, after all.

When they arrive at the hospital, the front desk clerk informs them that visiting hours are nearly over and suggests they come back tomorrow. But she's no match for Mr. Piquett's charm. In under a minute, she's ushering them toward the elevators.

He told the clerk they were there to see an old friend from the war convalescing and was directed to the third-floor men's medical ward. Instead, he and Mimi ride to the fourth floor and enter the septic ward. Mimi remembers the way from her nursing school days. The sharp smell of bleach mingles with the sickly sweet odor of decay. A steady chorus of moans rises from the room. Every bed is occupied. A few straggling visitors remain, fussing at their loved ones' bedsides. Thankfully, no policemen are there.

Mr. Piquett has a different story for the nurse in charge of the ward, who at first protests their arrival, then happily shows them to Mrs. Rawlings's bedside, batting her eyes at Mr. Piquett before returning to her work. Mimi is relieved to find Mrs. Rawlings sitting up in bed, drinking a glass of water. A stack of pillows is propped beneath her back. Her cheeks are pale and movements languid, but she appears in far better health than many of the patients around her. A man in worn overalls sits at her bedside.

"Who are you?" he asks them.

"Who are you?" Mr. Piquett counters.

"I'm her husband."

"Ah, very good. Might I have a word with you in the hallway?"

Mr. Rawlings doesn't move, his brown eyes full of suspicion as they move between Mr. Piquett and Mimi.

"I'm Nurse—" Mimi says, but stops, thinking better of giving her name. "A nurse at the clinic where your wife had her—er—procedure."

"So you're the reason she's here," he says, loud enough to be heard several beds over. Mimi winces.

Mrs. Rawlings sets her water glass on the bedside table, then weakly pats his knee. "We knew the risks. Go talk with the gentleman."

Her husband grudgingly rises and follows Mr. Piquett out into the hall. Mimi watches them go, then takes his seat beside the bed.

"How are you feeling, Mrs. Rawlings?"

"All right." She tries to sit up straighter and winces.

Mimi lays a hand on her shoulder. "Don't overexert yourself."

"I know I should have called the number on the card you gave me, but when I woke in such pain, I got scared."

"It's all right. What matters is that you're okay."

"Robert took me to St. Mary's, but they refused to admit me. The doc there said he didn't want anything to do with my case when he found out . . . found out I'd had an abortion."

"So they sent you here?"

Mrs. Rawlings nods.

"I'm sorry that happened." The doctor was probably worried about legal trouble. That, or he shared her parents' narrow view of right and wrong. Either way, a doctor's job was to help people, not turn them away. "May I check your pulse?"

Another nod. Mimi carefully takes her wrist and feels for the radial artery. The thrum beneath her fingertips is a little fast, but reassuringly strong and steady.

"An infection," Mrs. Rawlings says, when Mimi releases her wrist. "That's what the doctors here say."

Mimi counts the rise and fall of her chest as she speaks. She sounds tired, but not starved for air. Another good sign. "Do you mind if I look at your chart?"

"Go ahead."

After a glance at the nurse on duty, Mimi pulls her chart from its holder at the foot of the bed. As Mimi suspected, Mrs. Rawlings initially presented with fever, abdominal pain, and foul-smelling vaginal discharge. In the two days since, her fever broke, and the discharge diminished. Mimi returns the chart to its holder. Barring a sudden turn for the worse, Mrs. Rawlings should be sent home in a few days.

"From what I can glean, the infection appears to be improving," she says. "Are you still in a lot of pain?"

"Not like before."

"Good." Mimi glances at the nurse again, then scoots her chair closer to the bed and speaks in a whisper. "I'm sorry to ask you this, but have you spoken to the police?"

Mrs. Rawlings shakes her head. "They were here the day after I arrived, badgering me with questions, telling me"—her voice breaks—"telling me I was going to die and might as well confess and say who done it. I was in such pain, and they kept asking and asking. But I didn't tell 'em nothing."

Mimi's hands curl into fists in her lap, anger overshadowing her relief. "Those brutes. They had no right to do that."

"I broke the law."

"And they broke the law of human decency . . . scaring you like that, telling you that you were going to die. . . . They're not doctors. They don't know." Mimi shakes her head and takes a slow breath to calm herself. "Anyway, thank you for . . . your discretion."

"I don't regret what I did." She winces as she reaches for her water. Mimi hands her the glass. She takes a long, slow sip, then hands it back. "We can't afford no more babies." She sighs and lets her head fall back against the pillows. "Is it true you have to worry clear up till forty?"

"More years than that, I'm afraid. In nursing school, I took care of a forty-six-year-old mother of twins."

Mrs. Rawlings closes her eyes, as if the very thought exhausts her. If she and her husband can't afford another baby, how will they pay the hospital bill? Mimi has no easy answer. Instead, she focuses on the more immediate problem.

"They might be back, the police," she says.

"I know. Don't worry. I won't talk. Robert thinks I should. He was pressing me almost as hard as them cops. He doesn't understand that we're in this together." She opens her eyes. Her stare is steady and direct, and Mimi understands by *we*, she not only means her and Mimi, but all women.

"Rest now," Mimi says. "I'll be back tomorrow to check on you."

Ada hadn't asked that of her, and tomorrow is Mimi's day off. But she can't leave Mrs. Rawlings to bear this alone, even if Mimi risks a run-in with the police.

In a matter of minutes, Mrs. Rawlings is asleep. Mimi stands and slips quietly away. Exiting the ward, she sees Mr. Piquett and Mr. Rawlings standing together, several paces off. They're so enrapt in their conversation, neither looks her way. She waits just beyond the ward entrance, not wanting to interrupt.

"We have a deal?" Mr. Piquett says.

After a moment, Mr. Rawlings nods. Then Mr. Piquett hands him a wad of money. Mr. Rawlings counts it—half a dozen twenty-dollar bills—and stuffs it in the pocket of his overalls.

"You'll pay the hospital bills too?"

"You have my card. Forward the bills to that address." He extends his hand, but Mr. Rawlings doesn't shake it. He's no more friendly to Mimi as he passes by her on his way back to the ward. If anything, the look he shoots her is steelier. Not very grateful for a man a hundred and twenty dollars richer. But Mimi knows it's likely fear driving his anger. He almost lost his wife, after all. The mother of his children. Fear, anger—he has a right to both, even if the target of those emotions is misplaced.

It's not yet four o'clock when they leave the hospital. Mr. Piquett fetches the car but lets it idle at the curb after she gets in.

"What's Mrs. Rawlings's prognosis?" he asks her.

"Do you mean will she live?"

He nods.

"Yes. Her infection seems to have been mild, and, in any case, it appears to be clearing up."

"And the police?"

"They came by, but she didn't give them information about the clinic."

"Good." He shifts into drive and pulls away from the curb. "What's your address?"

"Aren't we going back to the clinic?"

"Ada told me to take you home after we finished here."

Mimi gives him her address, and he steers the coupe toward Oakley Boulevard. This time, he doesn't turn on the radio, though Mimi would welcome the distraction. A heaviness has settled in her stomach, like she's eaten something that won't digest.

"Is that how this works?" she asks. "When a woman gets sick, you buy her family's silence."

"Every situation is a little different, but that's the gist, yes." The coolness of his reply jogs something in her memory. *Louis Piquett.* Several years ago, she read his name in the paper. He was John Dillinger's lawyer. He'd helped Dillinger escape before his trial, and later, went to prison for harboring someone in Dillinger's gang.

This man is Ada's friend? Mimi studies him from the corner of her eye as he drives. Should she be afraid? What had the paper called him? *The brains of Dillinger's mob.*

"I take it these dealings don't sit well with you, Nurse Lukas," he says after a stretch of silence. "Do you have a better solution?"

Mimi considers. It would be better if the women never got sick at all. But they've taken every precaution they can at the clinic—sterilizing the instruments, scrubbing their hands and forearms, disinfecting the room between cases, wearing clean smocks over their uniforms and caps over their hair.

Better still if the women didn't need their services at all. But Mimi thinks back to Mrs. Bates and the two cans of beans she'd had to feed eight people; to Miss Simms and the bruises on her face and wrists; to the twelve-year-old girl they saw in February.

Birth control, then. But even for Mimi, getting a diaphragm was costly and troublesome. Single women can't get one at all. And some doctors won't prescribe one, even if a woman is married. She's heard some states still outlaw diaphragms and other forms of birth control.

All right, it would be better if they didn't have to fear the police coming after them. But the police didn't make the laws. Like it or not, abortion *is* illegal. Mimi is as much a criminal for what she does as Mr. Piquett is for having harbored fugitive bank robbers.

"No," Mimi finally says. "I don't have a better solution."

Mr. Piquett nods. "Neither do I."

They ride the rest of the way in silence. The heaviness in her stomach doesn't go away. What is it that she's heard said? Misery acquaints a man with strange bedfellows. Perhaps necessity does, as well.

As Mimi makes her way up the walkway to the house, she sees the living room curtains part and Halina's face press against the window. No doubt she's taking note of the shiny Pierce-Arrow idling at the curb. Mr. Piquett may be part of Chicago's mob-infested underbelly, but he's also a gentleman and doesn't drive away until Mimi's safely inside.

"You're home early," Halina says, joining her in the entryway. It sounds more like an accusation than an observation.

Mimi unpins her hat and hangs it on the rack. "Yes."

Halina frowns, clearly expecting some explanation.

Mimi doesn't give her one. She passes by the living room and sees Stan asleep in his armchair. Jo's teasing about hungry glances comes back to her. He *had* looked at her that way once, like she was the only thing that existed in his entire field of vision. Like he could stare at her forever and never get enough. Like he couldn't wait to peel off her clothes and make love.

She imagines him waking, blinking a few times in the late afternoon, then settling his gaze on her. Mimi's skin flushes. In her mind, he crooks two fingers in her direction, and she wastes no time going to him. He takes hold of her hips as soon as she's within reach and pulls her between his knees. His hands drift to the hem of her skirt, tugging it upward. Then she's straddling him, the armchair groaning beneath their combined weight. He kisses her hard while his fingers sink into her backside. She fumbles with his buckle as he pulls aside her panties and—

"I leave dinner to you tonight then, yes?"

Mimi nearly jumps at Halina's words. She rattles her head, surprised to find herself still standing in the hall, while Stan snores away in his chair.

"Yes. I'll take care of dinner." Her words are husky, breathless, but her mother-in-law doesn't seem to notice. Mimi casts one more look in Stan's direction, but the fantasy is gone.

CHAPTER 25

The summer carries on. Penny and Junior spend their days playing hopscotch and kick the can with their friends. When Mimi has the day off and a few nickels saved, she takes them to the beach, the picture show, or Riverview Amusement Park.

One thing that's noticeably absent: baseball. In summers past, Mimi and the children went to nearly every White Sox home game. On fair weather days, Babcia joined them. She showed little interest in the goings-on on the field and complained about the hard seats, but when Stan was up to bat, she'd leap to her feet and cheer just as loudly as the rest of them. When a National League team with a winning record came to play the Cubs, Stan would often take the children to a game at Wrigley Field, as well. Before Junior could walk, he had a glove, and Mimi can't remember all the times she came home from Marshall Field's or Lehman's Grocer to find him and Stan playing catch in the yard.

This summer, they haven't been to a single game. After hearing "tomorrow, son" a dozen times, Junior's stopped asking his father to throw the ball with him. When a match comes on the radio, Stan cranks the dial to another station.

It breaks Mimi's heart to see Stan suffering like this, but she's at a loss about what to do. She makes his favorite foods, and he says he isn't hungry. She freshens up her hair before leaving work, and he doesn't notice. She suggests a night out at the theater, supper club, or dance hall, and Stan suggests she take the children or one of her nurse friends instead. What more can she do?

One morning in mid-August, Mimi wakes to the sharp ring of the telephone. Once. Twice. Then, it goes silent. A few weak threads of light slip through the crack in the bedroom curtains, but not enough to rouse her from bed. Stan snores beside her. She lets her eyes close but snaps them open a moment later, when a loud knock rattles the bedroom door.

Halina's voice sounds through the wood. "You have someone on the telephone waiting on you."

Mimi forces herself out of bed, knowing the call's for her. If it had been for Stan, Halina would have knocked more gently. She gropes for her housecoat and throws it on over her nightgown. Her slippers are around here somewhere, but she gives up and shuffles out barefoot.

Halina isn't in the hallway, and she's left the handset dangling by its cord from the small cutout where they keep the telephone. Mimi sighs. *Good morning to you, too.* She hauls up the handset and presses it to her ear.

"Hello?"

"Mrs. Lukas?" an unfamiliar male voice says.

"Yes, this is she."

"This is Mr. Martin."

There's a pause, as if the caller expects her to say something.

"Thomas Martin. Ada's husband. We met once at the clinic."

"Mr. Martin, of course! Forgive me, I'm—"

"I know it's early. I apologize for calling at this hour. There's been an incident at the clinic."

Mimi's chest tightens. "What's happened? Is everyone all right?"

"Yes, but Ada and Miss Kuder are being detained at Central Station."

Another raid. She moves closer to the wall and cups her free hand around the mouthpiece. "They've been arrested?"

"I'm afraid so."

Mimi's knees go weak. She glances over her shoulder down the hall. Thank goodness the children aren't awake yet.

"I saw them this morning," Mr. Martin continues. "It will be several hours before bail is set and I can get them out of there. In the meantime, Ada asked that I contact you for a favor."

"Me?"

"I'm tied up waiting for the judge, and. . . . Ada trusts you, Mrs. Lukas."

She thinks about Jo and Ada, locked up in that cold cell. "Go on."

"She needs you to go to the clinic and retrieve the key to her office on Dearborn Street. It's in the far back corner of her desk drawer. At the Dearborn Street office—" He pauses. "Do you have pen and paper?"

Mimi grabs the pad and pencil they keep beside the telephone. "Yes, go ahead."

"Behind the desk is a safe. Open it with the code 4-29-19."

Mimi's hand flags. Ada's office has a safe? Whatever for?

"Did you get that?" he says. Mimi blinks and repeats the numbers as she writes them down.

"Good. Inside you'll find a cashbox. Take out twenty-five hundred dollars and put it in an envelope. Then—"

"I'm sorry, did you say twenty-five hundred?"

"Yes."

The tightness in her chest grows. Twenty-five hundred dollars? That's over half the value of her home.

Mimi listens to the rest of Mr. Martin's instructions in a daze and then hangs up the telephone. In addition to the code to the safe, an address is scrawled in a shaky hand on the top sheet of the pad. She doesn't have to do this. She can tear off the sheet, wad it up, and throw it in the trash. She's a nurse, after all. Not a racketeer. This isn't what she agreed to when she took the job.

Her family is already stirring. Mattress coils squeak in the children's bedroom, and the faucet runs in the bathroom. They're counting on her, and not just to make breakfast.

But Ada is counting on her, too. If Mimi and the others hope to have a job tomorrow, next week, next month, she needs to do this. The sooner it can be accomplished, the better, Mr. Martin told her. She understands his urgency. This mess is like a stain. The longer it sits, the harder it is to get out. But is Mimi really willing to sully her hands in the cleaning?

She tears the sheet of paper from the pad. Instead of crumpling it up, she folds it once and slips it into the pocket of her housecoat.

In half an hour, she's dressed. A pot of water heats on the stove. She'll add the Cream of Wheat before she leaves, but Halina will have to watch it to make sure it doesn't burn. Stan shuffles into the dining room, still in his pajamas, as Mimi hurriedly sets out bowls and spoons.

"There's an emergency at work this morning," she tells him. "I have to go in."

He yawns in reply.

"I don't think I'll make it back in time for church." She pours four glasses of orange juice and grabs the sugar bowl from the buffet. "I'm taking the car."

That gets his attention.

"What?"

"I don't have time to ride the L."

"What about the rest of us?"

"The streetcar will drop you right in front of the church."

"We're not going to church without the car."

"Fine. Don't go. Imperil your immortal soul or whatever it is that you Catholics believe. But I'm taking the car." Mimi stalks back to the kitchen with the empty pitcher of orange juice. She's never talked to Stan like that. A wife doesn't order her husband around; she asks politely. But she's too busy thinking about the task before her to care. Part of her, though, wishes he'd followed her into the kitchen to continue their argument. Though they rarely fought, the old Stan hated to lose. Perhaps it's the sportsman in him. Now, instead of the bullish footfalls of a man coming to put her into her place, she hears a muttered curse and the strike of a match.

Cigarette smoke drifts through the pantry and into the kitchen as she dumps Cream of Wheat into the pot. A quick stir, and she leaves.

There's no mistaking what happened when she arrives at the clinic. The door is unlocked, and the lights are on, even though the reception room is empty. Chairs lie on their sides, and the desk drawers gape open. The daily logbook is gone. No wonder Ada insisted they only use the women's initials. The cashbox is missing, too.

It won't take the police long to pick the lock and pilfer the rings, watches, and medals inside.

The disarray feels like a violation, pointed and personal, and Mimi has to fight the urge to tidy up. To put right the damage. But she isn't here for that.

The back half of the clinic seems largely untouched. An unopened instrument case sits on the metal table in the procedure room. Clean sheets dress the examination bed. At least they weren't mid-case, then, when the police arrived.

Mimi continues to Ada's office. Papers lie scattered on the floor. The mug on her desk rests on its side in a pool of drying coffee. But it doesn't appear that the police rooted through her drawers or the filing cabinet that stands against the far wall. They wouldn't have found much, even if they did. Ada's far too fastidious for that. Now Mimi knows why.

She sits at the desk and opens one drawer at a time, feeling for a key. In the far back corner of the bottom drawer, she finds it taped to the drawer wall. After pocketing the key and cleaning up the coffee spill, Mimi leaves, turning off all the lights and locking the main door. She can't help but wonder how many women were detained along with Ada and Jo. Were they badgered with questions, the way Mrs. Rawlings had been? Threatened with arrest and exposure if they didn't speak?

She shivers and pushes the thought aside. If she can accomplish today's goal, she'll save those women from further humiliation and interrogation.

Mimi's never been to Ada's office on Dearborn Street, but the building isn't hard to find. She takes the stairs to the third floor and uses the key she got from the desk drawer to open the door. It's a small, single-room office with a desk, a couple of chairs, and a few file cabinets. Sunk into the wall behind the desk is an iron safe the size of an icebox.

Before opening it, Mimi closes the window blinds and double-checks that the office door is locked. Her palms are sweaty and fingers clumsy as she spins the dial. Her first try is unsuccessful, and she tries again. On the third try, the door finally swings open. Inside, stacks of notebooks several feet high sit flush against the back wall. She takes a notebook off the top of a stack and opens it. *July, 1939—*

November, 1939 is written on the front page. On the next page begins a list of each case performed during that period. It's a near-perfect transcription of the details on the patient intake card they complete in the clinic. Mimi flips quickly through the pages. There must be over five hundred entries in this book alone. She sets it back on top of its stack, doing a quick estimation. If all the other notebooks contain case records, too, there must be over fifteen thousand cases going back a decade.

As she searches for the cashbox, Mimi finds other documents, as well—a logbook concerning payroll, records of commission payments, envelopes filled with intake cards Mimi guesses have yet to be transcribed. At the bottom of it all is the cashbox.

Mimi opens the lid and gasps. Unlike the one they keep at the clinic, this one has thousands of dollars inside—more money than Mimi's ever seen in one place. Why keep all this here? It's the sort of thing she'd expect to find in a mobster's den in Cicero. The answer comes to her quickly. It's the same reason they don't accept checks for payment and why Mimi and the others are all paid in cash. There's no money trail the police can follow from one bank account to the next.

Still, it's unsettling how much the clinic's operations resemble the types of organized crime syndicates she's heard about on the radio. Especially when Mimi considers what she's about to do next.

In one of the desk drawers, she finds an envelope, then removes twenty-five hundred dollars from the cashbox. Not trusting her clammy, unsteady hands, she counts the money again before slipping it inside the envelope.

It's such an outlandish sum. Most families don't make this much in a year. She remembers what Daniel told her the first time they met in the tavern. Bribing a state's attorney costs more than a measly hundred dollars. A lot more.

Mimi tucks the thick envelope into her purse. She never would have guessed this is how much he meant.

It's only half past nine when Mimi pulls up to her next destination, though it feels much later. She parks the Packard alongside the curb and double-checks the address. It's correct, but the house—a modest, one and a half-story brick bungalow with a small porch and overgrown shrubbery—isn't what she expected. But then, an extra hundred dollars a month wouldn't buy you a mansion. Especially not when you have four daughters and a sickly wife.

Mimi takes a deep breath and fumbles with the car door handle. She can't imagine her visit here will be any more welcome than the six A.M. phone call she received. She's spent the entire drive from Dearborn Street trying to think what she'll say if Daniel doesn't open the door. She knows he wouldn't want his family to know the sort of thing he's involved in. So she'll have to play it off as a casual visit. But what good reason would a friend—no, not a friend, an acquaintance—have for showing up on someone's doorstep on a Sunday morning? A woman acquaintance, no less. It's not as if she can ask to speak to Daniel about borrowing a cup of sugar or a few clothespins.

For perhaps the tenth time today, a voice at the back of Mimi's mind reminds her that this wasn't what she signed on for. In what world does a nurse deliver bribe money to a corrupt police officer on a Sunday morning before church?

Hers, apparently.

She steps out of the car just as the Moriaritys' front door opens. A short, thin woman steps out first. The yellow dress she wears washes out her complexion, and a wide-brimmed hat too big for her slight features sits angled atop her head. But her face is undeniably pretty. Her hair—or what Mimi can see of it—is a rich walnut color offset with streaks of silver. A different-colored outfit and a dab of rouge, and she'd be more than pretty. Not that it matters what she looks like. But somehow, Mimi's glad the woman's wearing yellow.

Carole comes out next, followed by Margaret, Marie, and a young woman Mimi doesn't recognize. They all wear dresses of modest length and similar pastel shades. Daniel exits last, closing the door just before a small black-and-white dog slips out. They march down the porch steps single file and make their way across the lawn toward a Buick sedan parked a few yards in front of the Packard.

Carole spots her first, smiling and waving. This draws Daniel's attention, his carefree expression clouding when his gaze finds Mimi.

"Mrs. Lukas," he says, his voice tight. "Are you . . . lost?"

Mimi responds with an equally tight smile. "Sorry to drop by unexpectedly on a Sunday. I . . . er . . . needed help with some papers

I'm preparing for the assistant state's attorney. He's expecting them on his desk first thing tomorrow and—"

"I understand." He turns to his daughters and hands the key he's carrying to the oldest. "Joan, will you drive? I'm afraid this may take a while."

"You're not coming to church?" his wife says.

"I'll try to catch up with you. No sense in everyone being late."

"But it's Sunday." She turns her head toward Mimi and glares.

"I know. It can't be helped."

Daniel loops an arm around his wife's waist and steers her toward the automobile like she's too fragile to get there on her own. It's not just coddling; there's genuine tenderness in his touch. A burr of envy lodges beneath Mimi's ribs. He opens the passenger door and helps her inside, then holds open the back door for his younger daughters. Joan circles around to the front. He watches and waves as they pull away, waiting until they're halfway down the block before turning back to Mimi.

She expects a glare like the one his wife gave her—she's ruined his Sunday, after all—but his eyes hold only concern. "What's happened?"

"There was another—"

He holds up his hand and glances around. "Let's talk in your car."

Mimi tells him about Mr. Martin's telephone call and the mess she found at the office. Daniel sighs and rubs his forehead.

"Ada wanted me to give you this." She looks out the windshield at the quiet street before handing him the envelope.

He peeks inside but doesn't count the money.

"I'm sorry I came to your house on a Sunday. Mr. Martin gave me your address, and I didn't know what else to do."

He scrubs his face. "It's all right. You did the right thing. The sooner we can get ahead of this, the better."

"That's what Mr. Martin said, too."

"I need to figure out which attorney the case has been assigned to. Can you drive me to Central Station?"

Mimi's stomach clenches. "I . . ."

"No one at the station will see you. I'll have you park a block away and wait for me in the car."

Mimi looks out the window at the tidy rows of houses across the street. It's not unlike her street. Her neighborhood. The normalcy of it all is at such odds with what she's doing.

Daniel reaches over and touches her hand, drawing back Mimi's attention. His skin is warm, his fingers lingering a moment before pulling away. "I know you don't want to be any more involved than you already are. If you'd rather go, I understand."

When she was stuck in the Central Station jail, Ada worked to free her. Sure, she did it as much for the clinic's sake as Mimi's. But Mimi has a vested interest in the clinic now, too. More than that, Jo and Ada are her friends.

She starts the car, and they drive away.

Daniel assures her he won't be at the station any longer than ten minutes. After fifteen, Mimi starts to worry. All he has to do is figure out which state's attorney has been assigned the case. Could such a simple question rouse suspicion? What if they search him and find the envelope?

After twenty minutes, she fits the key back in the ignition, but hesitates before starting the engine. She parked a block away from the station house like they discussed. She could drive by slowly, but what does she expect—to spy him through the front windows? Daniel could be anywhere inside the massive building. She could drive away instead. If he's been discovered, they'll be coming for her next, right?

But can she just leave him here?

Her hands grip the steering wheel, but she can't decide whether to creep forward down State Street or swing the car around and speed home.

Home, she decides, pressing down on the gas and wrenching the wheel to the left. A horn blares, and she looks over her shoulder to see another automobile racing toward her. They swerve left while Mimi jerks the Packard to the right. Her front tire slams into the curb while the other car zips past, missing her by only inches. It honks its horn again and continues on, the driver's fiery hand gestures visible through the back window.

Mimi's heart is beating double time as she reverses enough to straighten out the Packard alongside the curb, then kills the engine. Her head falls back against the seat, and she closes her eyes a moment before getting out to inspect the damage.

The fender is scratched and slightly dented. So is the hub. Mimi wrings her hands. They're still shaking with adrenaline. Stan loves this car. He'll be furious when he sees the damage. She prods the wheel with her foot. At least the tire hasn't gone flat.

When she looks up, she sees Daniel walk out the front door of the station house, carrying a box the size of an apple crate. She gets back in the car and waits for him. His stride is nonchalant, as if he's out for a Sunday stroll. He tips his hat and smiles at the people he passes on the sidewalk. If only Mimi had such steely nerves.

He glances at the fender before getting in. Mimi sags forward, resting her forehead on the steering wheel. If Daniel noticed the dent after having seen her car all of once, Stan will certainly notice.

"What happened?"

Mimi winces, uncertain what to say. After a moment, she sits up and sighs. "I lost my nerve and tried to drive away. I got all of two feet before almost hitting another car."

Daniel laughs.

"It's not funny."

He only laughs harder.

Mimi frowns, but the rich, hearty sound soon gets the better of her. "It's not funny," she says again, but there's no bite behind her words, and she has to fight off laughter of her own.

"I'm sorry," he says, his twinkling gray eyes telling her he's not sorry at all. "Remind me not to take you along on a bank heist."

"Nonsense! I could be a good distraction. Drive into another car as you slip away."

"You have a good point there. You certainly are . . . distracting."

Mimi's cheeks heat, and she looks away. "My husband's never going to let me touch the car again when he sees what I did."

"I can fix the dent and buff out those scratches in ten minutes flat."

"That's what you said about the station house, and you were gone twice as long."

"Ah, that's why you lost your nerve?"

She nods. "I thought maybe they'd caught on to what you—what we're doing."

"Did you think I'd turn you in?"

When she doesn't reply, he puts the box down at his feet and takes her chin. "Mimi, I would never do that. If I get caught, I'm going down alone."

His earnest eyes hold hers, and she longs to believe him. But some promises aren't that easy to keep. They're already so intertwined—him, her, Ada, the clinic—it's impossible to see how one falls without toppling the others.

Reluctantly, she pulls free of his grasp. "What's in the box?"

Disappointment flashes across his face, but he recovers quickly. "The evidence the officers got from the clinic."

"The things they stole, you mean."

He shrugs. "I had a heck of a time getting the police custodian to hand it over. But I think it'll help things along."

"What do you mean?"

"Attorney Meyers is assigned the case. I'm going to give it to him."

"Why? What if he uses it to move forward with the case?"

"I don't think he will. You said the cashbox at the clinic had been looted, right?"

She nods.

"And that several pieces of jewelry had been inside." He gives the box a nudge with his foot, and she hears a soft tinkling sound. "It's all here."

"You mean for him to keep the necklaces and watch?"

"Think of it as sweetening the deal."

She looks pointedly at his jacket and the faint outline of the envelope beneath. "The deal's not sweet enough already?"

"Drive me to his house, and we'll see."

Mimi hesitates. The only place she should be driving is home.

"On second thought, maybe it's safer if I drive," he says.

Mimi fights off a smile and starts the car. "Not a chance."

Assistant State's Attorney Meyers lives in a lavish, three-story brick home in Hyde Park. Daniel instructs her to drive past it and park a few houses down.

He distracted her with small talk on the way over—the weather, the children and the approaching school year, Colonel Lindbergh's recent visit to the city—but now, the weight of this final task catches up with her. Daniel seems to feel it, too, for his hand hesitates on the door handle.

"Aren't you going to tell me you'll be back in ten minutes flat?" Even to her own ears, the levity in her voice sounds forced. So, too, is his replying smile.

"Let's hope, but . . ."

"I'll wait."

He nods. "Thanks."

"What happens if he doesn't . . . agree to quash the case?"

"He'll tell me to get the hell out."

"He won't . . ."

"Turn me in? Nah." And just like that, the confident man she'd seen walking out of the station house returns.

"And what about the clinic?"

"This is Chicago. Everyone has a price."

He opens the door and steps out, the box tucked beneath one arm. She watches him in the rearview mirror until he disappears into the house.

Is he right? Does everyone in this city have a price? The day is cloudy but warm, and she cracks open the front windows. It doesn't seem right that her price for breaking the law is a steady paycheck to feed her children while some men can command thousands of dollars—money they don't need—all just to keep the clinic open. But then, she's done worse for less. What right does she have to ask for more when she sold out her sister for a stupid pink ribbon?

Mimi shakes off the thought. A breeze steals in, ruffling her hair and the collar of her blouse, but the car still feels stifling. And what if Daniel isn't right? Will Ada and Jo go to jail? Will the police come for her, too?

She reaches for the window crank, but even though the oxygen seems to have bled from the car, she doesn't dare open the window any farther. The glass, thin and lucent as it is, feels like the last protection left to her.

A rattle at the passenger-side door startles her, and she smashes her elbow into the steering wheel. She's breathing a curse when Daniel climbs into the car.

"Did it work?"

"Yep."

"Really?"

"Really."

A tidal wave of relief washes over her, leaving her giddy. Mimi leans over and kisses Daniel's cheek, getting a deep whiff of his cologne. A ruddy color creeps up his neck as she pulls away. The air no longer feels thin, but heavy and electric.

He rubs the skin where her lips had just been. "What was that for?"

"I . . . I'm just glad it worked."

"I told you it would. And I think I made it back in under ten minutes."

"It was at least fifteen." She glances at her wristwatch, although she has no idea what time he left. The slender silver hands point to noon.

Surely, it's later than that. It feels like she's lived a year in the six hours since the shrill ring of the telephone woke her.

She looks up and sees Daniel watching her with an intensity that makes her skin prickle. Whatever quip she'd meant to make about the time slips her mind.

A charged silence opens up between them. Mimi rubs her elbow and tries to find a place to settle her gaze that isn't his handsome face.

"I'll . . . um . . . take you home."

"Yeah," he says after a moment.

Mimi reaches for the key, still seated in the ignition. Daniel intercepts her hand and pulls her toward him. His lips are on hers before she knows what's happening. He tastes different than Stan. Mint instead of tobacco. Firm, dry lips where Stan's are soft and pillowy. For a moment, she gives into the heat coiling inside her and kisses him back. His arm slides around her waist, and he clings to her like a drowning man clings to land.

Mimi is drowning, too. All heat and desire.

She's drowning, and she doesn't care.

Doesn't care until she's almost fully submerged; then, some part of her cries out, and she pulls away.

They stare at each other for a moment. Hunger flickers in Daniel's eyes, but there's something else there, also. Disbelief.

Or is it fear?

Mimi feels it, too.

The outside world comes back into focus. Leaves shudder in the breeze, and a car drives past. The sun breaks free from the cloud cover only to disappear a moment later.

Mimi scoots to the far side of the car and grabs the steering wheel like it's a life buoy.

"Sorry," he says, "I don't know what came over me."

Mimi swallows and says nothing. Her hands grip the wheel so tightly, her knuckles blanch. It's all she can do to peel one hand away to start the ignition. They drive the entire way to Daniel's house in silence.

CHAPTER 26

"We've got a special case today," Ada says, as Mimi hangs up her hat and purse in the hall closet.

Mimi's stomach somersaults, threatening to send back up her breakfast. "Another child?"

"No, no. Nothing like that."

Three weeks have passed since Ada and Jo were arrested, and things are just starting to feel normal again. On their first day back in the clinic, Ada thanked Mimi for her help in "smoothing over the situation" and offered her a hundred dollars for her troubles. That would more than cover new clothes and school supplies for the children, plus repairs to the Packard. But Mimi refused the money. To pay her for the nursing work she does is one thing. To pay her for a favor is too much like the mobsters in the radio dramas she listens to.

Assistant State's Attorney Meyers hadn't been able to make the case completely disappear like it had when Mimi was arrested. But when it came up in Felony Court, Ada and Jo's lawyer argued police entrapment. Mr. Meyers accepted the accusation without rebuttal. The case was acquitted, and the state's attorney's office filed no appeal.

Now, Mr. Meyers is all the richer, and it's back to business as usual at the clinic.

Mimi follows Ada back to her office and takes the intake card Ada hands her. At first, she doesn't see anything out of the ordinary—just a woman in her late twenties who missed her last two periods. Then she notices the name: Blanche McAllister.

"*The* Blanche McAllister?"

Ada nods. "She's shooting a new picture here and, well, finds herself in need of our services."

"She came into the clinic and scheduled an appointment?" Surely Jo would have said something if a film star walked in.

"No, I received a personal telephone call about the matter. It's not a difficult case, as you see. She's had a prior operation—not here—in California, but there shouldn't be any trouble on that account."

Mimi knows what she means. Sometimes, women came in who'd previously taken matters into their own hands or used an unskilled provider, and the doctors had to navigate around significant scarring.

"Her appointment is at eleven. Afterward, I want you to take the car and drive her home. The studio's putting her up at an apartment on Chicago Avenue near the lake. Stay with her until Miss Ranus arrives this evening to take over."

Mimi frowns. Sometimes, when a woman is more than a couple of months along or has some sort of underlying disease, around-the-clock observation is required for a few days after the procedure to ensure her full recovery. But there's nothing on Miss McAllister's intake card to suggest she needs such attention.

"Is there something else wrong with her?"

"Aside from an overly inflated ego? No. But she's paying well for the service, so best not to disappoint. I thought perhaps with your husband's career, you might have some experience dealing with . . ."

"Egoists?"

"Yes."

Mimi swallows a sigh. Although she loved the movie star's last picture, Miss McAllister's the last sort of person Mimi wants to spend the afternoon with. But the alternative would be to send Edna with her. And as much as Mimi likes Edna, she knows her friend doesn't have the patience for such a woman. Besides, maybe Ada's wrong about Miss McAllister. She always plays such sweet characters in the movies. It's hard to imagine her being as insufferable as Ty Cobb. So Mimi dredges up a smile and says, "I'll take care of her."

* * *

Blanche McAllister is just as beautiful as she appears on the screen—high cheekbones, pouty lips, silky auburn hair—and just as self-important as Ada said. She arrives for her appointment half an hour late and demands to be shown to the anteroom right away. Once there, she hands Mimi her hat, purse, and silk shawl, as though Mimi is her own private butler, dismissing her with a flick of her wrist. She refuses to wear a hospital gown, insisting instead on her own silk kimono. Then, just as Mimi's about to administer the gas, she warns her and Edna that if she wakes up to find her kimono even the slightest bit ripped or stained, she'll buy another and send the clinic the bill.

After Miss McAllister is asleep, it's all Mimi can do to keep Edna from pulling out a pair of surgical scissors and carving up the kimono like it's a paper snowflake.

"It's just nerves making her act that way," Mimi says. Edna only smirks.

But when Miss McAllister wakes after the procedure, her disposition doesn't improve in the slightest. From the back seat of Ada's DeSoto, she complains Mimi took too long to fetch the car. Complains that she's driving too slow, then too fast. That all the sharp turns are making her sick. Never mind that Mimi drives the posted speed limit the entire time and has turned only twice.

"I've known stunt drivers in bank-heist films who drive more smoothly than you," she says to Mimi when they finally arrive at the towering apartment building.

Mimi winces, but not at Miss McAllister's insult. She's remembering Daniel and his joke about not taking her along on any bank heists. Remembering their kiss.

She pulls up alongside the curb before the building's gold-trimmed glass doors. A man in a heavily starched blue and red uniform approaches the car.

"Don't spend all afternoon parking, and don't talk with the doorman on your way up," Miss McAllister warns her. "He's a first-rate busybody, and I'd rather not see my name splashed across tomorrow's papers." She reaches over the front seat and adjusts the rearview mirror to put on lipstick.

"Discretion is one of the first principles they teach in nursing school," Mimi says, hoping to remind Miss McAllister that she's not just some maid to be ordered about, but a nurse.

"Good." She pinches her cheeks, then leans back, not bothering to right the mirror. A moment later, the back door opens, and the uniformed man helps her from the car.

Mimi twists in her seat and waves a hand to get his attention. "Can you tell me if there's a nearby place to—"

The door closes on her words, and she watches the man hurry up the steps to see Miss McAllister inside. So much for finding close parking.

Mimi circles the block three times before finding a place to leave the car, then hurries back to the apartment building. Instead of letting her inside, the doorman eyes her uniform and says smugly, "Can I help you?"

"I'm here to care for Miss McAllister."

"She didn't mention anything about any"—he looks her up and down again—"visitors."

Mimi sighs. "Then ring her."

"She doesn't care for needless interruptions."

"You just saw me drop her off."

He cocks his head. "Oh? Are you a chauffeur in addition to being a maid?"

"Neither. I'm a—" Mimi stops. It's plain from her white uniform that she's a nurse. But whether it's to satisfy his own interest or because it'd make a better story for the reporters, he's clearly keen on getting as much information out of her as he can. Miss McAllister was right. "Let me in, or I'll ring Miss McAllister myself, and you'll really see how little she cares for needless interruptions."

He purses his lips and begrudgingly opens the door for her. Inside, the lobby is resplendent—polished marble floors, velvet furniture, a tinkling stone fountain. Even the elevator that carries her to the twenty-first floor is beautiful, its decorative brass work polished to a high gleam. And unlike the doorman, the operator only smiles at her and readily punches in the number she requested.

She knocks softly on Miss McAllister's door before letting herself inside. In the entryway, a circle chandelier with tiers of dangling crystals hangs over a stone table topped with a spray of freshly cut flowers. To the left is a large sitting room with plush furniture and a matching chandelier. Floor-to-ceiling drapes hide what must be a spectacular view of the city and nearby lake. Mimi's tempted to cross the room and peek outside, but Miss McAllister's voice sounds from the opposite direction.

"Is that you, nurse?"

Mimi shakes her head. She told Miss McAllister her name twice already. It isn't as if Lukas is a difficult name to remember. But she says only, "Yes, it's me," and follows the short hallway to a set of double doors. She knocks again, then opens the doors to the largest bedroom she's ever seen. Half of Mimi's house would fit inside it. To one side, near another bank of shrouded windows, sit two armchairs and a loveseat circled around a lacquered coffee table. To the other side is a satin-skirted vanity framed by three panels of mirrors and an arched doorway that leads to a marble bathroom. In the center lies a massive bed, topped with a sateen comforter.

Miss McAllister sits amid a coterie of pillows. "Oh, there you are. Fetch me my nail file, will you?" She gestures languidly toward the vanity. Mimi fights the urge to remind her she's a nurse, not a servant. But she doubts Miss McAllister would heed the distinction. In her world, everyone is a servant. And she is paying a lot to have Mimi here with her—money that helps keep the clinic's fees flexible, so those who don't live in swanky downtown apartments but in South Side shanties can also afford their services. And, of course, so they can pay off men like Assistant State's Attorney Meyers. But Mimi doesn't want to think about that.

After the nail file, Miss McAllister asks for tea. Then a hot-water bottle. Then her slippers. Then a magazine from the front room—no, not that magazine, the other one. Mimi draws the line at making her a martini. "No drinking until tomorrow," she tells her, and brings her warm milk instead.

Unlike the polished brass bar cart in the sitting room with its kaleidoscope of liquor bottles, the kitchen is positively barren. A sleek electric refrigerator sits beside the sink, but all that's inside is a jug of milk, a wedge of cheese, and a half-eaten tin of caviar. In the cupboards, she finds a box of biscuits and three jars of olives. The dishes are glass—but not the cheaply made kind you'd find in a Quaker Oats box. These have polished, molded seams and delicate swirls that could only have been done by hand. They're also covered in a fine film of dust. Does the woman ever eat? No wonder she has such a slim figure. Maybe Mimi should try a diet of olives and caviar, too.

After rewarming Miss McAllister's water bottle and turning on her favorite radio program, *The Guiding Light*, Mimi slips out to do some quick shopping. In her many turns around the block, she'd seen both a grocer and butcher. She buys what she needs for chicken soup (saving the receipt to give to Ada) and hurries back, fielding a second volley of questions from the doorman before making it inside.

"I'll be in the kitchen cooking up some soup for you," Mimi tells Miss McAllister when she returns.

"I'm not hungry for anything but a drink."

"I'll get you a glass of water."

Miss McAllister purses her lips and crosses her arms. "Not that kind of drink."

Mimi brings her water anyway, then starts on the soup. It's her mother's recipe, and she feels a teensy pang of homesickness as she chops the chicken and vegetables. She really should telephone her brother to check up on Ma. But it's harvest time. He'll be too busy to take her call. Or so she tells herself, ignoring that small part of her that's just waiting for the woman to die. She loves her Ma. She does. But she can't think of her without thinking of Ginny. Without hearing the venomous words Ma said to her that Easter. Maybe when her mother's gone, Mimi will finally stop remembering.

She knows life hasn't been any easier for her mother than it's been for her. A farm takes just as much as it gives. Mimi can't remember a time when Ma didn't seem tired. Except perhaps when she was singing. Sometimes it was just a little ditty while they sat together on the porch steps, shucking corn or shelling beans. Other times it was a few tunes at the piano after supper. Everyone—even her rowdy brothers—would drift into the living room and quietly listen. Mostly it was at church, where she led the congregation in song. Her voice—rich and robust—was known throughout the county. Neighbors called on her to sing at weddings and funerals. No fair or festival was complete without Ma belting "My Country, 'Tis of Thee" from the bandstand.

She tried to teach Ginny and Mimi to sing, too. They'd practice scales and harmonies at the piano while Ma played. Ginny had more talent but never took a liking to it. She wanted to sing the type of songs they heard at the soda shop in town. Ma forbade anything but hymns. As for Mimi, she didn't care what they sang, only that it was a break from her chores and school work.

After Ginny's death, though, the lessons stopped. The piano collected dust, and they shucked and shelled in silence. The only time Mimi heard her mother sing was in church, and even then, the notes had a certain hollowness.

But those early memories of scales and ditties are among Mimi's favorites.

She smiles now as she works and hums "My Country, 'Tis of Thee." Soon, the soup is simmering on the stove, filling the apartment with the scent of rosemary and thyme. When the flavors have melded together to her satisfaction, she ladles out a bowlful and brings it to Miss McAllister on a tray.

"I told you I wasn't hungry," Miss McAllister says.

"A few bites will do you good. Help build back your strength."

Miss McAllister sighs and accepts the tray. Mimi watches with satisfaction as she eats the entire bowl.

She's in the kitchen washing the dishes when Miss McAllister calls for her again.

"Fetch me the pill bottle from the bathroom, won't you?"

Mimi finds the bottle on the bathroom counter alongside an empty glass. Sleeping pills, she sees from the label. She puts the bottle down and returns to the bedroom. "No pills tonight, I'm afraid."

"What? I'll never sleep without them."

"You had nitrous oxide today. You don't have much left in your system, but who knows how it might interact with those pills. I'll not risk it."

"It's not your choice."

"I'm here as your nurse, not your mother," Mimi says. "I won't wrestle you to the floor if you get out of bed and get those pills yourself. But I won't stand by, either. If you take them, I'm leaving. Whatever the consequences are, you'll have to deal with them alone."

Miss McAllister scowls at her, crossing her arms over her chest again. Clearly, she isn't used to being told no. "Fine. But I'm telling your boss about this."

Mimi nearly cracks a smile. She sounds just like Junior when he's angry and says, "I'm telling Daddy on you." Or used to say before the accident. Now Junior tiptoes around his father like Stan is a sleeping bear. It breaks Mimi's heart to see, to think about, and she pushes the thought away. "Tell her whatever you wish. Now, let's get your hair pinned up and ready for bed."

Miss McAllister doesn't protest as Mimi grabs a brush and tray of pins from the vanity. Instead of having Miss McAllister come to her, Mimi slips off her shoes and crawls onto the massive bed.

"Don't brush out all the curl," is all Miss McAllister says to her. Mimi moves aside a few pillows so she can kneel behind her. Miss McAllister's hair is just as soft as you'd expect a movie star's hair to be. Mimi takes her time brushing it, then coils small sections and pins them to her head. When she's finished, she gets a scarf from the set of Oriental drawers in the corner and ties it over her hair.

"There."

"I'm not tired yet," she says.

"And I'm not done."

She moves aside still more pillows so that Miss McAllister can lie flat and refills the water bottle with hot water from the kettle. Miss McAllister curls onto her side, hugging the water bottle to her lower abdomen.

"You're not in too much pain, are you?" Mimi asks as she dims the lights.

"It's bearable," she says, then adds, "barely."

Mimi crawls onto the bed again and rubs Miss McAllister's back the way she'd learned to do in nursing school. After a minute or so, her shoulders relax.

"How's the pain now?"

"Better."

Mimi continues to rub small circles over her back.

"It was much worse the first time," Miss McAllister says, a hint of sleepiness in her voice. "I was seventeen. I'd been in California a year and just landed my first role. It wasn't much. A few lines in one of those cowboy pictures. But I would have lost the part if anyone at the studio found out about my condition." She takes a deep breath, and Mimi feels her back muscles tightening again as she continues her massage. "A girl at my rooming house knew a doctor. Well, she said he was a doctor, but I don't think he really was. She said it would cost forty dollars. I scraped together every penny I had, and it still wasn't enough. The girl loaned me the rest—ten dollars plus a quarter interest every week until it was paid. I met the man at some grubby little office downtown, and he did . . . whatever it is you all do without giving me anything for the pain. But first . . . first he made me sleep with him. Said he wouldn't do the procedure if I didn't."

Beneath the steady motion of her hand, Mimi feels a slight shudder and knows Miss McAllister is crying.

Nothing Mimi can say will lessen the pain of that memory. She's never endured such a violation but knows the loneliness of carrying something like that inside you. So she does the only thing she can do and continues rubbing Miss McAllister's back until the woman falls asleep.

Mimi's just crept from the bed and slipped on her shoes when she hears the front door open. She hurries to the entry, closing the bedroom doors behind her, and finds Emily hanging her cardigan and hat on the cherrywood hat rack in the entryway.

"She just fell asleep," Mimi whispers.

They move into the sitting room so they can talk without worrying about the noise. Mimi turns on the light while Emily flops down on a plush velvet-upholstered chaise. Instead of sitting beside her, Mimi goes to the window and parts the curtains. The view is just as spectacular as she'd imagined. City lights twinkle in the deep blue of twilight. Between the buildings, she glimpses Lake Michigan, a dark swath of satin stretching to the horizon.

Mimi catches herself trying to memorize what she sees. The picture-perfect beauty of it all. Whom does she have to tell about it? Neither Stan nor Halina care for such things. Ginny, though. This view would have stolen her breath away.

A soft thud sounds behind her, and she turns to find Emily's stockinged feet resting on the glass coffee table, her shoes tossed carelessly away.

"Sorry I couldn't get here sooner," Emily says, eyeing the bar cart. "We had a late case."

Mimi sits opposite her in one of the low armchairs, sinking deep into the cushion. "It's all right. It was . . . a nice change of pace from the clinic."

"Miss McAllister isn't as awful as Edna says, is she?"

Mimi thinks over the afternoon, the constant complaints and snippy comments, the dozens of times she crisscrossed the apartment to fetch this or that. But she also remembers the shuddering woman hugging her hot-water bottle. "Aggravating, yes. Awful, no."

"I can handle aggravating if it means I get to kick back in a swanky place like this for the next few days."

"There's chicken soup in the refrigerator. She'll tell you she's not hungry, but heat some up anyway. She likes her tea black and will drink warm milk, too. Try not to let her talk you into mixing a martini. And no sleeping pills until tomorrow night."

"Yeah, yeah," Emily says, waving a hand. "I'm a nurse too, remember."

"Sorry, it's the mother in me. Oh, and careful of the doorman. He's a snoop."

Mimi glances toward the door, but doesn't rise to leave. It's too late to make it home and catch the children before bed, so why rush? She misses them the days she works. Misses their smiling faces, their meandering stories, their innocence and wonder. Even their bickering. She'll slip into their room when she gets back. Penny will have fallen asleep with her flashlight on and book open. Junior will have kicked off his blankets and flung his teddy bear to the floor. Mimi will shut the book, right the blankets, rescue Teddy from the floor, kiss their foreheads, then turn off the flashlight.

She misses them but is also grateful for the reprieve. For the change in surroundings. For the chance to have a conversation that doesn't begin with *what's for dinner?* or *I can't find my shoes* or *I don't want to brush my hair.*

Does that make her a bad mother? Some might think so, but Mimi's no longer sure. She's a bit wearier and a lot busier on the days she's home. But she's also more patient now. More mindful. More appreciative of the little things.

Mimi removes her shoes, too, and curls her legs under her on the chair.

"How's that ballplayer of yours?" Emily asks.

Mimi hesitates.

"Let me guess—he's fine. Same as always." Emily gets up and goes to the bar cart. "You don't have to talk to me, but I can tell something's wrong."

If Emily can tell, why can't Stan? She hoped he'd see it right away. Hoped the minute she walked into the house that Sunday afternoon three weeks ago that he'd stop her and demand to know where she'd been and with whom. Couldn't he see the flush in her cheeks? The skittishness of her eyes. The timidity of her footfalls. But when she passed the living room, he hadn't even looked up from the newspaper. That night in bed, he hadn't rolled close enough to smell Daniel's cologne. The following Sunday when they all climbed into the Packard for church, he didn't even notice the dent in the fender.

Emily picks up one of the bottles—a diamond-cut crystal decanter—and gives it a shake. Amber-colored liquor sloshes inside. "Fancy stuff here. Brandy, do you think?" She unstoppers the bottle and sniffs. "Yep."

"We really shouldn't—"

"I know. I know." Emily puts the stopper back and returns the decanter to its place among the rest of the bottles. She examines a few more, then sighs and plops back down on the chaise. "You always were such a good girl, Mimi."

"I'm not," she says, her stomach twisting.

"Yeah?" Emily snorts. "What's the worst thing you've ever done?"

Mimi bites her lip. She hasn't told anyone about Daniel kissing her. Even though the memory of it has buzzed at the edge of her thoughts for the past three weeks. She knows she's done a terrible thing. Guilt steals upon her suddenly throughout the day, its effect so strong, it leaves her nauseous. But she can't muster any regret. Or the conviction she won't do it again.

"And don't tell me it's missing church one Sunday or lying to your next-door neighbor about how much you love her chicken casserole."

"My sister got pregnant when she was fifteen," Mimi blurts out. "I didn't know. I thought she was just getting fat. I got mad at her one day and teased her about it. There, at the supper table. In front of the whole family. Then our mother dragged her upstairs and made my sister undress so she could see for herself. Not fat. Pregnant. My sister didn't talk to me for two weeks, and then one morning she was gone."

"Gone?"

"My parents sent her to an unwed mothers' home in Des Moines."

Emily sits up. "Sheesh."

"She died during childbirth. Infection, hemorrhage, eclampsia—I don't know what from. I never saw the records. Her baby died, too." Mimi takes a deep breath and looks down at her knotted hands. "I've done other terrible things, but that's the worst."

"How awful. You must know it wasn't your fault, though."

"It was. If I hadn't—" Her voice breaks, and she squeezes her eyes shut against the threat of tears.

Emily hurries over and kneels beside the chair, clasping Mimi's hands in hers.

"I can't help but imagine how she must have died—alone, afraid, in pain. Abandoned by her family. Shamed by society. Betrayed by her own sister. All because of a stupid ribbon." Mimi pulls a hand free and wipes her dripping nose on her sleeve.

"How old were you?"

"Eleven."

"Eleven! Oh, Mimi. You were just a child yourself."

"It doesn't change what I did."

Emily pulls her into her arms, rocking her back and forth, while Mimi cries into her shoulder. They stay like that for several minutes. Finally, Mimi pulls away.

"Feel better?" Emily asks.

Mimi nods. She *does* feel better. Emily isn't the only one she's told. Stan knows the story, too. Neither one seems to understand the depth of her culpability. But neither one has run out on her, either.

She sniffles, and Emily hands her a handkerchief.

"Bet you didn't think I'd have you beat," Mimi says, and to her relief, Emily chuckles.

"I don't know about that." She stands and returns to the chaise.

"Does it have to do with Dr. Millstone?"

Emily pulls her bottom lip into her mouth and nods. "I started working for him not long after graduation and . . . and sleeping with him, too."

Mimi sits in shocked silence. She'd long ago guessed they were lovers, but hadn't realized they'd been together so long.

"He was still married back then," Emily continues. "When his wife found out, she brought adultery charges against us."

"Really?" Mimi manages to say. Adultery charges. Is that where she's headed, too?

"We were freed of the charges, Henry and I, but it was awful to go through. I never want to be involved in a court case like that again. I was so mad at his wife. For years, just hearing her name made my blood boil. But you know what? I was the one who wronged her. Me and Henry. But I . . . I couldn't see beyond my own feelings."

"They're divorced now, aren't they?"

"Ten years."

"And you and Henry, I mean, Dr. Millstone, you're still . . ."

Emily laughs despite the somber conversation. "You can call him Henry. At least when you're around me. And, yes, we're still—how did his wife put it?—fornicating."

"But you love him?"

"Madly."

"And he loves you."

Emily shrugs.

"He does. I see it when the two of you are together. He can't take his eyes off you, Em. You've never talked about getting married?"

"After what happened, Henry said he never wanted to marry again."

"What about you?"

Emily turns toward the window, and Mimi follows her gaze. The sky outside has darkened to a perfect black, the stars like mirrored reflections of the city lights below. Beautiful, Mimi thinks. But cold and distant seeming, too.

"I'd like to marry," Emily says at last.

"Have you told him?"

She shakes her head. "But I've hinted."

Now Mimi laughs. "Men don't get hints. They hardly see what's right beneath their noses. If you want to marry, you should tell him."

"What if he says no?"

"Then . . . at least you'll know."

Emily crosses her arms over her stomach and shakes her head again. "No. I can't."

"Tell him, see what he says, and you can decide what to do from there. Better than being in limbo forever." She waits until Emily meets her eye. "No matter what happened in the past, you deserve a chance at happiness."

Emily releases a shaky breath and smiles. "So do you, Mimi."

She doubts that's true. Not when her first thought was of Daniel.

CHAPTER 27

Mimi holds her breath as she watches the foreman at Seeger's Auto Repair Shop squat down beside the Packard's front right fender. She's never been in an auto service shop before, but it reminds her of a hospital operating room with all its specialized equipment—wires and tubes and blowtorches. The mechanics lean over the engine of a car or its stripped-down body with their wrenches and pliers with the focus of a surgeon.

She trusts the Packard's in good hands, but the cost worries her. When she walks into a butcher shop, she knows what she can expect to pay for a pound of beef loin or pork shoulder. At the bakery, she knows the cost of bread. Here, she hasn't any idea. And "car accident while engaged in underworld activities" isn't part of her monthly budget.

The foreman stands and circles around the front of the car, writing something on his clipboard.

"Don't look too bad, ma'am. Just a small dent and a few scratches," he says to her through the open window. "But I'll need to get underneath and check that there wasn't any damage to the axle."

"How much do you think it will cost?"

"Ten dollars. More if there's damage beneath."

It's more money than she'd hoped, but less than she feared.

"What happened?" he asks. "You hit a curb?"

Mimi's stomach does a somersault. Had he seen her that day by the Central Station police house? Seen her reckless attempt to flee the scene? Seen Daniel leave the station carrying away a box of evidence, and the two of them drive away?

"Um . . . yes," she manages.

He smiles and gives the Packard a little pat. "Don't be embarrassed. We see it all the time."

Mimi's so relieved, she has to choke back a laugh. Of course he hadn't been there that day. It was like a child walking into a doctor's office, cradling his arm. The nurse or doctor needn't have seen him fall to guess it's a broken bone.

"How long will it take to fix?"

He slides his pen into the breast pocket of his coveralls and tucks the clipboard under his arm, then rises onto his tiptoes, scanning the garage. "An hour. Maybe two. You're welcome to wait inside the office if you don't want to leave and come back."

"That would be nice. Thank you."

The foreman opens the car door for her and escorts her from the garage to a small waiting area between the parts department and the shop manager's office. Mimi takes a seat in one of the wooden chairs.

"If there's anything wrong with the undercarriage or axle, I'll let you know."

Mimi thanks him and says a silent prayer that there's not. Already she'll have to find ways to trim a few dollars off her weekly grocer's bills.

Maybe she should have taken Daniel up on his offer to fix the damage himself. But she hates the idea of returning to his house and running into his wife again. Stan might be oblivious, but Mimi's sure Elizabeth would read the guilt in her face as plain as if it were written there in marker. *Elizabeth.* It would be easier if Mimi didn't know her name. Easier if she hadn't seen her. Easier if Daniel hadn't told Mimi so much about her that it feels almost like they're old friends.

But they're definitely not friends. A friend would never do what Mimi did. A twinge of nausea stirs inside her at the thought, but by now, Mimi is used to it.

She could have met Daniel at the LaSalle Street Tavern and arranged a time to bring the Packard by when his family wasn't home. But that would invite trouble. The kind of trouble that just thinking about has her heart beating faster and skin tingling with anticipation.

"Mrs. Lukas?"

Mimi startles and looks up. A man in a gray, pin-striped suit stands above her. His deep-set eyes and large ears are familiar, but Mimi can't remember how they're acquainted.

"I'm sorry. I didn't mean to surprise you like that," he says. "Laura always says I shouldn't bother people when they're lost in thought. But it's been so long—what, two, three years?—that I couldn't pass by without saying hello."

The gears of Mimi's brain feel like they're coated in molasses. Why can't she remember this man? It doesn't help that she's certain her cheeks are flushed from the thoughts he interrupted. Can he guess what she was thinking, the way she can tell from Junior's face when he's ruined his dinner with penny candy from the drugstore?

"I'm so glad you did," she says, standing. "It's wonderful to see you again. How is . . . Laura?"

"Fine, fine. Same as always. She'll be tickled pink to hear I ran into you."

"Please pass on a warm hello for me." *Think, think, think!* How does she know this man?

"I will. And how's Stan?"

Mimi hesitates. It's hard to know how much to say without knowing who this man is. "He's . . . um . . ."

"It's such a shame about his leg. He had at least a few more good years left in him. Rob is still playing, and he's pushing forty."

Rob . . . he must mean Robert Klepper. Only someone who knew him personally would use his first name like that. Baseball is definitely the connection. The trouble is, Stan's played with dozens of men over the years. Add in all the managers, coaches, and support staff, and this man could be one out of a hundred different fellows.

"It's been hard for him, leaving the game so abruptly. It's all he's ever known."

The man's expression turns thoughtful. Even though she still can't pluck his name from her memory, she ventures she must have liked him. There's kindness in his eyes and a genuine warmth in his voice.

"I imagine it's almost like losing a limb," he says. "Hard to feel whole again. He's lucky he's got you."

His words hit her like a punch to the gut, but she manages a thin smile. "And what about you? Are you still with the same club?"

"Yep. They haven't gotten rid of me yet." He laughs, and Mimi forces out a chuckle, too.

She's out of safe things to ask, and silence grows between them. She could venture a question about children or—

"Say, what's Stan up to these—"

"Mr. Robinson," the man at the nearby parts counter calls.

Gary Robinson! Now Mimi remembers. He was the team's traveling secretary when Stan played for the Reds. The same year Stan was traded back to the White Sox, Mr. Robinson came to work for the Cubs.

"Excuse me," Mr. Robinson says. "It was a pleasure to see you again, Mrs. Lukas."

"You, too."

He walks over to the parts counter, and Mimi sits back down. Now that she knows how they met, she can picture Laura, too—a stout blond woman with a strong bridge game and easy laugh. Thank goodness she hadn't asked about children. They'd wanted half a dozen, but Laura had never been able to get pregnant. Mimi's instincts had been right; she *had* liked Mr. Robinson. Him and Laura. They'd talked about getting together once they were both settled in Chicago, but never had.

She watches from the corner of her eye as Mr. Robinson counts out a few dollars from his billfold and hands them to the clerk in exchange for a long, cylindrical part she guesses has something to do with the exhaust system. He glances over in her direction, and Mimi looks away.

Should she tell Stan about seeing him? The memories they shared are good ones. But Stan doesn't seem keen on reliving any part of that life. No, she won't tell him. Not today, anyway.

Mr. Robinson stops on his way out the door and hands her one of the auto shop's business cards. She looks up at him, confused.

"My telephone number's on the back," he says.

She flips it over. "Thank you. I'll be sure to give Laura a ring. It would be wonderful to see her again."

"She'd love that. But actually, I was thinking of Stan. Has he thought about coaching? I could pass his name along to the other club secretaries. You never know when a spot might open up, and with a record like his, he stands a fighting chance of being picked."

A coaching spot—why hadn't Gibbins thought of that? Mimi stands and throws her arms around Mr. Robinson's neck. "Thank you. I'll pass along the message tonight. He'll be thrilled to talk to you."

When she pulls away, there's a hint of red in Mr. Robinson's cheeks. "Happy to help if I can."

Mimi hurries home as soon as the mechanics finish with the Packard. She planned on stopping by the bakery for dinner rolls, but the day-old loaf in the bread box will do. With the good news she's got, it won't matter what they eat.

She hadn't even minded the cost of the repairs. What was ten dollars when Stan might have a coaching job soon? She feels a slight pang at the thought of giving up her work at the clinic, which she'll undoubtedly have to do unless Stan manages to land with the Cubs or the Sox. Possible, but unlikely. She pushes the feeling away. There'll be time enough to think about such things later. Tonight is for cheer.

"Stan, you'll never guess who I ran into today," she calls from the entryway, fishing the card from her purse before hanging the bag along with her hat on the coatrack. "Mr. Robinson."

Stan doesn't reply.

She hurries into the living room. "Did you hear? I ran into Mr. Robinson."

He looks up at her from his armchair. "Who?"

Mimi turns down the volume on the radio. Sitting in her usual spot by the window, Halina throws Mimi a scowl, but she's too excited to care. "Mr. Robinson. You remember him. He was the team's traveling secretary when you played for the Reds."

"Gary?"

She nods and hands him the card. "He gave me his telephone number and said you should call him. He said he could float your name to the other secretaries in case a coaching position comes up."

Stan looks at the telephone number, then flips the card over. "You ran into him at Seeger's?"

"Yes. And, Stan, he said he thought with your record, you'd have a good chance."

"What were you doing at an auto repair shop?"

Mimi sighs. Of all the times to start caring about where she's been. "Are you listening to me, Stan? He might be able to help you get a job. A job in baseball."

"Is something wrong with the Packard?"

"No." She points at the card. "Are you going to call him?"

"If nothing's wrong with the Packard, why were you there?"

Mimi takes a step back. "What do you think, that I'm having an affair with one of the mechanics?" She immediately regrets her words. But Stan doesn't seem to notice the flush burning its way up her neck.

"No. I think you did something to my automobile, and I want to know what."

"This isn't about the goddamned Packard, Stan!" She winces, realizing the children are probably within earshot.

"Ojej," Halina says, and crosses herself. Mimi shoots her a glare, biting down on her tongue so she doesn't say anything else she'll regret.

This is nothing like how she thought the conversation would go. Stan should be excited. Grateful. Not hung up on their stupid automobile. No, not their automobile. *His*. And he didn't ask about her. If something happened to the Packard, it stands to reason something could have happened to its driver, too. But he's not the least bit concerned about her.

Her hands begin to tremble. From anger? Hurt? Mimi can't tell. Both have her on the verge of screaming. She balls her hands into fists at her side and takes a deep breath.

"The Packard is fine. There was a small dent in the fender, so I took it to Seeger's to be repaired. It's as good as new now. Are you going to call Mr. Robinson?"

Stan looks down at the card, then tosses it onto the side table beside his ashtray. "Next time something's wrong with the Packard, take it to McLeery's. They do better work."

His deadpan voice makes Mimi's emotions flare all the more. She eyes the ashtray and imagines throwing it against the wall. Imagines the ash blooming in the air and the glass shattering. Imagines the horrified expressions on Stan and Halina's faces. Imagines leaving the mess for them to clean up.

Instead, she turns around and leaves the room. Much more of this, though, and she just might make good on her imaginings.

CHAPTER 28

Mimi parks the Packard in front of a handsome, two-story brick home on Lake Park Avenue. Three white pillars support the sloped porch roof, matching the carved wood balustrade. She checks her makeup in the rearview mirror before getting out of the car, tempted to blot away her deep red lipstick. It's the perfect shade for her complexion, the salesclerk had assured her, and a sure bet for turning heads. But is that what she wants, to turn heads?

Mimi leaves the lipstick on, uncertainty be damned.

The soft hum of music and voices can be heard from the porch. She listens for a moment, trying to make out who's already here. Jo's laugh is unmistakable. So, too, is Roberta's warm, even tone. The other voices are too intertwined to differentiate. He might be here. He might not. But she's determined to have a good time, regardless.

Ada's daughter, Jennie, answers the door when Mimi knocks. Her pretty blond hair frames her face in soft waves. She smiles, and Mimi's nerves settle. "Mimi! Come in."

She takes Mimi's coat and points to the right, where the foyer opens to a large sitting room. There, Mimi finds most of the clinic staff already gathered. It's fun to see them in swanky evening wear for once instead of cotton smocks and white uniforms. Mr. Martin hands Mimi a cocktail, heavy on the scotch but smooth going down.

A glance around the room reveals several new faces. The handsome, dark-skinned man beside Roberta must be Abe, her husband. Jo and Annie have brought along men, too.

"Where's Stan?" Jo asks, when Mimi joins her and her beau on the damask-upholstered sofa.

"He wanted to come," Mimi lies. "But he caught the stomach flu."

"What a shame," Jo says.

"He'll be all right in a day or two."

If only that were true. Last week, when Mimi showed him the invitation to Ada's house party, Stan responded with a *humph*—as if the idea of going was too ridiculous to warrant a reply. He tossed the invitation onto the side table like it was junk. It landed beside his overflowing ashtray and the forgotten auto shop card with Mr. Robinson's telephone number.

Of course, Mimi tells Jo none of this and is grateful when the conversation moves on to other topics.

Ada stops by to say hello, but only long enough to point out the sumptuous platters of food she's set out on the table in the adjoining room and to remind her husband to refresh everyone's drinks. The lovely green chiffon dress she wears suits her just as well as her staid work attire.

Louis Piquett arrives next and, shortly after, Edna. But Mimi's eyes keep drifting to the door. Was it foolish to think Daniel would be invited, as well? He'd mentioned coming to Ada's house before for parties and picnics. All day, he's been on her mind—while picking out a dress and painting on lipstick, while pinning up her hair and spritzing on perfume—and her disappointment grows with each minute he doesn't appear. Even as a tiny part of her is relieved.

Then he arrives. Alone. Mimi washes down her mixed emotions with a long sip of her drink.

Ada introduces him to everyone as Mr. Moriarity, not Officer Moriarity. It's a cocktail party, not a deposition, of course. But Mimi wonders how many of those gathered know what he does for the clinic.

She watches as he accepts a drink from Mr. Martin, and the two men chat beside the unlit fireplace. They haven't spoken, she and Daniel, in almost two months. He's probably forgotten all about the kiss they shared in her car.

Finally, he glances her way, pinning her with a gaze that would put even Clark Gable to shame. Mimi's lips part, and she exhales softly. He hasn't forgotten. For now, though, they keep to their own sides of the room. Daniel talks to Mr. Martin and then Mr. Piquett. Mimi chats with Roberta and her husband, then falls into conversation with Edna. She catches him watching her, though. Feels the delicious prickle of his attention.

Ada reminds them all about the food again. As the others slowly shuffle into the dining room to fill their plates, Mimi lingers, pretending to admire a stone vase on the sitting room mantle.

Daniel comes up beside her. "You look breathtaking tonight," he whispers. The words send a pleasant skitter down her spine. It's been ages since a man complimented her like that.

"You clean up pretty well yourself." She gives his tie a playful tug, her hand dallying a breath too long before she remembers herself and turns back to the vase.

"You got the fender fixed, I see."

She nods.

"I told you I would have fixed it for you."

"I . . . wasn't ready to see you."

"And now?" His hand surreptitiously brushes her hip.

"Now . . . now I'm—"

"Go, go. Get some food," Ada says, coming up behind them.

Daniel steps away from Mimi and turns his dashing smile on Ada. "You don't have to tell me twice. It smells delicious." He saunters off toward the buffet, glancing over his shoulder at Mimi with a look that tells her he's hungry for more than just food.

Mimi doesn't move. Her feet have melded with the floorboards, and heat licks through her core.

"It was my mother's," Ada says.

It takes Mimi a minute to realize she's talking about the vase. "Oh . . . ah . . . it's beautiful."

"No, it's not," she says matter-of-factly. "Isn't worth much, either." She grabs it from the mantle and hands it to Mimi to see.

It's heavier than Mimi expected, its surface grittier. Ada points out a chip in the base that had been hidden from view.

"Cheap, broken, ugly," she says, taking it back from Mimi and returning it to its place on the mantle. "But it reminds me of home." Ada's eyes cut to the dining room, where Daniel stands serving himself at the buffet—then back to Mimi. "Sure, I could replace it with a cut crystal vase from Marshall Field's, but it wouldn't mean anything to me when I looked at it. Wouldn't remind me of the brisk highland air or the craggy stone bluffs or my mother's cock-a-leekie soup." She gives the vase a loving tap. "No, I wouldn't trade it in for the world." Then she loops her arm through Mimi's. "Come on, let's get something to eat."

Mimi's finishing her food when another set of guests arrive: Emily and Dr. Millstone. They walk arm-in-arm into the sitting room, and right away Mimi notices the unchecked glee in Emily's face. When their eyes meet, Emily nods and holds up her left hand. A diamond ring winks from her finger.

Mimi flashes her a smile. She'll get all the details of the engagement later. For now, it's enough to see her friend happy. Dr. Millstone looks happy, too. They join a few of the others in the dining room, releasing their hold on each other only long enough to fill plates of food.

As Mimi watches them, her joy sours into envy.

"You look like you could use another drink, Mrs. Lukas," Mr. Martin says, coming up beside the sofa where she's seated.

A drink won't fix what she's feeling, but she accepts his offer nonetheless. It's just as strong as the first. She takes a cautious sip, then another.

Jo and Jennie are seated beside her on the sofa. Edna relaxes in a nearby armchair. They're flapping their gums about something, but Mimi's long since lost track of the conversation.

Edna makes a remark, and Jo and Jennie laugh. A moment later, another peal of laughter, this time from the dining room. Mimi doesn't need to look to know it's Emily's. She gulps down more of her drink, but the burn only intensifies her envy. Her loneliness.

Across the room, Daniel catches her eye and nods toward the door. A shiver passes through her. One more sip to shore up her courage, then Mimi sets the half-finished cocktail aside. This is what she wants. The real reason she came tonight. The reason she wore her lace-cuffed stockings and new red lipstick. One kiss and all these ugly feelings will be forgotten.

Mimi gives a nod of her own. But before she can get up to say her goodbyes, Emily squeezes onto the sofa between her and Jennie.

"Is that an engagement ring?" Jo asks, pointing at Emily's hand.

"Well, I didn't want to steal all the attention tonight, but . . ."

Mimi does her best to listen while Emily delves into her tale. She feels Daniel's eyes on her, but she can't leave mid-story without seeming rude.

"Ten years, and you still love the man!" Jo cries when Emily's finished.

"Good for you," Edna says, then turns to Jo. "Some things in life are worth sticking with for the long haul."

"Some people, you mean," Jennie says in that quiet, dreamy way of the young. She reminds Mimi of Ginny. Reminds her of herself. At least of who she used to be.

"I guess so," Jo says. "Just be sure he doesn't make you wait another ten years before saying *I do*."

Emily smiles. "Henry and I have already picked a date for next summer."

"How thrilling!" Jennie says, scooting closer to Emily. "Do you know what you'll wear?"

The conversation moves into dresses and flowers and cakes, but Mimi's only half listening again. Edna and Jennie are right. Some people are worth the long haul.

She glances out the window at the darkened street. It's too late for her and Stan, though. He can't be bothered to care, and she's . . . dear God, she's about to sleep with another man.

Someone says her name, and she turns back to the women. "What?"

"What kind of wedding cake did you have?" Jennie asks.

It takes Mimi several seconds to wrangle her thoughts. White cake with buttercream frosting, that's what they'd had. Plain but delicious. Behind Jennie, the weathered vase on the mantle snags Mimi's eye. She stands. "I have to go."

Jennie stands, too. "Right now? Is everything all right?"

"Please give my thanks and apologies to your mother."

Mimi hurries out of the house. She's halfway down the steps when the door opens behind her.

"Your coat," Jennie says, handing it to her.

Mimi takes the coat and gives Jennie a quick hug. "Thank you."

"Are you sure everything's okay?"

Mimi nods, bounding down the remaining steps. It's not all right. But maybe, just maybe, it can be.

She's almost to the curb when the door opens again. She turns at the sound, expecting it to be Jennie with something else she's forgotten. It's not.

It's Daniel.

Their eyes meet, and her entire body feels his pull. A heartbeat later, she tears her gaze away, searching the darkness for the Packard. The porch steps creak, and his footfalls grow louder. She fights the urge to turn around. There—two houses down across the street—there's the Packard. Daniel grabs her arm before she can start toward it.

"Where are you going?"

"Home." She says the word like a prayer.

He drops her arm and rakes a hand through his hair. "I thought . . ."

"I can't."

"I see." His gaze lowers to the sidewalk.

Guilt twists inside her, but it's not enough to change her mind. She reaches out and cradles his cheek in her palm. "You're a good man, Daniel."

His hand covers hers, pressing it closer as he shakes his head.

"You are. You don't drive a fancy car. You don't wear expensive suits. You don't throw your money away on bookies. You do what you do for your family. Your girls. Your wife."

His eyes flicker back to hers, and she sees the pain in them.

"It's hard, I know. But you and I, we're just . . . lonely."

"I love you," he says.

"No, you love your wife. And I love my husband. Whatever this is between us, it's not worth hurting them."

He moves her hand from his cheek to his lips and kisses her palm. The heat she felt that day in the car stirs, but it's no match for her sudden resolve. As she tries to pull away, his hand tightens. Then he sighs and lets go.

"Goodbye, Daniel," she says, turning around without waiting for a reply. She can feel him watching her all the way to her car, hoping she'll turn around. A small part of her still wants to. But she starts the engine without looking back and drives away.

* * *

The living room light is still on when she arrives home. Thank God! She parks without bothering to check how close she is to the curb and hurries from the car as if that light might flicker out, and with it, her chances. Her heels click-clack over the pavers and up the steps at the same breakneck pace as her heart. She doesn't stop to haul Junior's bicycle from the lawn or straighten Penny's roller skates. Even the slightest hesitation, and she'll lose her nerve.

Inside, she throws her coat and purse at the rack on her way to the living room. "Midnight Serenade" plays softly on the radio. Both Stan and Halina are where she expects them, seated in their respective chairs, her slowly working her crochet hook, him flipping through a magazine. Neither glance up at her arrival.

"Mamo, I need a moment with my husband. Alone."

"But, I—"

"I'm not in the mood to fight with you," Mimi says, surprised at the firmness of her voice. "Please, just give us a few minutes."

Halina scowls but gathers up her crochet supplies and wintergreen oil and shuffles off.

Mimi turns her attention to Stan, who's looking at her now with that weary annoyance he so often wears these days. It's enough to make her hesitate. But just for a moment. Then her feet are moving again. She switches off the radio and drags over the ottoman, sitting so close her knees brush his.

Stan scoots back in his chair so their legs are no longer touching. "What's the deal, eh? I'm tired." He reaches toward the pack of cigarettes on the side table, but Mimi intercepts his hand.

"Please, don't. I have to tell you something, and I need you to listen. Really listen. Okay?"

"Fine," he says, sighing. He lowers his arm but doesn't pull free from her grasp, and Mimi doesn't let go.

"We're in trouble, Stan."

"If this is about me finding a job—"

"It's more than that. This family is in trouble. *You and I* are in trouble."

His nostrils flare, and he looks away. "Here we go with the melodrama. Our lives aren't like those washboard weepers you listen to on the radio, Mimi."

She takes him by the chin with her free hand and turns his head to face her again. The stubble on his jaw scratches at her skin. "Last year, after your accident, I went to the doctor and got a diaphragm so I wouldn't . . . so I could be sure I didn't get pregnant again."

There's a flicker of pain in his eyes as her words register. "You don't want to have any more of my children?"

"We were barely getting along as it was. A baby . . . a baby would only have made it worse."

"You should have talked to me about it first."

"I wanted to, but you were so angry all the time. And when you weren't angry, you were just . . . indifferent."

"You still should have told me."

Mimi nods. "I'm sorry. I'm sorry for a lot of things. I'm sorry I wasn't more sympathetic. More patient. But Stan, I was scared. Terrified. Not just about what the neighbors would think when they saw our new refrigerator being hauled away or the paint on our house chipping. Terrified that we'd end up in one of those shantytowns."

He shakes his head and pulls his hand away from hers. "This is what I mean—melodramatic."

"I've seen how people in the slums live. The choices they have to make. We're lucky we didn't end up like that."

"So this *is* about me finding a job."

Mimi sighs and starts yanking the bobby pins from her carefully styled hair. "Stan, you're miserable. And you're miserable to be around, too. Penny, Junior—they're afraid to even talk to you. They hide outside or in the basement so they don't have to hear you yell." She sees that flash of pain again in his eyes, but continues. "They don't laugh like they used to. Penny's getting into arguments with her friends. Junior destroyed Mrs. Davenport's flower bed twice this summer."

"That's because you're not around like a mother should be."

She jabs a fistful of bobby pins in his direction. "No, it's because their father takes no interest in them anymore." She pauses, her hand dropping to her lap. "And they're not the only ones you no longer take an interest in."

Stan snickers before turning away from her as if the conversation is boring him.

Mimi's heart beats fast again, a rising thud against her breastbone. Anger burns away her other emotions, and when she speaks, her voice is soft, flat, deadly. "I almost slept with another man tonight."

Stan's head whips around. "What?"

"And I'm starting to regret that I didn't."

His jaw tightens, but he says nothing.

"I wanted to. I've wanted to for weeks."

Stan's hands curl into fists as he draws in another breath. The rage in his eyes matches her own. It's the most alive she's seen him in months. "Why didn't you, then?" he bites out.

"Why? Why!" Mimi throws the bobby pins at him. "Because I love you, you idiot!" Hot tears stream down her face. "I love you and I want to fix this."

"I don't know how to fix this," he yells back at her. Then, so quietly she can barely hear him. "I don't know how to fix any of this. I made one little mistake. One little mistake. That's all it was." His voice rises again. "Coach was telling me to hold up at first, but I wanted to show 'em I was still good for more than a lousy single. I thought I could make it. Thought if I just ran fast enough. Pushed hard enough." He's crying now, too. He screws his face as if to hold back the tears, but they keep falling. "And then . . . just like that, it was all gone . . . I play the moment over and over again in my head. Maybe if I'd swung harder, reacted quicker, slid sooner. Because if I can't get something like that right, how can I get any of this right?" He gestures wildly around them.

Mimi's anger shatters. She scoots to the edge of the ottoman, fitting her legs between his, and cups his face in her hands. "I don't know. But the only way we'll figure it out is together."

CHAPTER 29

More tears flow that night, followed by *I love you*s. A kiss that rivals those of their early years. Then Mimi's diaphragm is put to good use.

She knows change won't happen overnight, but incrementally. In fits and starts. Yet by Christmas of that year, life in their household has indeed changed.

Stan is the first one dressed for Christmas Eve Mass. He smokes outside now, and only on occasion, and finishes his cigarette as the rest of the family piles into the Packard. The next day, he welcomes Penny onto his lap and listens intently as she tells him all about her new doll. Then, despite a fresh dusting of snow, he takes Junior outside so they can try out the boy's new baseball mitt. That evening, after the roasted goose and potatoes and green peas and rolls have gone around the table, he compliments Mimi's fine cooking.

For her part, Mimi gives him room to grieve. She finds ways to be encouraging without being pushy. When he wants to talk, she listens. Not the kind of listening she'd done before—half-hearted and distracted—but really listens. No judgment. No assumptions. No running through tomorrow's grocery list in her head.

These are small things, yes. But a change, nonetheless. A bigger change comes just after New Year's when Stan works up the nerve to call the number on the back of the auto shop card.

As luck would have it, the Cubs are looking for a new line coach, and the team's manager, Mr. Wilson, would like Stan to travel with them to Catalina Island for spring training and give the position a try. Suddenly, March can't come fast enough.

But the new year brings another change, well before March arrives, when Mimi receives another telephone call from her brother.

Ma is dead.

Mimi packs her black dress and hat in a daze while Halina readies the children. Stan's waiting behind the steering wheel when she shuffles out to the car. They drive all night through a blizzard, making it to the farm just before dawn. Stan carries the children one by one to the upstairs bedroom before falling asleep himself. Mimi's exhausted, too, but knows there's no point in lying down. A farm doesn't stop, even for death. So she seats herself on the worn living room couch and watches through the window as the sky lightens.

Ma's piano still sits in the corner of the room. Did she ever take up playing again? Singing? Not likely, considering her emphysema. Last year, when Mimi and the kids visited, Ma had tried to mutter her way through a few of the Easter service hymns only to wind up breathless and coughing. What a cruel turn of fate that she was robbed of the one thing that always seemed to bring her joy.

Soon, floorboards creak, and shuffling footfalls sound from the hallway. Mimi doesn't need to turn around to know it's her father. He's early. The sun's just a pale sliver on the horizon, and the chicken coop remains silent.

"We didn't wake you coming in, did we, Pa?" she asks when he passes through the living room en route to the front door.

He stops and shakes his head. "I was already up."

For a moment, she thinks he might come sit beside her. Might hold her hand or let her rest her head on his shoulder the way he had when she was young. Instead, he continues on to the door, stuffing his feet into his boots and shrugging on his coat. His movements are slower than she remembers, and he looks as if he's aged ten years since Easter. But maybe she was too focused on Ma to really notice him during that visit.

"Want some help?" she says.

He raises a brow.

"I'm not such a city slicker that I've forgotten how to feed the hens or milk a cow."

"Rosie will be round to do that."

She can't tell if he means the words as a jab or whether he's simply stating a fact, but she feels them just beneath her ribs, where her body's soft and unprotected. It's not that she doesn't like her sister-in-law, Rosie. But she can't help feeling like she's been replaced. Like she's an interloper now. Maybe she always was. Isn't that the nature of daughters? Was that why they were so quick to send Ginny away? Had it been one of her brothers, would Ma and Pa have acted differently?

It's a pointless question to follow. It couldn't happen to her brothers. One more way daughters are a liability.

Pa opens the door, but closes it again and turns back to her. "The undertaker will be round after lunch. You could"—he stops and swallows—"pick out something for her to wear."

"I will."

He nods, then opens the door again and stomps out into the frigid dawn.

There are only half a dozen dresses in her mother's wardrobe. Mimi takes out each one in turn, examines it in the growing light, then lays it on the bed. The faint scents of mothballs and lavender cling to the fabric, transporting Mimi back to all those afternoons spent with her mother in the kitchen or beside her in the garden or seated next to her at church.

Ma never was the affectionate type. Never doted on any of them, not even the boys. When Mimi had left for Chicago to begin nursing school, Ma waited in the Ford while Pa walked her to the train. With the whistle blowing, Mimi hurried aboard, stopping on the top step for a final wave. But Pa's attention was on the porter carrying her trunk to the baggage car. Ma's head was turned away from the platform, as if the nearby rows of corn were of more interest than Mimi's departure. She waited there as the train lurched into motion, one hand gripping the rail, the other hovering, ready to raise and wave should they look her way. Neither did.

They didn't approve of the city. Didn't see the point of an education beyond being able to read the Bible and subtract this year's seed prices from last year's earnings. But when she'd gotten to her room at the nurse's home and opened her suitcases, she found a box of Hershey's Kisses inside.

She looks now at the dresses on the bed, a dull ache spreading through her chest. The pale blue one with small white flowers that Mimi remembers from Easter. And her checkered gingham day dress. The one of black wool could be the one she wore to Grandmother's funeral, but Mimi isn't sure. The others are unfamiliar. Unanchored in her sea of memories.

They smell like her, though. They're cut in the same modest fashion she favored—high neckline and low hem. Have the same boxy shape. Maybe Rosie would be a better person to choose, just like she's a more reliable milker. But Pa asked *her* to choose, and even though she's no longer a child, she can't help but want to prove she's good for something.

Mimi settles on a plum-colored dress with long billowing sleeves and dark, opalescent buttons. Next, she rummages through Ma's drawers for a fresh set of underclothes. After sifting through a heap of wool stockings, she finally finds a pair of silk ones. There's a run in one of the knees, though. Mimi tosses the pair aside and searches for another. Her mother may be dead, but she'd haunt Mimi all the way to Chicago if Mimi handed the undertaker a pair of ruined stockings. In the end, Mimi slips upstairs and retrieves one of her own pairs. They might be a little tight, but Ma would much prefer that to a run.

She folds everything carefully and wraps the entire bundle in a clean flour sack. Ma has only one pair of dressy shoes, which Mimi polishes to a shine before stowing them in another sack. All that's left is a hat. Her navy wicker hat still hangs on a peg by the front door. But surely, she has another. Something she brought out for holidays and weddings. Hadn't she worn some sort of flowered affair at Easter?

Standing on her tiptoes, Mimi feels along the wardrobe's top shelf. First, she pulls down a long, slender box that contains a christening gown yellowed with age. Next is a small notebook with her mother's maiden name inked inside. Between its blank pages are pressed flowers that crumble into dust at the slightest touch. At last, in the far back corner, Mimi feels the round, smooth contours of a paperboard hatbox. She coaxes it forward with her fingertips, then pulls it down. Whatever's inside is too heavy to be a hat.

She pulls off the lid and finds several bundles of letters and a scattering of postcards inside. Pa will be back wanting breakfast soon.

Penny and Junior waking. But Mimi can't resist sitting down on the bed to sift through the box's contents.

There's a postcard stamped 1893 from Ma's older brother. A faded picture of the Chicago World's Fair adorns the front. There are stacks of letters from Mimi's grandmother. Others from her aunts. Another postcard from her uncle—this one with a picture of a tree-lined waterfront and the words *Door County, Wisconsin* written on the bottom. The top seam of each envelope has been neatly sliced, and Mimi can picture Ma seated at the kitchen table with her silver letter opener in hand.

Mimi doesn't read the messages scrawled on the backs of the postcards or remove any of the letters from their envelopes. Her mother was always a private person and wouldn't want Mimi nosing around in her things any more than necessary. She's about to reach for the lid when a tidy, familiar handwriting catches her eye.

She brushes aside a few more faded postcards to get a better look at a stack of envelopes beneath. They're tied together with coarse twine. Her hand freezes as she reaches for the stack. Not only her hand, but her entire body. It's several moments before her lungs release the air they've been holding, and her heart remembers to beat.

It's definitely handwriting she recognizes. And the name in the top left corner of the envelope confirms it: *Virginia Gunther.*

She unknots the twine with a shaky hand and picks up the first envelope. It's addressed to both Ma and Pa. The return address below her name is Des Moines. The year on the post office stamp reads 1918.

Ginny had written after being sent away? Why hadn't her parents told her? The omission feels like a lie—one told over and over again every time a new letter arrived. The envelope is like a hot coal that's been thrust into her hand. She wants to drop it and never let it go at the same time.

Unlike the other letters from Ma's family, the top seam hasn't been cut. Mimi gingerly flips it over, expecting to see a torn or loosened flap, but the envelope hasn't been opened at all. She grabs the entire stack and examines the seams. Not a single one has been ripped or sliced open.

Ma and Pa didn't read the letters? Not even after Ginny's death? She tries to give her parents the benefit of the doubt—grief and regret and all that. They may not have shown such feelings, but surely they felt them. Surely, they hadn't written her off the day her pregnancy was revealed.

With Ma dead, Mimi will never know. But the tenderness she felt only moments ago going through Ma's things is already burning away, leaving behind only bitterness.

Mimi returns to the top envelope and, after a glance through the open doorway and down the hall, slips her fingernail beneath the flap. The glue, brittle with age, releases easily. She stops again and listens. The cockerels and roosters are crowing now. What would Pa say if he caught her with the letters? What would she say to him?

She pulls out the letter and unfolds it. It's dated April 18, 1918—four days after Ginny left. Mimi runs her hand over the page before reading it. Brings it to her nose and smells it. Must and . . . rose water? Mimi knows it's her imagination. Ginny hadn't brought her bottle of drugstore perfume (the one she kept secreted at the back of her sock drawer) with her when she left. Mimi knows because she used to pull it out and sniff the nozzle those nights when she felt particularly alone.

She inhales again, and this time, there's only must. She lowers the paper from her nose. Her eyes settle on the page, taking in the shape of letters and words. Ginny always prided herself on the neatness of her handwriting. It wasn't enough to be a fast typist, she told Mimi. Your penmanship must be exemplary, too, if you want a shot at the best positions. At the time, Mimi had wished she'd play dolls with her instead of practicing with her pen.

Now, well . . . she smooths a hand over the page again. She's stalling. Afraid of what the letter might say. The look in Ginny's eye, when she spied Mimi watching from the hall as their mother cursed the swell of her belly, said it all: *How could you?*

She hasn't cried once since her brother called, but tears now well in her eyes. She takes a steadying breath and forces herself to read.

Dear Father and Mother,

The head matron urged me to write and tell you of my safe arrival at the home. It's a big brick building on the edge of town, about an hour's walk from the train station. There are four other girls with whom I share a room and twenty girls in total. You'll be happy to know we're kept busy throughout the day with chores and such. All the cooking and cleaning and mending is done by us girls. Sunday morning, we gathered in the downstairs sitting room for a visit from the pastor. Even though we weren't in a proper church and the pastor is a Methodist, the service was much like home. We gather in the evening, too, and one of the house staff reads from the bible before bed.

The food isn't bad here either. Not like farm cooking but edible.

Your Daughter,
Virginia

P. S. I'm sorry. Can I please come home?

Mimi turns the page over, but there's nothing on the back. Except for the very last line, the letter is so . . . sterile. No trace of Ginny's bright personality. But the postscript. Mimi's eyes had dried by the time she reached it, only to be flooded again.

Ginny's voice rings in Mimi's head. *I'm sorry. Can I please come home?* It's her older sister's voice, yes, but also the voice of a frightened fifteen-year-old. One who, for all her worldly affectations, knew so little about life.

The bitterness Mimi feels toward her mother deepens, knowing Ginny's question went unanswered. After another few letters, Ginny would have taken their parents' silence as answer enough and stopped asking.

Yet there are at least a dozen letters in the stack, so she kept writing, even in the face of that silence. Perhaps it was some requirement of the home. Mimi can imagine the staff patrolling the sitting room as the girls sat with their pens and paper, urging them to tell their families how well they were getting along. A kind of penance for their sins.

Mimi isn't sure she wants to read more of that. More words that aren't really Ginny's.

Footsteps sound on the front porch, and Mimi hastily stuffs the letter back in its envelope. The front door opens, whining on rusty hinges.

"Mimi?"

It's her sister-in-law, Rosie.

"Mimi? Do you need some help getting breakfast on?"

"I'll be right there," she calls, swiping at her eyes and searching for the box's lid.

From the front room, she hears the door close and Rosie stamp her feet on the rug. Mimi finds the lid at the foot of the bed but doesn't return Ginny's letters to the box before closing it. Those she shoves beneath the strap of her garter belt, as Rosie's footfalls sound in the hallway. She's not sure she can read any more of them. But she can't let them go, either.

She's straightening her skirt just as Rosie enters.

"You poor dear," Rosie says, sitting beside her on the bed. "I've been crying all morning, too. At least she's not suffering anymore and is with God in Heaven."

Mimi nods, even though her tears aren't for Ma.

CHAPTER 30

Three weeks later, back home in Chicago, Stan sits at the kitchen table as Mimi fries a ham steak. She'll throw a few eggs into the pan after the ham is done, but there isn't time for potatoes. Instead, she cuts a few slices of bread for the toaster.

"They had a pretty middling season last year," he says to her. "They certainly can play better on the road." Last week, Mr. Robinson dropped off a notebook with page after page of numbers—everything from how many games the Cubs won last season and by how many hits, to how many strikeouts their pitchers threw, to how many runs each player boasted. Stan has been studying it ever since.

"Who were the best hitters?"

"Jim Gleeson had a knockout year, but we traded him to the Reds."

Mimi likes how he says *we*, even if he's not part of the team yet. That will depend on how things go during spring training. But his chances are good, according to Mr. Robinson. And Mimi's just glad to see him engaged with life again.

"Hank Leiber had a pretty good season, too. You remember him. He used to play for the Giants."

"Mmm," she says, flipping the ham steak. "What position?"

"Center field."

"Sure, I remember him." But she doesn't. He's thrown dozens of names at her in the last week. Some she recalls. Most she doesn't. Either way, she wants to keep him talking.

She hadn't realized how important it was to belong to something. It's obvious now in the way Stan pores over that notebook.

In two weeks, he leaves for Catalina Island. She's nervous about being apart when they've only just found their stride again. Nervous, too, that he won't get the position. But she tries not to show it.

She moves the ham steak from the skillet to a plate, then cracks four eggs into the pan.

"Kids, breakfast," she calls down the hall, before starting the toaster. A glance at the clock above the table reveals it's later than she thought. She hauls the children's lunch sacks out of the icebox along with her own, then hurries back to the stove to flip the eggs. The toaster chimes, and she feeds it two more slices of bread.

"Remind your mother about the casserole in the icebox. She can heat it for dinner."

"You're leaving?"

"I'm due at work in half an hour." She sets the ham and eggs on the table, followed by a stack of toast. "Make sure the children leave for school on time."

Stan grabs her arm and tugs her onto his lap. He trails a line of kisses from her collarbone to her ear. "Don't go."

"I have to. I'll be late." But she lingers a moment longer, laughing as he nips her earlobe. Part of her burns to stay. To telephone the office and say she's got the flu. To spend the day in bed with Stan, making love and listening to him rattle off baseball numbers.

Another part of her is eager to go. The clinic is the only place she's entirely free of the strange mix of grief and anger she's felt since returning home from her mother's funeral. The only place she can slip free of her role as wife, as mother, and just be herself.

She turns her head and kisses him, then breaks free of his grasp.

Stan sighs, giving her a swat on the rear as she straightens her uniform. "Once the Cubs sign me, you won't need this silly job anymore."

"It's not silly."

"You know what I mean."

She turns away to hide her frown, grabbing her lunch from the counter. She's been so concerned with getting Stan back to his old self, Mimi hasn't thought about after. Something between panic and sadness stirs inside her at the thought of leaving the clinic. But she pushes it down. They can have that conversation later, when things aren't still so delicate between them. When he returns from California, job in hand.

For now, she just wants to enjoy the happy normalcy they've managed to find again.

"Do you have any questions?" Mimi asks.

The woman looks down at the card of instructions Mimi's given her and shakes her head.

"You can rest longer if you like."

Another shake of the head. She's a slight woman with dark hair and olive skin. She's said all of five words to Mimi since waking from the gas. Not enough for Mimi to place the accent. Sicilian, maybe? Greek? Mimi takes her hand and waits for the woman's eyes to meet hers before saying, "The important thing is to telephone if you feel unwell. All right? The number's right there on the card. And don't forget to come back in three days so we can check up on you."

The woman gives a weak smile. "*Sì*, yes."

Mimi walks her out to the reception room, where another dark-haired woman waits for her. Sisters, she thinks, her heart squeezing.

"Grazie," the woman says to Mimi as they leave.

She waits until they're out the door before glancing at her watch. It's only 11:15, but already her stomach is grumbling. She was so distracted by Stan's kisses that morning (and his comment afterward about giving up her "silly" job), she forgot to grab a piece of toast on the way out.

"When's our next patient due?" she asks, turning to the reception desk.

Jo looks down at the schedule book. "Our eleven-thirty canceled, so . . . not for another hour."

Mimi's grateful for the short reprieve. She scarfs down the apple from her lunch sack while chatting with Jo at the reception desk, then returns to the back of the clinic to get things ready for the next patient.

She hums "Only Forever" as she gathers the dirty linen and wipes down the cot in the anteroom. Hopefully she and Stan can pick up where they left off when she gets home tonight. After finishing up in the anteroom, she checks the gas level in the canisters and length of time left on the sterilizer. It's nice not to be in a rush for once, and she takes her time tidying the instrument cabinet.

Aside from her humming and the soft whir of the sterilizer, the back rooms are quiet. Roberta left after their last procedure to run a few errands over her lunch break. Dr. Millstone returned with Emily to his clinic in Grand Crossing to see his regular patients. Dr. Snyder, who's scheduled this afternoon, has yet to arrive. Likely, he'll stride into the clinic as they finish strapping down and shaving the next patient. He's a good doctor but doesn't like to waste time.

The quiet is soon broken by voices in the reception room. Mimi hopes it's Roberta, so she can hand off the last tasks and eat the rest of her lunch. It's been unusually warm for early February, enough to melt some of the January snow. Maybe she'll take her sandwich and walk to the river, though she'll have to be careful of the puddles of slush and mud. The door to the back rooms opens, and the voices draw near. It's not Roberta, but Ada and Mr. Piquett. They carry on their conversation down the hall to Ada's office and close the door.

Mimi sighs and returns to her work. A moment later, though, another voice sounds in the reception room. A man's voice, and one she doesn't recognize. With it comes the clomp of several pairs of feet. Mimi freezes.

"Where are your customers?" the voice bellows.

Mimi thinks of Jo and hurries toward the reception room. Ada and Mr. Piquett have heard the voice, too, and beat Mimi to the door. She follows after them, her blood turning as cold as Lake Michigan the moment she enters. More than a dozen policemen are squeezed into the room. She quickly scans their faces and is relieved to find that the short officer with pastrami breath isn't among them.

"Where are your customers?" the officer at the front of the group asks again, looking from Jo, to Ada, to Mr. Piquett. He's tall, with strawberry blond hair and small, pale eyes. Above the badge on his chest is a gold nameplate that reads, *Captain Duffy.*

It takes all Mimi's courage not to slink back the way she came.

"I don't know what you're talking about," Ada says, her cool, even voice easing the worry twisting inside Mimi's gut. This isn't the first time the police have shown up, Mimi reminds herself, and she's not alone. There are no patients here to bully and interrogate. No panicking doctor. Just her, Ada, Jo, and Mr. Piquett, and they've all been through this before.

Captain Duffy nods toward the open doorway behind Mimi. Two officers push past her into the back rooms of the clinic.

"Your men are not allowed back there," Ada says, the pitch of her voice rising slightly.

"My men can go wherever they please."

"Have you got a warrant?" Mr. Piquett asks.

"We don't need a warrant to go into a place like this anymore."

A clatter sounds from the back. No doubt the men are wreaking havoc in the procedure room. The instruments she just brought out will have to be resterilized. The linen washed. The floors scrubbed clean of their muddy boot prints. She and the other nurses will be scrambling all week to make up for the time lost to this intrusion.

"If your men damage my equipment," Ada says, "I'll hold the department liable."

Captain Duffy smirks and saunters over to the reception desk. Jo stands and backs away at his approach. He picks up the schedule book and flips it open. His smug expression falls a little as he glances down at the coded entries. "What is this? What does this all mean?"

"It's just a schedule book," Jo says.

"I know that. But it's written in gibberish."

Jo shrugs and glances at Ada. The look that passes between them seems to say, *Don't say anything more.*

Captain Duffy throws the book down on the desk, then comes around to the back and rummages through the drawers. He finds Jo's purse and dumps out its contents, his face flushing with what Mimi suspects is both irritation and embarrassment when only a wallet, compact, lipstick, and package of Kotex tampons fall onto the desk.

One of the officers returns from the back. He catches Captain Duffy's eye and shakes his head. The captain's cheeks flush an even deeper red. "We know you do criminal abortions here. Where do you keep your records?"

"I told you," Ada says. "I don't know what you're talking about."

"Fine," he says. "You don't want to talk to me, you can talk to the state's attorney." He picks up the telephone on Jo's desk and dials a number. "This is Captain Duffy. I need the wagon and a moving truck at the State Lake Building." A frown crosses his face. "When do you think? Now!" He slams down the receiver.

"Last I checked, this was still a country of laws," Mr. Piquett says, his voice as unperturbed as Ada's. "On what grounds do you mean to detain us?"

"Conspiracy."

"Conspiracy?"

"Conspiracy to commit abortion."

Mr. Piquett chuckles. "On whom? I don't see any pregnant women here. Do you?"

Captain Duffy's nostrils flare in an almost laughable way. He's like the cartoon rendering of a policeman in the funny pages. But men like him are still dangerous, and Mimi isn't sure it's wise to rile him further.

Ada seems to agree. She puts a hand on Mr. Piquett's arm and says to the captain, "If the state's attorney would like to speak to us, we're happy to oblige. But surely you can do us the courtesy of allowing us to take a cab to his office. I have a son in the service and a daughter in school. There's no need to treat us like abject criminals."

"You are criminals as far as I'm concerned. You'll go in the wagon."

Ada flashes him a contemptuous look—the kind that could melt winter ice—but doesn't say anything more.

Captain Duffy instructs his men to handcuff Mimi and the others, then corrals them in the corner of the reception room. While they wait for the police wagon to arrive, the policemen dismantle the office. They bag every scrap of paper from the desk, empty the contents of the cashbox, and even take the pictures from the walls.

Who knows what sort of damage they're doing in the back. From the sounds of things—breaking glass, clattering metal—they aren't taking much care. Without their equipment, it will take longer than a few days to be up and running again. Some women can't wait that long, leaving them no option but to turn to less skilled hands—or worse, their own.

Mimi shudders at the thought and tries to block out the policemen's ruckus. These men, with their dirty boots and billy clubs, are like vandals. Each messy print they leave on the floor, each nick in the desk, each piece of equipment they break, feels like a personal affront. A violation. An unwelcome hand sliding over her skin. She's almost glad when the wagon arrives, and she no longer has to bear witness to it all.

The clock in the state's attorney's office reads twelve-thirty when they arrive. Strange, so much has happened in so little time. Roberta will have returned from her errands by now, and Dr. Snyder will have arrived. Their next patient. Hopefully they all saw the police cars parked alongside the curb and steered clear of the building.

Though it isn't the same office she was taken to before, it looks nearly identical. Dark wood paneling. Generic watercolor prints. Hard wooden chairs. The secretary is an older woman this time, with thick glasses and unpainted lips pressed together in a no-nonsense expression.

Mimi, seated at the far end of the row of chairs, tries to mirror Ada's straight, assured posture.

"They'll likely question us separately," Ada says quietly when Captain Duffy moves out of earshot to talk to the secretary. "Don't tell them anything."

Mimi and Jo both nod.

"The state's attorney hasn't any legal grounds to compel you to talk," Mr. Piquett adds. "He's skating on thin ice here, and he knows it. With any luck, he'll turn us loose before supper."

But luck, it turns out, isn't on their side. Like the last time Mimi was here, the state's attorney leaves them to wait for over an hour before opening his double-wide office doors and sauntering out. He's an average-looking man, the kind Mimi passes every day on the street and never looks twice at. His hair is thinning at the top. His bulbous nose a shade redder than the rest of his face. His pant legs bunch around his ankles, though certainly a man in his position could afford a proper tailor.

He glances at them with a look of practiced disinterest, then strolls over to his secretary, leaning on her desk with his back to them. They talk quietly for several minutes. Long enough for Mimi to grow bored with the charade. Captain Duffy left shortly after depositing them here, but his second-in-command remains. After the state's attorney tires of gabbing with his secretary, he goes and speaks to the officer. Midway through their conversation, the officer points at Ada, and the other man nods. But it's Jo he calls to his office first.

Mimi watches the hands of the clock tick away as Jo remains behind the closed doors. Her nerves have come alive again, a harrying buzz beneath her skin. Last time, the attorney didn't interview any of them. Not really. He just let them go. That, she knows now, was thanks to Daniel. But where is Daniel now?

Perhaps he's at least partly to blame for her nerves. She hasn't seen him since that night four months ago at Ada's party. Surely, he doesn't hold a grudge against her. In walking away, she did them both a favor. But maybe she should have tried to see him again and smooth over any hurt feelings. In truth, she hadn't trusted herself in those early days. Things were improving with Stan, but it wasn't an overnight change. It was slow and sometimes painful for them both.

Now, however, she can scarcely believe she let Daniel kiss her and kissed him back.

Still, relief wins out over any consternation when he finally arrives. He first speaks to the officer, then the secretary. Both nod in deference to whatever he's saying, though the secretary's lips pinch together more tightly. He doesn't linger after, but as he exits, his eyes lock with Ada's, and he gives a slight, almost imperceptible nod. Then they slide to Mimi and soften. There's no grudge or hard feelings in his gaze, just a flicker of longing.

She's all the more certain of his feelings when, shortly after he leaves, the secretary brings them paper cups of water and begrudgingly allows each of them a turn at the telephone to call their families.

"One minute's all you get," she tells Mimi when it's her turn. "And I'll be listening, so no funny business."

Mimi's grateful when it's Stan who answers. His steady voice is a further balm for her nerves. She hates to lie, but there's no sense in worrying him, so she gives the same excuse as last time about needing to stay late to help on the ward.

"When will you be home?" he asks her.

"I'm not sure. Tomorrow morning at the latest."

He sighs, and she can't help but think back to his comment this morning about her silly job as they say their goodbyes.

Jo returns soon after, looking like she's drunk spoiled milk. She slumps into the chair beside Mimi's and crosses her arms and legs. The state's attorney beckons for Mr. Piquett to follow him into his office and closes the door behind them.

"Are you all right?" Mimi whispers to Jo.

Jo nods but doesn't meet her eye.

"He kept you for an awfully long time." She hands Jo the rest of her water. Jo's hand trembles when she takes the cup.

"He's not like the fellow last time," Jo says after gulping down the water. "That man didn't seem to care one way or the other if I talked or what I said. But this fellow"—she juts her chin to the set of closed doors—"he's slippery. The kind of fellow that plays it cool all evening, then throws a fit if you refuse him a goodnight kiss."

Mimi hadn't dated many men before Stan, but she knows the type.

"Did you . . . talk?"

Jo meets her eye for the first time and shakes her head.

Mimi doesn't press her further, especially after she sees the secretary eyeing them with a scowl.

Mr. Piquett is out in half the time Jo was. But twice during his interrogation, Mimi could hear raised voices through the door. Whether it was Mr. Piquett shouting or the state's attorney, she couldn't tell. Maybe both. Regardless, Mr. Piquett doesn't seem very rattled as he walks back to his seat. Then again, considering he associated with bank robbers and did time in a federal penitentiary, it'd probably take an awful lot to rattle him.

The state's attorney doesn't look rattled, either. He fiddles with his nose a moment, pinching and tweaking it as if it might itch, then points at Mimi. She glances at Ada, who gives her a reassuring nod, and then at Jo. Her friend's still hunched and sickly looking. Instead of fear, it sparks a flame of anger inside Mimi. It's one thing to work over a man like Mr. Piquett. Quite another to do it to someone like Jo.

She follows him into his office, and he closes the door behind them, gesturing to a chair opposite a massive polished wood desk. Everything atop it—from the pen tray to the lamp to the sheaf of stacked papers—seems to be aligned just so, tidy and uniform, each item parallel and equidistant to the next.

"Please sit down, Mrs. . . ."

Mimi sinks slowly into the chair and doesn't reply.

"Come, now. I'll find out your name soon enough."

When she remains silent, he shrugs and sits in the plush, leather-upholstered chair behind the desk. He opens a notebook, flipping through several ink-filled pages before arriving at a blank one.

Were those notes he took during his questioning of Jo and Mr. Piquett? Mimi's pulse ticks faster. Her palms are suddenly sweaty. She moves to wipe them on her skirt and finds him watching her. She stops. This is what he wants. She straightens, her anger sharpening, and claps her hands in her lap. Jo said she hadn't talked, and Mimi believes her. Those pages of notes might have been taken from his talk with Mr. Piquett, but if they are, they're not useful. Mr. Piquett's too smart for that.

"I'm one of the assistant state's attorneys, Mr. Papanek," he says, taking his time in selecting a pen from the tray. "And you? You're a nurse. . . ? No need to answer. It's plain from your uniform. Unless . . ." He sets the pen atop the open notebook and leans back in his chair. "Unless you're impersonating a nurse."

Mimi's jaw clenches before she can catch herself.

"I thought not. I'm a good judge of people, see? But I had to ask. You never know with these criminal operations."

Criminal operations. The words sour her stomach, but she keeps her face neutral.

"How long have you been employed there, at the clinic?"

Mimi breaks from his gaze and lets her eyes wander around the room. The dark wood wainscoting carries over from the other room, but above it, the walls are painted the same forestry green color her brother wore in France. Had Mr. Papanek served, too? He certainly looks the right age. What will happen if America joins Europe's new war? Will men like him, like her brother, be called to serve again? What about Stan? Her interlaced fingers tighten around each other. Thank God Junior's just a boy.

"Ma'am."

Mimi turns her attention back to Mr. Papanek.

"I'm sorry, did you say something?"

His lips flatten, and she feels a stab of satisfaction.

"Ma'am, I think you've underestimated the trouble you're in here."

"Oh?"

"Conspiracy to commit abortion is a felony."

She looks down and brushes an invisible speck of dirt from her uniform, hoping to appear bored even as her pulse is bounding again. It had taken Daniel all of fifteen minutes to convince the last state's attorney to drop the case against the clinic. Mr. Papanek might take longer, but what had Daniel said? Everyone has their price.

The thought is enough to calm her, and she meets his eyes again. He tries a different technique—painting her as a hapless victim caught up in Mr. Piquett's sweeping abortion ring. She has to stop herself from correcting him. Of course he would assume a man was in charge of things.

Next, he tries to bargain with her, promising she can go free if she'll just tell him where the clinic's records are kept. Then he turns threatening again. She'll never be able to work as a nurse again if she's convicted, he tells her. When that doesn't work, he spends what seems like twenty minutes straight (the walls are notably bare of a clock) asking variations on the same question, all angled to get her talking about the patient records.

Mimi stays silent through it all. Clearly, he hasn't guessed she's a mother and used to a litany of questions. At one point, she reaches out as if to admire the brass lamp on his desk, running her fingers down the beveled stand and moving it ever so slightly to the right. Mr. Papanek tries to carry on but loses track of what he's saying. He leans forward and straightens it before continuing.

Finally, Mr. Papanek stands, seeming tired of her silence, and leads her back to the row of hard chairs in the adjoining room where the others wait. Ada is eyeing her expectantly, and Mimi gives her a tiny nod. Ada smiles. She's next in line for Mr. Papanek's questioning and follows behind him to the office with a slow, dignified step.

The doors close, and Mimi glances at the clock. It's ten minutes to five. By the time Mr. Papanek's doors open again, it's half past six. Mimi's stomach is grumbling. She hasn't eaten anything but that apple all day. Now that he's finished questioning them all, she hopes they'll be released. Or, if not, at least taken to jail, where she can expect a meal. Not a good meal, but even stale crackers and watered-down soup sound good right now.

As if Mr. Papanek can read her mind, he says to the four of them, "Hungry? I know I am." Then he turns to his secretary. "It's going to be a long evening, Mrs. Larson. I think I'll run to Spiegelman's Deli. Shall I bring you back a sandwich and maybe some potato salad?"

Mrs. Larson replies in the affirmative. The police officer who's been with them since they arrived accepts Mr. Papanek's offer of a sandwich, too. He doesn't ask Mimi or the others.

After Mr. Papanek returns from the deli, he leaves his office doors open as he eats his sandwich. It looks and smells delicious, as do Mrs. Larson's and the officer's, and Mimi's stomach churns with longing. When he finishes eating, he makes a telephone call, speaking loudly enough for them to know he's talking with Captain Duffy at Central Station. Then he calls each of them into his office again for another round of questioning.

It's nearly eleven before he finally gives up and tells the police officer to take them to jail. Mimi's heart sinks at the idea of another night stuck behind bars. She'd give anything for a warm meal and soft bed. But she doesn't show it as the officer leads them away.

Unlike before, Mimi and the others aren't thrown unceremoniously into a cell. This time, they're properly booked—names recorded and pictures taken. Ada doesn't look concerned, so Mimi tries not to be, either. But as the camera's bulb flashes and she's led away half-blind to the women's holding cell, she can't shake the disquieting feeling something is different. There's a record of her arrest now. Photographic proof. But records disappear, she reminds herself. And even if hers doesn't, in a city like Chicago, it will be buried beneath a hundred other records in a week's time.

Won't it?

CHAPTER 31

"That shirt looks nice," Mimi says. It's surreal to be here in the bedroom with Stan after having been released from jail only a few hours before. Stan, of course, thinks she spent the night working an extra shift at the hospital, not on a hard bench in a foul-smelling Central Station jail cell.

"It's too tight in the middle."

"I can see about taking it out a bit."

Stan unfastens the buttons and shrugs out of the sleeves. "No. It's no good." He tosses the shirt atop a steadily growing pile of clothes that don't fit or aren't right for the balmy California weather. Meanwhile, the stack of clothes that *are* suitable for his upcoming trip to Catalina Island for the Cubs' spring training could fit in a sugar sack.

"Won't you be given a uniform to wear anyway?"

"Yeah, but I'll need something for evenings. And meetings." He reaches into the wardrobe for another shirt.

Mimi rubs the bridge of her nose and sighs. Beneath the heaps of trousers and socks and sweaters, the bed—and the much-needed sleep it promises—calls to her. Even with Ada and Jo as cellmates, Mimi hadn't slept a wink last night. In the morning, they were brought before a judge and released on bail (paid by Mr. Martin). As they exited the jail, Ada reassured Mimi and Jo there was nothing to worry about. Her connections—by whom Mimi assumed she meant Daniel—were already working to smooth things over.

Stan huffs, and she's drawn back to the present.

"That one fits well," she says, even though her tired eyes can barely focus.

"I don't know, Mimi. I've got to look the part."

"You will. What about the blue suit you wore at Christmas?"

"It's mohair. Too hot."

"What about the navy suit? That's lightweight and cool."

"Sure, but I need more than one."

Barring the blue period after his accident, when he wore the same old undershirt and wrinkled trousers, Stan had always been a neat dresser. Not preening, exactly, but certainly a dandy. They joked that he dog-eared more pages in the catalogs than Mimi. But it had always come easily to him. Not something he fussed over.

Mimi knows it's nerves causing him to fret. He hasn't said so, but she can tell how much this shot means to him. A lifeline tossed to a drowning man. She ought to be more patient. More thoughtful. What does an assistant baseball coach wear to spring training?

It doesn't help that he's not as trim as he was when he was playing. She's already got a stack of trousers and two suit coats to let out. He's still handsome. So much so, she feels that old stirring of unease—the kind that sat like a stone in her stomach whenever he played a long stretch of away games. It wasn't Stan she didn't trust, but all the pretty girls—younger girls—who liked to sit along the first-base line and bat their eyes at whatever player was at the plate.

She used to tell him, *keep your eye on the ball*—another joke between them and one she won't be making this time. Not when she was the one whose eye strayed.

"What about heading to the Loop tomorrow?" Mimi says. "Mandel Brothers is bound to have something. A new start like this deserves a new outfit."

Stan's facing away from her, but their eyes meet in her vanity mirror, and he frowns. He's been funny about money lately. He never minded asking her to buy cigarettes when they could barely afford bread, but now that they've got a few spare dollars in the bank again, he doesn't want to spend it. Not on movie tickets or an evening out or, apparently, a new suit of clothes.

"I know they'll still have their winter fashions, but I'm sure you can find something. Think . . . Humphrey Bogart or Gary Cooper. Hollywood's just a stone's throw from Catalina, after all." She dredges up her best smile. "Wouldn't it be something if you met them at the casino and were wearing the same suit?"

"Gary Cooper doesn't wear ready-made clothes."

"You don't know that."

"Besides, I'm not spending your money."

Mimi sinks onto the bed, stunned. That's what this is all about? "It's not my money. It's *our* money."

Stan grabs the last shirt in his wardrobe, its empty hanger making a high-pitched singing sound as it rocks back and forth on the rod.

"And what, the last eleven years before you broke your leg, I was spending *your* money?"

"That's different," he grumbles. "The natural way of things."

Mimi rises to her feet again. She didn't sit all night in jail to have him tell her the hard-earned money she made was no good. Hell, she's become a goddamned criminal to keep this family afloat! She can't say that, of course. He'd insist she quit right away. Besides, in a few weeks, all this trouble with the law will blow over, just like last time. Just like Ada said.

"Now you listen to me, Stanislaw Lukasewicz," she says, her voice edged with anger. Only Halina calls him that, and only when she, too, is angry. Mimi catches his eye in the mirror again and sees she has his attention. "I'm going to get the paper, and we're going to sit down and look at the weekend advertisements. You're going to pick out a suit. And shirt. And a new hat while you're at it. I don't care if it's what Gary Cooper would wear or not. But tomorrow after church, we're going downtown, and *I'm* going to buy it for you with *my* money. Money that I worked hard to earn. Money that's just as good as yours. Got it?"

Stan looks chastened. He nods.

"Good," she says brightly, turning on her heels to fetch the paper from the living room. When she returns, she hands half the pages to Stan. "Start looking."

He gives her a mischievous grin. "You're kind of cute when you're bossy like that."

Mimi can't help but smile, too, even though she's far too tired to entertain the idea of putting in the diaphragm and making love tonight. She sits on the edge of the bed with her section of the newspaper. Stan sits down also, pushing his shirts to one side of the chair and resting his feet beside her on the bed, like he's settling in for a leisurely read.

"Your socks stink," she says.

He responds by wiggling his toes and moving his feet closer so they brush against her hip. She bats at them with the newspaper but doesn't scoot away. She'll take smelly feet over bickering and cold indifference any day.

"The Bears just dropped their quarterback," he says.

"We're looking for suits, remember?"

"Oh, yeah."

She turns her attention to her own section. Most of the ads are toward the back, so she flips through the first pages quickly, stopping cold on page eight when a headline snags her eye.

Abortion Suspects Quizzed After Raid on Loop Office

Her heart stumbles, tripping over itself before settling into a frantic rhythm. She glances over at Stan. His attention is still fixed on the paper—probably that article about the Bears. Thank God she'd handed him that section instead of this one. She angles the paper away from his view and reads on.

The office of a physician at 190 North State Street was raided yesterday by the Central District Police. According to Assistant State's Attorney Samuel Papanek, he intends to present evidence to the grand jury that abortions had been performed there.

Two women office employees and a nurse were taken into custody and held pending an investigation of seized office records. Another suspect, disbarred attorney Louis Piquett, was also apprehended. Piquett, who was formerly imprisoned in a federal penitentiary for harboring a member of the notorious Dillinger gang, insisted he had no connection to the office and was freed.

There's a nudge at her hips, and she startles, closing the newspaper.

"What are you reading?" Stan asks, poking her with his toes again.

"Ah . . . er . . . nothing."

"We're looking for suits, remember?"

He says it playfully, but Mimi's mouth is so dry, all she can do is nod. She opens the paper, glancing at the article again before hurriedly flipping to the next page. Suits . . . spring training . . . Catalina Island. She says the words to herself as she stares at the spread of black and white before her. But it's no use. Her eyes can't focus, let alone her brain.

News of the raids hasn't appeared in the paper before. Thank God her name wasn't listed alongside Mr. Piquett's. She remembers the nod Daniel gave Ada yesterday. He's probably already convinced Mr. Papanek to drop the case. And, no matter what the article said, there hadn't been any records at the office to seize. Ada's too smart for that. No records. No case.

But the words *grand jury* scare Mimi—even if she's not entirely sure what a grand jury is. And she can't quite chase away the feeling that this isn't the end of things, but just the beginning.

CHAPTER 32

Mimi returns to the office the following Friday. Three chairs remain in the reception area. Everything else is gone. The back rooms fared little better. The police took the cot, the linen, the instruments, the gas canisters, even the sterilizer. They likely would have taken the exam table if it wasn't so heavy.

Her purse and coat are missing from the hall closet, along with everyone else's. The men didn't even leave behind her lunch. By now the food will have long since spoiled. Hopefully it's stinking up the entire Central Station evidence room.

The worst part is the mess the police left behind. The muddy boot prints, the shattered glass from the broken supply cabinet, the spilled iodine condensed into sticky goo. She picks up a trampled sanitary belt from the floor, rights a toppled trash bin, and tosses the belt inside. She can hear what the officers would say in defense of themselves: don't break the law, and we won't break your things. But the words ring hollow to her. Life distilled to a simple adage doesn't reflect life at all.

Mimi isn't the only one Ada's called to come into the office. Jo, Roberta, Edna, Annie—they all arrive shortly after Mimi and, after a few gasps of shock, begin sifting through the ruins of the place. There's no easy chatter today. No teasing and laughter. Just a sort of stunned silence.

Soon, Ada calls them all together in the reception room.

"By now, you're all aware of what happened last week. And I

imagine some of you might be worried—for your safety, for your jobs. But this isn't any different than before."

"They've taken all our furniture," Edna says, her normally calm voice edged with alarm. "They've never done that before."

Ada purses her lips. She has the stern look of a mother with no patience for a child's hysterics. "True, and I don't expect those brutes to be returning it anytime soon. But furniture and equipment can be replaced."

"Surely, they've got their eye on this place now. Who knows when they'll return," Jo says.

"I'm handling the police. But anyone who wants to quit is free to do so."

Mimi glances at the others. Each looks uncertain, like they're waiting for someone else to swallow their nerves and commit. Stay or go. It doesn't matter which, so long as they don't have to decide themselves.

A strange panic rises in Mimi. Not that the police will return or that the investigation against her will continue, but that she'll lose all this—these women, this place, their shared sense of purpose. Herself.

"I think I'll be going then," Roberta says at the same time Mimi says, "I'll stay."

Their eyes meet, and they smile, warm and rueful, as if they're both a little envious of the other's decision. Mimi thinks back to that evening they rode together on the streetcar and understands why Roberta would leave. The risks are greater for them all now, but doubly so for her as a black woman. All the more reason Mimi must stay. She'll miss Roberta dearly, though.

"I respect your decision, Mrs. Powell," Ada says. "Come by my house next week, and we'll settle your wages."

There's a flurry of hugs and promises to keep in touch; then, Roberta leaves. No one else goes with her.

Ada explains that for the next several weeks, while things cool down with the police and she refurnishes the office, they'll work out of Dr. Millstone's clinic.

"But the women won't know to go there," Annie says.

"That's why two of you will be stationed here—Miss Kuder and one of you nurses. We'll take appointments as usual, but when the women arrive for their procedures, we'll drive them to Dr. Millstone's. It's not far. And it gives us an extra layer of protection. For now. Like I said, I expect this whole thing to blow over in a few weeks."

They spend the rest of the day cleaning up the clinic and taking inventory of what the police left behind that's still in working order. It isn't much. Ada says she has a few supplies at her other office. She asks Mimi to come and fetch them with her.

They drive for several minutes in silence before Mimi says, "There was a write-up about the raid in the paper last weekend."

"I saw that."

"It said the state's attorney plans to present evidence to the grand jury."

Mimi went to the library earlier that week, pretending she needed to pick up a few books for Junior and Penny. Instead, she sought out the reference section. It might have been quicker if she'd accepted the help of the overly friendly librarian who dropped by to check on her, but Mimi, flushed with guilt and panic, shook her head and said she was fine. After nearly half an hour of searching, she found the explanation she was looking for. A grand jury was a private proceeding in which jurors decided if the evidence police had gathered constituted "probable cause" that a crime had been committed. If so, an indictment was issued against the accused, and a formal trial ensued.

In this case, the accused are Mimi, Jo, and Ada.

"Mr. Papanek is just spouting off," Ada says now. "He doesn't have the evidence needed for a grand jury."

"And Daniel?"

"Mr. Moriarity will approach Mr. Papanek when the moment is right."

"Last time he—"

"Last time, the police didn't have a warehouse's worth of things to sort through. I'm sure Mr. Papanek is still hoping they'll find a trove of evidence in some secret desk compartment or hidden within the stuffing of a chair. Once he realizes they have nothing, he'll be more . . . amenable to negotiations." They stop at a traffic light, and Ada turns to look at Mimi. She's got a mothering look again, but it's one of tender indulgence. "Patience, my dear. No sense in fretting over a future that isn't yet written."

She nods. Of course, Ada is right. Mimi's been telling herself the same things for days now, but it's nice to hear someone else say it. She leans back in her seat, breathing easier than she has since her library visit. They talk the rest of the way about their children—how Junior and Penny are faring in school; where Ada's son Robert is now stationed; what Jennie's plans are when she finishes school.

A few minutes later, they arrive at the office building on Dearborn Street. The elevator takes them to the fourth floor, and Mimi follows Ada down the hallway. They're talking now of the terrible situation in Europe. It's clear Ada's worried Robert will be deployed if America enters the fray, and Mimi's once again grateful her own son is so young.

Suddenly, Ada stops, and her face slackens. At first, Mimi thinks it's all this talk of war. She puts her hand on Ada's arm and starts to say something reassuring, but goes silent as her eyes follow Ada's gaze to a door several paces down the hall. It's cracked open a few inches and sits askew in its jamb.

"My God!" Ada says. She approaches the office as though it were a bear's den, her steps slow and cautious. Mimi follows. This can't be Ada's office, can it? She's only been here once and can't remember the number, but the sickly feeling in her stomach tells her this is the door.

Whoever was here before them must have kicked it in to gain entry. The top hinge is broken, and there's a boot print beside the knob. As best as Mimi can tell from the narrow opening, the office is dark and empty, but she holds her breath as Ada pushes the door fully open.

The hallway light spilling in around them illuminates the room enough to see that it's been ransacked—furniture overturned, papers scattered, books unshelved. But it isn't until Ada reaches inside with a shaky hand and switches on the overhead light that the worst of the destruction is laid bare.

Mimi's heart plummets. The safe has been drilled open, its combination and lock knocked completely off the iron door. Everything inside is gone.

CHAPTER 33

A few weeks later, Mimi attends Mass with Halina and the children. Stan's been on Catalina Island for only a few days—barely time enough to unpack his suitcase—but Mimi says a prayer that he's already made a good impression on Mr. Wrigley and the other team bigwigs.

After the final hymn, the congregation shuffles out of the pews, dipping their fingers in holy water and crossing themselves as they exit. As always, Mimi skips the water. But she smiles at Father Kowalski and shakes his hand. He asks if she's given any more thought to being baptized into the Catholic faith. Again, Mimi demurs. Perhaps when this business with the police blows over, and Stan returns, and life is finally back to normal, she'll consider it.

After praising the Father's sermon and pulling him toward her to kiss his cheek, Halina shuffles off to gossip with her friends. Hopefully, she won't take too long. Through the open doors, Penny and Junior spy other children playing on the snow-covered lawn outside. They look up at Mimi, and she nods. Before she can tell them to mind their nice clothes and not throw snowballs, they race out.

She's nearly to the doors herself, the cold morning air stinging her cheeks, when someone grabs her arm. She turns to find Zofina Dabrowski. From the grave look on Zofina's face, Mimi can tell she didn't stop her to discuss afternoon pleasantries or the Catholic Daughters. She nods with urgency toward the sanctuary, and Mimi follows her, threading her way through the stream of parishioners heading in the opposite direction.

Once they're back inside the nave of the church, Zofina hastens to one of the side chapels. Mimi walks a few steps behind, unnerved by Zofina's tightly set shoulders and clenched hands. Had she seen the article in the *Tribune* about the raid on the clinic? But that appeared a month ago. Why wait this long to talk to Mimi? The paper hasn't said anything about it since—she scours its pages every morning to be sure.

Could there be some issue with Zofina's health? Maybe she and her husband are ready for another baby, and she just wants assurance that the procedure she had won't stand in the way. Maybe she knows of another woman in trouble and wants to check with Mimi before referring her.

Zofina enters an empty side chapel where the statue of a saint—a man in bishop's robes, carrying a crooked staff—stands behind a bank of flickering tea candles. She lights one of the candles, then sinks onto the kneeler positioned before the saint. Mimi kneels beside her.

"Bow your head," Zofina hisses.

"What?"

"It's supposed to look like we're praying."

Mimi laces her fingers together and drops her chin. From the corner of her eye, she sees Zofina glance over her shoulder.

"Why didn't you tell me your clinic was raided by the police?" Zofina whispers.

"You saw in the paper?"

"No, I got a letter."

"A letter? From whom?"

"The state's attorney's office."

Mimi's chest tightens. "What did it say?"

"It said my name had been uncovered during a police investigation and that I had to appear at the Criminal Court Building."

"Did it say what the investigation was about?"

"No."

A seed of hope takes root inside her. Maybe this has nothing to do with the raid.

"But as soon as I saw it, I knew. I just knew they'd found out about my . . . procedure."

"Did you go?"

"The letter said I had to appear under penalty of being taken forthwith on a subpoena before the grand jury."

Grand jury. Mimi rubs the gooseflesh from her arms, and then, remembering she's supposed to be praying, clasps her hands again atop the kneeler.

Despite the records stolen from Ada's office, Mimi had hoped the case would be dropped before the grand jury was summoned. She doesn't see Ada much, not with all the procedures still taking place at Dr. Millstone's office, but every time she does, Ada assures Mimi this whole mess will soon go away.

Has Mimi been a fool to listen?

"What happened when you got there?"

"I met with this man. Mr. Papavich . . . Papacek . . ."

"Papanek."

"That's right. He told me your clinic had been raided and all the records seized. Seized! You should have—" The *click-click* of footsteps sounds in the aisle behind them, and Zofina goes silent.

The footsteps stop not far off. Mimi doesn't dare turn around and see who it is, though. That would look too suspicious.

Beside her, Zofina's entire body has gone rigid, her knuckles blanching around the rosary she clutches in her hands.

Then a voice sounds from the back of the sanctuary. "Susie! There you are. You know better than to be playing in here."

"I wasn't playing," a child's voice calls back. "I wanted to light a candle."

"Not today. Come along."

The footsteps they'd heard approaching in the aisle retreat. Once they're lost to the murmur of noise in the vestibule, Zofina lets out a heavy breath.

"You should have told me about the raid," she says.

In truth, it hadn't even occurred to Mimi. It frightened her enough to think that Mr. Papanek had the clinic's records. She never fully thought through how he might use them.

"I'm sorry, I didn't think—"

"What if my husband had gotten to the letter first?"

"You said the letter didn't specify what the investigation was about."

"What else is he going to think? That I was caught betting on horses? He's not stupid, Mimi."

Mimi winces. How many other women received letters like Zofina? How many husbands opened them to find their wives had been summoned to the Criminal Court Building in connection with a crime? Even with the best of lies, it would be hard to smooth over. While Zofina's husband would have been angry, hurt, ashamed, he didn't seem like the kind of man to take his feelings out with his fists. Not all women were so lucky.

"What else"—Mimi's voice is shaky, and she takes a steadying breath—"what else did Mr. Papanek say?"

Zofina drops her voice to the barest of whispers. "He said he knew I'd had an abortion. When I tried to deny it, he showed me this card with my name and address and how many weeks pregnant I'd been before the procedure."

Her patient intake card from the safe. How did Papanek even learn about Ada's other office? She's been asking herself this question for weeks and still has no answer. Mimi hadn't told him. She doubts Jo or Mr. Piquett had, either. Certainly, Ada would never give up the address. It probably wasn't even leased in her name. Had they followed Ada there? If so, how long had they been tailing her? Or had someone else turned?

"Mr. Papanek said if there was a trial," Zofina continued, "I might have to testify." She rests her forehead atop her clasped hands and begins to sob. "What am I going to do, Mimi? If Peter finds out, he'll never forgive me."

Mimi starts to reach out to her but catches herself. That would just draw attention to them. "He won't find out," she says, with more conviction than she feels.

Zofina wipes her eyes on her coat sleeve and turns her face to Mimi. Her expression is both wild and pleading. "If they call me to testify, I have to tell the truth. I can't add the weight of another sin to my soul."

Mimi swallows, fighting down her own wild dread. "I know."

CHAPTER 34

Mimi must talk to Daniel. The information Zofina told her—the letter she received and her meeting with Papanek—proves the case against them is still going forward.

She stops by the LaSalle Street Tavern several times after work, but Daniel's never there. Each time, she nurses a beer—it's better than that bathtub gin, but still barely drinkable—and fights off the advances of men who think she's there to pick up customers. She knows Halina's watching the clock and smells the smoke on her clothes when she returns home. Her excuses—a new admission to the ward, a last-minute surgery, an emergency blood draw she had to assist with—sound thin, even to her own ears.

Halina won't say anything to Stan, though. They mustn't upset or distract him while he's vying for this coaching spot. But that doesn't keep her mother-in-law from scowling at Mimi or muttering Polish curses or conveniently forgetting to put their ice order in the window to make known her disapproval. As if Mimi doesn't have enough to worry about without an icebox full of food about to spoil.

Even if it weren't raising Halina's suspicions, Mimi can't keep going to the tavern night after night. But a visit to the Criminal Court Building is far too risky—for both her and Daniel. And as badly as she wants his reassurance, she won't go to his house. If their roles were reversed, she wouldn't want him coming by unannounced. He'd be the one having to make excuses then, and Mimi doubts Halina would be any less suspicious than his wife.

After her fourth unsuccessful stop at the tavern, with the taste of stale beer still on her tongue, Mimi remembers something Daniel said when they ran into each other at the zoo. A milkshake. The city's best in Chicago, by Daniel's reckoning. He and his colleagues ate lunch at the diner every Wednesday without fail just so they could order one. But what was the name of the diner? She racks her brain on the way home but can't remember.

Halina gives her a sidelong stare when she arrives. "Another emergency?"

"Yes," Mimi says. She doesn't need to feign exhaustion. She hasn't slept well since Zofina cornered her in church. Worries repeat like a radio advertisement in her head. *Tonight's insomnia is brought to you by Assistant State's Attorney Papanek. One can't help but marvel at how he sways the members of the grand jury. And watch out if you're on the stand! He'll wear you down with questions until you can't tell truth from falsehood.*

And she misses Stan. Just having him asleep beside her is a comfort.

She hangs up her coat and hat, hoping that's the end of it. But Halina says, "Another hospital emergency, I told my son as much when he called."

My son. As if she has supreme claim on him. But tonight, Mimi's in no position to argue. "What did he say? Does he want me to telephone him back?"

"No," Halina says simply, and walks stiffly back to her chair in the living room.

Mimi hates that she missed his call. She'd give anything to hear his voice right now.

"He said something about dinner at the casino. One of those bands he likes to listen to on the radio is playing there tonight. You could call the hotel, but I'm sure he won't be in."

Mimi's hands ball into fists at her side. She'd like to throttle the woman. Stan's described the casino to her before, including the top floor ballroom overlooking the sea. It's impossible not to imagine him dancing with some Hollywood beauty there. And that's just what Halina wants her to imagine.

She takes a deep breath and uncurls her fingers. She knows her mother-in-law thinks Mimi met a man tonight. She'd think the same thing in Halina's shoes. And Mimi *had* gone out after work to see a man. A man she once kissed. *But it's not what you think*, she wishes she could say. She wishes she could collapse onto the couch and tell Halina everything. The true nature of her work. The recent raids. The looming grand jury. Keeping it all inside is like a growing infection, eating away at her flesh from the inside out.

But in Halina's mind, Mimi's true secret would be worse than an affair.

"Did the children get to talk to him?"

Halina nods.

"Good, thank you. I . . . I appreciate how well you look after them."

Halina narrows her eyes and frowns. *"Proszę bardzo."*

It's the most begrudging *you're welcome* Mimi's ever heard. But it's a start.

In the kitchen, Mimi warms some leftover soup on the stove and searches for the telephone directory. She finds it beneath a stack of old church bulletins in the top cupboard. There are hundreds of listings for restaurants. She reads the name of each one as she eats her soup. In the end, she's still not certain which one Daniel said he frequents. A handful sound familiar, but only two are close to the Criminal Court Building: Vic's and Grandma Suzy Q's. As luck would have it, tomorrow's Wednesday. But if Mimi guesses wrong between the two, luck won't matter. She'll have to wait a full week before trying the other. The thought makes the soup in her stomach roil, and she pushes the bowl away. Then it dawns on her. She isn't the only one who might remember.

The next morning, as she dishes oatmeal into the children's bowls, she asks, "Do you remember the name of that diner Mr. Moriarity recommended to us?"

Penny looks up from her book. "Mr. Who?"

"Mr. Moriarity. You met him at the zoo last summer."

Penny shrugs and goes back to her book. Junior's so focused on the piece of paper he's folding, Mimi doubts he's even heard her. So much for that idea.

"You know the rules, Pen. No reading at breakfast," Mimi says, sitting down at the table with her cup of coffee.

Penny grumbles but closes her book.

"The same goes for you, mister." Mimi taps the edge of Junior's bowl with a spoon. "No paper airplanes."

"But I'm almost done."

"You have to leave for school in fifteen minutes. Would you rather have a full belly to start your day or a paper airplane?"

"An airplane!"

Mimi sighs. She should have known better than to ask that question of a nine-year-old. "Well, I'd rather you have a full belly." She holds out her hand, and he begrudgingly relinquishes the half-folded paper. "You can finish your plane tonight."

They're halfway through their oatmeal when Mimi gets another idea. "It's a shame you don't remember the name of that diner. Mr. Moriarity said they have the best milkshakes in all of Chicago."

Both sets of eyes look up at her, wide and eager.

"I thought we might go Saturday afternoon and try them out. But I guess we can't. Oh, well."

"I remember!" Junior says. His eyebrows scrunch together the way they do when he's trying to recall where he left his mittens or schoolbooks.

"I thought it might be called Vic's," she says after a moment. "Or maybe Grandma Suzy Q's."

"Grandma's!" they say in unison.

"Are you sure?"

They both nod. Mimi wonders if they truly remember or just like the name, but it's better than picking one at random. If she has to wait another week without seeing Daniel and knowing where things stand with the case, she'll go mad.

"Can we really go on Saturday?" Junior asks.

"If you finish your breakfast and get to the bus on time."

They both dive back into their oatmeal.

She feels slightly bad having involved them in her hunt for Daniel. But she feels worse about how short-tempered and distracted she's been since her conversation with Zofina. Hopefully, they've got the right diner, and Daniel can put her mind at ease.

Mimi arrives at Grandma Suzy Q's at 10:45. It's a little early for lunch, but she can't risk missing him. She chooses a stool at the far end of the lunch counter and orders a cup of coffee. By the time the waitress pours her a second cup, Mimi's stared around so long, she could recite the details of the place—from its gray linoleum floors to its peach-striped wallpaper to its green-and-red vinyl booths—by heart. A small bell hangs on the front door. Each time it rings, Mimi's head turns like a trained circus animal. Each time, she's disappointed when the latest customer isn't Daniel.

By noon, she's on her third cup of coffee. Her hand shakes a little as she brings it to her lips. Soon every seat at the counter is occupied. The booths and tables are filling, too. She orders an open-faced roast beef sandwich with mashed potatoes and peas—not because she's hungry, but because the waitress has started to eye her with annoyance. It's tastier than expected, the gravy rich and the peas as plump as the ones they grew on the farm. She takes her time eating it, though, cutting each bite slowly and chewing for a full thirty seconds, like the reducing articles recommend.

She could certainly stand to lose a few pounds, but right now, her only concern is holding her spot at the counter as long as she can. With nearly every seat taken, it's grown loud in the diner, and she has to listen carefully to hear the bell. Still no Daniel.

Did she and the children get it wrong? Is he a few streets down, seated in the corner booth at Vic's? Or at another diner with a name that didn't even register. Maybe he and his partners have stopped going to lunch altogether.

She finishes her roast beef, and the waitress pointedly asks if she's ready to be rung up.

A rush of desperation fills her, traveling from her gut to her fingertips and back like electricity along a wire. She can't bear another week of sleepless nights. Of random waves of panic. Of utter distraction, no matter the task at hand.

"Actually," Mimi says. "I've heard you make the best milkshakes in all of Chicago."

The waitress smiles at this and takes the pencil from behind her ear. "What flavor?"

Mimi orders chocolate. It comes with a cloud of whipped cream and a bright red cherry on top like a sundae. Daniel's right—even though she's full from lunch, her first spoonful is delicious. Dare she hope she's in the right place?

The minutes tick by, and her confidence flags. Come Saturday, the children will be in heaven here. But right now, despite the rich, chocolaty taste coating her tongue, Mimi's much closer to the opposite side of paradise. It's past one o'clock, and the lunch crowd is nearly gone. She can hear the bell clearly now, but it hardly rings. A few bites more, and she'll leave.

She's about to get the waitress's attention and pay her bill when the door opens with a chime. Her head turns, and this time, she doesn't look away disappointed. The man Mimi remembers from her first visit to the Criminal Court Building walks in, his crooked nose immediately recognizable. Another man she doesn't know follows him in. And then, at the rear: Daniel.

The crooked-nosed man meets her eye. (His eyebrows still need a good trimming.) His stare lingers long enough to know he recognizes her, too. He gives Daniel a nudge, nods in her direction, then saunters toward a booth. The other man, the one she doesn't know, follows him, seemingly oblivious, while Daniel remains rooted by the door.

She can tell from his expression he's not only surprised to see her, but also alarmed. Mimi bites her lip and swivels on her stool, facing forward again, hoping he'll come sit beside her.

He doesn't. Mimi switches from a spoon to a straw and forces down the rest of her milkshake in slow, punctuated sips, waiting. She hears the men order lunch and watches the waitress bring it to them a few minutes later.

"Can I get you anything else?" the waitress asks Mimi, after dropping off the men's orders.

She holds up her glass, giving it a swirl, and smiles. "Almost done."

It's impossible not to seem suspicious after sitting here for nearly three hours, but now that the diner isn't so full, the waitress doesn't seem to care. She goes back to wiping the counters and putting out new place settings. Mimi, meanwhile, stares forward, continuing her slow, labored sips of milkshake. The glass pie case on the back counter offers a blurred reflection of Daniel and his colleagues. She watches them eat. Unlike her, they make quick work of their meals.

Surely, Daniel won't leave before talking to her. There's no mistaking that he saw her. But as the men scoot out of their booth and stand, suddenly she's unsure. The urge to turn around and call to him is so strong, Mimi has to grip the edge of the counter to keep from doing it. However much she wants to know about the case, she can't jeopardize him to do it.

She keeps her eyes fixed on their reflections in the pie case. Two of them move toward the cash register at the far end of the counter. The other crosses the diner and sits a few stools away from her. A sidelong glance reveals it's Daniel.

Mimi listens to the clink of coins and ding of the cash register as the other men pay. The small bell on the door tinkles, but she knows better than to turn around and watch them leave. Daniel orders a vanilla milkshake, then moves to the stool beside her, looking over his shoulder before sitting down.

"Did Ada send you after me?" His voice is quiet but sharp.

"No. I came on my own. You mentioned at the zoo you like to come here on Wednesdays for lunch. I thought I might be able to run into you here without it looking suspicious."

His shoulders relax. "You do fit in better here than at the tavern."

She doesn't tell him she went there looking for him, too. The sharpness is gone from his voice, and she doesn't want it to return. The waitress brings him his milkshake, and he thanks her. Before bustling off, she gives Mimi a knowing look and winks, as if to say she'd wait three hours for a man as handsome as Daniel, too.

But it's not his handsomeness Mimi notices today. He's changed in the months since she saw him last. Shadows hang beneath his eyes, and there's a gauntness to his cheeks. His cuticles are red and ragged, the way Penny's get sometimes before a big test at school.

"What do you think of the milkshake?" he asks her.

"It's good," she says.

Daniel raises his eyebrows, perceptive as ever. Good to see that hasn't changed.

"Honestly, I'm two sips away from being sick."

They both laugh.

"How long have you been sitting here?"

"Since a quarter to eleven. I didn't want to risk missing you."

"I'm glad you came. It's good to see you." He reaches out and brushes the back of her hand. Mimi pulls away.

"Daniel, I—"

"Sorry, I know you're here about the case."

"It's good to see you, too. Maybe if things had been different, if I'd met you—"

"In another world, another time. I know." He shrugs and sips his shake, but the nonchalance of it all doesn't reach his eyes. "So what do you want to know?"

"I heard Mr. Papanek might bring the case before the grand jury."

"He is. The proceedings have already begun."

Mimi knots her fingers together, squeezing so tightly, her nails bite into her skin. She can barely speak around the growing thickness in her throat. "He did?"

"Last week."

"Is that . . . it, then? Am I going to prison?" The threat of tears carries on her wobbly voice.

Daniel swivels on his stool to face her and reaches for her hands again. This time, she lets him take them. "No, they might not issue a true bill."

"A true bill?"

"An indictment. They might find the evidence lacking."

"They have our patient records, Daniel. Mr. Papanek's sending letters to the women, telling them they might need to testify."

He hangs his head. "I know."

"Is there no way to convince Mr. Papanek to drop the case?"

He lets go of her hands and turns back to the counter. His fingers curl around the frosty milkshake glass, but he doesn't drink. "When I approached him last month, he wouldn't take the money."

"Can't you try again?"

"Jesus, Mimi, it's not that simple!"

Mimi winces at the volume of his voice. The waitress glances over at them, then quickly away. *A lover's spat*, she must be thinking. Better that than the truth.

Daniel takes a deep breath, but his knuckles remain white around the glass. "I'm trying. But it's not like before. Papanek's like a goddamned dog with a bone when it comes to this case. He wants to go after everyone—not only you, Ada, and Jo, but Dr. Gabler, too, and anyone else he can tie to the clinic. The feds are even sniffing around."

"The feds? Like J. Edgar Hoover?"

Daniel gives a small, mirthless laugh. "No. Federal revenue agents. They suspect tax fraud."

"Oh." Mimi reaches for her milkshake. She can't bear another sip, but at least it's something to hold on to. The brown liquid inside has grown runny, the glass no longer cold to the touch. "Daniel, what should I do?"

"Is there any place you can go?"

"You mean, leave Chicago?"

He nods.

Mimi presses her lips together. She may well be sick after all.

"Are things really that bleak?"

"I don't know." He takes off his hat and rakes a hand through his hair. "I'm gonna try again with Papanek, but the case is too hot right now. I need more time." His voice is rising again. "Tell Ada I need more goddamn time."

Mimi puts a hand on his arm. She's not sure who's trembling, her or him. "How much did she give you?"

"Three thousand."

Three thousand, and Mr. Papanek turned it down? Not many men could resist that much money. Despite a stab of guilt at the thought, Mimi hopes he won't turn it down a second time.

"I'll tell Ada," she says.

"Thanks." Daniel glances down at his wristwatch. "I've got to go."

He puts his hat back on and stands. "I'll get your meal."

"You don't have to do that."

He nods toward the waitress. "It's part of the ruse. What kind of fella lets his best gal pay for her own lunch?"

Mimi manages a smile. She owes him that, at least. Never mind the dread roiling in her stomach alongside her food. "Thank you. For everything."

She kisses him on the cheek and leaves, throwing up in an alleyway on her way to the L.

CHAPTER 35

The next few weeks pass much the same as those that came before. Mimi washes the clothes and hangs them to dry in the weak March sunlight. She scours the oven and waxes the kitchen floor. She packs the children's lunches. She makes soups and casseroles and meat pies that can be reheated for dinner on the days she works. When Stan calls, the whole family crowds around the telephone, eager for a turn. He's getting along swimmingly with the players and other coaches. Mr. Wilson, the manager, has hinted a contract will be waiting for him when the team returns to Chicago.

Mimi sends her cheeriest voice down the line, even though her sleep's been even more fretful since her meeting with Daniel. *I miss you*, she tells Stan. *I miss you too, peach*, he says, and she passes the phone to Junior before her voice betrays her.

Though plenty of women must have read the *Chicago Tribune* article back in January about the raid, it doesn't stop them from coming to the clinic. With all the back-and-forth to Dr. Millstone's office, Mimi and the other nurses are busier than ever. Some women complain about the inconvenience of being driven from the State Lake Building to another office, but most just accept it, having already committed to see their choice through to the end, no matter what they must endure. Those who've come from Indiana, Michigan, Wisconsin—the clinic always served its share of out-of-staters—likely see it as just another leg of their long journey.

The curdled vestiges of the milkshake still sit in Mimi's stomach, or at least that's how it feels. The very sight of chocolate—everything from Ovaltine to a Hershey's bar—makes her gag. But when she's with the children or puts on her nursing uniform, she tamps down her nerves and swallows that sickly feeling. People are relying on her: Penny, Junior, her patients. In some ways, slipping into that skin—mother, nurse—is a relief. A reminder of who she is when everything around her is so uncertain.

"Can we add chocolate chips?" Penny asks, licking the sugar from her fingers.

Mimi shakes her head. "These are for your father, and he likes raisins best."

"Will he be here when we wake up?" Junior asks.

"No. His train doesn't arrive until late afternoon." She hands them both an egg to crack into the bowl. After five weeks on Catalina Island, Stan's finally coming home tomorrow.

"That's why we have a special dinner planned, dodo," Penny says to her brother. "Not a special breakfast."

Mimi sticks a finger into the batter to fish out a piece of eggshell. "Be nice to your brother."

Penny sighs dramatically, like it's the most onerous request she's ever heard.

The doorbell rings just as Mimi starts to whisk together the sugar, eggs, and vanilla. "Can you get that, Mamo?" she calls over her shoulder toward the living room. It's probably a traveling salesman peddling knives or encyclopedias. Hopefully, Halina will turn him away.

But a moment later, Halina hollers Mimi's name. There's a high-pitched edge to her voice, and Mimi knows suddenly it's not a traveling salesman at the door. She hands Penny the whisk and tells the children to stay in the kitchen.

As she walks down the hall, she wipes her trembling hands on her apron. Two men stand in the front doorway beyond Halina. Despite their police uniforms, she hasn't let them in. Mimi's never been more grateful for that indomitable stare she knows her mother-in-law has unleashed on the men.

"Are you Miriam Lukasewicz?" one of the men asks as Mimi approaches.

"I am."

The man reaches for the handcuffs fastened to his belt while the other says, "You need to come with us, ma'am. You're under arr—"

Mimi holds up a hand. "Wait." She's no longer trembling. A singular focus has taken root inside her. "Please. My children are home. I'll go with you, but please, let's do this outside."

The officers frown. They look at each other, then back at her.

"Fine," the one with the handcuffs says. "No dawdling, though."

Mimi unties her apron and hands it to Halina, whose cheeks have gone pale and eyes wide, as if she's just seen the dreaded bebok or some other creature from the folktales she tells the children. "Finish the cookies with them, please. The recipe's on the counter. I'll be back"—she glances askance at the men—"well, as soon as I possibly can."

Halina nods gravely.

Mimi glances over her shoulder toward the kitchen. Penny and Junior are arguing about who will get to lick the spoon once they've finished the batter. Mimi's heart squeezes, but she refuses to cry. She grabs her coat from the peg on the wall, then joins the men on the porch, closing the door behind her.

"Thank you," she says, holding out her arms for the handcuffs. Across the street, the Davenports' front window curtains are drawn wide. Mimi can't help but laugh, even as the tears she's been holding back threaten to come. This is far more of a show than when the men came for her electric refrigerator.

When she arrives at the jail, she finds Ada and Jo already there. Jo gives her a fierce hug, and they sit together on the cell's wooden bench. Ada paces.

"What now?" Mimi asks, regretting she hadn't spent more time at the library researching what happens *after* a grand jury indictment.

"Mr. Martin is getting in touch with our lawyer."

A lawyer. Mimi hadn't even thought of that. She doesn't know any lawyers. Does Stan?

Stan.

Her chest tightens. He's probably just boarded the train in Los Angeles. Mimi pictures him relaxing in his sleeper or enjoying a drink in the dining car, blissfully unaware of what awaits him at home.

"I don't have a lawyer," Jo says, an edge of panic in her voice.

"My attorney, Mr. Smith, is a good man and an even better lawyer. He can represent us all."

"Will we be here through the trial? In jail, I mean," Mimi says.

"No." Ada stops pacing and sits down at the end of the bench. "In a day or two, we'll go before a judge and be released on bail."

"Are you sure?" Mimi asks.

Ada rubs her eyes. Her lipstick has settled into the grooves and crevices of her mouth, making them more pronounced, while the fleshy parts of her lips are bare and pale. "I'm not sure of anything anymore."

Early the following afternoon, Ada's prediction is proved right. In the company of Mr. Smith—a tall man, with unruly brown hair but keen eyes—Mimi, Jo, and Ada are brought before a judge. He reads the grand jury's indictment and charges them with conspiracy to commit criminal abortions. Even though she's been expecting it, hearing the words spoken aloud turns Mimi's blood as cold as lake water.

Bail is set for each of them at two thousand dollars. It's a staggering amount, and far more than Mimi could scrape together, but Ada offers her house as a surety for all of them. Her generosity is not unplanned, for Mr. Smith has a valuation of the property ready to present to the judge.

How long has Ada anticipated this outcome? Perhaps Daniel or some other contact at the state's attorney's office had been feeding her information about the grand jury proceeding. A flush of anger creeps into Mimi's cheeks. Ada ought to have told her all she knew right away. Not a dribble here and there as she saw fit.

But as quickly as it came, Mimi's anger subsides. What would she have done with the knowledge besides worry more? Sure, she might have made the oatmeal cookies in the morning instead of waiting until the afternoon, but that hardly matters now. Stan won't enjoy them for long. Perhaps, if she'd known what Ada knew, she might have told him the truth already. But she can't blame Ada for her own cowardice.

The judge accepts the property bond, and they're released and ushered into some remote hallway of the Criminal Court Building so the next arraignment hearing can begin. Mr. Smith pulls them aside into a small alcove. There's a bench and window overlooking the western edge of the city. Mimi doesn't sit. She's been sitting all night and half the day. She wants to get home. Must get home. If she hurries, she might beat Stan there. There may even be time for the special dinner she'd planned.

Mr. Smith says something, and she rattles her head. He's talking about court dates, and plea filings, and she's thinking about chicken cacciatore. It all feels so . . . surreal. As if it isn't her standing here facing criminal charges, but some other woman.

"I'll get your information from Ada and meet with you both separately over the coming days," Mr. Smith is saying to her and Jo. "Of course, you're welcome to hire your own lawyer, but it's best we coordinate our plan of attack."

Plan of attack. He talks as if they're heading into a battle. Maybe they are. Suddenly, Mimi feels woefully unprepared. She's a nurse, not a soldier.

Mr. Smith is looking at her, and she realizes he's asked her a question. Mimi nods, hoping she hasn't just agreed to pay him thousands of dollars or take the witness stand and lie. He must see that she's rattled, for he smiles warmly and pats her shoulder. "We'll go over all this again when we meet on Monday."

Monday. Monday? What day is it? Wednesday, she remembers. She looks between him and Ada. "But I'm scheduled at the clinic on Monday."

"I think it best if you steer clear of the clinic for a while," Mr. Smith says. Ada nods in agreement.

"Of course." She rattles her head. "Of course." She glances out the window. The sun hovers just above the buildings, like a perfectly balanced ball. "May I go?"

"Yes," Mr. Smith says.

She starts to walk away but turns around. "What do I tell my husband?"

Jo knows Mimi hasn't told Stan anything, and looks at her now the way she would a man on his way to the electric chair.

"Tell him you're in good hands," Mr. Smith says. "I'm going to do everything I can to see you don't go to prison."

Mimi swallows. She isn't sure what's worse: Jo's look, or Mr. Smith's reminder that she's facing prison time.

"Thank you," she croaks, before turning back around and urging her feet onward to home.

CHAPTER 36

Mimi pays for a cab instead of taking the L home, using the dollar she keeps in the inside pocket of her coat for emergencies. Now, more than ever, she needs to be careful about spending money, but this definitely counts as an emergency.

The children rush to the front door as soon as she opens it. They were expecting their father, no doubt, but indulge Mimi in a long, tight hug nonetheless.

"How come you left yesterday?" Junior asks. "We hadn't even finished the cookies."

She ruffles his hair and plants a kiss on his forehead, which he promptly wipes away. "Work, darling."

"But it was your day off," he says.

"I know. I'm sorry. It couldn't be helped." She practiced what she'd say to them on the way home, but it doesn't make the lie come any easier.

"How come they came to the house to get you?" Penny asks. "Doesn't the hospital have a telephone?"

Just then, Halina makes her way from the dining room. "Let your mother be, children. No doubt she's had a long night." She looks Mimi up and down, as if to be sure she's made it back in one piece, before crossing her arms and glaring.

Thank you, Mimi mouths, shrugging out of her coat.

The children return to the living room, where *Little Orphan Annie* plays on the radio. Mimi's got only minutes before Stan arrives home, so she hurries to shower and change. On the way to her bedroom, she passes the dining room doorway, where Halina still stands.

"I owe you an explanation, and you will have one. But please, let's don't spoil Stan's homecoming. I'll tell you both after supper, once the children are in bed."

Halina narrows her eyes. "Everything."

Mimi nods. "Everything."

Mimi's buttoning her dress when she hears the front door open and the children squeal. Her heart feels as if it's being torn atrium from ventricle, but when she checks herself in the mirror, her face is composed and eyes dry. She coaches herself through each movement before she takes it: open the door; step into the hall; smile.

Stan looks as happy and well as she's ever seen him. His duffel bag and suitcase lie abandoned by the door, and he has an arm around each of the children. He returns Mimi's smile with a radiant one of his own and makes quick work of the distance between them. Open your lips, she tells herself as he kisses her. Wrap your arms around his waist. Don't cry.

She makes it through dinner in much the same way. Bake the chicken. Slice the bread. Pass the butter. Take a bite, chew, and swallow. Take another bite. Stan regales them with stories from spring training. The grand slam one of the players hit during a practice game. The shark he saw swimming just beyond the dock. The buffalo—yes, buffalo!—that would occasionally meander down from the hills and block the road.

Mimi tells herself to listen. To watch. To remember. But she can't seem to hold on to any of it. Not Stan's carefree stories. Or Penny's gap-toothed smile. Or Junior's snorting laughter. They're like the lightning bugs the children chase across the lawn. You think you've caught one, only to open your hand and find it empty.

While Mimi gets the platter of cookies and pitcher of milk from the kitchen, Stan sends Junior to fetch his suitcase. Inside are gifts for each of them—a sand dollar for Penny, a shark's tooth for Junior, a silk scarf for Halina, and a necklace of tiny strung seashells for Mimi.

"Put it on," he says.

Put it on, she tells herself. Don't tremble. But her fingers don't entirely obey, and it takes three tries to secure the clasp. The shells sit smooth and cool against her skin. "It's beautiful."

He smiles. "So are you. Pretty as peach pie."

Beneath the table, she balls her hands into fists, relishing the stinging prick of her nails against her palms. Mimi hasn't hated herself this much since she watched through the cracked-open door as her mother forced Ginny to undress.

After dinner, the children play pirates in the living room, taking turns hiding their new treasures while the other searches. Usually, Mimi would insist they help with dishes or clearing the table, but tonight, she's happy to let them play. She's determined to shield them from the awful business of the trial. Even so, their little world won't remain the same much longer.

Besides, shaking out the tablecloth, scrubbing the dishes, wiping the crumbs from the counter—these things require no great show of will. She doesn't have to pretend for the soap bubbles that everything is all right.

When bedtime comes, the children beg to stay up a little longer. They've crowded around Stan on the sofa, eager to hear more stories. They might not be tired, but Stan is. Mimi can see it in the droop of his eyes and sag of his shoulders. She can't have him falling asleep before she has a chance to come clean. Already, her nerve is flagging.

The promise of a cookie in tomorrow's lunch gets the children into their pajamas and brushing their teeth. After a goodnight kiss from Stan and Babcia, Mimi shoos them into their bedrooms and tucks them into bed. She lingers momentarily in their doorways before turning off the light, loath to lose sight of them. She's not going to prison tonight. Hopefully, she won't go to prison at all. But she can't shake the feeling that come tomorrow, nothing will be the same. Or maybe she's dawdling.

There's nothing else but to walk to the living room, turn off the radio, and tell Stan and Halina everything.

But where to begin? She realizes, standing before them, that she should have planned exactly what to say. Perhaps it's best just to start at the beginning.

"I've something I must tell you."

"Can it wait till morning?" Stan says. "I'm beat."

"No."

His brow furrows, and he glances from her to Halina and back. "All right. I'm all ears." He scoots to one side of the sofa, making room for her beside him. She takes a step toward him but stops, ignoring her body's urge to cuddle up next to him. She'll lose all her willpower that way. Halina sits in the chair beside the window, and Mimi angles herself so she can speak to them both.

"For the past year and a half, I haven't been working at Chicago General Hospital."

Confusion settles on both of their faces.

"You'll recall I did have a job at Memorial Hospital, for a short time after the accident, but they let me go—I told you that—and I tried to find another job, at Chicago General and elsewhere, but no one was hiring. At least, no one was hiring a nurse absent ten years from the profession, with no experience and two children at home. But I ran into an old friend"—she turns to Stan—"Emily—you might remember her; she came to our wedding. Anyway, I ran into her—this was while I was still working at Memorial—and well, she told me about this place, a clinic, on State Street and, well, she didn't actually tell me about it, she gave me the address and name of the doctor who ran the clinic and—" Mimi stops. Their looks of confusion have deepened into incomprehension. "Sorry, none of that's really important. What you need to know . . . what you need to know is this." She takes a deep breath. "For the past year and a half, I've been working at a clinic that performs abortions. Illegal abortions."

Mimi waits, giving them a moment to process what she's said. A frown spreads across Stan's face. It starts as a slight downturn of the lips. Then his cheeks join in, dimpling and tensing, as if he's tasted something bitter. Then his eyebrows pull together, and his skin flushes.

"There's more," she says, before he can interrupt her. "In January, the police raided the clinic. They detained me and two of the other women who work there. The next day, they let me go but—"

"That was the night you telephoned," Stan says. "You told me there was a hospital emergency."

She winces. "I didn't want to worry you. I thought—"

"Worry me? You'd been arrested!"

To Mimi's surprise, Halina cuts in. "Hush, Stanislaw. Do you want your children to hear this?" She turns to Mimi and nods for her to continue.

Mimi does. She tells them about the second raid at Ada's office on Dearborn Street; the stolen patient records; the grand jury; the arrest, arraignment, and impending trial.

Stan's expression has morphed again. The frown is gone, and in its place sits bewilderment. He looked this way when the doctor told him about his leg—the severity of the break, the difficulty they'd had setting it, the need for weeks of traction. "Yes, yes, but how many games will I miss?" he asked. The doctor removed his glasses and wiped them on his jacket. When he put them back on, he blinked several times before answering. "The rest of the season, certainly. After that . . . well, we'll just have to see."

Now, Stan pats his breast pocket, then glances to the side table beside his old chair. Cigarettes, she realizes. He's looking for cigarettes. He hunts behind the throw pillows and gropes between the sofa cushions. He's muttering to himself, but Mimi can't make out the words. She tries to catch and hold his gaze, but his eyes are slippery, unfocused. He abandons the sofa and searches his chair, upending the seat cushion and throwing the doilies to the ground.

He's about to ransack the coffee table when Mimi gives in and points to the lacquered box atop the radio cabinet. Stan raids the box and lights a cigarette. After a deep inhale and long exhale of smoke, he finally meets her eyes. She waits, thinking he's going to say something. Instead, he shakes his head and takes another drag.

Halina speaks instead. "All these many late nights, what you said were emergencies at the hospital, it was this?"

"Yes."

"You were at this . . . this clinic?" She points her crochet hook at Mimi. "The truth now."

"Not always at the clinic. Sometimes I visited the women at their homes afterward to check on their condition. I did other things on occasion, too. Clerical things for the owner, Mrs. Martin." Perhaps it's a stretch to classify the delivery of bribes as "clerical," but it's not an outright lie. "Otherwise, I was at the clinic."

"At the clinic?" Stan says, almost mockingly. "On State Street? You expect us to believe this sort of criminal operation took place right in the open in the middle of the goddamned Loop?"

She knows Halina's thinking it, too, wondering how such a thing is possible, for she doesn't flinch at Stan's profanity. Was it so easy to believe Mimi operated out of an alley somewhere, luring wholesome and unsuspecting women into sin?

"An office in the State Lake Building, yes. It's been operating for over a decade. Licensed physicians do the procedures and always under the cleanest of conditions."

"And that makes it better?" Stan says. He takes another drag, then begins to pace, padding the short distance to the door, then back to the far wall where the radio cabinet sits. It's a narrow pass between the couch and coffee table, and she can't help but worry he's going to bang his leg.

"How could you do this, Mimi? How could you be so . . . so . . . stupid. . . ? I never should have let you go back to work in the first place."

Mimi stands there, stunned.

"It was that woman. She talked you into this."

"What?" Does Stan think Mimi has no mind of her own?

"That friend. Emma . . . Erma . . . Etta—"

"It's Emily, and no, she didn't talk me into this."

"Who, then?"

"No one. I made the decision on my own."

He stops, looks at her, rattles his head, and begins pacing again. "Did you ever stop and think how this could affect us? My career. Our family."

"Someone had to work around here!"

Now it's Stan who looks stunned. He stops mid-stride. The growing ash at the tip of his cigarette breaks off and falls to the floor, smoldering atop the rug. He doesn't bother to stamp it out.

Mimi wraps her arms around her midsection. Silence grips the room, so complete she can hear the rug's fibers softly sizzle. Her mother-in-law sits on the edge of her chair, gaping at Mimi as if she's never seen her before. Stan is staring at her, too, every muscle rigid, as if he's just been struck by a wild pitch and is debating whether or not to rush the mound.

"Who else knows?" he says finally, his voice calm but razor-sharp.

"The Davenports saw me leave yesterday with the police, but they don't know why. Other than that, no one."

"Good. Keep it that way." He walks past her out of the room, smoke trailing behind him.

CHAPTER 37

For the next week, Stan's about as warm to Mimi as a bag of frozen peas. He eats the breakfast she serves each morning with his nose stuck in the paper. If he needs salt or butter or cream for his coffee, he asks Halina, Penny, or Junior. If they're not nearby, he goes without.

For her part, Mimi tries to keep busy. Mr. Smith stops by Monday morning to discuss her impending trial. She boils coffee and watches as he heaps three spoonfuls of sugar into his cup before laying out the facts. He's been granted three weeks to review the state's evidence. His plan is to enter a plea of abatement. Mimi admits she doesn't know what that is.

"The crux of it is this," Mr. Smith tells her. "Both the raid at the State Street clinic and the Dearborn Street office were conducted without a search warrant. Therefore, all the evidence obtained therein and any testimony gathered as a result should, by right of law, be thrown out. The plea is just a formal way to bring that to the judge's attention."

She pours him another cup of coffee (she'll have to refill the sugar bowl if he drinks much more) and asks what happens if the judge doesn't accept their plea. He rattles off other legal mumbo jumbo he'll pursue—a motion to quash the indictment, a demurrer to the indictment, a motion for a bill of particulars, a petition to suppress evidence, a motion to vacate—before finally getting to the main point. If, in the end, Mimi's found guilty, she'll face up to five years in prison and two thousand dollars in fines.

Mimi's so shaken, she takes a sip from the milk pot before realizing it's not her coffee cup. Such a steep fine would cost them the house. And five years in prison! She'd miss out on so much of Penny's and Junior's childhoods.

If Mr. Smith notices her distress, he doesn't show it, aside from a pat on the hand and a breezy reassurance that everything will be fine. As soon as he's out the door, Halina, who's been eavesdropping from the living room, takes out her rosary. Mimi's so worried, she's tempted to join her. Instead, she performs a more familiar penance: cleaning.

She starts with the laundry, not just their dirty clothes and week-old sheets. She washes the curtains, the tablecloth, the picnic blanket stowed away in the cellar. What's washed, of course, must be dried, then starched and ironed, and folded or rehung. This sees her through Tuesday afternoon. Then she attacks the rugs, hauling them from the house, hanging them over the clothesline, and beating them with the broom until her arms ache. The living room rug, the one with the cigarette burn, gets an extra few whacks.

There's always hope that Daniel will succeed in fixing the case. But Mimi only allows herself to indulge that hope in small, occasional sips. The rest of the time, she cleans.

Wednesday, she dusts and polishes the furniture. Thursday, she does the marketing and cleans out the icebox. Friday, she scours the bathtub. Saturday, she reorganizes the kitchen cupboards. Sunday, she accompanies the family to Mass.

Sitting on the hard wooden pew between Halina and Junior, she tries to pray, but finds the task hopeless. Instead, she makes a mental list of what else there is to clean. The cellar, the attic, the stove. . . . It's not enough to see her through the next week, let alone through to her court date at the end of the month. But when she reaches the end, she can start all over again at the beginning. It's a comforting thought. Also a depressing one. Is this how she spent her days before her job at the clinic? Had it always been this unfulfilling? If Stan hadn't broken his leg, would she have gone round and round like this forever?

But surely that would be preferable to where she is today—or will be in a few months, once Mr. Smith uses up all the pleas and motions and petitions—wouldn't it?

* * *

"How come Daddy gets to read the newspaper at breakfast, but I can't read my book?" Penny asks a few weeks later.

Mimi waits for Stan to answer. When he doesn't, she says, "Your father's an adult. When you're all grown and have your own house, you can read at the breakfast table, too."

Penny frowns and crosses her arms. "I will. And at lunch and dinner, too."

"Not if your husband has any say," Halina says with a chuckle. Judging from the way Penny's expression further sours, she doesn't think it's funny.

"When I'm a grown-up," Junior says, "I'm going to play jacks at breakfast and only eat donuts."

"And ice cream," Penny says, still pouting.

"And marshmallows!"

"And . . ."

Mimi doesn't hear what the children say next, even though they're close to shouting. She's staring at Stan. Or rather, at the newspaper held up in front of his face. A headline on the back page has caught her eye:

TWO ABORTION CHARGES FILED
AGAINST LOOP PHYSICIAN

She leans so far forward, the front of her blouse is swimming in her breakfast bowl along with her cereal, but she can't make out anything else. Does this have anything to do with the clinic? There are dozens, if not hundreds, of physicians with offices in the Loop. She wouldn't be surprised if one or two of them were abortionists on the side. Only last week, she read that the League for Planned Parenthood estimated that between 700,000 and 1,000,000 abortions are performed each year in America. Of course, they might be inflating that number a bit to support their crusade for better access to birth control. But however many abortions there are and however many physicians perform them, Mimi has a sinking, sickly feeling this article refers to someone she knows.

She sits up and dabs the milk from her blouse. Stan will just ignore her if she asks to see the paper. The only thing he's said all morning is, "Pass the sugar bowl." Besides, she doesn't want to draw his attention to the article. Any reminder of the subject, whether it's directly related to Mimi or not, will only further flame his anger. So, no matter how fast her heart is beating, she'll have to wait until he leaves.

But before he does, the telephone rings. Mimi startles, nearly knocking over her coffee. Stan lowers the paper enough to peek over the top and glare at her, as if this mess with the clinic is the only reason someone might be ringing them at such an early hour. She leaves her half-eaten cereal and goes to the phone, all the while hoping it's the Cubs manager, Mr. Wilson, or someone else with the team, so Stan can't blame her for the interruption.

When she picks up the phone and answers, however, it's a woman's voice on the line.

"Mimi, thank God, it's Emily. The most awful thing happened."

Mimi waits for her to continue, but only muffled sobs come down the line. The article in the paper immediately comes back to her. The physician mentioned in the headline must be Dr. Millstone.

"Em, are you all right? Is Dr. Millstone all right?"

The mention of Dr. Millstone's name only makes Emily cry harder.

"Are you at home?"

Mimi hears what she thinks is an *um-hum*.

"I'll be there as soon as I can."

"No, not here," Emily says with a shaky voice. "Can you meet me at Washington Park?"

They arrange to meet in an hour on the lagoon side of the park by the boathouse. It won't give Mimi much time to dawdle, but if she leaves as soon as the children are off to school, she can make it.

"Who was that?" Stan says when she returns to the table. She's so surprised to hear his voice directed at her that it takes her a moment to answer.

"A friend."

"A friend?"

"Yes, we're meeting for a stroll at Washington Park."

"It's raining."

Mimi looks out the dining room window. Swollen gray clouds blanket the sky, and raindrops pelt the ground.

She knows Stan wasn't telling her out of concern she'll get wet. He doesn't trust her. Annoyance prickles inside her. But can she blame him?

"Thank you, dear. I'll be sure to bring my umbrella."

An hour later, she finds Emily pacing in front of the boathouse. No one's out on the water today, and empty boats bob along the lagoon's edge. Emily lowers her umbrella and throws her arms around Mimi, sobbing against her shoulder.

"He's so upset, Mimi. I've never seen him so upset."

Mimi loops an arm around Emily's waist, leading her into the boathouse and out of the rain. It's less a boathouse, really, and more like a set of open-air Grecian temples. The kind she read about in history class, with stone pillars and low-pitched roofs. Two of the buildings are long and narrow and belly up to the water. A third building sits between them, set back a short distance from the lagoon. In warmer months, the buildings are packed with parkgoers who've come to rent a boat or sit beneath the shade and watch the water. But on a wet April day like today, there's hardly anyone here.

She closes her umbrella and sits with Emily on one of the boathouse's wooden benches. Before leaving the house, she grabbed the newspaper Stan left on the table beside his breakfast dishes and read the article on the L. It wasn't long—only three paragraphs—and some details were vague. But it was enough to learn that "police raiders," under the lead of Mr. Papanek, arrested Dr. Millstone and two nurses at his downtown office. They were accused of conspiracy to commit abortion, which all three parties denied, and were released on bond.

Likely, Emily hasn't seen the article, and knowing about it would only distress her further, so Mimi doesn't mention it. Instead, she takes Emily's hand and says, "Tell me everything, from the beginning."

It takes Emily a moment to calm herself enough to speak. Her hands are cold and trembling. "The police showed up at Henry's office Friday morning," she begins. "A whole gang of them. They tore the place apart and arrested Henry. Annie and Edna were there, readying for a procedure. Those rotten coppers arrested them, too."

Mimi's chest tightens. So Annie and Edna were the two nurses referred to in the article. Clearly, Roberta was right to quit when she could.

"What about you?" Mimi asks.

"I wasn't feeling well, so I'd stayed home that day. But, Mimi, they came there, too. They ransacked the rooms we use as an office, along with the entire first floor. Even the kitchen! There was coffee, milk, broken eggs—practically the whole damned pantry—spilled across the floor when they left."

"They didn't arrest you, too?"

Emily shakes her head. "But they will." She starts to cry again. "It's only a matter of time."

"You don't know that." Mimi rummages through her purse for a handkerchief and hands it to Emily. "Did the police take anything? Anything that incriminated the doctor?"

"We had a few records out on the desk at home, and a patient was still recovering from her procedure in the downtown office. I'm sure they questioned her. Henry keeps a safe at home. The police hounded me to open it, but I refused. I guess they didn't have whatever they needed to open it themselves, so they sealed it up with police tape. They told me if I tried to open it and remove what was inside, they'd know."

"What *is* inside?"

Emily shrugs. "Patient records, I think. Financial papers. That sort of thing."

"And the police mean to come back and open it?"

"I think so. But they haven't yet."

Mimi looks out at the lagoon. Raindrops trouble the water. She thinks about what Ada had told her: *No sense in fretting over a future that isn't yet written.* It wasn't bad advice, and had calmed her at the time. But then, that was right before they'd discovered Ada's safe drilled open. Perhaps it's better if Mimi keeps such advice to herself.

"What happened next? After the police left?"

"They kept Henry in jail overnight. And oh, Mimi, it was awful. Was it awful for you? He said it was cold and dank and smelly. There was no place to lie down, so he was up the whole night. The rats were so bold, one of them came up and sniffed at his shoe. He had to kick him away to keep from being bitten."

"Rats?" Mimi shivers. There weren't any rats on the women's

side. At least, none that she'd seen. But it doesn't surprise her, with how filthy and dank the place is. "That *is* awful. Go on."

"The next morning, Henry went before a judge. He had to use our home as collateral to be released. He's supposed to appear in felony court today, but I'm not sure he's going to show."

"He said that?"

"Not in so many words, but he's been so upset since the raid. When he came home Saturday and saw what they'd done to the house and how they'd sealed the safe, he became positively despondent. I could hardly get him to eat anything. And yesterday, he refused to go to church. We always go to church. He loves Dr. Bradley's sermons and leaves so inspired and uplifted." Emily looks down and fingers her engagement ring. There's a second band beneath it, Mimi notices, one of plain silver.

"Em, did you and Dr. Millstone marry already?"

A sheepish smile spreads across her face. "We did. Three weeks ago."

"What about your summer wedding?"

"Henry thought we shouldn't wait."

Mimi wraps her up in a hug. "Congratulations!"

"It was a small ceremony. Just the two of us. We didn't even bring along any witnesses. The organist and the groundskeeper signed for us. But we're still planning on a big party in June with flowers and champagne and—" The smile falls from her face, and she looks away.

June. Mimi can picture it—the fully leafed trees, the warm sunshine, the blooming flowers—but she can't picture herself there. Mr. Smith warned her the trial could go on for several months. Will she be home in June, tending her garden and accompanying the children to the lakeshore? Or will she be in prison? The thought sours her stomach. Emily must be having the same trouble picturing her future.

Despite the uncertainty, Mimi takes her hand again and says in her cheeriest voice, "I, for one, can't wait for the party."

Only after she's said it does the dark irony of her words register. *Can't wait*. It's enough to make her want to laugh and cry at the same time. With effort, Mimi manages to keep both impulses schooled.

She doubts Emily caught the irony, but regardless, her smile doesn't return. Mimi tries another tactic. "An arrest is not the same as a conviction. Remember last August when Ada and Jo were arrested? A few weeks later, they were acquitted."

She doesn't mention the twenty-five hundred dollars it took to buy off Attorney Meyers or the three thousand dollars Daniel's got now to fix the case with Mr. Papanek.

"I told Henry so, but he insists this time is different," Emily says. "You should have seen him as he was packing his bag this morning. Pulling at his hair and muttering nonsense."

"Packing his bag? Where did he go?"

Emily glances around, as if someone might have snuck up on them and is listening. "I'm not supposed to tell anyone, but he's taken a room at a hotel. Just for a few days. He says he's so tired and needs time to think."

Mimi's shoulders tighten. Is he running, going on the lam? But if so, why leave Emily behind? Maybe he means to get settled someplace and send for her later.

"I called you as soon as he left. It will only upset the coppers more if he doesn't show up in court this morning, don't you think? But there was no talking sense into him."

Mimi has no reassurances to offer, so she only nods.

"I've got a bad feeling about all this, Mimi." She begins to cry again, talking through her tears. "It's here, just below my sternum, like my stomach is eating itself from the inside out. It's warning me that something is wrong, but I'm not sure what."

Mimi gives her hand a reassuring squeeze; never mind she's got a bad feeling about this, too. "Whatever it is, we'll face it together."

CHAPTER 38

Two days later, Mimi and Halina sit alone in the living room. Stan left last night for a two-game series against the Cardinals, and the children are in bed. Halina knits, and Mimi flips through the pages of *Ladies' Home Journal* while the radio announcer reads the latest news. After days of fighting, Greek troops have retreated, and the Nazis now occupy Athens.

Every day it seems there's more bad news in Europe and the Orient. How long before the war comes for America, too? With everything that's going on here at home, it's too much for Mimi to take. She reaches for the radio dial.

"In local news, doctor bares shocking details about abortion ring, then kills himself."

Mimi's hand falls to her lap, and she scoots to the edge of her chair.

"Loop physician, Dr. Henry James Millstone, killed himself yesterday in a room he had rented at the Hotel Rienzi. He was forty-four years old. Dr. Millstone was facing two felony abortion charges as well as a federal tax fraud investigation. Police found his body in bed, propped against pillows, after he had taken an overdose of a powerful narcotic. While waiting for the drug to take effect, he wrote letters to his wife, a bride of only a month; the coroner; and the police. It appears the man continued writing until death stilled his hand.

"In one of the letters, addressed to Assistant State's Attorney

Samuel Papanek, Dr. Millstone disclosed the workings of a so-called 'million-dollar syndicate' of Loop abortionists. The state's attorney's office is currently investigating this ring. In his letter, Dr. Millstone suggested the ring had framed him 'to deflect suspicion from themselves.'

"The coroner and his chief investigator are looking into Dr. Millstone's death and affairs.

"And now, back to our show."

Mimi reaches out again. Instead of turning to another station, she bats at the on-off knob until the radio goes silent, then rushes from the room.

Mimi sets the coffee pot on the table beside the sugar bowl.

"Will your husband be joining us today?" Mr. Smith asks.

"No. The club doesn't get back from St. Louis until this evening."

"I see. Well, he's welcome to come by my office when he gets back if he has any questions. Especially in light of these—er—latest developments."

He can only mean Dr. Millstone's suicide. She puts a hand on her stomach—her gut has wound itself into knots—until she's sure this morning's breakfast won't come up, then pours the coffee.

"I'll tell him."

Stan hasn't shown the slightest interest in the case. That would require speaking to her. But it's more than that. Like with his leg, he seems to think that if he ignores the truth of the situation, it might somehow disappear. Unlike his leg, the stakes here have become life and death.

Mr. Smith unzips his satchel and pulls out a leather-bound folio and two manila folders. "Strictly speaking, Dr. Millstone's case is tangential to yours, but it does . . . complicate things."

"The letters."

"Yes." He retrieves a piece of paper and passes it to her. "It's a facsimile, of course, but you can see it speaks directly of Mrs. Martin."

The words on the paper are typed, not handwritten, but she can't help but think about what she heard on the radio. *The man continued writing until death stilled his hand.* It's only been four days since Dr. Millstone's death. Three since the police found his body. "How did you get this?"

"A contact at the state's attorney's office. We'd get it through discovery anyway, but the more time we have to consider the evidence, the better."

Mimi's insides twist a little tighter. It's strange to think of a dying man's letters as evidence. Mr. Smith stares at her intently, and she knows he's waiting for her to read it. Mimi takes a deep breath and directs her eyes toward the words.

Assistant State's Attorney Samuel Papanek &
Captain Thomas Duffy

Gentlemen: I want to thank you both for the courtesy you have given me, but I deeply regret that you did not call me into your respective offices. I assure you I would have given you information and could very easily have cleared up your entire case for you.

I am going to ask a favor of you, Sam. Please be fair to that innocent little bride of mine. She is absolutely innocent, Sam. I know you will do the gentlemanly thing by her.

Mimi stops reading to blink back the tears from her eyes. Emily's been on her mind all weekend. How devastated and frightened she must be. Mimi's rung her half a dozen times over the past three days, but Emily hasn't answered.

About the whole setup of this syndicate, Sam. This guy, Dr. Max Gecht, is the brains of the whole affair. He made his million and is reposing in a castle in the hills of Hollywood.

I think I am getting a little incoherent as my head is going around. The outfit is the remains of the old Gecht regime. Dr. Gabler herself is now retired with close to a million and an estate which I understand is one of the show places of Florida. She was muscled out by Mrs. Martin and Mr. Piquett, who by the way are supposed to be sweethearts.

Mimi feels herself bristling. *Syndicate, outfit, muscled out*—he talks like they're a bunch of gangsters.

In the next few paragraphs, Dr. Millstone extols his early accomplishments—graduating from Rush Medical School, practicing alongside the famed surgeon Dr. James Neff. He speaks of his divorce from his first wife as the beginning of his first slump and then the gradual skid to his present predicament.

> *The end—my vision is getting blurry—I feel faint—had a glass of cold water and it has helped. I never knew any of these people. They are slickers and used me for a football. They actually framed me by forcing cases into my office so that I would be caught. In this way it would take the heat off them. Can't you see, Sam, how I was innocently roped in?*

Mimi slides the paper back to Mr. Smith.

"Can you dispute or corroborate anything the letter says?" he asks.

She hesitates. Even though it's filled with falsehoods, it feels awful to speak ill of the dead. Especially a man she'd been friendly with and the husband of a dear friend.

"Anything you say, Mrs. Lukas, is protected by attorney-client privilege."

"Dr. Gabler owned the clinic when I began working there. I don't know who owned it before her."

"And that was the fall of thirty-nine."

"Yes, October. I'd been there three months when Dr. Gabler left, and Ada took over. It seemed like an amicable arrangement. Dr. Gabler said she was retiring. As for Mr. Piquett, I couldn't say his exact role in it all. He stopped by the clinic from time to time and . . ."

"Go on."

"Sometimes—it didn't happen often—a woman who'd been seen at the clinic would suffer complications and wind up in the hospital. When that happened, Mr. Piquett would intervene with the woman and her husband, if she had one."

"Intervene how?"

"Offer them money if they agreed not to tell the police about the clinic."

"I see. And Dr. Millstone?"

Her fingers close around her coffee cup, but she doesn't drink. Warmth radiates through the porcelain, but it doesn't touch the chill that's settled inside her since she learned of the suicide. "He started working at the clinic as soon as Dr. Gabler left. He wasn't the only physician, but one of two or three main ones." And a favorite among the nurses for his mild temperament and steady hand, Mimi included. It makes his characterization of the clinic as greedy and corrupt and him its hapless victim all the more stinging.

"What does he mean when he says they framed me by forcing cases into my clinic?"

"After the State Street clinic was raided and our equipment was taken, we started taking patients to Dr. Millstone's offices for procedures."

"Whose idea was that?"

"Surely you've talked to Ada about this."

"I have. But I'd like to hear your understanding of things."

"I don't know. Ada's, I presume. But she must have discussed it with Dr. Millstone in advance, because he was always ready for us when we arrived and never seemed put out by the arrangement."

Mr. Smith rubs his chin. There's a scar there. A thin white line she hadn't noticed before. It could be the result of a hundred types of accidents—a slip on the ice, a stumble on the stairs, an uppercut from the schoolyard bully. Mimi prefers this last idea. She imagines him staggering back, eyes fluttering. He lifts a hand to his chin, and his fingers come away bloody. The bully approaches—a freckle-faced boy nearly twice young Mr. Smith's size. He rears back for another swing, but Mr. Smith ducks before delivering a knockout blow of his own. The other children in the schoolyard cheer.

"That must be how they got him," he says.

Mimi rattles her head. "Hmm?"

"Dr. Millstone. The police probably learned what was going on and sent a woman or two up to the State Street office to ask for an abortion, then followed you to Dr. Millstone's." He rubs his chin again. "Could constitute police entrapment, but we'll look into that later if the need arises."

Mimi pushes her coffee cup away. Even the smell is making her sick. She knows when he said *followed you*, he didn't mean her. She hasn't stepped foot in the State Street clinic or either of Dr. Millstone's offices since the grand jury indictment several weeks ago. But she still can't shake the feeling of being partially responsible. If she and the other nurses hadn't agreed to Ada's new plan, the raid on

Dr. Millstone's offices and the awful events that followed wouldn't have occurred. Or maybe they would have just found new nurses. And what of the women? Not the police's moles, but the women who'd actually needed their services. Was it worth it?

Mimi doesn't know. Certainly, Emily wouldn't say so.

"What about the letter Dr. Millstone wrote to his wife?" she asks.

"Oh, that? It doesn't contain anything useful vis-à-vis this case."

"Was it delivered to Mrs. Millstone?"

"No, I don't think so. It's still classified as evidence."

"Do you have a copy?"

Mr. Smith frowns but opens the manila folder again and passes her another typewritten paper.

My dearest love, it begins. Mimi reads no further. "Emily deserves to have this. You said it contains nothing relevant to the case. May I have this copy to give to her?"

His frown deepens. "You really shouldn't be seen together. Certainly not at her house. I don't think the police are watching you. But in all likelihood, they're watching her. They may even have her telephone tapped. She's facing similar charges as you, you know?"

Mimi hadn't known, only suspected. No wonder Mimi's calls had gone unanswered. "She wasn't among those arrested when they raided Dr. Millstone's office."

"No. It happened the day of his suicide. According to my contact at the state's attorney's office, they raided his offices again, looking for him and other collaborators."

"She's not a collaborator. She's his wife." The words come out sharper than Mimi intended, but Mr. Smith doesn't flinch.

"She didn't assist him in procedures?"

Mimi looks out the window. Clouds blot out the sun.

"Mrs. Lukas, as your attorney, I strongly advise you against seeking out Mrs. Millstone. Anyone associated with the case, really. Including Mrs. Martin and Miss Kuder. But, as a husband . . . well, you may have the letter."

CHAPTER 39

Mimi puts a can of fruit cocktail into her shopping basket, then another just for good measure. It's amazing how much Junior's eating these days, and he's not even nine. She'd better grab another can of Malt-O-Meal, too.

It's been a week since her meeting with Mr. Smith. She heeded his advice not to go to the Millstone house but has tried several more times to reach Emily by phone. No answer every time. All Mimi knows is what she reads in the paper. Tuesday, an article ran about the coroner's inquest into Dr. Millstone's death that included a picture of poor Emily testifying. It described how she became hysterical mid-testimony and had to be excused. Reporters love to throw that word around—*hysterical*—especially when describing women, but in this case, Mimi suspects it's true. If Stan had killed himself and she'd been forced to testify in front of the coroner, she'd be hysterical, too.

Wednesday, she learned from the *Tribune* that Louis Piquett had been arrested again along with Ada's bookkeeper, Mr. Frank Senft. Both men were quizzed about their connection to the abortion ring described in Dr. Millstone's suicide note. Thursday, the paper reported Mr. Piquett had been charged with conspiracy to commit abortions and released on an eight-thousand-dollar bail. Mr. Senft remained in Papanek's custody for further questioning.

Friday, a short article on page twenty-four reported that a felony court judge granted Mr. Papanek a two-week continuance in the charges he'd placed against Mr. Piquett, Emily, Annie, and Edna. Mr. Papanek was quoted as saying he expected grand jury indictments soon.

Thankfully, the weekend passed without any more bad news. This morning, Mr. Smith filed a plea with the judge handling their case. In it, he charged that no legal evidence had been introduced against Mimi and the others, as the names of the women who appeared before the grand jury were all obtained through the unlawful seizure of records. They won't know for a week or two if the plea is accepted, but Mr. Smith is—how had he said it?—*cautiously optimistic.*

Even so, the knots in Mimi's stomach haven't gone away. Her dress is noticeably looser through the waist. If she makes it through all this, she'll write to "Bonnie Knows Best." Never mind boiled cabbage or grapefruit and toast. Facing down felony charges is the surest reducing plan there is.

She laughs to herself as she grabs the Malt-O-Meal and starts toward the checkout counter. Better that than crying. Halfway down the aisle, she spies a young woman staring at the shelves of canned vegetables. She reaches for a can, hesitates, then reaches for another. After examining the label, she puts the can back and sighs. As Mimi draws closer, she recognizes the girl. Her first thought is to keep walking, but the frustration on the girl's face—brow furrowed, lower lip clasped between her teeth—is plain.

"Miss Moriarity?"

She startles and spins around to face Mimi, eyeing her without recognition.

"Marie, right? I'm Mrs. Lukas. We met at the zoo last year. I'm a friend of your father's."

She continues to stare at Mimi without speaking.

"You might not remember me. You were there with a boy, and the rest of us, well, we were just tagging along behind."

A blush spreads across Marie's cheeks, and she stops biting her lip long enough to flash a sheepish smile. "I remember," she says.

"Can I help you find something?"

"It's these beans. I'm not sure which I should get."

"What are you making?"

"Tomato hamburger soup."

"Hmm." Mimi looks at the shelf of canned goods. "Fava beans are a good choice."

"Thanks." Marie grabs a can of fava beans and adds it to her basket. The only other thing inside is a can of stewed tomatoes. Up close, Mimi sees dark circles under Marie's eyes and odd creases in the fabric of her dress, as if someone with a less-than-expert touch took an iron to it. Mimi can't remember how old Daniel said she was. Fifteen? Sixteen? She should be in school, but Mimi doesn't say so.

"What else does the recipe call for?"

Marie drops her gaze and shuffles a foot atop the linoleum floor. "I don't know. It's my mother's recipe. But she's . . . unwell."

Mimi remembers what Daniel has said about the fragile state of Elizabeth's nerves and her near-constant aches and pains. "Well, soup's just the thing to make her feel better. You might throw in a can or two of mixed vegetables, some tomato paste, a bay leaf—do you have dried bay leaves at home?—maybe some potatoes and . . ."

Fifteen minutes later, Marie's grocery basket is well-stocked, and Mimi's walked her through the general steps of making soup, from browning the meat to adding salt and spices to letting the pot simmer for a while so the flavors have a chance to meld. They wave goodbye on the street, and Mimi's happy to see a new lightness in Marie's step. She loads her groceries into the Packard and drives to the bakery, her last stop before home.

The delicious scent of freshly baked bread hits her when she enters the store. Her stomach grumbles. Not in the way it has of late, angry and constricting, but with genuine hunger, giving Mimi hope she'll be able to eat more than a few bites of supper. At that, her thoughts go to Marie. A crusty loaf of bread would accompany the soup perfectly. She should have suggested it. On impulse, she buys two loaves instead of one when she gets to the counter. The Moriarity house is only a mile or two out of her way. She'll drop off the bread, then head straight home.

To her surprise, Daniel answers the door. She thought he'd be at work. He's dressed in an undershirt and wrinkled trousers. His hair, usually slicked back, falls in oily clumps around his face. He looks surprised to see her, too. No, not surprised. Spooked. His eyes skate past her, darting up and down the street. She looks over her shoulder, as well. Surely, no one followed her here. The street is the same as when she arrived. Quiet and peaceful. The sidewalk's empty save for an old man walking his dog.

"Ada, again, huh?" he says to her, his voice gravelly, as if they're the first words he's said all day.

"What? No, I . . ." She's so rattled by Daniel's appearance that she forgets why she's come until she looks down and sees the loaf of bread in her hand. She holds it out to him. "I brought you this. Well, not you. Marie. I ran into her at the grocery store."

He hesitates before taking it. "Bread?"

"Marie mentioned she was making tomato hamburger soup. I thought they would go well together."

Daniel gives the loaf of bread a squeeze, the paper bag crinkling beneath his fingers. Then he sticks his nose in the mouth of the bag and inhales. "Bread," he says again.

"Just bread," Mimi says, although she can't figure out what else he might think is in there. "Why aren't you at work?"

He glances over her head again at the street, then sets the loaf on a small entry table beside the door and steps out. After closing the door behind him, he grabs Mimi's arm and tugs her down the front steps. His grip isn't painful, but it isn't gentle, either. She thinks for a moment he's walking her to her car, but when they reach the bottom step, he veers left, cutting across the yard instead of continuing down the front path to the street.

She tries to pull away, but his grip tightens. "Daniel, you're hurting me. Where are we going?"

He drags her through the narrow space between the houses and into the back alley, then lets her go. Mimi rubs her upper arm. There's a lingering throb where his fingers had been.

"It's not safe to talk out front like that," he says.

"Safe?"

He begins to pace the narrow alley. Garbage cans line the fences. A dog barks from a few yards away. "You shouldn't have come. Did Ada send you?"

"I already told you, no. I haven't seen Ada in weeks. Daniel, what's wrong? What's going on?"

"Papanek won't take the money. I tried, Mimi. I did. The case, it's too damn hot right now. Dr. Millstone and that damned letter. Every day, they're picking up someone new. And not just them. Federal revenue agents are in on it now, too. And Ada!"

"What about Ada?"

He enmeshes his fingers in his hair and pulls at his scalp. "She's harassing me daily. Calling, stopping by. Always asking, did I get the fix in? Did I get the fix in? I told her I can't touch it right now." He stops pacing and stalks toward her. "You know what she said to me?"

Mimi takes a step back, glancing over her shoulder at the way they came. She's never seen Daniel like this, so scattered and irate.

"You know what she said?" he repeats, drawing her gaze back to his. She shakes her head.

"That bitch threatened me. Threatened me! She said if she goes to prison, she's taking me with her."

"I'm sure she didn't mean it. She's just scared. Same as the rest of us."

"So you're on her side?"

"I'm not on anyone's side."

He backs up a few steps and resumes pacing. "What will happen to my family if I go to prison? I can't. I just can't. There's no way out of this. No way out."

Mimi glances down the narrow walkway between the houses again. But instead of fleeing, she turns back to Daniel, closing the distance between them and capturing his hands. He stops pacing. His skin is clammy, and his nail beds are even more ragged than when she'd seen him at the diner. With Daniel in such a state and her mother unwell, it's no wonder Marie seemed so downcast and bedraggled at the grocers.

"You have to calm down. I'll talk to Ada. Tell her to ease up on you and be patient. But you can't go around acting like this. Like a madman."

He frees his thumb and traces it over her knuckles. "We could have been something, you and me. Something real special. We shoulda . . ." His voice trails off, and he glances at the sky, as if imagining some alternate life they could have led.

Slowly, gently, Mimi pulls her hands free. "We're friends, Daniel. That's all. I'll talk to Ada, and you—"

"They're on to me, you know? They got my office filled with wires and dictographs. They're trying to get me, too. Just like the rest of you." His eyes meet hers again, but his gaze is unfocused, like he's looking through her at something else.

Are there really wires in Daniel's office, or is he paranoid? And whom does he mean by *they*? Papanek and the other men investigating the case? Considering Daniel approached Papanek with a bribe, it makes sense that Papanek would suspect him. But why not just report Daniel to his superiors?

"There's no way out," he says again, this time in a whisper. Then, his feet are in motion again, tromping back and forth over the rutted dirt alleyway. "She thinks she can put all this pressure on me, threaten me, cause me all this trouble. Well, I'll show her. I'll show her. It's the only way. The only way out."

"Dad?" Marie's voice calls from the house. "Are you out there, Dad?"

Daniel freezes, his face going pale. His eyes find hers again, clearer now and more focused.

"Dad?" Marie calls again.

Mimi nods to one of the garbage cans.

"Just taking out the trash," he calls over the wood-slatted fence, his voice a little thin but otherwise normal-sounding. "I'll be right in."

Mimi nods again, this time to the back gate, and forces her lips into a reassuring smile.

Daniel smiles, too, an eerie, doll-like grin that makes her skin prickle. A moment later, he disappears through the gate, leaving Mimi alone in the darkening alley.

CHAPTER 40

Mimi gets little sleep that night. Daniel seemed so unlike himself, his behavior so erratic. She made up her mind when she got home to go see Ada as soon as the children were off to school the next morning. But after lying awake for several hours, she decides it can't wait. The bedside clock reads five o'clock when she gets up and dresses. Stan's in Boston for the start of a long stretch of away games, so she needn't tiptoe around the bedroom or worry about turning on the lamp.

She sets out breakfast dishes and a box of Wheaties, leaving Halina a note that she's out running errands. The sky is just beginning to lighten as she leaves the house, the first rays of morning sun reaching above the still trees and quiet houses to the east. A bite lingers in the air, but there's not a cloud in sight, and the day promises to be a warm one. After her talk with Ada, she'll try to enjoy it. Walk the children to school, perhaps. Ready her garden for spring planting. Spread out a blanket in the back and nap in the sun.

The pleasant thoughts dull the edge of her unease as she drives to Ada's. It's only a few minutes past six when she arrives, rather early for an unannounced visit, but Ada's certainly not the type to linger in bed. Still, Mimi knocks quietly, in case anyone else in the house is still asleep.

The maid, Delia, opens the door. "May I help you?"

"Is Mrs. Martin awake? I'm a—er—friend, Mimi Lukas."

"Yes, I remember you. Just a minute."

Delia returns a moment later and lets her inside.

"Sorry for the early call," Mimi says, belatedly remembering her manners. Delia takes her coat and escorts her down a hall that flanks the staircase into a large, sunny kitchen. Ada and Mr. Martin are seated at a small table, sipping coffee. Mr. Martin is dressed and shaven. Ada's still in her housecoat, her hair tied up in a scarf. Neither seems to mind Mimi's early intrusion, though. Mr. Martin flashes her a warm smile then goes back to his paper. Ada motions for her to join them at the table, and Delia brings her a cup of coffee.

"How have you been, my dear?" Ada asks.

Mimi adds a splash of milk to her cup and stirs. "All right, considering. You?"

"Fine."

If Mimi didn't know Ada better, she might believe her. Even this early in the morning, without makeup or finished hair, she radiates poise and confidence. But there's a weary edge behind her calm demeanor Mimi hasn't seen before. Like the act of seeming normal—seeming fine, confident, and poised—takes considerable effort. Mimi knows that feeling, that weariness well. So, too, it seems, does Daniel.

"I'm here because . . ." She glances at Mr. Martin, uncertain how much he knows, but Ada nods for her to continue. "Yesterday I was at the market and—"

A knock at the door interrupts her. Delia shuffles from the kitchen to answer it.

"Probably just the milkman," Ada says. "He knocks sometimes if he's got extra cream. Go on, dear."

"Yesterday at the market, I ran into one of Mr. Moriar—"

A commotion sounds from the foyer, followed by the thud of footsteps up the stairs. Mr. Martin rises from his chair. "What the devil?"

"Delia?" Ada calls. But her voice is drowned out by the sound of gunshots. For the span of a heartbeat, the entire world freezes. Except the sound. *Bang! Bang! Bang!* Then everything is in motion again, including Mimi. She races behind Ada and Mr. Martin to the foyer. The front door is open wide, and Delia cowers beside it. Mimi's eyes rake over her, searching for blood. None.

Another shot rings out. The origin of the sound is clear: upstairs.

Ada gasps. "Jennie!" She staggers toward the steps. Mimi's faster, taking the stairs two at a time. She arrives on the landing and sees an open door. It's dim inside, but she can just make out the figure of a man standing at the foot of a bed. Though he must have heard

Mimi scrambling up the stairs, he doesn't look her way. He takes something out of his pocket and throws it into the air above the bed. Slips of dark paper rain down. Mimi takes a step closer, then stops, her heart leaping into her throat. It's Daniel.

There's a faint glint of metal in one hand. The gun. He brings it to his temple and pulls the trigger.

Mimi turns her head, wincing. But the only sound is a soft click. Then another. "No, no, no!" he shouts. She looks back just as he begins smashing the barrel of the gun into his forehead.

Ada's at her side now. "Jennie!" she says again, and they both rush into the room.

Jennie lies on the bed, one arm draped over her face, moaning. Dark stains spread across the bedclothes. Paper is scattered all around. Ada climbs onto the bed and shakes Jennie's leg. Jennie startles and cries out, weakly batting Ada away.

"It's me, baby. It's Mama."

Mimi clambers onto the bed, too, and pulls back the covers. They're heavy and wet with blood. So is Jennie's nightgown. Mimi needs to figure out where she's injured and stanch the flow, but the room's still so dark, it's difficult to see.

"Light," she says to Ada. "And we need to call for an ambulance."

Ada doesn't move except to crawl to the head of the bed and drag Jennie into her lap. "I'm here, baby. It's going to be okay."

Mimi jumps off the bed and throws the curtains wide. A moment later, she's back at Jennie's side. "Telephone the police," she calls to no one in particular. "We need an ambulance!" She lifts Jennie's nightdress. Using her own shirtsleeve, she wipes the blood away from Jennie's midsection. Three bullet holes riddle her abdomen. There's another in her upper leg and one in her right shoulder. None of the wounds is spurting blood—a good sign—but the flow is constant, and the internal damage likely significant.

She takes one of Ada's hands and places it over the wound on Jennie's shoulder. "Keep pressure here."

Ada nods, tears streaming down her face. "She's going to be okay, isn't she?"

Before Mimi can answer, Ada turns back to her daughter, kissing the girl's brow. "You're going to be okay, baby. You're going to be okay."

Jennie's face is crumbled in pain. Her breathing is fast and labored. Sweat dapples her skin. She coughs, and red-tinged spittle dribbles from her lips.

Mimi rips the pillowcase off one of the pillows and ties it around Jennie's leg where the bullet had entered, then turns her attention to the girl's abdomen. Already, it's wet with blood again. She picks the two holes bleeding the worst, and flattens her hands atop them. It's little use when the damage is deep inside, but she must do something.

Slowly, Mimi becomes aware of a banging noise, loud and rhythmic. The door? Have the police and ambulance arrived? She turns her head and sees that it's Daniel banging his head against the wall. A splatter of red mars the paint.

"Stop!" she cries. "Stop it." But Daniel doesn't seem to hear her or even register that she and Ada are there. He might do himself real harm—he's certainly trying—but Mimi can't leave Jennie's side. The girl's breath has become a rattle, her face waxy and pale.

There's more banging, but Mimi doesn't realize it's footsteps until the first police officer appears in the doorway. He stands there a moment, mouth agape. Another officer appears behind him.

"Where's the ambulance?" Mimi yells.

Her voice seems to startle the men into action. "On its way," one says, as the other barrels toward Daniel. The men tussle. In the end, it takes both officers to subdue him. By the time Daniel's in handcuffs, the ambulance has arrived.

"Five gunshot wounds," she tells the ambulance physician. "One in the leg and four in the torso."

But even before he pushes her aside and places a stethoscope on Jennie's chest, Mimi knows it's too late. She hasn't heard or felt a breath in well over a minute, and the flow of blood has slowed.

The physician removes the stethoscope from his ears and shakes his head. "I'm sorry."

Ada screams—a high-pitched, heartrending cry any mother would know. She pulls Jennie's body to her breast, rocking back and forth as she sobs.

Mimi stumbles off the bed, backing away until she hits the wall. The room goes in and out of focus. Officers are leading Daniel away. Blood is everywhere—on the bed and the wall, on Mimi's clothes and hands. The dark strips of paper Daniel threw into the air aren't paper, but money. Twenties and fifties and even hundred-dollar bills.

Dozens and dozens of them lie scattered throughout the room. She doesn't need to count it to know it's the bribe money Ada gave him.

Someone hands Mimi a towel. Her cheeks are wet with tears, though Mimi doesn't remember when she started crying. She wipes them dry and holds out the towel.

"It's for the blood, ma'am."

Mimi turns and sees that the man speaking to her is a police officer. A young man. Little older than Jennie.

"Oh," she says, and wipes her hands. She blots her skirt and blouse, too, but it does little good. "Is this Ada's towel?"

The policeman shrugs. "It came from the hall closet."

"It's going to stain." Mimi purses her lips and looks around the room. "It's all going to stain if we don't get these linens soaking soon." Cold water and vinegar will work best, though she doubts it will be enough. She steps forward and reaches for the tangled sheets she'd pushed to the foot of the bed.

The officer grabs her wrist. "That's evidence, ma'am."

Evidence. Mimi recoils, the sound of gunshots replaying in her ears.

"Let's get you out of here, okay?" The officer puts his arm around her and leads her from the room. He takes her down the stairs and into the living room.

"Why don't you sit, ma'am?"

She'd like to sit; her legs are wobbly and back sore, but she doesn't want to get blood on Ada's good furniture. There's a wooden chair in the kitchen. Along with her coffee. It's likely gone cold, though. And she really ought to be getting back home if she hopes to catch Penny and Junior before they leave for school.

"Can you get me my coat?" she says to the officer.

"Are you cold?"

"School starts at eight."

"Ma'am, you really ought to sit down."

His words sound funny, like she's hearing them under water. He leads her toward a chair, but Mimi resists. Or tries to. Her legs scarcely seem under her control.

"I'll take it from here, officer," a voice says. The familiar timbre cuts through the fog in Mimi's mind. She turns her head just as her knees give out. It's Mr. Papanek.

CHAPTER 41

The officer helps Mimi to the chair. She doesn't protest. Never mind the threat of the stain.

"Fetch her a glass of water," Mr. Papanek says to the officer, and then to her, "Wait here, Mrs. Lukas, and don't try to run."

Run? She can barely stand.

The officer brings her a cup of ice-cold water. She thanks him and drinks it, even though she's shivering. It helps clear her mind. There are dozens of policemen milling about the house now. At a word from Mr. Papanek, they begin searching the rooms, opening cabinets and drawers.

Mimi sees Delia and Mr. Martin escorted out of the house. The maid looks pale and frightened; he looks bereft.

Next, Ada is brought down the stairs, an officer on either side of her. She's no longer in her housecoat, but a blue and white day dress. Her stockings slouch, bunching at her ankles, as if she's forgotten to fasten them to her garter belt. "What about Jennie? Can't I be with my Jennie?" she asks.

"She's getting along fine," one of the men says, handing Ada off to another policeman. "Go with the officers now."

Ada looks back toward the stairs, craning her neck as if she might be able to see into Jennie's room. "Are you sure?"

They walk her out of the house without answering.

Getting along fine? Has Mimi misremembered what happened

in the room? The labored rattle of Jennie's breath. The blood-soaked sheets. The shake of the ambulance physician's head.

Mr. Papanek returns to the living room and hands her a set of clothes. "Put these on."

"Is Ada's daughter really all right? The physician didn't hear a heartbeat. I was there and—"

He hoists her up by the arm. "Never you mind that."

In the hallway water closet, Mimi changes out of her blouse and skirt into the dress Mr. Papanek gave her. It's a few sizes too big and smells of Ada's perfume. She scrubs her hands and forearms at the sink, watching the red-tinged water swirl down the drain, but she can't get all the blood out from under her nails before there's a sharp knock at the door.

With her ruined clothes folded and tucked under her arm—she couldn't very well leave them in Ada's bathroom—Mimi's escorted to the back of a squad car and driven to the Criminal Court Building. Ada rides with her, while Mr. Martin and Delia follow in another police car.

"Do you think Jennie's all right?" she asks Mimi on the drive. "I'm so worried about my Jennie."

Mimi doesn't know what to say, so she takes Ada's hand in her own and gives it a squeeze.

They wait for hours in Papanek's office. No one offers them a cup of water. When Mimi asks to use the telephone to call Halina, the dour secretary tells her no.

Seated on the hard, wooden chair, Mimi plays the morning's events over and over again in her mind. It's all so strange and nightmare-like. She wonders whether it happened at all. But then she'll look down at her hands and see the dried blood beneath her nails, or glance at the folded clothes beside her, stained so completely bright red it can't have been a dream.

Around midday, Papanek calls her into his office. What was she doing at Ada's so early in the morning? he asks. Why was she there at all? Does she know Officer Moriarity? Where did she meet him?

She keeps her head down and answers short. Several times, she loses track of the question, her mind stuck on the *Bang! Bang! Bang!* of the gun. She can tell by the edge in Mr. Papanek's voice that his patience with her is wearing thin, but Mimi can't muster the will to care.

Eventually, she looks up and cuts him off mid-sentence. "Throw me in jail if you want. I'm done answering your questions."

"A young woman is dead, Mrs. Lukas."

The finality in his words hit her like a fist to the stomach. No dream. No misremembering. Jennie is dead. She shakes her head. "Why would he want to kill Jennie?"

Mimi says it as much to herself as to Mr. Papanek, but of course, he has an answer. "My men who interviewed him at the hospital said he thought he was shooting at Mrs. Martin."

She knots her hands together in her lap, squeezing her fingers so tightly they begin to lose feeling. If only she'd arrived at the Martins' sooner. Maybe then, Jennie would still be alive.

"You seem less surprised by that than the notion Mr. Moriarity would kill her daughter. Care to tell me why?"

Mimi stands. "This whole thing has gotten so awful and ugly, nothing surprises me anymore. Put that in your goddamned report."

He glares at her, but doesn't stop her as she stalks from the room, joining the others on the hard chairs out front.

Delia's subjected to his questions next, though he keeps her in his office for only a few minutes. Thankfully, he has the decency not to badger Ada or her husband.

In the early afternoon, two men dressed in cheap, ready-made suits come into the office.

"Mr. and Mrs. Martin?" one of the men asks.

Ada and her husband stand.

"Where would you like us to take your daughter?"

"What do you mean?" Ada asks.

"We're from the coroner's office, ma'am. Is there an undertaker you prefer?"

Ada falls back into her chair. "Undertaker? I don't know any undertakers." She turns to her husband, her voice growing shrill. "What do we do? We don't know any undertakers. Our Jennie, our baby, she needs . . . she needs . . ." Ada begins to sob. Every muscle in Mr. Martin's face is taut, as if it's all he can do to keep from sobbing, too.

"I know an undertaker on Forty-seventh Street," Mimi says, thinking of a quiet gentleman from church. He wears a yellow bow tie every Sunday, except Christmas, when he dons a red-and-green-checkered one. "Mister . . . Pulaski."

Ada wipes her eyes on her sleeve. "Is he . . ."

"He's very kind and . . ." What does one say of an undertaker? "Skilled."

"Thank you," Ada says, then turns back to the men. "Please take my Jennie to Mr. Pulaski on Forty-seventh Street. And please . . . be gentle with her."

The men nod and leave.

It's three more hours before Mr. Papanek releases them. Two squad cars return them to Ada's home. When they arrive, the police open Ada's door, but instead of getting out, she turns to Mimi. "I don't know if I can go back in there."

Mimi nods. If it had been one of her children murdered, she can't imagine getting within ten blocks of her home again. But not going inside won't change what happened, and they can't stay here in the squad car. "I'll go with you."

Mimi and Delia walk on either side of Ada and help her inside. Mr. Martin walks behind them, his steps slow and heavy. The house is dark and quiet when they enter, and even though Mimi knows no one is there, a chill skitters up her spine.

Delia turns on the foyer's overhead light, and Mimi shivers again. The house has been ransacked. Jackets and scarves litter the ground, as if the entire coat closet has been emptied onto the floor. A half-open umbrella sits beside a pair of galoshes. A lone mitten lies inside an upturned hat. A fur coat and a rubber rain slicker tangle on the marble entry table beside a toppled vase.

If the foyer looks this bad, Mimi has no doubt the rest of the house lies in worse shambles. Delia's mouth is a grim line, while Ada stands between them, slack-jawed. "What have they done to our house? Tom, look what they've done."

But Mr. Martin hardly seems to register the disarray. He shuffles into the living room and straight toward the bar cart, not bothering to turn on the light or step over the jumble of magazines and doilies and throw pillows in his way.

"Never mind the mess, Mrs. Martin," Delia says. "Let's get you to bed."

Once Ada is settled, with the curtains drawn and a cool cloth draped over her forehead, Mimi helps Delia strip the bloody sheets and blankets from Jennie's bed. Never mind if it's evidence. Clearly, the police have already taken all they wanted. She vaguely remembers thinking this morning they ought to have been started soaking in water and vinegar, but the idea now is so ridiculous, she almost laughs.

They throw the bedclothes in the trash bins behind the house, then Delia helps Mimi find her coat and purse amid the clutter in the hall.

Once she's alone, seated behind the wheel of her car, Mimi's entire body begins to tremble. It takes her three tries to fit the key into the ignition. She cranks on the heat, even though the car's already warm, and takes a deep breath before pulling away from the curb.

Her mind is blank the entire drive. She navigates the roads like an automaton, turning this way and that, braking and accelerating without conscious thought to do so. Not until she's parked in front of her own house does her brain kick back in.

She can't go inside like this—dazed and shaking. How will she explain her daylong absence? What will she fix for dinner? Her eyes snag on Junior's bike, its back wheel crushing her newly blooming daffodils, then blur with tears. She cries uncontrollably for several minutes, her nose dripping and body heaving. Then, slowly, she pulls herself together. Noodles with weenies and butter. That's what she'll cook for dinner. With a side of canned pears. The rest—an explanation for Halina, the bloodstained clothes folded on the seat beside her—she'll deal with after supper and a hot shower. Right now, she only wants to hug her children.

CHAPTER 42

That night, even though Mimi knows Daniel's under police guard at the hospital, she takes a pillow and blanket from her bedroom and sleeps in the hallway in front of the children's rooms. The floor is hard and cold, and every creak startles her awake, but she'd sleep worse in her bedroom without the slim reassurance that any madman with a gun who entered would stumble over her first before reaching the children.

Is Daniel a madman? He certainly seemed mad there in Jennie's bedroom. And the night before, too, as he'd paced the alleyway behind his house. If not mad, certainly unsettled. Should she have gone to see Ada right away? Would that have saved Jennie's life? Upset as Daniel was when they spoke, Mimi never would have thought him capable of such an act. He must have felt his life was falling apart around him. He'd said as much, hadn't he? *No way out.* Mimi can certainly relate, even if she can't fathom his actions. Her own world feels like a sandcastle with the incoming tide lapping at its walls.

If only Stan were here. It doesn't matter that he's still not speaking to her. His presence would be enough. She can't remember if the team's in Boston today or Brooklyn. All she knows is he won't be back for another fourteen days.

She makes pancakes for breakfast. An unusual midweek treat, but Penny and Junior's delighted surprise is worth the extra effort. Only Halina doesn't look pleased. No doubt she's still haunted by the story Mimi told her last night. Mimi spared her the grimmest details—Jennie's writhing agony, the thud of Daniel's head against the wall, the blood-slickened money scattered about the bed. The story's tragic enough without them.

The telephone rings shortly after the children leave for school as she's scrubbing syrup from the last of the breakfast dishes. Her lungs fill with a greedy inhale. Could it be Stan?

Mimi hastily wipes her hands on her apron and hurries to the telephone.

"Good morning, Lukas residence."

"Mimi?"

It's Emily's voice, not Stan's. Even though Mimi's been trying to reach her for over a week, a knot of disappointment twists inside her. "Em. Where have you been? Are you okay?"

"They got me, Mimi. They got me, too." There's a quiver in her words, as if she's on the brink of tears.

"I heard. I'm so sorry."

"And did you see today's paper?"

Mimi avoided the newspaper this morning, taking it straight from the front porch to the trash can. She doesn't need any reminder of yesterday's horrors. "You mean about Ada's daughter, Jennie?"

"Murdered! I can't bear all this tragedy. I just can't. Poor Henry, and now this."

Mimi searches for something to say as the line goes quiet but can't find the words. Everything that comes to mind rings false or glib.

"I'm scared, Mimi."

"Me, too."

"Do you think God's punishing us?"

Mimi pulls her bottom lip into her mouth, and her eyes drift upward, as if she might find the answer hovering just below the plaster-white ceiling. Edna or Roberta would be better to ask. They'd readily reply *no.* And surely that's what Emily needs to hear. Father Kowalski would have a ready answer, too. That visiting professor who'd seduced Ginny all those years back could speak on the subject for hours. The thought turns her stomach. "I don't know God's mind, Em. And I don't much trust anyone who says they do. But I don't think it's as simple as that. Good and bad. Right and wrong. Nothing about any of this ever felt simple."

"You don't regret it? Don't wish I'd never run into you at Memorial and given you the clinic's address?"

"I don't know." She knows this isn't the answer Emily's searching for, either, but it's the best she can give. "Do you?"

"Yes . . . no . . . I don't know."

"Just because you regret something doesn't mean it was the wrong thing to do."

Emily begins to cry, a muffled, tremulous sound that breaks Mimi's heart to hear. "I miss him so much, Mimi. I can't believe he's gone. I don't think I can face this all alone."

"You're not alone."

The line is silent except for the murmur of tears.

"You're not alone, Em. We've still got each other."

At this, Emily sobs quietly, but she doesn't speak.

"He left you a letter."

"Henry?"

"The police didn't tell you?"

"Henry left me a letter?"

"My lawyer, he got a copy. We can meet at Washington Park this afternoon, and I'll give it to you."

"No."

"I'll come to the apartment, then." Mr. Smith's warnings be damned.

"Can you . . . will you read it to me over the phone?"

"Sure, but—"

"Thank you, Mimi. You've always been a swell friend."

Mimi sets the phone down and retrieves the letter from her bedroom. After making sure Emily's still on the line, she takes a deep breath and begins to read aloud:

My dearest Emily,

Our time together—sweet as it was—has come to an end. You can sell a detailed account of our experience with the million-dollar syndicate to a confession magazine and be set up real good.

I have this rendezvous with death and wanted to take you with me—but felt I wanted someone to retain this spark of goodness that I might have done in the world. Please, darling, be good and think of me once in a while. I am leaving this world with no regrets as I have lived as no one has lived. I have done some good and a little bad but have been persecuted by people that are trying to save their necks.

I am getting heavy and sleepy and my vision is starting to get a little blurred. I will continue to write until this pen gets too heavy.

Now about the hereafter, I shall try to return to you nightly with my little words of tenderness and advice. I wonder, wonder deeply, if we shall meet. I am going to try to give you my feelings as I depart from this mortal world—from you. Don't let anyone see me as I want them all to remember me as alive and vibrant.

Our years together were the best and dearest of my life. I hope—

"I hope what?" Emily says when Mimi stops.

She flips the page over, but it's blank. "That's the end. I think he may have . . ."

There's a soft gasp on the other end of the line, followed by the sound of renewed tears. It's all Mimi can do to keep from crying, too.

"I'm so sorry, Em. Please, let me come over and bring—"

"No. I just . . . I just need to be alone for a while."

"Tomorrow, then."

There's a pause before Emily says, "Tomorrow. Thank you, Mimi. You really are a good friend."

There's a click, and the line goes dead before Mimi can say the same.

CHAPTER 43

The next morning, there's no avoiding the bad news in the paper. It's printed in large letters across the top of the front page:

MILLSTONE WIDOW ENDS HER
LIFE OVER ABORTION PROBE

Mimi's halfway across the yard on her way to the trash bin when she sees it. She falls to her knees and retches up last night's dinner. The newly greening grass is covered in cold dew. It bleeds through her housecoat, turning her skin to gooseflesh. She wipes her lips with her sleeve, then shoves a fist in her mouth so no one hears her scream.

As the Packard idles at a traffic light, Mimi catches sight of herself in the rearview mirror. She's done her best to cover the dark circles beneath her eyes and pin her limp hair into something resembling a chignon. Her hat hides the worst of it—greasy, unwashed roots—but she still looks like a ghost of herself. The head-to-toe black she wears doesn't do her sallow complexion any favors. A grimace reveals pink-smudged teeth.

She pulls a tissue from her purse to wipe the lipstick from her teeth when a car honks behind her. The light's gone green. She abandons the tissue and jerks the car into gear. Better to wait until she gets to the church anyway. Since she read of Emily's death in the paper two days earlier, she hasn't been able to stop gnawing at her lips.

Yesterday's ordeal at the county morgue—an hours-long recounting of every detail of Jennie's murder for the coroner and his jury—only made the tic worse.

At the next light, Mimi spies a run in her stocking. Not some little thing she can dab with Run-R-Stop and hope no one sees, but a gaping tear from knee to ankle. She glances at her watch and then back to the road. If the darn light hurries up, she'll have enough time to stop at Woolworth's. Dark circles and limp hair are one thing, but she'll not attend Jennie's funeral with a run in her stocking.

At Woolworth's, Mimi winds through the crowded aisles to the stockings counter. Time's taken on the herky-jerky quality of a dilapidated roller coaster, and she forgot today was Saturday. Woolworth's is always busy on Saturdays.

She reaches for a pair of stockings, but another hand grabs them first. The next pair is too big. The next too small. They can't be out of her size, can they? She continues to rummage through the packages of stockings until she finds a pair that will fit, then joins the long line of other women waiting to pay.

Another glance at her watch has her foot tapping impatiently. Directly ahead of her is a knot of three women chatting and laughing. Each holds an armful of goods, none of which seem as important as stockings for a murdered friend's funeral. If she told them she was running late for such an occasion, would the women let her cut ahead in line?

Mimi inches closer to ask—she'll leave out the part about the murder—but stops when she catches an earful of their conversation.

"Poison. That's what the paper said."

"Poison?"

The first woman nods.

Mimi's chest tightens, and she bites down on her lip. Surely they're not talking about Emily. But who else could it be?

"Guess she thought it'd be quick and painless. But it seems like it was anything but."

Mimi closes her eyes, willing herself not to break down weeping in the middle of Woolworth's. She hadn't learned any more than what *The Tribune* printed, but it's enough to know the woman is right. Emily's death wasn't quick or painless. She dressed in her crisp white nurse uniform and wrote a parting letter to Henry:

Darling, I am following you. Please forgive me for the way I am taking out, as I don't know how to do it as you did. I love you so.

Then she drank the fateful draught. When the agony became too much to bear, she stumbled from the apartment, moaning and gasping, and collapsed in the arms of her neighbor. The police were called, but arrived too late to save her.

"Was she part of that same criminal operation as the crooked cop?" one of the women asks.

Mimi opens her eyes in time to see the first woman nod again. "He's tried to kill himself three times at the hospital and now is on a hunger strike in jail."

"I heard it was a mistake," another of the women says. "That he meant to kill Mrs. Martin, the head of the syndicate, but shot her daughter by mistake."

The other two women give a pitying shake of the head, as if it's nothing more tragic than spilled grape juice or a fallen soufflé.

Daniel. Jennie. Emily. It's too much for Mimi to bear. And to hear strangers talking so casually about them, swapping bits of information like recipes, makes her blood hot.

"He wasn't the only one on the take," one of them says. "I overheard my husband say that two fellas from the state's attorney's office were fired, too. Both had taken bribes from that abortion racket."

Mimi's fingers tense and curl, throttling her purse straps in one hand and the package of stockings in the other. *These are people's lives*, she wants to scream. It grows in her throat, the words jockeying to be free, and she bites down harder on her lower lip.

"You know who else was involved in the clinic's sordid dealings," the first woman says. "The wife of, oh, what's his name . . . that washed-up ballplayer . . . the Polack . . . Smashin' . . . Slashin' . . ."

The scream building in Mimi's throat dies. She'd seen her name printed in the paper alongside the other "million-dollar abortion ring conspirators" but hoped people wouldn't connect Mrs. Miriam Lukasewicz to—

"Slammin' Stach Lukas?" one of the women supplies.

"Yeah, that's the one."

The women wag their heads again. Then their conversation changes direction. Something about a new picture playing at the Chicago Theater.

Mimi's flexed hands are trembling now. Thank goodness Stan's on a bus hundreds of miles away, headed from Boston to Brooklyn for tomorrow's matchup against the Dodgers. But if these strangers made the connection, others will, as well. It's only a matter of time before news reaches him, too.

The women's voices blend into those around them. Everyone is talking now—shoppers, salesclerks, diners at the nearby lunch counter—and the noise is deafening. *Did you hear?* says the doorman to the gentleman who enters. *Did you hear?* says the waitress with her coffee pot. *Did you hear?* says the clerk, dropping coins into the till. *Did you hear, did you hear, did you hear?*

"Enough!" Mimi screams.

A hundred pairs of eyes turn in her direction, and everyone goes quiet.

"Enough," she says again, half whisper, half sob. She pushes past the women in front of her and slaps a dime down on the counter. Then she hurries from the store, chatter resuming in her wake.

CHAPTER 44

"*Świnie,*" Halina says under her breath.

Mimi doesn't need to know what the words mean to know Halina's upset. She says them like a cat hacking up a hairball. It's not the sort of thing Mimi expects to hear from her mother-in-law in church, and it's enough to make her raise her head and look around for the first time since they arrived.

Father Kowalski is reading from the Bible—the Gospel of Matthew, though Mimi still doesn't understand enough Polish to know which verse. More than the usual number of people aren't listening. Instead, she sees dozens of heads bent together, lips whispering. Other parishioners are craning their necks to steal a backward glance in her direction. One man a few rows ahead has the gall to point.

After yesterday's debacle at Woolworth's, she should have expected this. But time and reality still have that fuzzy, jolting feeling of a dream. No, not a dream. A nightmare. This morning, she walked out of the house with her shoes on the wrong feet. It wasn't until she nearly turned her ankle on the porch steps that she noticed.

Father Kowalski clears his throat and waits until the whispers quiet and heads turn forward before continuing to read. When he finishes, the congregation sits, more than a few taking the opportunity to steal a glance in her direction while they reach for their hymnal or tuck their skirts.

Mimi's cheeks barely muster a blush. She's so tired, and these people have never liked or accepted her. But then Penny leans close and whispers, "Mama, why is everyone looking at us?"

At that, Mimi's heart breaks anew. The Polish Day Parade is set to begin shortly after Mass, and Penny's wearing her traditional folk costume. Most of the children and half the adults are dressed similarly. But Penny fingers the strand of red beads around her neck, as if her costume might be the cause of their stares and scorn.

"They're not looking at us, darling. I'm sure it's just a bird or something trapped inside. Pay attention to Father Kowalski now."

But there's no way around it when they arrive at the start of the parade route after Mass. Hundreds of people have gathered at the intersection of Noble and Division Streets, and at first, it's easy to disappear into the crowd. Musicians lug their instruments. Other participants carry flags, wreaths, or banners. It's a riot of colors, ribbons, and flowers. The route follows Division Street to Humboldt Park, where there'll be food, music, and speeches. Even Mayor Kelly is slated to give an address.

In the past, Mimi's always enjoyed the festivities, despite feeling like an outsider. And the children look forward to it all year long. But for Halina, it's as important a day as Christmas, and one of the few times Mimi sees a look of unbridled joy on her mother-in-law's face.

But today, as Halina is helping straighten the tulle apron Penny wears over her red flower-print skirt and Mimi is wiping away the smudge of dirt that's somehow found its way onto Junior's kaftan, Mrs. Rozmarek comes up to them. She, too, is dressed in an elaborate costume of bright colors and detailed embroidery. As secretary of the Polish National Alliance and chairwoman of its education department, she's the one they're supposed to report to as soon as the children are ready to march. Mimi's met her several dozen times over the years, so by now is used to her cramped smile and brusque manner.

"Mrs. Lukas, might I speak to you a moment?"

Mimi gives Junior's kaftan a final look, then stands. "Of course."

Mrs. Rozmarek steps away from Halina and the children, and Mimi follows, her stomach tightening. People are staring again. Or perhaps they've been all along, only Mimi hadn't noticed.

"Some of the board have been talking, and we think it best if Penelope and Stanislaw don't march in the parade today."

"What?"

"For their own sake and the sake of other children."

"I don't understand."

Mrs. Rozmarek's eye twitches, but her tight smile holds. "While I'm not one to condemn a child for their parent's sins, I'm not sure we can count on everyone else to be so . . . magnanimous."

Mimi's hands tingle with heat. There's nothing magnanimous about excluding her children from the parade.

"And just what do you think is going to happen?"

"Well . . . a fight could break out among the children."

"A fight?"

"Children know more than we give them credit for. Why, some of the older ones probably even read the paper. Someone might say something and, well . . . it's natural for a child to want to defend their mother, even if her actions aren't worthy of defense."

The heat travels up Mimi's arms and into her neck. She splays her fingers to keep them from balling into fists. "My children know better than to rise to the provocation of bullies."

"Be that as it may, it's just not the sort of thing we can chance on a day like today. Not with the whole city watching."

"Please, Agatha. My children have nothing to do with . . . with the charges against me. They'll be so disappointed if they can't be part of the parade. They've marched every year since they could walk. You're a mother. You must understand."

"As a mother, I would have thought more about my family before involving myself in criminal activity."

Mimi glances around, desperation clawing at the back side of her ribs. Penny and Junior will be devastated. Across the street, she sees Zofina fussing with her own children's outfits. Mimi catches her eye. Zofina and Mrs. Rozmarek are cousins, or second cousins, or relations of some order, and they've always appeared chummy. Surely, Zofina can talk some sense into Mrs. Rozmarek.

But just as Mimi raises a hand to wave her over, Zofina looks away, suddenly engrossed in adjusting the flower wreath atop her daughter's head. Mimi watches her a moment, hoping she'll look back and come to Mimi's aid. She doesn't.

In all the years Mimi's been coming to the parade, she's never felt more alone.

She turns back to Mrs. Rozmarek. "Please, I'm begging—"

"Let's not cause more of a scene. The board's already decided. Good day, Mrs. Lukas."

Mimi feels her composure slipping. The urge to cry wars with the urge to pull her hair out and scream. Her hands are still hot and tingling.

Mrs. Rozmarek's afraid of causing more of a scene, is she? As if just speaking to Mimi is tantamount to scandal. Well, Mimi will show her what a real scene looks like. She glances around for something to throw. Finding nothing, she takes off her shoe and hurls it at Mrs. Rozmarek. It hits the woman squarely in the back. She hollers in surprise and spins around. If everyone wasn't watching before, they are now.

Mrs. Rozmarek looks down at the shoe, then up at Mimi. No cramped smile now. Her mouth gapes open, and her cheeks flush the same red color as her necklace.

"Did you . . . did you . . ."

Mimi saunters over and picks up her shoe. "You might want to close your mouth, Agatha. The whole city's watching, remember?" She plants a hand on Mrs. Rozmarek's shoulder to steady herself as she slips the shoe back on.

Mrs. Rozmarek remains stock-still, as if she fears what else Mimi might do.

"Stan's not the only one with a strong arm and good aim," Mimi says. She turns to her family. "We've been asked to leave. Let's go."

They must have seen her hurl the shoe, for they follow wide-eyed behind her without uttering a word.

"Mama threw her shoe at Mrs. Rozmarek, so we weren't allowed to be in the parade," Junior says into the telephone. Mimi winces. At least he's no longer crying. There's a pause, then Junior repeats, "Her shoe."

Mimi sighs and returns her attention to the sink of dirty dishes. Halina will tell Stan the entire story—in Polish, no doubt, so Mimi won't understand when she calls Mimi *a lunatic* and *a disgrace* and whatever other insults she's been thinking up all afternoon. Mimi's surprised Halina hasn't said so in English right to her face. Despite Halina's obvious disappointment that the children couldn't march, she's said very little and refrained from her usual nasty looks. Maybe she's afraid Mimi will throw a shoe at her, too.

Mimi's elbow-deep in suds when Junior calls out for her. She wipes her hands on her apron and goes to the kitchen doorway. Junior's holding out the telephone to her. "Papa wants to talk to you."

Mimi hesitates before taking the telephone. It's the third time Stan's called since leaving for the East, but the first time he's asked to speak to her. "Hello?"

"A shoe!"

Mimi pulls the handset away from her ear, grimacing. Then, seeing Junior's watching, forces a smile. "So nice to hear your voice, too. How's the road been?"

"A shoe," he says more quietly. "You threw a shoe at Mrs. Rozmarek?"

"Yes, I did."

"Mrs. Rozmarek, secretary of the alliance?"

"Yes."

"What in the devil's name for?"

Still smiling, she shoos Junior toward the living room. Once he's out of earshot, she whispers, "She wouldn't let the children march in the parade."

"Why should she? You threw a goddamned shoe at her. What if she'd been hurt?"

"I threw the shoe after."

"After what?"

Mimi sighs. "After she said the children couldn't join the parade."

"Why?"

"Because she's a mean-spirited old hag, that's why." Mimi leans back against the wall and sighs again. "And . . ."

"And?"

"And she knows. They all know. About the charges against me."

The line goes silent.

"Stan, are you still there?"

"What do you mean she knows? How? I told you to—"

"It was in the paper. My name, where we live, the charges, everything."

Stan goes quiet again.

She closes her eyes, cradling the phone against her cheek. After their short exchange, she'd forgotten how painful his silence was. "I'm sorry, Stan. I was trying to help our situation. Not make it worse."

"Well, you did make it worse. A whole lot worse."

Mimi's voice trembles. "I know." Thank goodness the radio's on in the living room, and the children can't hear her. When he says nothing, she continues. "I thought maybe you would have heard the news."

"Here? In New York? Thank heavens not. They might have fired me. Shit, they might fire me when we get home and they *do* hear about it."

"Stan . . . I'm scared. What if . . . what if I go to prison."

He exhales into the telephone. "I don't know, Mimi."

Do you still love me? she wants to ask. *Do you forgive me?* Instead, she says, "When do you come home?" and holds her breath.

She already knows the answer. Nine days. Mimi's always had a good head for remembering his schedule. But it's a game they used to play whenever he was on the road. She'd ask when he was coming home, and he'd say, *Tonight, peach, if you want me to.* She always laughed and told him no, but it was nice to know he would have.

Tonight, all he says is, "The thirteenth."

CHAPTER 45

The nine days until Stan's return come and go without any more shoe-throwing incidents. *The Tribune* runs a few more stories, but these are relegated to the back of the paper, alongside headlines like GARFIELD PARK FLOWER SHOW OPENS and NEW FEATHER HATS BAD NEWS FOR CHICKENS.

The day Stan's due back in town, Mimi gets an early telephone call from Mr. Smith. Judge Haas is ready to rule on the plea in abatement they filed. She dresses in her nicest suit and arrives at the appointed time at the Cook County Criminal Court House. Ada and Jo are there, too, along with Mr. Smith. Aside from Mr. Papanek's boss—State's Attorney Thomas J. Courtney—and the bailiff and clerk, the courtroom is empty.

They all rise when Judge Haas enters, and he wastes no time reading his decree. "This Court, hearing counsel in support of the motion on plea in abatement, as to defendants Ada Martin, Josephine Kuder, and Miriam Lukasewicz, as well as in opposition thereto and being fully advised in the premises, doth overrule said motion and orders that said plea in abatement in this case be hereby overruled accordingly."

Mr. Smith whispers a translation to Mimi and the others through gritted teeth. "Our plea was denied."

After another hour of back-and-forth between Mr. Smith and the judge—none of which Mimi fully understands—the case is continued until three weeks hence, and the courtroom is dismissed.

In the grand rotunda outside the courtroom, Mr. Smith explains that while the judge's decision is disappointing, it was not unexpected. He'll meet with each of them in the coming weeks to prepare them for the next steps. Though he's well-practiced at keeping his demeanor cool and voice even, Mimi can tell today's decision was a serious blow to their case.

On her way out of the court building, she stops at the drinking fountain. The somber news has left her mouth dry. When she turns around, Mimi finds Assistant State's Attorney Papanek lounging against the wall behind her.

"A word, if you have a moment, Mrs. Lukasewicz. Or, it's Lukas you prefer, isn't it?"

Mimi looks down the hall and out into the great entryway, scanning the bustling crowd for Mr. Smith. His tall, lanky form would be easy to spot, but he isn't there.

"I won't keep you long. I know you're expecting Mr. Lukas home this evening. Four wins in the last five games should be cause to celebrate."

That he knows anything about Stan unnerves her, but she squares her shoulders and straightens. "I didn't take you for a baseball fan."

"No?" He gestures toward the nearby bank of elevators. "Shall we?"

"Do I have a choice?"

"Ah, that's precisely what I want to discuss."

It's not much of an answer, but after a glance at her wristwatch, Mimi follows him to his office.

"No interruptions, please, Mrs. Larson," he says when they pass by his secretary.

Mimi sits in the same chair she's sat in twice before. The last time, she had Jennie's blood beneath her nails and staining the knees of her stockings. She rubs her arms and tries—unsuccessfully—to push the thought from her mind. "As you say, I haven't much time, so please be direct."

He sits down and smiles at her. "Very well. We have twenty-four women lined up to testify against you. Women who received illegal surgical attention at the State Street clinic. Women who can identify you as the nurse who assisted in their procedure."

Mimi's mouth goes dry again. It isn't new information. Mr. Smith told her several women were called to testify at the grand jury and would likely be called again for the trial. But Mr. Papanek paints a more vivid picture: a woman seated in the witness box, turning her gaze on Mimi and pointing directly at her. *She did it. She's the one. She's guilty.*

It's all Mimi can do not to shiver at the thought. But that would give Papanek the upper hand. He wouldn't have sought her out if he didn't want something. And whatever it is, she's determined not to give it to him.

"Twenty-four women," he says again. "Plus the testimony of Mrs. Martin's bookkeeper. Should be an open-and-shut case." He leans back in his plush leather chair, twirling a pen deftly between his fingers. "We'll be pressing for the maximum sentence, of course. Five years in the state penitentiary and two thousand dollars in fines."

Mimi knows this, too—what the maximum sentence could be—but that doesn't stop the bile from inching up her throat.

"Have you been to the Oakdale Reformatory, Mrs. Lukas? It's not a nice place."

"If you brought me here to scare me, I have better things to do with my time." She starts to stand.

"Of course." He makes a great show of glancing at the wall clock. "Penny and Junior should be getting home from school in just a few minutes, shouldn't they?"

Mimi's knees buckle, and she sits back down. It's one thing to know about Stan and the Cubs' latest winning streak. But her children?

"Junior's what, nine?" Papanek continues. "And Penny's got a birthday next month, doesn't she? Her twelfth. Almost a young woman. A girl really needs her mother at that age. Wouldn't you say?"

"My children are none of your business."

"I have a family, too," he continues, as if she hadn't spoken. "Two boys. I can't imagine life without them. . . . So much can happen in five years. Children grow up. Spouses move on. Abandonment is cause for divorce, you know. And what is imprisonment if not de facto abandonment? It's an easy case to argue."

Divorce? Stan wouldn't do such a thing, would he? Uncertainty pricks at her skin like an icy breeze off the lake. But she mustn't show it. Mimi grabs the arms of her chair and makes to stand, though she's not sure her legs can yet be trusted. "You're wasting my time."

"What if I could offer you a deal? Immunity from prosecution on the condition that you testify against the other members of the syndicate."

"You mean Ada and Jo?"

"Them and the others, yes."

By *others*, she guesses he's referring to Annie, Edna, and the doctors who worked at the clinic. Maybe Dr. Gabler and Mr. Piquett, too. And Em and Dr. Millstone, were they still alive. Her friends and colleagues. People she's spent the last year and a half trusting and who've put their trust in her.

"And the charges against me would be dropped?"

"Yes. Gone forever. No fine. No prison. Provided you cooperate fully."

Mimi studies his face. He wears an earnest expression, but she still doesn't trust him. "How do I know you're not just trying to get me to confess?"

"If you agree to turn state's witness, Mrs. Lukas, we'll draw up an official contract that outlines the terms and your guarantee of immunity."

"But I . . . I'll have to take the witness stand?"

"Yes."

The image she'd constructed in her mind earlier morphs into her in the witness box, pointing down at Ada and Jo. *They're the ones who did it, Your Honor. They're guilty.*

This time, she can't stop herself from shuddering.

"Do we have a deal?"

Mimi's hand drifts to her necklace. It's the pink shell one Stan gave her. "Why me?"

Mr. Papanek regards her a moment, and she can tell he's debating if and how much of the truth to give her. "You're a small player in all this, Mrs. Lukas. And you have the most to lose."

She nods, her hand still at her throat. Stan, the children, her freedom—she stands to lose everything. "When do I have to decide?"

Mr. Papanek frowns. "What reason could you possibly have for turning down such a deal?"

"I'm not turning it down. I'm asking for time to consider."

"I'll tell you what, Mrs. Lukas—the trial begins in three weeks. Take all that time if you need it. If you're still uncertain, listen to the first day of testimony." He takes off his glasses and wipes them with a hankie. "Twenty-four women . . . we'll get through at least half of them. I guarantee by the end of the day, you'll be begging me to let you turn state's witness."

CHAPTER 46

"All rise for the Honorable Judge Haas."

Mimi stands alongside Jo, Ada, and Mr. Smith. Unlike with Mimi's earlier court visits, today the benches behind them are peppered with spectators. Some, like Mr. Martin, Mimi recognizes. Others she doesn't, though she suspects a few are reporters. She wishes Stan were here. Wishes with a fervor she hasn't felt in a long time. But he's back in Boston for a four-game series against the Braves. Then it's on to New York to play the Giants. He's on thin ice with the club as it is, on account of the trial. Taking time off to sit behind her in the courtroom might mean a demotion. Or worse. A tightness grips Mimi's chest. By the time Stan gets home, she might be locked away in an Oakdale prison cell.

Judge Haas, a balding man whose deep-set eyes and sagging jowls remind Mimi of a hound dog, takes his place on the platform at the front of the room. He sits, and the rest of them do likewise.

The courtroom feels more like a cave than a house of justice, windowless and cold with towering ceilings and flat gray walls. Pendant lamps hang high above their heads, robed in dust and cobwebs, their pale light unable to penetrate the corners of the room.

Mimi glances askance at the prosecution's table. Mr. Papanek isn't there, but she knows well enough how to find him. Over the past weeks, she thought of little else but his offer. Twice, she'd made up her mind to accept, determined to drive to the court building first thing in the morning, only to wake up and find her resolve gone.

Stan would think it an easy decision. Would drive her to Mr. Papanek's office himself and place the pen in her hand to sign. But Mimi hasn't told him. She hasn't told anyone.

The clerk rises and reads from a sheet of paper. "Ada Martin, Josephine Kuder, and Miriam Lukasewicz, on March thirty-first, 1941, the Grand Jury indicted each of you on charges of conspiracy. What is your plea, guilty or not guilty?"

As planned, Mr. Smith responds for them. "Not guilty as to all three."

"Jury waivers heretofore signed?" the clerk asks.

"That is right," Mr. Smith says.

This, too, was planned. Mr. Smith felt a jury trial would only lengthen and encumber the process, not improve their odds.

What are *our odds*, Mimi had asked when they were discussing it. Mr. Smith took off his glasses and rubbed his eyes. "This isn't like a horse race, Mrs. Lukas," he said, "a quick lap to the finish line. The police violated your constitutional rights when they raided the clinic without a warrant. To my mind, all evidence and testimony gained thereafter is void. This judge doesn't agree, but the next one might. We may lose this case but be victorious in the end."

Those weren't the odds she was hoping for. It was easy to play the long game when you weren't the one sitting in jail, separated from your family. And who was to say the next judge would agree with Mr. Smith's interpretation of the law any more than Judge Haas did?

The conversation did answer one thing: why Mr. Papanek offered her a deal. He might have dozens of women willing or coerced into testifying that they'd received illegal abortions, but all those women's names were obtained in the raids. His case would crumble if such testimony were later ruled inadmissible. But if Mimi were to turn state's witness, her testimony would stand regardless. She would, for all intents and purposes, be sealing Jo and Ada's fates. Assuring that a guilty verdict—if rendered—would not be overturned.

It's this realization that makes her decision about the deal so grueling. Even now, facing the judge, she's still uncertain.

Mr. Nash, the lawyer for the prosecution, stands to deliver his opening statement. He's a middle-aged man with a farmer's build but a slickness borne of the city. The pin-striped suit he wears likely cost four or five times her weekly salary, and even from a dozen feet away, she can smell his amber-scented cologne.

"May it please the Court," he begins. "A grand jury for the county of Cook in the state of Illinois present that one Ada Martin, one Josephine Kuder, and one Miriam Lukasewicz unlawfully, maliciously, wantonly, knowingly, and wickedly conspired to cause a large number of women, each pregnant with child, to abort and miscarry when such abortions and miscarriages were not necessary for the preservation of said women's lives, contrary to the law and against the peace and dignity of the people of the state of Illinois."

Mimi blinks several times, trying to concentrate. His words are like a rat's nest, impossible to fully untangle. But she gets the gist. She and the others broke the law—wantonly and wickedly—by performing abortions outside of the narrowest medical indications.

Apparently, the judge is not impressed with the lawyer's convoluted language, either, for he waves his hand in a let's-move-along motion and says, "We're all aware of the Grand Jury's findings, Mr. Nash."

"Of course," he says, bowing his head slightly. "The State expects the evidence to show, Your Honor, that Ada Martin and her co-defendants conspired to commit criminal abortions. That this conspiracy was a long-continuing one, and that Mrs. Martin solicited hundreds of doctors and druggists to send business to her office and paid those persons commissions."

Mimi tries not to bristle. Mr. Smith coached her to remain impassive, no matter what was said. But the picture painted by the prosecution is a false one. Yes, doctors and druggists referred patients to their clinic, but the women came to them looking for help, not the other way around.

Mr. Nash continues. "The prosecution will show that a great number of women came to the office at One-Ninety North State Street, and that here, criminal abortions were performed on these women. Not for the purpose of preserving or saving these women's lives, but for pure profit."

Mimi hides her hands in her lap and knots them together in a stranglehold. It's easy for Mr. Nash to say the operations weren't performed for the preservation of life when he hadn't visited these women's frigid and impoverished homes, hadn't seen their bruises.

He concludes by saying, "The State expects to call twenty-five witnesses out of a list of approximately seventy witnesses furnished to the defense, and that by their testimony, to conclusively prove the allegations of this indictment beyond a reasonable doubt."

He swaggers back to his seat and nods at Mr. Smith, who rises.

"We waive, for the present, the opening statement."

The State begins to call its first witness, but Mr. Smith interrupts, "Just a minute, if the Court please, I think it not amiss to call the Court's attention to the fact that the witness who now appears is an accessory. According to the bill of particulars, she is the one who participated in the crime, if there was a crime committed, and I think she should be warned of her constitutional rights, that she does not have to testify to any fact that might incriminate her."

Mr. Nash rolls his eyes. "The defense has no purpose other than to frighten the witness."

"Scare them with the Constitution?" Mr. Smith replies. "You did the scaring."

A few muffled laughs sound behind them in the gallery. Mimi's lips quirk with a smile.

The judge raps his gavel. "Contrary to other jurisdictions, a woman who is aborted in the state of Illinois is not regarded as a party of the crime, but a victim. She need not be admonished and apprised of her Fifth Amendment rights."

"Very well, Your Honor." Mr. Smith sits heavily and shrugs. "It was worth a try," he whispers to Mimi and the others.

A Mrs. Bernice Strauss is brought from the witness room and sworn in. She's a middle-aged woman with light brown hair tied back in a simple bun. Her dress is impeccably pressed but has the faded look of a few too many washes. Mimi doesn't recognize her, though perhaps she came into the clinic on one of Mimi's days off. She sits stiffly in the wooden witness chair, her back straight and ankles crossed, gaze locked on the prosecution table. Only her hands, which grasp her purse strap like the reins of a racehorse, betray her nervousness.

Mr. Nash's first questions are simple ones. Her name, her address, whether or not she's married, how many children she has. Then he asks if she ever visited the State Lake Building.

"Yes," Mrs. Strauss replies.

"About when was that?"

"The eighteenth of November."

"What year?"

The room's high ceiling swallows her reply.

"What year was that?" Mr. Smith asks.

"Nineteen forty," Mr. Nash says; then, to Mrs. Strauss, "Do you remember where you went in that building?"

"To the office of Dr. Josephine Gabler."

"After you got into the office, did you talk with anyone?"

"Yes, I talked with the receptionist."

Jo tenses and draws in a shaky breath. Mimi reaches beneath the desk, taking Jo's hand. Her normally soft skin is rough and chapped, her fingers clammy.

"Do you know the receptionist's name?" Mr. Nash continues.

"No, I do not."

"Do you see her in the courtroom?"

"Yes."

"Will you point her out, please?"

For the first time since she entered the room, Mrs. Strauss glances at Mimi and her colleagues. She raises her arm and extends a finger in Jo's direction. "Sitting there in the tan coat and hat."

Jo's hand tightens around Mimi's. Otherwise, she remains perfectly still, her face impassive, just as Mr. Smith instructed them.

Mimi can't help but feel a flush of anger toward Mrs. Strauss on Jo's behalf. She knows the woman was likely bullied into testifying, but Jo and the others at the clinic had been there to help her when no one else would.

Mrs. Strauss's gaze darts away, as if she can sense Mimi's anger. She lowers her arm and takes hold of her purse strap again, her knuckles blanching. Mimi hopes it's not only nerves she feels, but shame.

"What did you talk to her about?" Mr. Nash asks.

"I made an appointment for the next day."

Mr. Smith stands. "Objected to."

"Overruled."

"Exception," Mr. Smith says, and sits down.

Mr. Nash smirks and continues, "Will you tell Judge Haas what conversation you had with the receptionist?"

"I just made an appointment to come back the next day."

Mr. Smith rises again. "Pardon me, Judge, to save time, may it be understood that I am objecting to all of this? The entire testimony of this witness."

Judge Haas frowns. "On what grounds?"

"On the grounds that have been heretofore covered in the motion to suppress. The bedrock upon which the prosecution rests its case is unconstitutional."

Mimi doesn't fully understand what all this banter is for but suspects it has something to do with what Mr. Smith told her about losing this case but being victorious in the end. Does that mean he's already given up on winning this one? Or does he think these objections might stand? Her stomach clenches. None of it will matter if she turns state's witness.

"All right," Judge Haas says wearily. "So noted."

"Thank you."

"May I at last proceed, Your Honor?" Mr. Nash asks, after flashing Mr. Smith a side-eyed glare.

"Surely. Let us conduct this case with absolute courtesy between respective counsel. After all, this is just another case."

Mimi bites down on her tongue to keep from glowering. It's not just another case to her. In the end, the judge and lawyers, they'll all go home. But Mimi and the others may well go to prison.

Mr. Nash asks Mrs. Strauss again about the conversation she had with Jo.

"Well, there wasn't much said that evening. I just made an appointment to come back the next day."

"Yes, but tell us what you said to her."

"Oh, my, I don't remember." She gives a nervous chuckle. "It was quite a while ago."

Mr. Nash sighs. He has the look of a frustrated school teacher. "Did you tell her what you were there for?"

Mr. Smith objects on the grounds that the question is leading. Judge Haas sustains the objection, which Mimi has realized means the question is not allowed and does not need to be answered.

"State to the best of your recollection just what was said by you and what was said by Miss Kuder."

"She says she doesn't remember, Judge," Mr. Smith says.

Judge Haas turns to Mrs. Strauss. "Do you remember what was said between you? Answer yes or no."

Mrs. Strauss clutches her purse to her breast, wringing the strap with such force, Mimi thinks it might snap. "Well, I can . . . just like you make any other appointment . . . I gave my name and address, and I made a . . . set a time, a time to come back again."

"Object to that," Mr. Smith says. He's been on his feet for nearly the entire testimony.

"I will let it stand, for what it's worth," the judge replies.

Mr. Nash then walks Mrs. Strauss through what happened the next day—with a few more objections by Mr. Smith. She identifies Ada as the person who led her from the reception to the anteroom and gave her a hospital gown to change into. She describes the procedure room in vague terms—an operating table, a case of instruments—and says there was another woman in there besides Ada, but she does not know her name and doesn't see her in the courtroom. Then her eyes were covered by a handkerchief, she tells the judge, and she was given gas. That's all she remembers.

"Had you missed any of your menstrual periods? Prior to the time you went to Dr. Gabler's office?" Mr. Nash asks.

Mrs. Strauss's cheeks color, and her eyes flee to her lap. "Yes. I missed one."

"What was your condition when you went to the office at One-Ninety North State Street on November nineteenth?"

Mr. Smith stands. "Object to that."

"On what ground?" Mr. Nash says, the exacerbation plain in his voice.

"Well, it's a conclusion. How does she know what her condition was? We're interested in facts here. Her condition was not a fact."

"No one could know better than she." He grabs a bound stack of papers from his desk and brings them to the judge. "In People versus Patrick, this question was asked repeatedly, and the court permitted it to be answered."

"That question in that case was more specific than this one," the judge says.

"Very well." Mr. Nash turns back to Mrs. Strauss. "Were you pregnant at the time you went to the clinic on State Street?"

"Object to that," Mr. Smith says, rising for what seems to Mimi like the hundredth time today. "There isn't anybody in the world that would know that without the proper tests."

Judge Haas pulls a pair of spectacles from his robes and hangs them on his nose. "Let me look at Patrick." He flips through the pages Mr. Nash handed him.

"Page two-seventy-seven, Your Honor," the prosecutor says, approaching the bench. Mr. Smith joins him.

Watching the men, Mimi shakes her head. This feels more like a circus than a trial. A woman knows when she's pregnant. She may deny it, blame her morning sickness and fatigue on something else, but deep down, she knows. Especially a woman like Mrs. Strauss, who's been pregnant before. Yet here these men are, arguing back and forth and consulting past cases to determine whether or not she can be believed.

In the end, the men let Mrs. Strauss reply. Yes, she tells the court, she was pregnant when she went to the clinic.

The prosecution has no more questions, and Mr. Smith begins his cross-examination.

"As I understand, you went into this room, and you were given gas while you were laid on the table, is that right?"

"Yes."

"You don't know what was done to you?"

"No."

"You did not *see* any instruments of any kind or nature used, did you?"

"Well, I didn't see any instruments used, no."

"So you don't actually know whether any instruments were used on you at all, do you?"

Mrs. Strauss shifts in her chair, her gaze skittish. "Well . . ."

"Yes? Please speak up. It's hard to hear in here."

She closes her eyes a moment, then clears her throat and straightens. "Before I completely passed out with gas, I . . . I felt an instrument inserted for examination."

"I see. Inserted where?"

The flush in Mrs. Strauss's cheeks deepens, climbing all the way to her ears. "Must I answer that?"

"You must," Judge Haas says.

She shrinks down in her chair, her gaze falling to the floor. "My privates."

"I'm sorry, I can't hear you, Mrs. Strauss." Mr. Smith gestures to the ceiling. "It's a very large room. You must speak up."

"My privates," she says, only a tiny bit louder.

"I'll need you to be more specific than that, I'm afraid."

"Objection," Mr. Nash says, rising to his feet. "She's no doctor."

"And yet we allowed her to speculate on whether or not she was pregnant. Certainly, then she can describe where exactly the aforementioned instrument was inserted."

"Your Honor, I—"

"A vaginal examination," Mrs. Strauss hollers, her voice thin and quavering, as if she's on the verge of tears. Mimi's anger toward her softens into pity. None of them deserve this.

"And as far as you know, that is all that happened, isn't it?" Mr. Smith asks.

"Yes." She takes a steadying breath. "Yes. Then I passed out."

"Thank you," he says, then turns to Judge Haas. "No further questions."

Mrs. Strauss hurriedly stands. She's about to step down from the witness box when Mr. Nash says, "Excuse me, Your Honor, one more question I forgot to ask."

Mrs. Strauss looks stricken as she glances longingly toward the door. She turns to the judge, who nods, and she sits back down.

"After you left the office of Ada Martin on November nineteenth, 1940, were you pregnant any longer?"

Mr. Smith is back on his feet. "That is objected to."

"She was permitted to testify that she was pregnant. Certainly, she should be permitted to answer if she was not any longer."

Mr. Smith throws up his arms. "There ought to be an end to this somewhere. The prosecution now proposes to prove *by her* that she was pregnant when she went there, and then something happened, something she does not know anything about, and presto change-o, she was not pregnant when she came away. Your Honor, the evidence should be limited to knowable facts and circumstances."

All eyes go to the judge. Mimi holds her breath.

"I am going to let her answer."

The court recorder rereads the question.

"No," Mrs. Strauss says, glancing at Mimi and the others, then quickly away. "After I left the office, I was no longer pregnant."

Several more witnesses are called to the stand. Their testimonies are much the same. Mr. Smith continues to lob objections, though they're frequently overruled.

Many of the witnesses, Mimi recognizes. Some point her out as the nurse who assisted in their procedure. She remembers the stories of women accused of witchcraft from her high school history class. How they were weighted down with stones and thrown into a lake. If they floated, they were guilty. If they sank, they were innocent. Either way, they were dead.

Each woman's testimony is another stone.

Late that morning, Mr. Nash summons Zofina Dabrowski to the stand. She walks in the picture of poise, her stride easy and chin high, as if this were a Catholic Daughters meeting, not a conspiracy trial. Her blue dress and matching hat are modest and muted. She answers Mr. Nash's questions loudly and without hesitation. The only glance she spares in Mimi's direction is when Mr. Nash asks her to identify the nurse she encountered at the clinic. When they meet hers, Zofina's eyes are as blank as a doll's. Had they ever held any warmth, any fragility, any kindness, or had Mimi imagined it?

Zofina raises a manicured hand but can't seem to extend her arm. Instead, she draws her thumb to her mouth, gnawing at the cuticle.

Mr. Nash repeats his question. Zofina doesn't move. Doesn't speak.

"Mrs. Dabrowski, will you please indicate for the court who—"

"I heard you," she snaps, before pointing a shaky finger at Mimi. Her thumb is bleeding, and though it's hard to tell from where Mimi sits, the rest of her cuticles look just as raw.

After Zofina's testimony concludes, the judge orders a recess for lunch. But Mimi cannot eat. She, Jo, and Ada sit on an alcove bench outside the courtroom. Light streams in through the window, the sun winking at them from a cloudless sky. After hours in the dimly lit courtroom, the sunshine stings Mimi's eyes.

Ada doesn't eat, either. She wears the same distant look she's had since Jennie's death. Jo scarfs down her sandwich and half of

Mimi's, then excuses herself to the washroom. She returns with a fresh coat of lipstick and watery eyes.

"Rotten what those women said up there on the stand," she says. "As if they weren't the ones who sought *us* out to fix their trouble."

"They weren't given a choice," Ada says, her voice flat.

"It's still rotten. If we're going to jail over it, they should be, too."

Mimi nudges Jo with her shoulder. "You don't mean that."

"I do. And you're lying if you say you don't."

She knows how Jo's feeling. Angry. Betrayed. Scared. Mimi feels the same. "None of us should be going to jail over this, that's what I say."

Ada snorts and juts her chin toward the courtroom. The prosecutors stand beside the doorway, talking. Mr. Papanek is there, also. "Tell that to them."

How much more rotten will it be if Mimi agrees to Papanek's deal and takes the stand? Her insides twist, and she's all the more glad she didn't touch her sandwich.

Mr. Smith comes up beside them. "It's time to go back in, ladies." He looks none the worse for wear, despite the number of times he jumped to his feet to object that morning.

Ada and Jo stand and follow him inside. Mimi takes a final glance out the window at the glaringly blue sky. It ought to be cloudy. Storming. Spitting rain and hail. But what does the weather care for the troubles of women? What does anyone care?

She starts toward the courtroom, but Papanek, still hovering by the doorway, waves her aside.

"I hear Mr. Nash is doing a fine job, and it's not looking good for you."

"I wouldn't know," Mimi says.

"Oh, I think you do. Have you made your decision?"

Mimi bites her lip and looks through the open courtroom doors.

"Listen to the rest of the testimony today," he says, his voice dripping with smug confidence. "Then go home to your family. I'll be in the office at seven A.M. tomorrow. I'm sure I'll see you there."

CHAPTER 47

That night, after the children have gone to bed, Mimi sits slumped at the kitchen table. She stares straight ahead at the calendar hanging on the wall, but the dates and scrawled appointments blur in and out of focus. Her head swims with thoughts of today's trial. Sixteen women testified, with more slated for tomorrow.

Mimi reaches for the anger and indignation she felt earlier in the day but finds only pity. Pity for the women forced to talk publicly about such private matters. "Speak up," they were repeatedly told by the lawyers and the judge. Yet, for the women's entire lives, these had been matters they were shamed into not speaking of at all. *Menstrual period, douche, vagina*—these were words whispered only among women, if at all. Mimi's own mother never even used the word *pregnant*. A woman was *in trouble* (if she wasn't married) or *in the family way*.

If Mimi accepts Mr. Papanek's deal, she'd not only be betraying Ada and Jo, Annie and Edna, Em and Dr. Millstone, but all their patients, as well. Every woman who came through the clinic door expecting her most private health matters to remain that—private. It was an implicit promise Mimi made, a fundamental tenet of being a nurse.

But she's not just a nurse. Mimi's a mother. The two most important people in the world are asleep a few doors down. When they wake, they expect her to be there. Not just tomorrow, but the day after, and the day after that. She made a promise to them, too. A promise to kiss their scraped knees and cheer them on at baseball matches. To clap wildly at school pageants, even when they flub their lines, and tuck them into bed at night. To listen to their dreams and steer them away from wrongdoing.

No matter what choice she makes, she'll be breaking a promise.

She hoped Stan might call tonight. Had listened all evening, ready to dash to the telephone. Surely, he must be wondering how the first day of the trial went. Another glance at the wall clock—nearly ten o'clock, eleven o'clock in New York—and she gives up hope. He's always in bed early the night before a game, even though all he does now is stand by first base and coach the runners when to stay put and when to steal second. She recalls what Mr. Papanek said about imprisonment being grounds for divorce. Is Stan thinking the same thing? Is that why he didn't call?

The thud of footfalls sounds in the hall, and the bright scent of wintergreen oil invades the air. Mimi stifles a groan. Halina. She comes to the kitchen doorway and leans against the jamb, crossing her arms. "You look—"

"Please, Mamo, not tonight. I don't want to hear that I look haggard or bloated. I just want to be left alone."

"What I was going to say is you look like you could use some tea." Halina shuffles to the stove and grabs the kettle. "All this time, I thought you were running around with another man."

"I know." That she wasn't entirely wrong only makes Mimi feel worse.

"But no, you were out there working for this . . . this—how do you say?—abortion clinic." She fills the kettle with water and sets it back on the stove to boil, then goes to the cupboard for teacups.

Mimi props her elbows on the table and lets her head fall into her hands. She knows where this is going. She's been waiting for it ever since she told Halina the truth of what was happening. Killing unborn babies is a far worse sin than adultery, Halina will tell her. And what was Mimi thinking, putting her family at risk like this? They're pariahs at church. The children are teased at school. Halina's friends refuse to come by the house for tea and coffee cake. Stan's job is hanging on by a thread.

The kettle whistles, and Halina pours the boiling water into the teapot. She carries everything over to the table—sugar, milk, cups, spoons, pot—then sits beside her. Mimi straightens and braces herself.

"When I was a young girl in Polska, I had a friend named Beata. Like sisters, we were. We did everything together. We even dreamed of moving to America together." Halina pauses, as if lost in thought. Then she sighs and pours the tea.

Mimi's heard dozens of Halina's girlhood stories. *Polska* this and *Polska* that. But she's never heard her mother-in-law mention the name Beata.

"And did she? Move to America, too, I mean?"

Halina shakes her head. "A few years before I left, when we were sixteen or so, a young man from the railroad company took an interest in Beata. Filip was his name."

Mimi takes a sip of her tea. Halina was right; the warm, fragrant drink is a welcome balm for her overwrought nerves. Halina, however, doesn't drink. Her knobby hands circle the cup, and she stares down at the liquid as if she can see her memories playing out across its dark surface.

"At first, Beata liked the attention. What girl wouldn't? Filip was handsome. He had a good job. But one night, Beata came to my window, crying. Her face was red and swollen. Her stockings were torn, her dress bloodied."

"Filip did that?"

"*Tak*, yes."

Halina doesn't elaborate, but Mimi has a good idea of what happened.

"She stayed away from him after that," Halina continues after a moment. "But a few months later, she realized she was pregnant. If there were places like your clinic in Kraków, we didn't know about them. Her father was furious when he found out. He made her tell him who'd done it, who'd put the baby inside her. Then he gave Filip two hundred korona to marry her."

"Didn't she tell her father what Filip had done?"

Halina shrugs. "He didn't care. All he cared about was not having the shame of a bastard grandchild."

Mimi can't help but think of Ginny. The shame was all their parents seemed to care about, too.

"What happened to her?"

"She married him. No other choice."

"And did he . . ."

"Every time I saw her, she had a new bruise. And a new baby. Three by the time I left for America. We wrote, but eventually the letters stopped coming . . . who knows how she is today." Halina frowns down at her cup. "Sixty thousand Poles killed when Hitler invaded. That's what I see in the paper. I pray not Beata." Her frown contorts into a sneer. "But God willing, Filip was."

Mimi's never heard her mother-in-law speak with such vitriol. But she doesn't blame her. Mimi's wished death upon the professor who got Ginny pregnant a million ways over.

Mimi takes another sip of her tea. Halina drinks hers in a single gulp like it's moonshine, then stares at the empty cup.

"I don't know what you did at that clinic of yours, but if you were helping women like Beata, it was a good thing. A brave thing."

For a moment, Mimi's too stunned to speak. "Your friends at church don't think so. They won't even come over to the house anymore."

"They will eventually. None of them make as good of *drożdżówka* as I do."

A tiny smile finds its way to Mimi's face.

"Besides, who knows what they think."

"I may go to jail, Mamo."

"I didn't say it was smart what you did. But it was good." She grabs their empty teacups and stands. "You have to decide for yourself what matters more."

A little after midnight, Mimi gives up on sleep. Her thoughts are an endless spiral: Ginny, Beata, the trial. She's no more certain now what to do about Mr. Papanek's offer than yesterday. She turns on the bedside lamp and gets up. In the closet, she rifles through her clothes for her robe, only to remember she spilled coffee on it the morning before last and tossed it in the hamper. There's a spare somewhere on the top shelf. As she pushes aside hats, long underwear, and a stack of folded sweaters, she sees the box she took from her parents' house. Ginny's box.

She stares at it a moment, then pulls it down and sets it on the bed. Will her own life be reduced to a box of knickknacks someday?

What's the point of keeping these things, anyway? Ginny's dead, and nothing in here will bring her back.

Mimi upends the contents onto the bed. Among the cards and old school flyers, she sees the stack of unopened letters bound together with twine. She forgot she'd secreted them away after her mother's funeral and added them to the box, meaning to pull them out and read once her emotions were less raw. That's not tonight, but if she doesn't take Papanek's deal, it may be her last chance.

She sits cross-legged on the bed and unbinds the letters. She already read the top one, so she casts it aside and carefully opens the second. It's as stale and formal as the first. No trace of the true Ginny on the page, as if her bright and tenacious personality bled out on the way to Des Moines. Her lovely handwriting—so neat and artful—is the only testament Ginny wrote them at all.

The next several letters are the same: lean, lifeless descriptions of her days at the home. She doesn't even bother with a postscript appeal to return to the farm after the first two. Mimi's about to give up and toss the lot of them—read and unread—back into the box, when she sees her name scrawled on one of the envelopes.

She stares at it a moment before picking it up. Every day the summer Ginny had been away, Mimi hoped for a letter. That none came only sharpened Mimi's guilt. She'd made a grave mistake revealing Ginny's secret, and her sister had not forgiven her.

Now, Mimi's hands tremble as she breaks the time-weathered seal. She hates her parents for having kept this from her, yet she hesitates before pulling the folded pages from the envelope. What if Ginny had written to tell her what a rotten sister she was? To say Mimi ruined her life, and they'd never be friends again. Fair enough things for a frightened fifteen-year-old to write. But Mimi knows now it was not her fault. Not all of it, anyway. There's plenty of blame to go around. That rotten professor is owed the lion's share. Ma for telling them nothing about how babies were made. Pa for caring more about the family's good name than his own daughter. Every goddamned rule and custom that added weight to men's side of the scale.

Mimi takes a breath and unfolds the letter. It's dated May 30, 1918—just over a month after Ginny left. Immediately, she can see it's not like the other letters.

Dear Mimi,

I suppose you think I'm cross with you. And I was. Rip-roaring mad, to tell you the truth. Did you have to go and open your big old mouth on Easter of all days? You know how holier-than-thou Ma and Pa get on days like that. Anyhow, I wanted to write and tell you I forgive you. If I'd come out and told you about my trouble, I know you would have kept my secret for me. I guess I was hoping it would go away on its own and I wouldn't have to tell anybody. Least of all Ma and Pa. But I guess they would have figured it out eventually.

Now, don't you spend the whole summer moping just because yours truly isn't there. But don't you go forgetting about me either. I'm still your big sister. And you're about to be an aunt. An aunt! It's strange to pen those words. Even stranger to think that I'm gonna be a mother before too long. Ma and Pa say I've got to give the baby up if I want to come home, and I reckon that's what I'll do. Many of the girls here don't have a home to go back to, so I guess I ought to count myself lucky. I don't feel lucky much these days, though. Funny that I should be so lonely in a house full of other girls. I miss home. And you.

Please write back if you can.

Your sister,
Ginny

There are four more letters in the stack addressed to Mimi. She reads them, her anger toward Ma and Pa growing each time she breaks an envelope's seal. How could they have kept these from her? Surely, they saw how much she grieved Ginny's absence. After her death, it would have been impossible to ignore. Mimi hardly ate, and cried herself to sleep for weeks on end. But maybe their grief blinded them. That, along with their pride.

A deepening sadness tempers her anger. Whether it was talk of the war or a loud creak in the night, Ginny always wore a brave face for Mimi. Her letters are no different. But her carefully chosen words don't fully mask her fear. Not to Mimi's adult eyes. Fear, loneliness, uncertainty—it's all there, a shadow behind the lines. Written and unwritten. By the third letter, it's clear she wanted to keep the baby. No more talk of typist school in Chicago. Instead, she speaks about a laundry service in Des Moines willing to hire unwed mothers. She wonders if Mimi might come out next summer to look after the baby—a boy, she's certain. Could Ma and Pa spare her around the farm? Probably not, Ginny concludes, and Mimi knows she's right. Even if they could have spared her, they never would have let Mimi go.

The last letter, written only a week before the stillbirth and Ginny's death, is the hardest to read. Ginny knows the birth will hurt—all the girls at the house say so—but how badly? Most girls don't return with their babies and stay on for only a handful of days after. They're pale and tired, and their breasts ache. Some don't talk about their babies at all. Others talk on and on about them—their pretty eyes and cute noses, their tiny little toes and soft skin. It's these girls Ginny pities the most. They still have hope. Hope that they'll be able to make a life for themselves and somehow get their babies back. Ginny knows that won't happen. That's why she doesn't want to leave the hospital without him, her baby, when he comes.

Some of the staff are encouraging. Laud her for owning up to the consequences of her mistake. Her sin. Others tell her she's being selfish. Thinking about herself, not the baby. She's not fully made up her mind, she writes Mimi. *Do you think Ma and Pa will ever forgive me if I keep him? Or will they disown me? I can live with that*, she writes, *but you and me, Mimi, we're sisters forever, right?*

She signs off by saying all she can do is follow her heart. When the time comes, and she's holding her son in her arms, she'll know the right thing to do.

It guts Mimi to know that all Ginny's letters, her pleas for reassurance, for forgiveness, went unanswered. And hasn't Mimi been searching for the same thing ever since? Forgiveness. It was here all along, and she never knew. At least now she knows. Ginny never got that reassurance. Not from Mimi or their parents. But somehow, she trusted herself enough to know she'd find the right path.

She'd always been brave like that, Ginny. Mimi sees now how hard-won that bravery was. Fear and doubt dogged her, the same as everyone else. Her sister wasn't the unflappable idol Mimi thought her. And Mimi loves her all the more for it.

There's a final envelope in the stack. This one's slightly larger and more official-looking. The lettering is typed, not handwritten. It's addressed to Mr. and Mrs. Donald Gunther. When she goes to break the seal, she sees the top edge of the letter has already been cut open. So this one, her parents did bother to read.

Inside is a single sheet of paper. In stark, typewritten lines, it informs her parents of Ginny's death. Postpartum hemorrhage. Lifesaving interventions were attempted but ultimately unsuccessful. Please inform the home as to arrangements for the body. If no instructions are given, the body will be interred in the potter's field beside the hospital. Also, send word regarding the infant. Sex: Male. Height: 21 inches. Weight: 7 lbs. 8 oz. Eye color: Blue. If no claim on the infant is made within thirty days, he will be placed in an orphanage.

Mimi drops the letter. It drifts down to the bed, landing atop the stack of envelopes, its words staring up at her. A live birth. A son! The only piece of Ginny left in this world. How could her parents have let him go unclaimed?

She does the math quickly in her head. He'd be a young man now, nearing his twenty-second birthday. Was he adopted, or did he spend his boyhood at the orphanage? Does he know about his birth mother? A hundred other questions flood her mind—too many to sort through tonight, alongside far too many emotions.

She picks up the letter again and holds it to her breast, breathing in deep but ragged. A few more inhales, and her mind clears enough to fold the letter and place it back in its envelope. She stacks it on top of the rest and binds them up with the pink ribbon, tying it off with a neat bow.

Mimi knows now what she must do.

CHAPTER 48

The next morning, Mimi arrives at the Criminal Court Building early. The great entryway and branching hallways are just beginning to fill with people—workers, mostly, carrying lunch pails and briefcases and steaming thermoses that scent the air of coffee. She takes the stairs to the second floor and easily finds her way to Papanek's office. His secretary isn't in yet, but the double doors that lead from the front room to his private sanctum are open, and light shines from within.

Mimi finds Mr. Papanek seated at his desk, reading some memo or other. It's one of a stack of papers planted in the center of his desk. A new case, perhaps. A new villain to pursue. She'd like to hate the man, so certain and dogged in his cause he's no time for decency or humanity. But he didn't write the laws. Not the laws laid out in the neatly shelved books behind him nor those unwritten laws that exert such unequal pressure on their lives. He thinks himself a hero. And maybe when the histories are written, he will be.

To Mimi, he's just a man. She knocks on the jamb but doesn't wait for him to look up before entering.

"Mrs. Lukas." He stands and glances down at his wristwatch. "Cutting it a little close, aren't you? You're due in court in thirty minutes."

She sits, and Mr. Papanek does likewise.

"Let's get started," he continues, moving the stack of papers aside. "Good thing for you, I had Mrs. Larson prepare the paperwork yesterday. When she gets in, I'll have her run to Mr. Courtney's office and fill him in. I'm sure Judge Haas will permit us an hour or two's stay."

He reaches for a manila folder at the far edge of his desk. Mimi reaches for it, too, placing her hand flat atop it before he can open it. "I'm not taking your deal, Mr. Papanek."

"Excuse me?"

"I've decided not to be a witness for the state."

He looks at her like she's grown a second head, blinking as he slowly leans back. "You know Judge Haas will assuredly find you guilty."

She nods.

"This isn't some game, Mrs. Lukas. There won't be time later to change your mind."

"I shan't change my mind."

"Mr. Nash will ask for a swift and aggressive sentencing. That's five years in prison."

"You've said."

He snorts. "I suppose Mr. Smith's filled your head with nonsense about winning on appeal."

Mimi clasps her hands and meets his stare. "I've already lost, Mr. Papanek. I lost my dear friend Emily and her husband. I lost Jennie." She doesn't mention Daniel or Ginny, though she counts them among the losses, too. "The most I can hope for is to honor my convictions and preserve my dignity. If I took your deal, I'd lose all hope of that, too."

"What about your family? You can't possibly believe this is what's best for them." He sits up, puffing out his chest while his neck and ears flush red. "Who . . . who will see your children dressed and off to school in the morning? Who will cook them supper and tuck them into bed at night?"

"A mother is more to her children than a cook and maid."

"Exactly! Who will see to their moral upbringing? Teach them right from wrong?"

"Me," she says simply. "That's why I can't take your deal."

Mimi makes it to the courtroom before the others and paces the hallway until they arrive. There's a strange emptiness inside her where all the doubt over Papanek's offer once twisted and churned. She thought her step would feel lighter. That it would be easier to square her shoulders and raise her head. But the weight has only shifted, not disappeared. As much as she dreads Judge Haas's decision, she'd rather have it now than sit through another day or two of testimony.

The trial begins much the same as yesterday. Mimi, Jo, and Ada sit at the defendants' table with Mr. Smith, while Mr. Nash and the others from the state's attorney's office open briefcases, shuffle papers, and whisper among themselves at the table to the right. A scattering of people is again perched behind the rail in the gallery.

Judge Haas arrives. They all stand, and the clerk delivers his official preamble. The People of Illinois versus Ada Martin, et al, is now in session.

Everyone sits except Mr. Nash, who calls the first witness just as the back doors open with a groan. Mimi catches the scowl on Judge Haas's face as she turns around. A man strides into the courtroom, the slightest limp in his otherwise confident step. *Stan!*

Mimi stands. His clothes are rumpled, and eyes bloodshot. He must have ridden the train all night to make it here. He pauses halfway down the aisle, as if uncertain where to sit, but when his gaze meets hers, he smiles. Not that megawatt smile of his, but one more humble and true. Mimi exhales and smiles back.

"This is a courtroom, not a ballpark, Stach," the judge says. He's still wearing a scowl, but there's a twinkle in his eyes that wasn't there before. "The view's the same no matter where you sit."

Stan removes his hat. "Yes, Judge."

"Your Honor."

"Your Honor," Stan repeats. He walks to the front row and takes a seat directly behind her. "I got here as soon as I could," he whispers.

Mimi sits, too, swiveling to face him. "Don't you have another game today in New York?"

"Being here's more import—"

Judge Haas clears his throat. Mimi mouths *thank you* and turns around.

Mr. Nash calls his witness, and the second day of the trial begins in earnest. Nine more women testify along with Mr. Senft, Ada's bookkeeper. Like yesterday, Mr. Smith riddles each testimony with objections. Like yesterday, most are overruled.

In his testimony, Mr. Senft speaks about leasing the office on Dearborn Street under an alias with money given to him by Dr. Gabler and, later, Ada. He also tells of the commissions they paid to doctors and druggists who referred patients to the clinic. When asked about the clinic's employees, he identifies Jo and Mimi by name.

During Mr. Smith's cross-examination, Mr. Senft admits that after his arrest in April, he was held in custody for three days and told if he didn't make a written statement, he'd be indicted.

He doesn't seem remorseful about taking the deal, though Mimi notices him squirm in the witness chair when his gaze meets Ada's. Mimi doesn't begrudge him for turning state's witness. Well, not entirely. She'd almost turned herself. But he does strike her as a man who'd testify against his own mother if the price were right. And Mimi's glad she's not up there with him.

After Mr. Senft steps down, Mr. Nash turns toward the defendant's table and stares directly at her, as if giving her one final chance to switch sides. Mimi lifts her chin and looks away. She's scared as the devil inside, but damned if she'll show it.

"The State rests, Your Honor."

Mimi feels all the eyes in the courtroom turn toward the defendant's table as Mr. Smith rises.

"At this time, I move the court to strike all witness testimony on the grounds that the evidence was unlawfully obtained from an illegal search and seizure. Any evidence the witnesses subsequently gave came from that tainted and polluted source."

"Motion denied," Judge Haas says.

"I now motion the court to discharge the defendants on the ground that there is insufficient evidence to support a verdict."

"Denied. That's up to me to decide."

Mr. Smith sighs. He makes a great show of plucking a handkerchief from his pocket and removing his glasses. The courtroom sits in silence as he wipes the lenses. Only once the glasses are back on his face and the hankie tucked away does Mr. Smith speak. "Very well. The defendants rest."

Mimi knows her side has no witnesses to call, but the finality of

Mr. Smith's words is still crushing. Her palms grow sweaty, and her pulse thuds loudly in her ears. She glances over her shoulder, grateful to find Stan still there.

The judge asks the clerk the time, and Mimi's surprised to hear it's only a quarter after one. These past hours have been among the longest of her life. Even labor was less grueling.

"Well, gentlemen," Judge Haas says, leaning back in his chair and crossing his robed arms. "To be perfectly frank with you, in the face of all this evidence, there could not be a finding of not guilty. We can adjourn for lunch, or I can render my verdict now."

"It seems you already have, Your Honor," Mr. Smith says flatly.

"My official verdict."

Mr. Smith turns to Mimi, Ada, and Jo. Mimi can't imagine eating, but part of her wants to stave off the inevitable as long as possible.

"I think we ought to wait," Jo says, her voice high and thin. "Maybe he'll have a change of heart."

Ada shakes her head. "Let's just get this over with."

Mimi takes a deep breath. The judge won't change his mind, and Ada's right. Things have dragged on long enough. "Now."

Mr. Smith nods. "We'll hear your verdict, Your Honor."

Judge Haas bids them to rise. They do.

"Let the record show a finding of guilty as to each defendant of conspiracy, as alleged and charged in the indictment." He bangs his gavel once, as if to punctuate the finality of his words.

Guilty. Mimi had expected that verdict, but it doesn't lessen the blow. The air rushes from her lungs. For a moment, she remains like that, lungs collapsed, nerves firing in panic; then she feels Stan's hand on her shoulder, warm and steady. The pain of impact remains, but she manages to breathe again.

"We come now to the question of punishment." Judge Haas turns to Mr. Nash. "Has the State any recommendation?"

Mr. Nash stands. "I respectfully call to Your Honor's attention that not one scintilla of evidence has been offered to contradict the charges as testified by the twenty-four women who stated they had been criminally aborted. In light of this, Your Honor, the State asks that all three defendants be sent to the penitentiary for the maximum term allowed, five years."

The judge nods, then looks to Mr. Smith. "Do the defendants have anything to say, any motions to make, any evidence to offer in mitigation?"

"If the Court please, the State talks of their evidence. Your Honor, the state's attorney's office invaded these women's place of work. Why, they invaded Ada Martin's very home. Every single scintilla of evidence was obtained ruthlessly and in absolute violation of the Constitution of the United States and the Constitution of the State of Illinois.

"I have contended from the start that in view of the filthy mess that was procured here, these women should be set entirely free." He pauses and shakes his head. "But here we are, and it is in Your Honor's power. We know you will do what you think is just and will temper that justice with mercy."

Judge Haas purses his lips. His gaze moves from Mr. Smith to Mimi, Ada, and Jo. Beneath the table, Mimi takes hold of her friends' hands. "The sentence will be three years in the penitentiary."

Mimi's breathless once again. Three years. Three years of her life, gone.

"To which we object," Mr. Smith says. "And, of course, I'd like to make a motion to vacate."

Judge Haas stands. "Gentlemen, that is my sentence, and that's the end of the story."

Stan's hand on her shoulder slackens, and she waits for it to slip away. Instead, he gives her a gentle squeeze. Ada and Jo are still holding on, too. It's enough to keep back Mimi's tears. Enough to remind her why she chose this. Enough to not regret that she did.

EPILOGUE

That's the end of the story. Or so Judge Haas said. But Mimi has other ideas.

For the last year, she's been at the Oakdale Reformatory for Women in Dwight, Illinois. As far as penitentiaries go, it's not altogether bad. She lives in what the reform-minded superintendent calls a cottage, along with twenty-five other women. They each have their own room with a bed, a dresser, and a wicker rocking chair. A fireplace heats the common room, and the radio livens their evenings. The United States joined the Allies in December after the bombing of Pearl Harbor, and most of the women at Oakdale know someone—a son, a husband, a brother—gearing up to fight in the war, and they all squeeze around the radio when a news broadcast comes on.

Lucky for Mimi, Junior's far too young to enlist, and the draft board deemed Stan ineligible on account of his bum leg. It's hard enough to be apart from them without having to worry about bullet wounds and bombing raids.

After leaving New York so abruptly to attend Mimi's trial, Stan was demoted to head coach of the Janesville Cubs, a D-level farm team in rural Wisconsin, for the remainder of the season. He led the team to a second-place finish and was reinstated with the Chicago Cubs the following spring. Now, with so many players leaving for the war, he's talking with Mr. Wrigley about creating an All-American Girls League next season. Mimi likes the idea.

She didn't follow news of Daniel's trial, but she heard from Jo that he was found guilty of murder and is currently serving a life sentence forty-five miles away at Joliet Penitentiary. Jo said he appealed, but the Illinois Supreme Court affirmed his conviction. Whenever Mimi thinks of him, which is less and less these days, pity and remorse soften her anger.

Oakdale's a far more progressive institution than Joliet, but a prison's still a prison. The doors and windows are checkered with bars. A peephole allows the warden to look in on the women while they're locked in their bedrooms at night. Every letter Mimi receives from home is opened and inspected. She's well prepared for the long hours the women work—cooking, cleaning, sewing, laundering, gardening, tending to the prison's chickens and sheep. Sometimes, Mimi even helps in the infirmary. By the end of the day, her feet are sore and eyelids heavy, but she always makes time to write to her family before bed and is first in line for the telephone, which the women are permitted to use only on Sunday afternoons.

Ada and Jo live in another cottage, but Mimi sees them often around the grounds. Ada hasn't found cause to smile since Jennie's death, but Jo fares better. She juggles letters between two beaus—one in the Navy and one in the Army.

The women appealed their conviction, and the Supreme Court has agreed to hear the case. Mr. Smith filed a brief on their behalf and expects a ruling any day now. If the new judge sides with them and remands their case to the county courts for retrial, they may be permitted to leave on bail. The prosecution's case will be gutted, and the state's attorney will have no choice but to drop the charges against them. Or so Mr. Smith says. Mimi appreciates his persistence and optimism but keeps her hope in check.

Whether she remains at Oakdale for one more day or two more years, Mimi's at peace with her fate. But she does miss her family terribly.

Her bedroom walls are covered with postcards from the towns Stan's visited for away games, and handcrafted cards and drawings from Penny and Junior. (Halina insists they write to Mimi regularly.) The family motors down to Oakdale every weekend Stan's in town. Mimi cherishes their visits, but it breaks her heart anew when they leave without her. Penny looks more like a young woman each time Mimi sees her, and Junior's half an inch taller. They're bursting with stories about school and friends, sometimes talking over each other in their excitement to fill her in. But she knows there's so much of their lives she's missing. Stan, too, has plenty to say—about the club, the war—and though he'll reach out sometimes and take her hand or stroke her arm, she sees the strain and fatigue in his eyes. It's there in Halina's face, too.

Fitting herself back into their lives will be no easy task. Things are irrevocably different now. Her family's different; she's different. But Mimi's determined to move forward together whenever she's let free.

Father Kowalski visits from time to time, too. Their talk of God and his abiding forgiveness comforts her. She still doesn't regret her work at the clinic or rejecting Papanek's deal. But Lord knows there's plenty else to seek forgiveness for.

And plenty to do whenever she's released. There's a war on, after all. Poverty and injustice haven't gone away. She'll start, though, with mending her family—and not just the five of them. Mimi has a nephew out there somewhere, too. She wrote to the unwed mothers' home in Des Moines. Their reply was short and to the point: they do not disclose information about past adoptees. It's better for the children that way.

Mimi disagrees. And she won't give up until she finds him.

AUTHOR'S NOTE

Before writing this story, when I thought about abortion in the pre-*Roe v. Wade* era, I imagined dark alleys, dirty equipment, and unskilled practitioners. In many cases, that wasn't far from the truth. In 1930, for example, abortion was reported as the official cause of eighteen percent of maternal deaths. But that wasn't the whole truth.

First, abortions were legally performed in hospitals and clinics when a physician deemed that the mother's life was at risk. If you go further back, to the first half of the nineteenth century and before, ending an unwanted pregnancy before quickening—when the mother first feels the fetus move inside her—was not a crime at all. (Although there were few safe and reliable means to do so.)

Second, even after laws were passed criminalizing abortion at any stage of pregnancy, some physicians continued to perform them beyond the narrow scope of therapeutic exceptions. As the understanding of germ theory and aseptic surgery increased, so too did the safety and efficacy of such procedures.

In the early part of the twentieth century, clinics like the one described in this book existed in Chicago, Los Angeles, San Francisco, and New York. Smaller operations existed in Baltimore and Detroit. And those were just the ones I uncovered in my research. Likely, most cities in the United States had physicians who performed safe, albeit illegal, abortions. Alongside them were numerous others, most with dubious skills, who employed far less safe techniques.

Around the 1940s, the scope of what constituted a legal, therapeutic abortion narrowed. Hospital boards and committees took over much of the decision-making. At the same time, enforcement of anti-abortion laws increased. This led to few safe options for women seeking to terminate their pregnancies and more instances like I had imagined, where procedures were performed in the shadows by dirty, untrained hands.

The clinic Mimi works at in the book is based on a real clinic that opened sometime in the 1920s or early '30s in downtown Chicago's bustling Loop neighborhood. It was first run by Dr. Max Gecht, then by Dr. Josephine Gabler, and then by Ada Martin. Indeed, almost every character in the book, except Mimi and her family, is based on a real person. The details of the raid and ensuing trial largely follow the historical record.

To ensure accuracy, I pored over countless newspaper articles and hundreds of pages of trial transcripts. Some parts of the narrative, such as the suicide notes left by Henry and Emily Millstone, and parts of the courtroom dialogue, were taken verbatim from the historical record.

Of course, this is also a work of fiction, and I changed some details to better suit the story. Josephine Kuder, for example, was married at the time of the trial, not single. Emily Millstone had been in prison for possession of narcotics until only a few months before the first raid. While Daniel Moriarity was on friendly terms with the Martin family and perhaps other clinic staff, his relationship with Mimi was entirely of my imagining.

For pacing purposes, I greatly compressed the timeline of the trial. In the book, it's mere weeks from the grand jury indictment to the women's conviction. In reality, Ada Martin and Josephine Kuder were not found guilty of conspiracy to commit abortion until April 16, 1942—a full year after the grand jury endorsed a true bill against them. Initially, there was a nurse, Edna Bullock, on trial with them, but she was granted a separate trial after being injured in a car accident.

As in the story, Ada Martin and Josephine Kuder were convicted and sentenced to prison. Their lawyer, however, immediately filed an appeal, and the women were released on a three-thousand-dollar bond, pending the appeal, instead of going to prison. In November 1942, the Illinois Supreme Court ruled the evidence used in the case was illegally seized, including the name of nearly every witness, rendering their testimony inadmissible. The initial ruling was reversed and the case remanded (i.e., sent back) to the lower court for retrial. Ultimately, the charges against the women were dropped due to a lack of admissible evidence.

Despite this victory, the fallout from the case cannot be overstated. Officer Daniel Moriarity murdered Ada Martin's daughter, Jennie, at the outset of the trial. He was found guilty and sentenced to life in prison. He died at Joliet Penitentiary in 1946. Henry and Emily Millstone both died by suicide the same month Jennie was murdered. Needless to say, the clinic never reopened.

In the 1930s and '40s, abortion was not the lightning-rod issue it is today. It was illegal across the U.S. and objected to on moral grounds by most Christian institutions. Some physicians advocated for liberalizing the therapeutic indications for abortion, but they were the minority. As for everyday Americans, many were ambivalent on the matter. What's not materially different is the number of pregnancies that ended in abortion. Similar to today, best estimates are twenty to twenty-five percent.

I wrote this book to better understand and explore the complicated picture of abortion in pre-Roe America. What I found was something far more nuanced than the proverbial back-alley butcher but, in many ways, just as tragic. I wrote this book because I believe we must know our past to fully understand our present, navigate what lies ahead, and build a better future.

ACKNOWLEDGMENTS

This book greatly benefited from the keen insights of several early readers, including Wendy Randall, Jenny Ballif, Angelina Hill, Connie Mayo, Reine Bouton, Veronica Klash, and Patricia Tudosa. With all my heart, I thank you.

My enduring gratitude also goes out to my agent, Michael Carr, for championing my stories and helping me grow as a writer.

Many thanks to my wonderful editor, John Scognamiglio, and the entire team at Kensington, for making this book possible. Michelle Addo-Chajet, Vida Engstrand, Alexandra Nicolajsen, Kristin McLaughlin, Kait Johnson, Andi Paris, Matt Johnson, Carly Sommerstein, Jackie Dinas, Susanna Gruninger, Lori Glick, and so many more—your wisdom, enthusiasm, and dedication mean the world. I'm also deeply grateful for the sharp eye of my copy editor, Scott Heim.

Thank you to Jay Jorgensen and Alex Ip, my go-to sources for all things law-related. To Gary Jorgensen for sharing his love and knowledge of baseball. And *dziękuję* to Aneta Studzińska for helping me with the Polish words and phrases. Any errors or embellishments are my own.

And always, thank you to my family. Your encouragement and support give me wings. Steven, I couldn't ask for a better partner. Finally, spending so much time in a story world set in the 1930s and '40s made me think often of my grandmothers—Miriam and Carolyn—two women with strong minds and generous hearts. I thank you for the examples you set and the love you shared.

ACKNOWLEDGMENTS

This book greatly benefited from the [illegible] of several [illegible] friends: [illegible] Wendy Kendall [illegible] Angelina Hill [illegible] all my heartfelt thank you.

My enduring gratitude also goes out to my agent [illegible] for championing [illegible] and helping me [illegible].

Huge thanks to my wonderful editor John Scognamiglio and the [illegible]

[illegible]

[illegible] finally, [illegible] spending so much time in a story world [illegible] Carolyn, two women with strong minds and generous hearts. I thank you for the example you set and the love you shared.

A READING GROUP GUIDE

ABOUT THIS GUIDE

The suggested questions are included to enhance your group's reading of Amanda Skenandore's *When No One Else Will*!

DISCUSSION QUESTIONS

1. How does Mimi change and grow over the course of the novel? What lessons does she learn?

2. Regret is a recurring theme in the novel. Do you think it's possible to live a life without regret? How does regret or fear of regret drive people's choices?

3. After his accident, Stan struggles to move on. Have you ever experienced a life-changing setback? How did you move past it?

4. As detailed in the Author's Note, this story is based on an actual abortion clinic in downtown Chicago in the 1930s and early 1940s. Does this surprise you? How did the story align with your understanding of abortion and abortion access in this era? How have attitudes toward abortion changed?

5. Emily, Dr. Millstone, and Ada's daughter Jennie all died on account of the trial. Do you view their deaths as unnecessary tragedies of an unjust system or the unfortunate consequences of criminal activity?

6. What role does gender inequality play in the story?

7. What place do you think controversial topics like abortion have in literature?

8. In the end, Mimi refuses Papanek's deal. Do you think she made the right choice? What choice would you have made?

9. How does faith influence Mimi and other characters' choices? How does faith—religious, spiritual, humanistic, or otherwise—influence *your* choices?

10. Many of the characters' actions are motivated by the desire to protect or support their families. Mimi, Daniel, and many of the women who seek abortions at the clinic are driven by this desire. Does this change how you view their actions?

www.ingramcontent.com/pod-product-compliance
Lightning Source LLC
LaVergne TN
LVHW030908080826
845145LV00010B/2805

* 9 7 8 1 4 9 6 7 4 1 7 0 7 *